Mrs.

Mrs.

A Novel

CAITLIN MACY

Little, Brown and Company

New York Boston London

Little, Brown and Company
Hachette Book Group
1290 Avenue of the Americas, New York NY 10104
littlebrown.com

First Edition: February 2018

Little, Brown and Company is a division of Hachette Book Group, Inc. The Little, Brown name and logo are trademarks of Hachette Book Group, Inc.

The publisher is not responsible for websites (or their content) that are not owned by the publisher.

The Hachette Speakers Bureau provides a wide range of authors for speaking events. To find out more, go to hachettespeakersbureau.com or call (866) 376-6591.

ISBN 978-0-316-43415-7 (hardcover) / 978-0-316-52376-9 (Canada)
LCCN 2016963001

10 9 8 7 6 5 4 3 2 1

LSC-C

Printed in the United States of America

For Jeremy

To anyone else she was defiance; but she knew
that it was only going on. You just go on.
— John O'Hara, *BUtterfield 8*

Mrs.

Chapter One

Look at you in your fur! You were so smart to wear it!"

"It was my mother's. I never wear it. I really never do. But today I just thought, *Why not?*"

In the cold, the mothers gathered outside the school. One after another, like children being summoned in a schoolyard game, they came battling off of Park Avenue into the leeward hush of the side street.

"...sick the whole time, all five of us."

"...quit over the phone..."

"...got to be kidding me..."

"...torn ACL the very first run of the very first day..."

"...Doug will *only* ski in March."

"Called me up—said she wasn't coming back from St. Lucia."

It was January, the first day back after Christmas break—freezing out, with a surprisingly cutting wind. When Gwen Hogan, standing at the outer remove of the crush of mothers, turned her head to look up the block, the cold hit her cheeks and went right through the hood of her parka, making her temples ache.

Not that she minded—not in any nonphysical, existential way. You had to earn spring, after all.

"...something to be said for the tropical Christmas..."

"...Tom's mother's camel-hair coat. A gift certificate to Best Buy..."

"Yup, yup—do the reverse."

"...because I don't need snow at Christmas. I like it, but I don't *need* it."

"...paid her the entire summer while we were away. If I had known—"

The school, St. Timothy's, was a brick-and-limestone town house with a mansard roof on East Sixty-Third Street. It had been built at the turn of the nineteenth century as the rectory of the church that was just around the corner. By the turn of the next, it was no longer clear whether St. Tim's the Preschool was still Episcopalian, or even Christian. (If pressed, the administration would have copped to the denomination before the religion; *Christian* suggested Jesus a little too pointedly for this parent body.) The building itself had been ceded bit by bit, at first, by rooms and then by floors, until this past decade when it was given over entirely to the widely desired, deep-coffered preschool.

The front door was of a heavy-paneled forest green on which a brass knocker in the form of a lion's head snarled menacingly. Above the door hung the school flag, whipped every which way today by the wind. On a quieter morning you could see that it had a white cross on a red background. Gwen Hogan kept her eyes on the flag, watched it flutter and snap. *Me? Oh, no—I was just thinking about what to make for supper!* was the response she kept at the ready, should someone take pity on her for standing alone and address her. In her mind she was always having to set potential empathizers at ease. In fact, they never materialized—these

4

kindly souls who would feel themselves implicated in her solitude—although she was occasionally mistaken for Lally Stein's au pair, to whom, it was true, she bore a passing resemblance (the ponytail and the youthful, makeup-less face; the jeans and running shoes).

"It's not *about* the money! I just can't get over the selfishness of it."

"Well, I *refuse*—"

"We *refuse*—"

"Ron refuses on *principle*—"

But one was never to learn what it was that Ron's moral code had prompted him to reject, for at that moment, a violent gust assailed the women. "Agh!" They cringed; gloved hands flew protectively to girlish faces. Really! This weather was unbelievable! When the wind died away, a ripple of laughter went down the line as the women gave in to the giddiness anyone feels in the face of such brief, surmountable challenges that never actually interfere with comfort.

"Well, I'm glad I wore fur today! I'm glad I dragged it out!"

A taxi pulled up, and before the women even turned, they knew who would emerge from it—who among them would risk being late for pickup on the very first day back. Sure enough, she unfolded the almost excessive length of herself till she stood, nearly six feet tall, in an ankle-length black-and-tan shearling coat and a fur hat: Philippa Lye. Gwen hadn't seen the hat before, wondered briefly if it was a Christmas gift. Its fluffy gray-brown flaps framed Philippa's face becomingly: those cheekbones, unconciliatory in the extreme; the arrogant jutting triangle of a nose; and then—as if to give it some wanted thematic contrast—the large, watchful brown eyes. Watchful—in a woman who, for so many reasons, you'd think wouldn't give a shit. Her hair, which fell to her shoulders from underneath the hat, was chocolate-Lab brown; Gwen privately felt it made suckers of all these dyed blondes.

"He says I owe him money," Philippa announced, her voice just loud and insistent enough to carry over the wind. A couple of the nannies, who waited on the east side of the school, closer to Park, looked over at her, keeping their expressions vague, and then looked away. Cravenly, Gwen Hogan also veiled her expression; she couldn't afford to get involved any more than the nannies could.

"The driver, you mean? Well, what does the meter say?" said Ann DeGroat, detaching herself from a conversation about limestone versus soapstone countertops.

"Yes—what are you implying?" said Betsy Fleming, rubbing her upper arms to keep warm as she joined Ann. "He's trying to cheat you?"

"That's the thing." Philippa sounded amused. It was the other women who moved and spoke impatiently, attempting to get to the bottom of things on her behalf. "The meter's broken! He said I should estimate."

"Sir! Sir!" This was Emily Lewin, a former prosecutor, taking on the cabbie.

Philippa went on without rancor: "I take this cab every day. It never costs more than twelve. Twelve *with* tip. He's very angry with me. I don't *have* any more. I gave him everything I have." With that, she turned her coat pockets inside out—an irrelevant gesture had she carried a handbag, but, in typical fashion, Philippa Lye seemed to have walked out of her apartment with nothing but the coat on her back and the hat on her head.

"That's not the point," Betsy said, sharing an exasperated glance with Ann. "We can *give* you money."

The taxi driver, who had been leaning out the window following this exchange, began to yell, accusing Philippa of things.

Gwen still hung back so as not to be the one who loaned Philippa money if it came to that, for the others all could— indeed, would be thrilled to have her in their debt. She watched Philippa watching the other women haggle over it, as if the scene, though of mild interest, were unconnected to herself. Gwen thought her beyond beautiful—no mere specific example, idiosyncratic in its variation on a theme, but the embodiment of some Platonic form that had always existed in her mind. *Always,* as with all things, meant since preadolescence. In a coincidence that would have mattered little to most of the women here but figured largely in her own thoughts, Gwen had known Philippa Lye's face a long, long time—since she was eight years old, in fact. Consciously or unconsciously, for most of her life, Gwen had judged all other faces on how they compared to it.

"Exactly how much did you give him?" Ann DeGroat persisted.

"Fourteen, I'm sure, because I had a dollar in coins and I gave him every penny."

Betsy groaned— "You paid in change?" —but Emily went on the attack. "Look, sir!" She leaned into the driver's-side window. "It's clear that, in fact, you've been overpaid for this trip!"

Decades before New York had made its queer claim on her life, Gwen had been in Girl Scouts with Philippa's younger— plainer—sister, Rosemary, in Nautauqua, Massachusetts. Hard to imagine such a humble pursuit and place could have any connection with as exalted an event as pickup at St. Timothy's in the aughts. To be fair, the Lye sisters were from Dunning, the next town over; the nicer town, with the pristine Main Street and the twin white steeples of the Congregational and Unitarian

7

churches. Nautauqua, where the Girl Scouts met, had the traffic circle and the fast-food franchises. But still: thirty years ago, Gwen Hogan—Gwen Babineau then—had spent afternoons playing dress-up at the Lyes' house—not so very many of them, for her friendship with Rosemary had limped along rather than taken off. Then again, it had limped along awhile, as if neither girl was willing to be the one to call a halt. What Gwen remembered most was the feeling of luck she had when Philippa—who everyone said was going to be a model and who was already in a newspaper ad for the local Ford dealership—having no better options on the particular day, would join them. Both Gwen and Rose lacked imagination. Philippa Lye created the fantasy and then took you along on it. Rosemary complained often, to their mother, but Gwen was tickled to be lady-in-waiting to Philippa's queen, the long-suffering hairdresser to her movie star. When Gwen thought of Philippa over the years, hearing snippets about her success—catalogs and a magazine cover; a stint in Japan—she felt complacent, as one does when one's own opinion is corroborated by the universe.

Rosemary she thought of not at all.

In a stream of disgust, the taxi driver gesticulated violently and skidded off. "It's fine—it's fine." Emily put up a staying hand as she turned back to the group, though Philippa hadn't yet thanked her. "It's okay!"

There was an impatience in Emily's voice, as there often was when the women spoke to Philippa. They snapped at her more often than you would expect adults to snap at another adult. They seemed to feel it their due, though the impatience, Gwen had noticed, stopped short of harshness. No one yelled at Philippa Lye. Not for now anyway. One wondered what would happen if the money suddenly disappeared—if her husband's bank fell prey to one of those rogue traders who were jeopardizing the bigger establishments. But one didn't wonder long. Skinker, Farr was an old institution, its establishment nearly a century ago now less remarkable, Gwen's husband, Dan, had informed her, than the fact that it had remained in the Skinkers' hands through the 1980s, when most of the private banks were disappearing.

Skinker, Farr meant something. Even the extremely rich hedge-fund wives—even Lally Stein and Belle Ostergaard—and their husbands gave the Skinkers a certain deference.

One could snap; one could not yell.

"How will you get home?" This was Betsy, who perhaps had been upstaged by Emily.

"Oh, gosh—I don't know!" Philippa caught Gwen's eye. Gwen hid a smile because she, too, found the question ridiculous. "We'll take the bus!" Philippa proposed. "Or even—walk!"

But the mothers of St. Timothy's didn't, as a rule, do comedy.

"Walk?" Looking alarmed, Ann gestured to the sky. "In this weather?"

"Here, take a twenty." Betsy reached into her purse, fumbled for her wallet.

Ann was the quicker draw, from a shallower pocketbook: "Take mine. Take it."

A brief argument ensued over who would loan Philippa the twenty.

"Just take both," Emily decided. "In fact, you know what, I'm going to give you twenty too. You may need it."

"All right," Philippa said gravely. "Thank you."

The women, looking pained by their own generosity, turned away with jerky, defensive movements. It was Philippa who stood, tall and unslouching in the magnificent hat. She reminded Gwen of a medieval bishop receiving patronage. She glanced happily at the bills as a child looks at money for candy—frankly counting—and crushed them into her pocket.

At twelve sharp, the green door swung inward. "Hello, hello!" Mrs. Davidson cried spiritedly, as if something unexpectedly pleasant had befallen her in the fact of these women waiting to collect their children. Beside her, Ms. Babcock, her assistant head—and henchwoman, so people said—might have been delighted as well, or she might have been filled with extreme loathing at the sight of the mothers, which she covered up with a kindly smile. The women surged forward as the ceremonial handing-off of their excuses for existence began. Mrs. Davidson cried, "I have Virginia DeGroat! I have Willie Haskell!"

On the tailwind of another gust, as the names continued, one final mother blew in. Why, it was the new mother! Ah yes. Everyone, turning, having forgotten her entirely, observed her with curiosity: the New Mother. Her daughter had started just that morning, a rare midyear admittee. Coffee conversation after drop-off had concluded that strings must have been pulled or, rather, lines yanked, cut, and resealed. Nobody got into St. Tim's midyear. Short but not petite—trim and muscular, in fact—she was darkly attractive. In giant sunglasses and hustling, though not in a panicked way, more as if she enjoyed the challenge of the clock, and with her arms heavily laden with shopping bags, the New Mother swept down on St. Tim's in the same wildly high-heeled pumps she'd been wearing at drop-off. Minnie was her name, was it? Minnie Something? "Like the mouse?"

Emily Lewin had asked her provocatively. "Yes!" had come the disarming reply. "My mother loved anything Disney, and she named me after the cartoon!"

She looked good-humored as she flipped her sunglasses up and glanced around. Her manner, as if in imitation of her name, was congenial in a giggly, little-girl sort of way. Here—here, they all felt—was something new. She didn't seem to notice that the mothers, who were keeping an ear cocked for their children's names, were all glancing at the labels on the shopping bags and turning back to one another with raised eyebrows. Most people would have stowed them at home or in a waiting car. The New Mother—Minnie—was apparently ignorant of these subtleties. Or perhaps—the idea presented itself uncomfortably—she was simply uninterested in them? Gwen stared at her shoes, unable to believe a person could actually walk in them. They must've been four inches high, the metal heel spiked to a fine and frightening point, as if the point she made by wearing them was far beyond ambulatory. But walk she did—triumphantly, weaving confidently through the crowd, her shoulders thrust back, her balance as light and careless as if she were in the old running shoes that Gwen herself wore. And that was the only way to wear shoes like that, thought Gwen, who, despite the fact that she took no time at all with her own appearance, could be exacting about others'. In shoes that high, any telltale hunch of the shoulders, slump of the back, or grimace, and you looked—well, you looked like a prostitute at the end of a long night.

"Philomena Stein! Lila and Dickson Dilworth!"

In the middle of the calling of the names, a curious little side drama began, apparent only to Gwen, because she habitually hung back. The New Mother went straight up to Philippa, of all people—and introduced herself. "Philippa? Philippa Skinker? I'm Minnie Curtis."

But Philippa was the sort of person who might not answer even a direct address if she didn't feel like it. She looked vaguely at the woman as she went on, recounting some tenuous connection.

"I have Peter Felekonaides! I have Emma Eliot! I have—" Mrs. Davidson hesitated for a second, and stolid Ms. Babcock, lips as wooden as a dummy's, might have been feeding her the name: "I have Mary Hogan!"

Gwen made her way to the door, took Mary by the hand, and accepted the unwieldy pile of construction-paper collages Ms. Babcock delivered smugly. "Some artwork you'll want to take home and display."

Still, for a moment, the brutality of the city fell away in her joy at seeing her daughter, at the feel of the warm little hand in hers.

"Did you have a good day, honey?"

Dreamy and not given to small talk, Mary didn't answer but gazed off toward Park Avenue as if she were trying to recall something. Gwen gave her hand a squeeze and pulled her gently as she started through the crowd—"Let's go, honey"—clamping the artwork to her side with an elbow. On the way out she brushed by Philippa, who was pressing forward at the summons of "Ruth and Sebastian Skinker!"—the New Mother chattily in her wake. "Just such an amazing coincidence! I've been so looking forward to trading stories with you about the place! I've heard your name so often, I feel like I already know you!"

"What's for lunch, Mom?" Mary tugged at Gwen's hand.

"Um…the leftover meat loaf from last night," Gwen mumbled, reluctant to have these women overhear the humble nature of the food she fed her child. There was a shame over here on Sixty-Third and Park in cooking from scratch, in not simply serving chicken nuggets and other branded, microwavable products—Go-Gurts and Veggie Stix. Perhaps it reeked of the middle class, or seemed grungy. Gwen had quickly learned to keep silent.

"Hey," Gwen said to Philippa as she brushed by her.

"Gwen." Some sympathy passed between them, as it always did.

Their children had never been classmates, for Mary was older, in the Fours, while Ruth Skinker was a tiny Two and Sebastian a Three; the Skinkers' seven-year-old, Laura, had moved on to big school already. And despite the fact that both women were outsiders at St. Tim's, Gwen knew full well that the natures of their exclusion were distinct—hers innate, an extension of her personality and relative poverty, Philippa's more like that of a celebrity; she kept herself apart except when she needed something. Her children were the third generation of Skinkers to attend the school; their father, Jed, ran the bank; their paternal grandmother, Laura Winifred "Winnie" Skinker, a frequently photographed society matron, was on the board at Cleary, the most bluestocking of the Upper East Side girls' schools, where her namesake, little Laura, was now in second grade. Even the bank played its part in the lore; rather than occupying a few stultifying, fluorescent-lit stories in a midtown office tower, Skinker, Farr was housed in a Beaux-Arts mansion on West Fifty-Fourth that the Skinkers themselves owned. Stone gargoyles instead of elevator banks greeted the potential client, and the old Mr. Skinker, now deceased, was said to have named them all.

"He had another accident," Gwen could hear Ms. Babcock flatly informing Philippa. "Poo this time."

Waiting for the light to change, Gwen glanced back. Philippa was taking the news impassively. This seemed to vex Ms. Babcock, who likely expected flustered apologies from the mothers—prostrations and embarrassment. A flicker of annoyance crossed the woman's broad face, which came up to Philippa's bra line. "You really need to remember to bring in the change of clothes," she instructed Philippa's chest, the truculent note that Gwen instinctively avoided inciting sounding in her voice. "We've gone to the Lost and Found twice for him."

She didn't hear Philippa's reply, only glimpsed her haughty, indifferent body language, for at that moment the light changed, and Mary cried, "Walking person! Walking person!" Across the double avenue Gwen hurried her daughter the way her own mother had when Gwen was growing up in Nautauqua, Massachusetts. Camilla had always hurried her—into the car, out of the car, up the stairs to St. Agnes's, down the aisles of Donnelly's. Gwen had never, as far as she could remember, gone anywhere at a relaxing pace when she was little.

Chapter Two

Real winter day today," Gwen remarked to Mary as they came up the subway stairs at Eighty-Sixth Street and were slowed by the throng at the corner, the street merchants selling novelty hats, phone cases, handbags. Waiting for the crosstown bus, Gwen knelt to put Mary's mittens on, pulling them up over the little red hands. Gwen's mother, Camilla, had knit them. They were orange wool with a pale blue zigzag around the palm and they dangled, as Gwen's had as a child, from a string that went up one arm of Mary's coat, across the back, and down the other. "It's totally out of control! She refused to put on her mittens today!" Gwen would hear the St. Tim's mothers proclaiming about their own daughters. It was the kind of comment that made Gwen look away and hope not to be noticed. She couldn't imagine having that kind of adversarial relationship with her only child. Sometimes she would hear them querulously addressing their nannies: "Why is he wearing *those* pants? What happened to the ones I laid out?" As if motherhood were a battle which the toddlers were winning.

Mary had done a twos program in the basement of a Catholic

church up the block from where they lived; Gwen had planned for her to stay at St. Ephraim's for preschool. Then Dan came home one day with a tip from a female colleague of his at the U.S. Attorney's Office. "St. Timothy's is the best," he declared, and on his own he sought out an application. At the group visit the school required as part of the application, while the other rising three-year-olds sat blinking and mouth-breathing as they colored with crayons, Mary arranged all of the plastic animals by species and height and then created an elaborate game in which they all jumped over one another in order to get home. Gwen could have died, the hostility in the room from the other mothers was so intense. She swore she would never go back. Then they got in, though, and it gave her pause; even she recognized the rare honor that was being bestowed. Looking at the tuition—the deposit that was required immediately—she was ready to rip up the letter and throw it away. But the next day another letter arrived informing them of their reduced "commitment"—the significant scholarship they were being given. Dan laughed when she told him. "They want to pay for Mary to smarten up the place? Let 'em!" And who, after all, was she to deprive her daughter of music and movement, a huge padded rooftop playground, real water and sand in the play tables—a better school for less money? It was funny, though. In spite of the scholarship, Gwen sensed that the Hogans' presence among the chosen, as the months went by, was an affront to the administration, like that of a black-sheep relative whose ongoing claim of legitimacy rankled. Whereas Dan, having gotten invested in it and competitive for one brief moment, never thought about St. Timothy's again.

"The bus is here," Mary announced, pointing. She took pleasure in things working right, running on time; so did Gwen. "M Eighty-Six. Crosstown local. Next stop, Third Avenue."

"That's right."

They rode four halting blocks, Gwen clasping Mary in her lap, and got out at York. The young man whose family owned the corner deli was outside today, rearranging the banks of flowers under the covering sheet of plastic his father rolled down in the winter. Mary waved at him—"Mike!"—and he waved back. Gwen would see her neighbors chatting and laughing with Mike, post-purchase. Gwen, too, would have enjoyed the sense of community that might have come from patronizing the place. But she had so little use for the deli! It was one of the characteristics of New York that had made her feel most alien when they'd arrived a decade ago, when Dan took a clerkship out of law school on the Second Circuit: that this was a city of people who couldn't be bothered to cut up their own cantaloupe or push a grocery cart down an aisle to stock up for more than a day. It was a relief when she ran out of milk and had to run down and buy a quart—when she could show it wasn't personal.

The outer door of their building closed with a whump behind them. Kicking aside the scattering of takeout menus, Gwen dug out her keys and let the two of them through the second door. Mary went ahead, doing her posting-pony trot and clucking, while Gwen held the door for another tenant—an older man in a porkpie hat who walked with a limp. He didn't thank Gwen but proceeded through the door with an avaricious look in his eye and lumbered quickly toward the elevator in the back. He was carrying a tabloid newspaper in a plastic bag that swung manically from the crook in his arm. Gwen hurried, too, but stopped quickly at the phalanx of mailboxes to remove the mostly junk mail that was stuffed into their box, knowing how long it would take for the shambling elevator to return if she missed it.

"Look, there's a letter from Grandma!" she said to Mary, forcing herself not to run.

"I'm getting out on seven!" the man said as if it were a threat, his thumb locked against the button, as Gwen hurried the two of them in.

It was 2009, the winter after the financial crisis. The Yorkville building was filled mainly with old people who had hung on to rent-stabilized apartments and college grads new to the city—the smart, ambitious, but unsophisticated kind who filled the Second Avenue bars on Friday nights. There was one other young family besides the Hogans. At Halloween, they would emerge from an upper floor with older children in costumes that usually involved guns. The mother seemed to find Gwen's presence year after year irksome, as if she was an unwelcome reminder of the compromise of rearing children in this building from which other families had moved on. She made a point of not speaking to Gwen and would address her only through her children: "Say 'thank you' to the lady for the Twizzlers, Jack."

The Hogans' apartment was on five and consisted of two bedrooms in the back, a shared bathroom in between, and a living room in the front with west-facing windows that looked onto York. It truly was a "living" room; they did everything there—ate and watched television and played Sorry! and crazy eights with Mary. Dan lay down on the floor every morning to do the exercises that helped his back. A Pullman kitchen with folding closet-type doors ran along one side of the room. "Let's hang up our coats now," Gwen said as they came in, helping Mary with hers. Mary skipped away to her bedroom to commune with her stuffed animals, and Gwen took the meat loaf out of the fridge, sliced it into pieces, and put the plates in the microwave one at a time.

A decade ago, when they had moved into the building, they, too, had been recent grads—Dan a few months out of law school, Gwen working in the lab at Taurus, the pharmaceutical giant, and finishing up her master's at Rutgers at night but commuting on the weekends—strange to say it then, strange to recall it now—to New York to be with Dan. Describing her life at the time to her fellow technicians in the lab, Gwen would find herself being cagey, knowing that she was not one to have a "husband" in "Manhattan"—that wasn't her at all.

She poured two glasses of milk, which she placed on the round pine table, its legs resting half on the strip of kitchen linoleum and half on the parquet floor of the living room, balanced by strategically placed matchbooks. The trash was full so she tied it up and took it out to the landing, replaced the bag and rinsed her hands.

Married straight out of college, Gwen and Dan had been oblivious to the kind of sudden proprieties that beset couples who married later on. It didn't strike them as strange that they started out with a roommate, for instance. They were slight, slim people, she and Dan—runners, the both of them—and when Topher, who worked at Sotheby's and had aspirations to a fancier address, left for an illegal sublet on Sutton Place, they couldn't quite bring themselves to take over the bigger bedroom. They stayed on their Serta Perfect full-size in the dark back bedroom, leaving Topher's discarded futon frame where it was. "I'll have my mother down," Gwen decided, anticipating hosting Camilla now that they had the room. She hoped to correct her mother's impression of her life in New York City. Camilla, she had sensed, inferred pretension from the mere fact that it was not Boston.

The truth was, Gwen thought she'd better get her mother down to New York in a hurry because soon Dan's clerkship was ending and he'd be starting at a law firm. At that point, with the increased income, there probably would be pretensions—doormen and a cleaning woman. Camilla had made sure that all through elementary and high school, Gwen studied hard. For thirteen years, she had made sure. But Gwen's mother hadn't known—how could she—that in Gwen's generation, education would beget New York City would beget hired help, taxis, parking garages. Gwen would have to break her in gently.

Or so she thought.

It hadn't worked out like that, though.

A few weeks after he started at Buckland, Brandt, Dan came home with an itchy red patch on his forearm. Gwen's calamine lotion and baking-soda baths did nothing to soothe it. By Thanksgiving the rash had spread to his back, and by Christmas there were white spots on top of the red and they were creeping up his neck and down his legs, and Dan no longer rolled up his shirtsleeves.

When Gwen asked him how work was going, Dan made it clear he was succeeding—"I'm on my second trial in a year!"—but he'd also get a lunatic look in his eye such as she had never seen there before, as if his alacrity, his scathing ambition as the second youngest of the five sons of Perry Hogan, lawyer in Biddeville, New Jersey—even his high-school wrestler's scrappiness had never predicted the likes of a corporate law job in the early 2000s. He would get that look in his eye and he would begin, unawares, to scratch. One night she found him in the bathroom, naked but for his wire-rimmed glasses and his briefs, standing in the tub pouring rubbing alcohol on his thighs.

"I'm thinking of trying to get into the U.S. Attorney's Office," he said impatiently, wincing a little as the alcohol hit the rawer patches.

"Okay," said Gwen.

Later, she mentioned Dan's new coup of a job to her supervisor. "Are you okay about the money?" the woman asked boldly. The query was so unexpected that it took Gwen a minute to understand, and when she did, she burst into unhinged-sounding laughter. It was the moment she realized that she wasn't living in Nautauqua, Massachusetts, anymore. The colleague cheerfully cited the debt her own husband—also an attorney—had accrued in law school, which had sent him to a corporate firm straightaway. Gwen hoped she didn't sound condescending when she said quietly, in the explicitly unadorned tone people use to talk about the things that truly matter to them, "My husband doesn't have any student loans. He turned down Harvard Law and went to Rutgers on a full ride." "No one does that!" the woman had said, waving her arm as if batting away an absurdity. "He doesn't believe in financial leverage," Gwen had continued, "of any kind."

That was nearly a decade ago. But even today Gwen felt a spark of vanity when she thought of her husband's drive—his iconoclasm and powers of renouncement. Even today she could hear the refrain they had lived by for so long starting in her head, that *they were different.*

Even after everything.

"Mary! Lunch is ready!" Gwen put down a bowl of raw carrot sticks she had peeled and cut up earlier, then took a paper napkin for each of them from the napkin holder that sat in the middle of the table.

"I forgot Lambie!" Mary froze before the table, eyes wide with the oversight. "Be right back!"

She charged away down the short hallway. An only child,

she was good at creating her own dramatic tension, making her own fun.

Gwen drew back a chair, and a play of light on the window made her turn her head so she caught a glimpse of herself. Her long wheat-colored hair was pulled back into a low, indifferent ponytail, today with an actual ponytail holder, other days with a rubber band. She ought to have moved on from her preteen vanity of having notably long hair, she knew. She sat down and took a sip of milk. "Coming, Mom! Coming! Lambie and I are coming right away!" But this younger sibling from a former mill town (the blown-out factory buildings overhung the Nautauqua River); this scrappy, penny-pinching adolescent who had worked at Dunkin' Donuts and Friendly's, then as a clerk and eventually a floor manager at Nelson's, the family-owned department store in downtown Nautauqua, who had nurtured a secret passion for punk rock and had a Sex Pistols poster on her bedroom wall; this close-to-full-scholarship Yale chemical engineering major who had hung out with Dan Hogan and his roommates freshman year because they were familiar to her when no one else was; this skilled technician who had been called, embarrassingly, by her boss at Taurus a "rising star" and urged several times to apply to the PhD program—this woman refused to cut off her hair.

She cinched the ponytail up tight now by pulling on two hanks.

In college, she hadn't seen the need for change. As she got older, maybe her long hair was a little bit defiant, like continuing to wear the fleece jacket her brother, Bobby, had handed down to her when she was in eighth grade.

But now—she felt along the length of the ponytail—now it was something more, this vestige of her sixth-grade self.

For it turned out the striving—the job at Friendly's, from

whose fry basket she had a small white scar on the back of her right hand; the midnight runs to the Taurus lab to get the samples, collect the data, for whatever experiment she was working on—could take you only so far. Camilla and Robert had taught her to do well, to work hard. No one in her family, least of all Gwen, had grasped the paradox that those principles ultimately bore. Her brother, Bobby, had also done well. He had not dishonored his family—far from it. He was a sergeant in the Dunning, Massachusetts, police department, the next town over, and he and Beth had three children, the youngest of whom, Nina, was severely learning-disabled, which had required Beth to quit her job as an ER nurse at Dunning-Nautauqua Memorial.

And Gwen—Gwen had quit her job too. She was no longer a chemical engineer—it was several years ago now; Mary had turned five just after the new year. Sometimes she still missed it—not the desk work that she had segued into eventually but the experiments, the moment of discovery that no one else shared.

Motherhood could be a little like that, on some days.

Returning with the pink stuffed lamb, which she sat on the chair next to her, Mary shook her head. "He can't see over."

"No," Gwen agreed. "Do you want to get the dictionary for him to sit on?"

Mary thought about it. "No. He likes sitting low."

" 'Kay." Gwen didn't go in for the anxious interrogation that constituted most mothers' conversations—"So, did you have *fun?* Did you do a good *job?*"—so mother and daughter forked up their meat loaf for a little while in silence.

"Oh—your card from Grandma," Gwen remembered, rising to get the envelope.

Mary gazed at her mother with a far-off, pleased expression, chewing her carrots, and eventually looked down to examine the card, though she didn't tear it open. She was the least materially acquisitive child Gwen had ever encountered. The little girl tapped her mother's arm and pointed at the return address on the envelope, written in Camilla's didactically neat hand.

"Uh-huh," Gwen said, not sure what Mary was getting at.

"Grand*ma* lives in *Ma,*" Mary said, as if the point were obvious.

"*Ma?* Oh, yes—*M-A,* Massachusetts! Yes, she does."

"Ma in Ma," Mary said. "That's funny."

Gwen said quickly, sounding falsely cheery now, just like the other mothers, "Sometimes Grandma comes to New York to see us, though," and wasn't surprised when Mary didn't respond to what was, after all, a non sequitur.

Camilla had been down to see them just twice in fact. She'd taken the Greyhound from Worcester, buying a coffee at Dunkin' Donuts and a newspaper to read on the bus—the *Globe,* not the *Times.* Bobby's wife, Beth, took care of Gwen's dad while Camilla was away; he had had a stroke the summer Gwen graduated (salutatorian to Paul Pierson's valedictorian, by a tenth of a percent) from Dunning-Nautauqua High. "It's such a hassle for you to get down here. Why don't you fly, Mom? Or take the train?" Gwen had suggested the second time her mom came to visit, when the bus had been held up by an accident near the Bruckner Expressway for the better part of two hours. This was when Mary was two, Gwen was pregnant with their second, and Dan was fresh from winning a complicated fraud trial and was considering taking a job at a firm again—"I'll take my time; make sure it's a good fit." Since Gwen had left Taurus to become a stay-at-home mom, Dan's idea of a large family sustained her. They spent their evenings Googling real estate outside of the city—Dan preferred New Jersey, Gwen Connecticut. Despite his public-sector job, they had managed to save a little. Gwen was feeling flush and happy—always a danger around Camilla.

Camilla had a way of not answering those questions she deemed irrelevant. She'd been braiding toddler Mary's hair at the time, and she had a ponytail holder stuck in her mouth. When the braids were done, embellished with pink and blue grosgrain ribbons, and Mary was sitting in her high chair and patting them with her fingers, enjoying the tight perfection of them, Camilla said, combing the hairs briskly out of the brush before putting the brush back in its drawer, "Fly, huh."

There was a silence while Gwen finished stacking the dishwasher—her mother hurrying over with a spare cup and spoon and a nearly missed breakfast plate—and started the cycle. She turned around, having first formulated her statement. "Dan and I could pay for it." She cleared her throat. "We could fly you down." She had been planning on making this offer for longer than she would have liked to admit, had extensively researched flight times and prices to see if she could, indeed, make it. "Dan's talking about going back to a firm. He's thinking he'll make the move this summer. Time to cash in. Everyone says it's the second kid that does it. And of course, we mean to have more than two…" She repeated: "We could pay for it."

Camilla greeted this with a look of internal amusement, which Gwen caught just before it vanished. Mrs. Babineau had an exaggeratedly firm mouth in a face that had settled contentedly into deep lines, as if a dour sixty-two had been the age she had long targeted. Her complexion was so white, it sometimes had a bluish cast, as if it had never been exposed to the sun. And when Gwen thought about it, she doubted her mother had ever been tan. When would Camilla Babineau, of Nautauqua, Massachusetts, out of Quebecois Canada, have lain on a beach for the purpose of darkening her skin? Her hair, though, was dyed a darker brown than its natural color. She kept it short, set it with hot rollers before a special occasion. Perhaps Gwen *had* grown pretentious; in New York she was aware of how provincial her mother looked, how her eyeglasses with the up-curving arms looked secretarial. Gwen, who for years had rejected a colleague's kindly suggestion of a haircut "with my guy, who could do wonders!," itched to make over her mother. Despite the cold, they were taking Mary to the park this morning. Camilla was religious about going out in all kinds of weather. Gwen went to the door and got their coats from the closet. Both women wore old parka-type winter coats, with flaps and several pockets both internal and external. Mary had an old wool coat with a velvet collar, a hand-me-down from a cousin, Bobby's eldest, Taylor. Camilla got herself zipped up and knelt to help her granddaughter button hers.

The two women spoke few words as they finished getting ready. Gwen's suggestion of flying seemed to hang in the air, silly and gauche and implicating—the kind of offer a pretentious person who lived in New York City would make. "Here's your scarf"— followed by silence till Gwen said tightly to Mary, "All set?"

They stored the stroller on the landing between the fire door and the building's stairwell. Gwen started to back it out but Camilla said, with surprising scorn, "She doesn't need that!" Gwen turned to see her mother eyeing Mary conspiratorially. "You don't need that stroller, do you, Mary? You can walk, can't you? You're a big girl! Don't you want to walk to the park? Exercise is good for you!"

Intrigued by her grandmother's enthusiasm on this point, if not by the point itself, Mary nodded—a spark of enlightenment, or rebellion, coming into her eye. "Walk," she said. "Mary walk." So Gwen wedged the thing back in its place and jammed on its brake. She ought to take better care of the stroller, she thought, not constantly load it down with hernia-threatening grocery bags. It would have two or even three more passengers after Mary outgrew it. It needed to last. Four kids was a tall order for a light-weight, modern apparatus. Even this very afternoon in January, nearly three years later, sitting at the round pine table with the noon light making geometrical shadows on the cheap parquet, Gwen still had a clear tactile memory of putting the stroller back in its place, and an emotional memory of the rush of guilt she felt when, irritated by Camilla's oblique yet unceasing commentary on her life, she jammed on the brake with undue force.

Two weeks later Gwen ended up in the hospital. The placenta was growing into the scar she'd gotten from the C-section with Mary. *Placenta accreta,* it was called. She might have died. She lost the baby, and she would not have another.

Her parents, Camilla and Robert, had taught her to work hard—to do well. And Gwen had always—always—worked hard. Achievement had been her middle name.

When the two women got outside in the brisk winter morning, Camilla chuckled and at last responded to Gwen's suggestion. "Remember what Dad used to say? 'Time to spare, go by air.'" Gwen stopped on the sidewalk. An inchoate syllable of protest came out of her mouth. She quickly closed it. Camilla gave another chuckle, and they walked on toward the park.

Chapter Three

In a French café on Madison Avenue, at a quarter past nine on a Thursday morning, a group of St. Tim's mothers—Betsy Fleming, Emily Lewin, and Ann DeGroat—were considering in murmurs whether to invite the New Mother to join them. The place was bustling, nearly every seat filled, with parties waiting by the door, craning their necks to look for spots. Yet there was an air of laxness as well—the women spread out like high-end bag ladies, as if getting on with their days was the last thing they had in mind.

A green leather banquette ran along the back of the room, where the New Mother was sitting, alone. Ann, Betsy, and Emily didn't feel too bad looking over—practically staring—at her, for she seemed to invite observation. Despite the fact that points in this town had long ago ceased being given for grooming or comportment, Minnie Curtis's hair was blown out and styled, her clothes smart and expensively tailored, rather than expensively draped and drawstringed. Was that an actual matching skirt and jacket she was wearing—a suit? In the demure way she sat, her legs tucked under her, her spine straight as if so quaint a rule as good posture still mattered, she seemed to represent the standards of an earlier generation. Had they not recognized her from school, the mothers might have mistaken her for an upscale saleswoman or a professional fund-raiser, someone who needed to befriend the rich, when in fact, people said *she* was very rich.

"John Curtis is the husband," offered Betsy Fleming in an undertone.

"John who?" murmured Ann DeGroat. "Never heard of him."

"Do we know him?"

"Invictus."

"Invite-it what?"

"Martin Kerr's firm." This was Emily Lewin.

"No—no. I don't know it."

"Yes, yes. You do. Didn't Marnie Pete's husband work there?"

"Yes, I think James—"

"Who?"

"Seven billion under management," said Betsy.

"Marnie who?"

"You wouldn't know them. They were before us. Moved to Singapore."

"Ah . . ."

"Didn't James Pete leave under a cloud?" Emily said.

"Well, Marty does tend to hire the smart ones with the dodgy backgrounds," Betsy acknowledged. "He likes them hungry. But nothing's ever been proven." She gulped her quickly cooling latte. "I say go for it. It's all such a fuzzy line these days. You think these guys have job security? Bullshit. Those jobs have the half-life of a job at McDonald's. They get the big apartment, leverage up . . . next thing you know, the guy's not producing and his wife's gonna leave him and they're fucked." Betsy liked to tell it like it was and to swear. An equity saleswoman until recently, she had married late. She'd had three kids in four years yet still had the feeling sometimes that she was impersonating a mother of preschool children, as if a strong wind might blow Tommy and the boys and the baby away, and she'd find herself back on the trading floor listening to the morning call over her squawk box. She had five years on Ann and Emily.

The gazes of all three women flitted back to Minnie Curtis. At the moment, she didn't look like a woman who was going to leave her husband. She didn't look "fucked"—not in the least. She glowed with contentment. She exuded that satisfaction that the anxious, the guilty—the heathen—never can. When she unhurriedly removed a mini-bottle of hand sanitizer from her fancy pocketbook and rubbed her hands together, she seemed to take pleasure in how attractive they were and in her perfectly manicured nails (not too long, not too short). Watching her, each of the women had a sudden itch to sanitize her own hands.

"How do you know these things?" said Ann admiringly to Betsy, breaking her croissant in two and spreading butter on both halves. Wan, blond, and underweight her whole life, Ann wasn't ambitious enough to watch her diet for nutrition's sake, though lately she had been feeling she ought to get more cardiovascular exercise. "How do you know every last detail of all of these hedge funds? I can barely keep straight what Guy does for a living. Oil and gas—I know that's the industry, but—"

Betsy looked affronted. "I covered hedge funds for fifteen years!"

"Oh my gosh, I always forget that! You're so arty now. You're so 'mom,'" Ann said.

"I had to have a third child to get out of it!"

They nudged one another.

"Go say hi to her."

"Yeah, just ask her to come over."

"No—she's clearly waiting for someone."

The morning din of the café provided a soothing background to the speculation—the hiss of steam from the espresso machines, the clatter of crockery; laughter and shouts. The French café was preferred over the Italian across the street, which had been discovered to be a tristate chain. Once their preference had been established, the mornings had seemed to take on a feeling of mild importance, of commitment to a cause; loyalty manifest.

"He's her second marriage, apparently . . ."

"Oh, really? Not the father of—what is it?"

"Annabelle?"

"Arabella."

"She's in Pilar's class—in the Fours."

"She's really tall. The new girl's tall."

"Well, she ought to be—she's five and a half!"

"Five and a half? Jeez. The nursery kids just seem to get older and older."

"Competitive advantage! Everyone's after it. In my day, we prided ourselves on being *young* for our class." Betsy checked her phone before volunteering diffidently, "I skipped a grade."

"*Did* you?" said Ann, pleased with and impressed by her friend. "Aren't you smart. Is she"—she lowered her voice and said, with a little bit of a wince—"South American?," made tentative not by racism, which wouldn't have occurred to her, but because she was never quite sure which countries made up Central America and which South America.

"Venezuelan. It's a big oil family, people say."

"Oh, I thought it was sugar. I'm pretty sure I heard it was sugar."

"Yeah? Well. Raping-and-pillaging kind of fortune, anyway."

"Now, Emily…"

"Sorry, girls, but you're both wrong," Betsy said. "What I heard—what I *know*, because I heard it from a very good source," she added mischievously, tipping her cup up and wishing the coffee had lasted longer because she was trying to cut back, "was that she was John Curtis's secretary!" Now she had their attention. "His temp! They were all living in London and she was married to some other guy, some English guy, and she started temping at Invictus, to make a little money of her own, and the next thing you know, she's running off with the boss."

"Wow," said Ann, who never said a mean word about anyone, though whether out of kindness or an utter lack of discernment, Emily and Betsy couldn't have said. "That's…I mean—interesting!" She giggled. "Cool!"

"Oh, *Invictus*." Emily addressed Betsy. "Of course—Martin *Kerr* Invictus. It just clicked." She smirked at the other two. "They must be rich!" Emily, whose husband, Stephen Simon, came from one of the leading New York real estate families and was worth hundreds of millions, punctuated her observation with a wheezing laugh. "Really rich!"

Emily had grown up in the city with her divorced mother on the Upper West Side. She had been a smart girl, had gone to Cleary School and Harvard on financial aid, clerked for Justice Sandra Day O'Connor, prosecuted perps in the DA's office, and eventually segued into white-collar defense at Cravath. But at a certain point (the birth of her fourth child), the Simon money had made it ludicrous that she would go into an office in the morning. Jobless, she eschewed all accoutrements of wealth. She wore no makeup or engagement ring; her outfit today—a typical *ensemble*—consisted of a stretched-out, maroon-colored turtleneck over baggy threadbare corduroys with no belt. She picked her nails down to the quick (nice nails meant you weren't serious) and her laugh evoked a large sea mammal with respiratory trouble.

"The firm's done well," Betsy conceded with the sort of appreciative wistfulness she'd often felt since she quit.

"Who's your source on all this?" Emily asked.

Betsy grinned. "*She* is! She was telling that woman — Gwen? You know, Gwen...what's-her-name, the one who looks like Lally's au pair? — the whole story at pickup the other day. I was just standing there trying to smile in a friendly way. Couldn't help overhearing..."

"So you practically know her!" Emily squealed. "You're the one who should invite her over!"

"No, no, come on — I don't know her."

"Well, I don't know her at all!" Ann said defensively.

"I haven't been introduced!" echoed Betsy.

"Anyway, she's waiting for someone, I'm sure."

"I do feel bad not inviting her over." Ann sighed.

"I really don't think she cares, Ann. She doesn't look like she cares."

"We'll invite her over next time," Betsy said soothingly.

"Okay."

"Fine."

It wasn't that they had any plan to snub the woman. In fact, they'd spoken freely, rather giddily, just now, the mothers, because they liked her. They'd liked Minnie Curtis from the get-go. They liked the alert, arched-eyebrow, ready look of her. The money didn't hurt. Martin Kerr's Invictus was one of the funds people had heard of. Aggressive. Shady, perhaps? That too. No one cared, in the same way that no one cared whether the New Mother came from a South American sugar fortune or a temp agency. Either way, she provided interest. And who were they to judge? This wasn't a society in which one needed to know whether one's neighbor could be trusted—or had the same values one had. This was a society that ran on Lycra and imported Labradoodles, on making a virtue of a pervasive lack of any kind of necessity: deciding to pick up the kids yourself when you could have sent the nanny. They glanced again at Mrs. Curtis. (Surnames were still in use north of Forty-Second Street.) She was looking around the café with a cheerful, expectant air. There was nothing subtle about her appeal—one could venture, about any attribute of hers at all. She had shining hair of the darkest near-black brown and wonderfully white, perfect teeth, and her mouth was a pink bow. Her cheeks might have admitted some adolescent struggle with acne, which careful though plentiful makeup concealed. It was a little cheesy, the way Mrs. Curtis was made up, pink blush and glossy lips, but it worked. It was sweet, how polished she was, like a little girl before a birthday party. The handbag might be a little much for ten a.m.: a quilted black rectangle sitting beside her on the banquette, wrapped up in its clichéd gold chain of a strap. But this was a society of strivers who had achieved and gotten used to wealth. Real snobbery was rare. Maybe everyone allowed herself one accoutrement straight out of the aspirational era, one item she knew better than to covet now but that, then, had symbolized everything. A black quilted Chanel purse; how many years had Minnie Curtis née Colón desired such a thing before she felt she could afford it?

In the end, for this morning, anyway, the women—yawning presently and stretching, saying, "I gotta get to the gym," ordering second half-caff lattes, and looking, without remark, at the time on their phones—granted themselves the luxury of not inviting her over.

*　　*　　*

At her table, meanwhile, Minnie Curtis withdrew a pair of reading glasses from her handbag and picked up the menu that had lain before her for some minutes. She surveyed it suspiciously. When the waiter appeared, tall and dour, and roughly demanded her order, she did not rush to meet his tempo, as most of the women did. No; she made him wait. When the man had been inconvenienced enough to make an *ack*-type sound in the back of his throat while shifting his weight from side to side with increasing violence, Minnie raised her eyes and said coolly, "I'll have coffee." She paused. "Black," she added as he snatched the menu from her hands. Minnie's coffee date was Philippa Lye, and as Emily, Betsy, or Ann could have predicted, Mrs. Skinker was late. Perhaps Minnie could have predicted it, too, with the things she'd heard about Philippa and now observed, but Minnie had shown up precisely on time despite the expectation. Minnie Curtis was one of the few people who didn't automatically build leeway into their days. She shunned the easy exit, the free pass. She looked on perks with scorn, and people who complained to her that the weather had affected their plans, she greeted with the sort of smile one gives a senile person or, in the case of household help, fired at once.

Fordyce, Crandall. Seven floors of billable hours. How Minnie Colón had loved the place—the thrum of corporate efficiency; the creed of "support." It was the first nice place she'd ever been a part of.

Occasionally the other legal assistants would ask her to go to lunch with them—"to be nice," Minnie was sure, for that was their doctrine. She was the only professional paralegal among them, the other girls all killing time between a nice college and a socially acceptable career. Perhaps they expected her to learn from them at these lunches, model herself after them—start wearing ballet flats and understated makeup.

Stupid girls.

Stupid, spoiled girls.

But then, what would you expect? They hadn't been spanked as children.

At lunch, as they failed at their diets—yes, please, the Death by Chocolate with three spoons—they would speak in hushed voices of a vast and personal affront: a former member of their ranks who had left Fordyce not for law school or a job at an art auction house or a PR firm but to get married. Soon, Minnie had a composite of this girl—so tall, so thin, so apparently never in need of her colleagues unless she wanted them to show her, for the fourth time, how to get the Xerox machine to produce double-sided copies.

"She just comes in with that huge rock and announces she's getting married. Of all the people..." They would turn to Minnie and say condescendingly: "You didn't know her. She left before you started."

"It's like, she does nothing for two years and we're all covering her ass and then Jed Skinker waltzes in at the last minute...I mean, honestly!"

It was true that Minnie Colón, out of Spanish Harlem with a five-year sojourn in a shitty, racist town on the North Shore of Long Island, had never met this Philippa Lye. She could not join in the backbiting—not that she would have in any case. Didn't the girls see that their jealous chatter only betrayed their own weakness and desperation? Oh, Minnie could have taught those girls a few things if they'd cared to listen.

As far as the Death by Chocolate—goodness knows, Minnie never shared food.

The stepfather who had raised Minnie was not a religious fanatic but he was dogmatic, his favorite tenet that God was watching us all the time—seeing us no matter where we were or what we were doing. Hector Colón got up in the morning in order to rout out weakness in deportment, hygiene, grammar, posture, thoughts. He was compulsively neat himself and exacting with his children, though Minnie, his stepdaughter, was the only one in whom his efforts seemed to take. The boys were slobs; the younger, Jaime, was worse than that—a bad seed. By the time Minnie turned thirteen, on Long Island, where Hector had moved the family to get out of Harlem, he was in love with her. Minnie was aware of this and might even have expected it—wasn't it her due as a beautiful, perfect young woman who never shampooed without conditioning and who always left at least one bite of food on her plate to show self-restraint? She was less traumatized by Hector's continuing to kiss her on the lips at bedtime all through high school; by his squeezing her bare knees in the mornings when she sat in the front seat of the Ford Escort and then, after dropping off the boys, walking his fingers up to the bottom of her burgundy-plaid uniform skirt and slipping them a centimeter underneath the hem before, with a huge, renouncing groan, he would forbid himself any more of a transgression; by his coming home drunk after a Christmas party one night when she was fifteen and tipsily getting into bed with her and her having to fight him off with sharp elbows and even a kick to the shin when he tried to press *it* into her thigh and finally her being so tired and bored that she allowed him to sleep with his arm around her midriff whispering epigrams of love until he passed out cold; by his running joke that he ought to introduce her as his wife and his proceeding to do so on more than one occasion—she was less traumatized by all of that than she was by the A-minus she got junior year in Health. The fact was, as an adult, Minnie had standards that she kept to as naturally as breathing, no matter the setting. Hanging around in sweatpants with her hair uncombed, eating a bowl of cereal in front of the television—all habits her generation fell into without a blink—would not have occurred to her. Whether she owed her self-control to Hector, her own disposition, her life experience (her mother had descended into alcoholism when Minnie was nine and rarely got out of her sweats or combed her hair), or to the Roman Catholic Church she couldn't have said.

The truth of who she was could perhaps best be summed up by saying that, by surprising Minnie at home, one would gain no advantage whatever over her.

In the café, chairs scraped as the table of St. Tim's mothers got up to go, the women rising and turning studiously neutral faces toward Minnie as they gathered their things.

The group seemed to confer under their breath—they edged closer. After an awkward pause, Betsy laughed, and then Ann DeGroat said, extending her hand to Minnie in a sort of choppy dance movement, "I don't believe we've met!"

"Minnie Curtis!" said Minnie, making to rise, but Ann and Betsy protested, "Oh, no—don't get up! Don't get up!"

"We thought you might have been waiting for someone," Betsy said, arranging her scarf around her neck, "or we would have told you to come and sit with us."

"Oh—thank you! Philippa—Philippa Lye was supposed to come but it doesn't look like she's going to make it."

"Ri-ight!"

"Welcome to our world!"

"She's often late." Betsy frowned. "You see, I used to have a corporate job, and it really wasn't acceptable to be late for things."

Ann said anxiously, "Next time coffee with us, okay?"

The waiter dropped the check before Minnie with a grunt. Minnie glanced at it and opened her wallet.

"I, for one, had better be going," Betsy said brightly.

"It was *great* to meet you, Minnie!" said Ann. "I know Virginia wants to have a playdate with Arabella!"

Minnie took a hundred-dollar bill out of her wallet and placed it on the check.

"Is that a hundred?" said Emily as Betsy tried to edge the three of them away.

"It is." Minnie smiled. "I always carry a lot of cash."

"Do you?"

"Yes," Minnie said without clarification.

"Hmm."

"I don't know if they'll accept that! I really don't know. What do you think, Bets?"

Betsy shrugged. "Search me. But I really—"

"Your husband's at Invictus, isn't he?" Emily remarked, as if the bill had been a Rorschach test and an association had finally come into her head.

"That's right." Minnie raised her eyes to the three women and said softly, "I was married to another man when I met John. And of course I still love Tony. He's the father of my daughter, after all. But I felt I would have a better life with John."

"Sure, sure!"

"Of course. Of course!" The St. Tim's mothers couldn't have agreed more vociferously. Concurring with Minnie's statement all the way, they fairly charged out the door of the café. On the sidewalk they tittered and laughed outright and snorted through their noses—"Well, if that wasn't the overshare of the morning!" "A better life! Uh...yeah! Hedge-fund zillionaire, she means!" "Jeez." "Gosh!" But once they broke apart and walked home, each of the three by herself felt distinctly unsettled, as if the New Mother's attitude undermined the narratives they told themselves of their own lives. Betsy muttered aloud, "But I *did* want to have children!" and Ann thought, *It's not true that I don't like sex. It's just that Guy...,* and Emily's mind flitted to the raised eyebrows of an unbelievably droll but penurious Frenchman she had dated in her twenties, who, she could admit to herself now, she knew all along had been married, although not the part about the children at home in Lyon.

Maybe it was in our natures to eat too much and drink too much, to sleep off hangovers till one p.m. on Saturdays, to get behind on our credit cards because of clothes, to let attractive young men sleep with us on the first date but hope they would call, to be miserable and pick at our nails and develop anxiety disorders and feud with one another and have fallings-out and write in our diaries and make up only with better boundaries in place and become galvanized by self-help books we chanced upon on the sale tables of Barnes and Noble and feel real joy in spring and decide to focus on our careers and spend Sunday afternoons at copy shops amending our résumés: Objective: an entry-level job in communications.

But we suppressed all of this—all of it. We did the Zone diet and the Atkins diet and we went (practically, mostly, quite a good deal of the time) on the wagon and became smarter about clothes (even occasionally copying a trick with a scarf or a color combo we'd seen on Philippa Lye) and we did the cabbage-soup diet developed for cardiac patients pre-surgery and got haircuts on Madison on trainee night and learned to cook things out of The Silver Palate Cookbook *and did the grapefruit diet and the frozen-yogurt diet, all so as not to appear sluts.*

Whereas she—

41

Whereas Philippa Lye—

The girl was heading toward disaster. Even in our twenties, we could see she represented another time in the city, a laxer time, when background and the effects of personality could get you somewhere. But that was then! No one like that could amount to anything anymore. Not among the ascendant, increasingly well-hydrated, continually self-improving meritocracy. How many times did she *pound around the Reservoir in Central Park after dark to squeeze the run in? How many times did she go to church by herself when all else failed? A movie by herself? Try yoga? Brashly announce a dinner party then have to buy four new spices at $6.99 a pop, a tart pan with a removable bottom, cloth napkins; lug wine up the stairs of a sixth-floor walk-up by herself, go back down—twice—for fancy water? In what ways did she suffer or pay her dues?*

(As to the rumors about her past, her twenties—call them the lost years, the years in between her modeling career and her landing at Fordyce, Crandall as a legal assistant—don't go there. Not if you don't want to seem petty and sick...too sordid to even contemplate. So sordid and stomach-churning it probably wasn't true and that would be embarrassing—to gloat about something, then find it apocryphal. You see we had, after all, learned some lessons between college and now.)

And we weren't saying anything more than the truth when we said that, despite her looks, the girl might have been disposed of, as so many girls we knew who blew out their twenties were. She might have ended up, as Jen Kim (the witty one of us) had predicted, selling scented candles in Taos, partnering with some goateed nice guy she'd meet in recovery, life divided into the exciting but shameful "before" and the supposedly more honest fresh-aired pleasures of "after"...

Meanwhile, we dieted.

We ordered the tap water at restaurants to save on the bill—"without ice, please."

We tried to "take advantage of the city." We went hungover to Chinatown for dim sum. We saw odd independent films that we never quite forgot. We ate hamburgers on Jane Street. We embraced new drinks (a gimlet, Scotch and soda with a twist, bourbon and rye) at the Gramercy Park Hotel and over-tipped the Irishman who played piano.

"Fly me to the moon . . ."

And we waited.

Patiently, we waited. And just as it seemed comeuppance would slam down like the steel grille of a discount electronics store — she had been drunk at work, then took a shocking spate of sick days — she married out.

Wouldn't you know it; she married out.

Philippa Lye.

Just like that.

I admit that we looked, rather frantically, for the worm in the apple.

The story, in all its abysmal detail, became known.

It was a dive bar in Yorkville that people didn't go to even ironically. Word had it she was so drunk she'd forgotten to pay her tab and was stumbling out alone, knocking over chairs on the way, when Jedediah Skinker, the scion himself, sprang up, bodily stopped the pursuant bartender, and covered the check. Why he was drinking alone in that bar we will never know, though we certainly pos-tulated at length — and sometimes still wonder today. He put her in a taxi and refused to take advantage of her despite the many times she suggested it.

Married her.

Speedily she moved from whatever unsavory building she'd been living in (she never had us over and often received personal mail at the office, against firm policy) to an inherited apartment on Eighty-Ninth Street in one of those co-ops that look gastrointestinally pained (Jen Kim again) when someone ac-tually wants to take out a mortgage.

Yet it was nothing so specific as a material advantage in looks or influence that rankled. Standards of beauty had gotten broader by the nineties and we more or less liked ourselves for who we were. And college ties by then were the equivalent of family connections. It came down to the sense of entitlement she exuded. In her first year at the law firm, in the mid-1990s, traipsing aloofly around, she had spoken elliptically—maddeningly elliptically, had Philippa Lye. Naively, we had waited for the day—oh, the glorious day—when the music would end, when she would no longer be able to speak in those a-contextualized sound bites but would have to explain herself, as the rest of us had to, as the rest of us always fucking had to. But Jed Skinker proposed at the tail end of our collective career at Fordyce—nobody lasted more than two years. We were off to law school, to jobs in marketing, broadcasting, children's-book publishing, at Internet start-ups or Fifty-Seventh Street galleries—and damn if Philippa Lye hadn't ended by speaking elliptically: the Opera House Cup... Club 55... never actually met each other but my third-form year his sister... Seal... Neddie... black-tie landmarks thing... won the club doubles three years in a...

Fuck her.

Chapter Four

One person who had never come across Philippa Lye in his twenties was Dan Hogan. He had never come across any of them—not Jen Kim or Jessica Kaplan or Megan Crowley, though the last boarded the 6 train at the same stop he did (Seventy-Seventh Street) for two years in the late '90s, Dan Hogan with a JD so new, he felt like the impostor from the old TV commercial ("I just play one on TV") as he walked the crosstown blocks from York and tripped almost embarrassingly eagerly down to his Second Circuit clerkship. And while it was true that Dan's world and those girls' world, orbiting independently for so long, were suddenly accelerating toward each other through that transfiguring force of their generation—education—Dan, as if wanting to avoid the personal devastation that might result from a total collision, had gotten married right out of college.

"Dude, you wanna come out?" Matt Nast gave a rap on the open door of Dan's office. "We're getting a beer."

"Nah, better not."

The invitation was proffered with little expectation of its being taken up, Dan knew, but he stood right up from behind his desk. He didn't socialize with his colleagues in the U.S. Attorney's Office half as much as they did with one another, but he didn't like people to think he took them for granted. Mutual respect was the tone here in the storied office of the Southern District—the office that had prosecuted, well, everyone: the Rosenbergs to Ivan Boesky. Everyone who worked here was aware of taking his place in history, but Dan didn't like to flaunt his ambition in front of his peers. You didn't get through as the second youngest of five brothers by sticking your neck out on a regular basis. "Gotta deal with some stuff," he said.

"Hey—congrats, by the way." Open and easygoing, Nast clapped him on the back as Dan came to the door. "Park Avenue's lost a proctologist, huh?"

"Thanks, man." This was a reference to the defendant in Dan's latest trial, a Dr. Gene Torelli, who had managed to combine an Upper East Side medical practice with a money-laundering operation for the Gambino crime family. "Frank DiNapoli"—this was Dan's go-to agent at the FBI—"told me I'm gonna have to go elsewhere for my anal-retentiveness."

As Matt chuckled and ritualistically pressed him to come out, Dan made the small talk, fidgeting and rising on his toes, trying not to focus on the beer.

It was half past seven on a Thursday at the end of January and he craved one.

"You gotta celebrate! We're only having one. Well, maybe two. I'm outta here tomorrow morning."

"Yeah?" Dan felt his fidgeting intensify—gripped his right hand to still it. To an observer, he must look like a freaky motherfucker. Next to his laid-back colleague, he felt like an old-fashioned ticking alarm clock, like the one his wife, Gwen, had on her bed-side table, about thirty seconds from the bell. Nast, while smart and focused on the job, never really seemed hungry—he worked cases soberly, like a bright child given a puzzle to do. Perhaps something about Matt's contrasting style set Dan off. But then, something about nearly everyone in this town except maybe his wife and kid evoked Dan's impatience, his jumpy dismissiveness. Instead of his attitude mellowing with time, the longer he stayed in New York—he and Gwen were past the decade mark now—the worse it got, as if he were absorbing some toxic element out of the air.

"Vacation?" he inquired briefly.

Nast looked sheepish when he said, "Caribbean for a week." He added, in what might have been an apology or might have been a brag: "Nicole's parents."

"Mm."

Time was, Dan had been naive. He could wince, remembering his surprise at his colleagues' addresses in Tribeca lofts, doorman buildings on Central Park West; could shudder at his gullible as-sumption that they were all living off their salaries. He thought of himself as savvy and pretty tough, willing to do what it took to get ahead, but the moment that he realized that half his "peers" were bankrolled by trust funds or parents—that private-school tuitions, second houses, posh vacations had nothing to do with ac-tual income—had been like a knuckle to the head from his oldest brother, Donny ("*Duh*, McFly!"). He'd been a baby. Innocent as a lamb. Put it another way: a total fucking idiot. Yet it hadn't killed him. It might have, he supposed, but on further inspection, some part of him rejected the cushy existence enabled by the parental dole. Some part of him defined himself *against it*. Gwen defined herself against it too. In it but not of it, the two of them. Never of it. They were different. The Hogans were different. Pressing himself now, for instance, as he'd press a recalcitrant witness in court, he asked if his reaction was, actually, jealousy. Wouldn't he, really, on his $150,000-a-year job as an assistant U.S. attorney in the Securities Fraud unit, love to be kiting off to St. Somewhere, lolling on the beach with an umbrella in his drink on some fantasy in-laws' dime? At this, his nervous system gave an involuntary shudder. Nope; good to know. It was actually repulsion.

"Good for you."

"Should be fun. We're trying Nevis this year."

"Got it." To be clear, Dan had nothing against Nast himself.

"Last year we went to Antigua but Nicole thought it was kinda played."

"I see."

"So, Nevis is kinda hard to get to—two flights and all—so we're thinking that'll keep out hoi polloi..."

"Sure, sure." It occurred to Dan, as he took off his wire-rimmed glasses and polished them with his shirttail to give his hands something to do, that it was boredom, not rage, that would ultimately provoke one to violence, although, again, Nast himself was a good guy. During their first year here, both of them in General Crimes, Dan had bestowed on his colleague the epithet *a true intellectual*, each man understanding perhaps that the phrase combined respect and derision. This was in contrast to Dan's own intelligence, which had once been called *raw* and seemed to have remained so, as if the influences or pretensions that might have cooked it had never penetrated its core...Go ahead, call it a class issue. Dan would not be the one to take offense. After all, no one was keeping Dan down. From this office, he could go to a firm any time he liked, cop the big salary and be done with commuting by subway and staycations.

"Hey—heard you got a new case," Matt said. "John Curtis Take Two, is it? That guy's like the Weeble-Wobble of perps."

"Curtis? Yeah. He's haunting my dreams."

"Diane says he was at Yale with you? Hadn't realized that with Tamco."

"Yeah, we overlapped." Dan's stomach tightened—still, after all this time—at the mention of their female colleague, but he pressed on. "But I didn't know the guy. We 'moved in different circles,'" he added with the kind of self-ironic inflection he inserted for his own amusement, knowing no one would pick up on it. "Sure got to know him on Tamco, though."

Dan didn't even have a visual on John Curtis as an undergrad. During the case he pursued three years ago, he'd been able to remember him by reputation only—the rich, Euro crowd the guy had run with, some nasty rumors that had hounded him. Curtis had worked at Tamco, the bond company, then, some irregularity in his résumé keeping him from the Morgan or Goldman hire, when he'd apparently decided his track record wasn't quite good enough for the big promotion he was after. So he'd started cherry-picking trades to make himself look good—a relatively simple operation, when you got down to it. All Curtis had to do was delay the allocation of trades long enough to learn which ones were the good ones and then put those in whichever subaccounts would help his résumé. And fuck the ones that wouldn't. There had been a theme of flagrancy to the case, and Dan had been 100 percent sure Curtis, his fellow Yalie, was guilty.

"You tried to flip someone," Nast recalled.

Dan gave a nod. "Tried and failed. This woman from the middle office—young woman." Instead of cooperating with them, the woman had gone hard-loyal to her boss in such a slavish way, it gave Dan the creeps. He couldn't get the case off the ground and had to drop the thing pre-indictment and watch the SEC issue the $100,000 rap on the knuckles. "He ended up in London."

"London 'oliday while the air cleared?"

Dan gave a bark of a laugh, not at Matt's bad Cockney but because he suddenly remembered something he knew Nast would appreciate. "Get a load of this. Undergrad, he was John Curtis, right? Guy's name was John Curtis. And then when he was at Tamco, still the same John Curtis we all knew and loved."

"Mm-hmm."

"So, now—now he's John *D.* Curtis." Dan guffawed. "Motherfucker added the *D!*"

"No! Kidding me."

"Nope! Wanted to give his name more of a Rockefeller ring, apparently." Dan shook his head, for this fact was as incredible to him as anything the initial investigation had turned up since the SEC had briefed them on the new case. Frank DiNapoli had told him about it: "Moved to London, worked for a hedge fund, added a fake middle initial to his name, Danny, you know"—baby-faced DiNapoli had recounted in his trademark deadpan the other day—"as ya do."

"So the 'D' really doesn't stand for anything?" said Nast, and Dan could have kissed him—the classic straight man.

"Beyond *Dipshit?*" He cackled. "Oh, and by the way he also flirted with using 'Curtis Johns.' That appears here and there as well, when he was between jobs. It made me think—I mean, maybe I should start going as 'Hogan Dans.' Turn over a new leaf. Whaddaya think?"

Matt clapped him on the back. "I think Hogan Dans would definitely be coming out with us for a beer."

Dan chuckled. "Have a good vacation, man."

He watched Matt roll down the hall, then stop to pick up Tad Zalewski and Diane Costa. When Dan heard the latter say, "Let me just grab my bag," he retreated from the doorway and went back behind his desk, relieved that he'd committed to staying in and working. Diane was another pal from his General Crimes class. Another improbable friend of his made on the job. But now, seven years in, he and she were neck and neck in a horse race for deputy chief of the unit. Whoever didn't get the promotion would probably leave. (*But she doesn't have the trial experience I do!* he heard himself saying in a weenie-ish whine.) A straight shooter, outspoken (not to say aggressive), a go-getter (again, not to say aggressive)—Diane Costa, with her management-consulting Euro-husband Johann...Whoever did get the promotion would be made chief in a year—it was a fait accompli.

Dan sat down at his desk, clasped his fingers together, stretched his arms up, his palms facing outward, and half yawned, as if the easygoing posture might disguise his jumpy, hypercompetitive mind-set. For that was an illustrious position, chief of the securities and commodities unit in this, the southern—or, as they conceitedly but with good reason called themselves, the "sovereign"—district of New York. He tipped onto the back legs of his chair, balancing on his fingertips, then let the wheels drop to the floor.

Not so long ago, Dan had been set to go back to a law firm. It was after his fifth year, his third year in securities fraud, when colleagues who had initially enjoyed escaping the corporate grind were heading to white-shoe Manhattan firms in, if not droves, then predictable, pleasantly resigned clusters. Despite a minor reluctance to cash in, Dan was no martyr; even he, with his material desires well in check, was getting tired of the Yorkville ghetto. It was known in the office that it was the second kid that did it—that drew you instinctually toward the teat of corporate comfort. Gwen was pregnant again and Dan had no intention of stopping at two—"Screw these Isle of Manhattan control freaks with their one point seven children!" But—here he blinked his eyes rapidly—that wasn't how things had happened. That wasn't how it had worked out. It turned out Dan and Gwen were, in the common parlance, "done." Dan had even started using that stock, jokey phrase when people who didn't know better tried to goad him—"Oh, no, one and done!" he'd say, as if it were a cheery maxim he lived by. Gwen in the hospital, hemorrhaging, white as death, the baby lost at twenty weeks...

After they got past that, Dan felt irritated when he thought of a job in corporate litigation. As the weeks went by, he felt more so. Presently he felt enraged. That was the year the question *How dare you?* started to form on his lips in the most innocuous of situations—when getting a regular, light and sweet, from the stands on Center Street...when stopped in a tunnel on the express train up to Eighty-Sixth Street...when sitting with Gwen between courses at their neighborhood red-wine Italian, silently debating another bottle, as conversation lapsed.

How dare you? How fucking dare you?

Sometimes he'd wake up silent-shouting the question, sweating, his fists and jaw clenched, having been unable to get the words out in a dream.

How dare you?

Who the hell was this "you" and what galling presumption was he, she, or it visiting on Dan? Dan never defined it. But the sharpest prompt seemed to come, not from the miscreants he pursued, but from the job offers that came rolling in. The very job offers he'd been enjoying contemplating...Looking at an e-mail one afternoon from the head of the white-collar criminal-defense group at a firm where he'd had a second and a third meeting that read *We want to get you in as soon as possible to talk to Jim*—the managing partner—he'd barely fought down the career-suicidal desire to tap in the guy's number and rage into the phone, *How fucking dare you?*

And so he had stayed. He had stayed to become chief of the unit, apparently. Surely he had known that was in there even two years ago. Now that he knew he would never have four kids to support—or even two—there was just this: his ambition. His sadness, which he didn't acknowledge, and his ambition, which he did. No trajectory seemed too steep, no position too exalted now that his career had his single-minded attention. A federal judge-ship. U.S. attorney itself. Head of the frickin' FBI—why not? So many others who had come from his office had done as much. Or go on a tangent, just as good: he contemplated moving back over the bridge to New Jersey, running for Congress from his home state. Brian, his middle brother, the Rutgers poli-sci major, ran lo-cal campaigns—had been cited, in the last presidential race, as an "operative"...

From down the hall, he heard Diane Costa's unrestrained belly laugh.

"What does your wife think about all this?" he heard her saying back then, when he was letting himself—in a rare relaxation of his privacy standards—wax expansive over drinks one night about the firm job (and the money and the kids and the kind of house he wanted in Glen Ridge, a town whose real estate he had Googled many times) and how the cushier life would side-track probably forever his secret dream of a run at Washington someday. "She's fine with whatever," Dan said dismissively, not enjoying the entitlement of Diane's going around him, as it were, to get to his wife in some sisterly feint.

"She's fine with whatever? What the hell, Dan?"

And then she had to go all anachronistic feminist righteousness on him when she had no fucking idea of how his marriage ran. Diane was smart, Diane was committed, Diane would go far (though probably not as far as he himself), but Gwen—Gwen had it all over Diane. Dan couldn't even think of them as being in the same class of person, the same gender, the same conversation, anything. But you couldn't say that, could you? You couldn't explain, *Look, you're one of those women who get strident about who changes how many diapers on the nanny's day off. Gwen and I are beyond that. Gwen and I*—Then she'd actually run with it.

"What's your other kid—one and a half? Two? And didn't your wife used to have some big career? What was she? No, tell me! A scientist or something? Wait—a chemist, right?"

"Chemical engineer," Dan said tersely. Uneasily he fended her off.

The truth was he hadn't known how to reconcile his surprise finding, a decade ago, that intelligence in a spouse was a sine qua non for him (he had dumped another, dumber girl within a week of meeting Gwen) with his secret desire for a stay-at-home wife like his mother. Vanity, he saw now, had led him to picture himself as a partner in a firm with four or even five kids; the resigned—but in truth eager—move out to the suburbs...When he met Gwen, he'd been planning to marry his then-girlfriend, Amy. Amy, with her generous rack, her throwback sweater sets that showed it off, her Yale-football-obsessed dad—*what's not to like?* Amy was the picture of the wife of the politician Dan had already confided in her he wanted to become—at that point he wasn't secretive about the dream, not at all. Then one afternoon freshman spring, his roommate Brady brought Gwen into their suite. Brady and Gwen were of that rare, beleaguered breed, future engineers at a school where most kids had their sights set on something starrier; she'd come over to work on a few problems with Brady. At some shenanigan Dan had indulged in—he had made rude noises out the window at a buddy of his who was chatting up a girl in the courtyard—Gwen Babineau had given him a withering look, utterly unimpressed but far from humorless, such as his mother would give him when as a boy he'd acted out.

Amy was out by Sunday; he never looked back. Gwen's dim view of him drove him crazy. Amy was a big girl who tended toward fat and, like him, a big drinker. That had been fun while it lasted—getting trashed with a good-natured young woman who prided herself on keeping up with him, stumbling home to her dorm room, charming her roommates, who thought he'd make a great congressman, the sloppy sex afterward. Now, on Thursday nights, he would go out with his buddies and Gwen. She didn't insist on proper dates, the way Amy had. She didn't insist on anything. (On Valentine's Day, which fell a few months after they'd started dating, he'd panicked, realizing he should have gotten her something. When he sheepishly presented his last-minute gift, Gwen Babineau looked at it and said, "You bought me a drugstore heart of chocolates?" As he squirmed, "You mean to tell me you actually spent money on this?") Yet she had a hold over him that Amy had never had. It stayed like that, as the other guys' girlfriends came and went—the group of him and his roommates and Gwen. He would drink nine or ten beers while she nursed a pint. She was pale and freckly, and her large mouth and receding chin gave his girlfriend the look of a lass, a sister, a friend—a role Gwen played with all of his buddies, dispensing advice and sticking up for the girls in all situations. But underneath the turtlenecks and fleece jackets and jeans, Gwen Babineau had the most perfect body he had ever encountered—uptilted breasts on that small waist, athletic thighs and slim calves...That she hid it in those unremarkable clothes only made it sexier, as if it were a secret she kept all for him. Gwen herself paid no attention to her figure at all. She didn't know the word *diet* and her underwear was plain white cotton bought in multi-pair packs. Having sex with her those nights, so shit-faced he couldn't see and aware that she was stone sober and no doubt bored silly by his antics, he had been happier than he could ever remember being...

Sometimes the question was an enraged demand. Sometimes it was a low, menacing murmur. This dark January night, though, it came into his head like a sputter, like the blubbering plaint of a kid whom some practical joke had made a stooge of. He nearly choked over it as it interrupted his warm memory of college: *How — how dare you?*

That evening two years ago, Diane had thrown some toxic shit at him. Perhaps sexist was going too far, she'd conceded. But at the very least, she had concluded the evening by telling him — okay, they were both drunk and cocky, celebrating after the GenStar trial — he had a problem with women.

"Bullshit," he'd responded automatically. "Total bullshit."

On a note of self-disgust at his procrastination, Dan once more fell to surveying the unlovely documents before him — John Curtis's subpoenaed credit card statements. He knew what he'd find. The guys who thought they were smarter than the law, smarter than the Feds, they were spendy people, people who liked to splash it around — cars, art, houses. You didn't break the law so you could sock more money away.

Chapter Five

Two long days per week were required of the older children at St. Timothy's; they brought their lunch, and pickup was at three instead of noon. Ostensibly, this was to prepare the Fours for kindergarten, but the real reason, Gwen thought, was that they had to top the fees somehow, for Mrs. Davidson had refused to initiate the discrete morning and afternoon sessions most of the other preschools had caved to. "We are one school and we all come to school at the same time!" the head had apparently declared in one of those oft-quoted remarks that stood in for a creed among the parents.

Gwen hadn't gotten used to the long days. The usual pattern of the day revoked, she would anxiously check the time at home after the dishes and beds, after her run and shower. When at last the hour for pickup arrived, the event had a disorienting feel, as if one had come in error. As if to underline her sense of dislocation, last week the teachers had forgotten about spacey, tractable Mary in the top-floor room used for music and movement. After waiting till every child was handed out and Mrs. Davidson and Ms. Babcock had begun to close the door, Gwen had had to initiate a search. Ms. Babcock had huffed up the stairs behind her, forcing Gwen to wait on the landings—but without seeming to, so as not to play up the difference in physical fitness between the two of them. When they finally found Mary, sitting on the floor, humming "The Circle Game," and tightening her laces, the assistant head had made the kind of comment Gwen thought would have died out a generation ago: "What? Still putting on your shoes? No wonder you got left behind!"

January's brief correction of below-freezing weather had given way to the city's more typical, limpid, 30- to 40-degree days. As she hurried the last blocks, Gwen caught up to two nannies she knew. "Hi, Linda. Hi, Raquel."

"Oh, hi, Gwen," they said.

Walking beside the women as they closed in on the school, Gwen held herself a little stiffly, lest Linda or Raquel think she was presuming a friendship. Linda was the babysitter for Jeannie Haskell's son, Willie, a fellow Four of Mary's. Raquel was a specially trained twins' nanny, her charges two strawberry-blond Threes whose parents Gwen couldn't picture.

"What you making for supper tonight, Gwen?" asked Linda, maneuvering the stroller out of the sidewalk's walking path as they arrived.

"Me? Well, it turns out I had some chicken stew in the freezer. I just have to defrost it."

Gwen cooked the way her mother had—chops, chicken cutlets, stew, pot roast—and they always had homemade dessert. It soothed her, the cooking, and she let Mary help; she wasn't the type of mother who worries about a child chopping an onion. In the early weeks of the Threes class at St. Tim's, before Gwen had fully internalized her own strangeness, she'd had a classmate of Mary's over for the afternoon. The mom herself had come to pick the child up, trekking all the way to York from Park; Jessica Kaplan, one of those women who quit the law jobs to become yoga instructors. Jessica had stared at the week's menu taped to the fridge. "God," she had said, smoothing out a crumpled corner so that she could read the whole seven days' worth. "It's a lot of…meat."

"Maybe some green beans," Gwen continued to Linda. "I need to buy a vegetable. I've got nothing."

Linda gave a meaningful nod at Gwen's reply as if it only proved a point she was making. "Mm-hm."

"How about you?" Gwen asked.

"Oh, you know." Linda gave a put-upon sigh. "He want the chicken finger again and the baby carrot."

"Not again!" Gwen shook her head in commiseration.

"Can you believe it? This child gonna turn *into* a chicken finger."

"What about drumsticks?" Gwen suggested. "Or a whole roast chicken—maybe he could have that one time instead."

"Gwen, I *try* that. How many times I try that?" Linda turned to the older, more reserved Raquel, who gave a supportive nod.

"I tell my boss, but my boss say it's okay—she want him to be happy."

"She feel guilty because she work," Raquel suggested. "I know it."

"Used to be—he was two—edamame. Yams. He like everything! He the best eater! But she spoil him."

"She spoil him 'cause she feel guilty," said Raquel.

"I can understand that," Gwen said, to be diplomatic, though she would never say as much to Jeannie Haskell herself or let on that she knew about Jeannie's son's rejectionist diet or his habit, when his mother traveled for work, of lying down on the sofa in the television room off the kitchen and falling asleep in Linda's arms.

"So you doing that stew, Gwen?" Linda confirmed politely.

"I guess I'll do some rice with it too."

Raquel and Linda turned in on themselves to resume a discussion about Raquel's teenage daughter, and Gwen glanced at the sparse group of well-dressed mothers. Everyone here was very polite—it was part of the culture—but there was an undercurrent of fear in the air, something a horse or a dog would sense, though not, Gwen had to admit, the goofy yellow Labs the nannies sometimes led beside the strollers, squeezing in the dog walk with pickup.

Arabella Curtis stayed late on Tuesdays as well; Gwen looked around for Minnie.

Despite having made inroads with many of the mothers—she was apparently working her way through the class alphabetically, inviting each child over for a playdate—Minnie didn't seem terribly interested in joining any particular group. She stood next to Gwen most often when she came to pickup, which wasn't, actually, that frequently. Though she didn't work and had only the one child, half the time she sent the nanny, an unkempt, defeated-looking white woman who spoke to no one. True to her aspect the first day at the school, Minnie Curtis seemed to be an original. Besides the stilettos and the shopping bags, the thing that distinguished her here—the really odd thing—was that she didn't seem all that thrilled about motherhood. When her daughter emerged from school, she would frown uncertainly at her, as if she had been expecting something more, and last week when the girl had started to explain how she had hurt herself on the slide, showing off her Cinderella

Band-Aid, Minnie had interrupted, "You can walk, can't you? Save it for later. Mommy's late."

Apparently it was Gwen's turn for a playdate, for Minnie had e-mailed her just the day before to set one up. *Arabella will be thrilled to play with Mary! Just thrilled!!!* Minnie had informed her, amazing Gwen with how fast she had adopted the hyperbolic rhetoric of this place. The note ended in a string of *x*'s and *o*'s.

Gwen checked her watch, and when she looked up, a man had alit from an SUV that was idling across the street and was making his way toward them. It was disconcerting to notice the man, as if one had opened one's door unawares onto a crowd, without one's game face on. He didn't address anyone as he came up to the group of them but Gwen could see the other mothers looking harder into the middle distance, their conversations slowing, as if they were preparing to be recognized. Gwen herself felt some flicker of familiarity as the man took up a peremptory position in front of her, tapping an ugly black loafer on the sidewalk.

After a minute he gave an irritated glance around that included her.

Startled, Gwen said uncertainly, "Hi." She had recognized him.

She of all people had recognized someone. The flashy good looks that asserted themselves then dissolved on inspection—flesh where you wanted definition in his face . . . *I was just lying there and he . . .* The words came shockingly into her head from freshman year, as if no time at all had elapsed. She felt her face go red.

"I'm sorry?" he said rudely—the asshole, as if he were oblivious to the context they were in—but Gwen happily played the stooge.

"How've you been?" she practically gushed, some confidence from the circumstances in which she'd known him bubbling up and allowing her to take the lead.

Gwen had not realized he lived in New York—why would she have—and he was changed in some way beyond age that she couldn't immediately grasp. "Gwen Babineau!" she said heartily. She wouldn't let him cow her—oh no, she would not.

Ann DeGroat and a couple of her pals were casting curious glances Gwen's way, as if a spear-carrier in their star vehicles had suddenly leaped to center stage, and they weren't sure how to proceed to keep the audience from becoming alarmed.

"Gwen Hogan now," she added, surprised by the bragging note that came into her voice.

As the man tried to grope his way back to the connection, fear flickered in the brown eyes. Then they turned ingratiating. "Gwen? Gwen, is it?" He flipped back his hair—he still wore it longish as he had in college and parted it foppishly down the middle—and she realized then what was different. He'd gotten rid of the blond. "And…what was it—your last name?"

"Babineau." His look of insolence was gone too, replaced with something blanker; she almost missed the blond, petulant Curtis of yore. "It used to be Babineau. In college, I mean."

"College?" he said skeptically.

"Uh-huh."

"What college was that?"

She gave him a look. "Yale."

"Yale?"

"We were at Yale together," she said flatly. "You and I."

"No! You can't be serious. Jesus, you don't look old enough!" He glanced around at the others as if for confirmation. "I thought you were a babysitter!"

Now that Curtis had made a bid for the others' attention, his lack of interest in her was so total it was like a bodily rebuff. Still, Gwen was—perversely—enjoying the encounter. The gray day felt suddenly brought to heel. He of all people—the irony struck her at once—had legitimized her in front of the other mothers, few as their numbers were today, women who were always running into people they knew and exclaiming over it, as if it never ceased to be unexpected that friends of theirs skied at the same half dozen resorts, got the same sudden ideas about Caribbean islands.

He—whom she'd long ago had repeated dreams of throttling—had no idea who she was and never had.

Startled, she said, "You're Minnie's husband?"

The gaze flickered back in her direction but the man hesitated, as if he were waiting for her to marshal evidence.

"Minnie *Curtis*—of course!"

He flashed a cheesy grin and turned up his palms. "You got me!"

"Ah, okay. It's all becoming clear," Gwen said glibly, knowing he wasn't listening but going on anyway. "My daughter, Mary, is in Arabella's class. In fact, it's funny, we have a playdate coming up—"

"Hey, what time do you have?" He batted her shoulder with the back of a begloved hand. He wasn't speaking to her, to be clear—all conversation was transactional—he was using her to supply information. "Isn't it three? When do they let them out? I gotta be somewhere and if they're late, it's really gonna suck for me."

The verb on his lips repulsed her. "Um—now?" she said.

Indeed, the heavy green door swung open. Arabella Curtis darted around Ms. Babcock and came running down the steps. "John!"

"Hi, baby!" Curtis knelt and embraced the girl theatrically. The women watched with a look of uneasy approval—disapproving of the divorce implied by "John"; approving, in a general way, of men with money.

"Can we get crêpes, John? Can we go to the crêpe place again?"

Minnie's daughter was striking. She had uncertain blue eyes arrestingly offset by her mother's dark hair. A head taller than the other children, Arabella was old for the class, people said, but the girl had also had, Gwen guessed, that early unsustainable burst of height. Minnie couldn't have been more than five foot two. "She's so sweet," Minnie would say of Arabella as she and Gwen stood waiting. "So innocent"—rigorously abstract pronouncements delivered with an odd overlay of nostalgia, which made a marked contrast to her impatience when her daughter actually appeared.

Innocence, in Gwen's opinion, was not the quality the girl most obviously projected. Hugging her stepfather, Arabella was facing back toward Gwen. Gwen found herself looking away—loath to meet the quickly appraising eyes, like a dog that wants to avoid a fight.

As more children emerged, John Curtis stood and hoisted the five-year-old awkwardly up onto his shoulders. "Oh no, John! I don't want to go up!"

Mrs. Davidson looked over, looked askance—seemed to think better of saying anything. Gwen felt an odd pang of sympathy for the head of school—she seemed to see her age in that instant, see the compromises of a job that had become 90 percent fundraising. "The fucking new money," she was supposed to have remarked coming out of her office one night when she thought the building was empty.

"Let me down, John!" the girl said plaintively. "Really, let me down! It's too high! It's really too high!" The child was truly afraid, Gwen saw, her face screwed up, her back hunched to lower her center of gravity as she gripped the lapels of her stepfather's coat, some delicacy keeping her from holding on to his head, the way Mary had when Dan used to carry her like that. Undeterred, John Curtis quick-marched her over toward the waiting Escalade. "Wheeeeee!"

"Please, John! Let me down! *Please!*"

Mary came out and followed her mother's gaze. "Are we still having the playdate, Mom? Are we having the playdate with them?"

"It's next week, honey—not till next week." They watched Curtis load Arabella into the backseat and slam the door of the SUV—everyone did. It pulled quietly away from the curb.

"What are you looking at?" Mary asked when Gwen continued to stare down the street after the car turned the corner.

"Oh," Gwen said, in a voice calibrated to carry, "I just recognized someone I knew from college, that's all."

She took Mary's hand and began to walk east. "Shall we go to the park, honey?" she said, though it was a given they would go to the park.

I was just lying there and he . . .

Freshman-year math—multivariable calc. She hadn't yet met Dan Hogan or his three roommates. She used to walk over to class on Hillhouse with a guy from her entryway, Ryan Caughlin. Ryan had a T-shirt that said READ MY LIPS with a photograph of two men kissing on it. Yet somehow the T-shirt's message eluded her. It took Melinda Chu from across the landing to inform her, "Ryan's gay!" It was 1990 and Gwen had never known a gay person—it just hadn't occurred to her. Ryan didn't seem to mind. He took her at face value. They'd walk over to math together, Ryan going on about some new offense his jock roommates had committed, and she'd think happily, marveling, that this was what college was going to be like: just from showing up, you met amazing people who enriched your life.

It was Ryan who'd pointed out to her the remarkable sartorial evolution they came to refer to as "the Metamorphosis of John Curtis." An unremarkable young man at first, Curtis had sat in the row in front of them in dark, nondescript T-shirts and black jeans, as if he, too, might have hailed from Nautauqua, Massachusetts—although to be honest Gwen couldn't remember the guy's pre-preppification clothes all that well, just the hurt-looking scowl on his face and the humble messenger bag he'd carried. That and his compulsive fidgeting, the finger-drumming and shifting and neck-craning directly in front of them that was so distracting she muttered to Ryan, "Do you want to change seats?" "Are you kidding?" Ryan whispered. "This is way too much fun!" It was late September. Only that week, Curtis had started showing up in flashy madras shorts and polo shirts. Ryan elbowed her and pointed to his notebook, where he'd scrawled, *The Metamorphosis of John Curtis* and then *One day, John Curtis woke up and found himself transformed into a giant preppie.* Gwen laughed loudly, not because it was all that funny but because she was in on a joke and college was pure heaven. Curtis provided fodder for them all fall. Within a week he had replaced his plain black lace-ups with tasseled loafers and added belts to the shorts, canvas ones, adorned with motifs of golf clubs and Martha's Vineyard. "No, it isn't!" she hissed happily to Ryan when he said it was Nantucket. "Jeez, you should trust me—I'm from Mass.!" As the weather cooled, their classmate opted for faded Levi's and white oxford shirts, cotton baseball hats worn backward printed with MIKE'S BAIT SHOP or MOUNT GAY RUM. He started tying a navy-blue pullover around his waist after briefly trying it Euro-style, around his shoulders. This latter even Gwen could see was an affectation too far. Ditto the variegation of the shirts from innocuous white to hot pink and yellow, but what really floored her was the change, when they came back from Thanksgiving, in Curtis's hair. He'd been growing it out, apparently, although she hadn't really noticed till he started parting it down the middle. It was thick, luxuriously thick—the feature, had he been a woman, that might have been called his best—and rose in two brown waves from the top of his forehead. After Thanksgiving break, one of the waves was dyed bright blond. "Nice," Ryan said sarcastically, but there was some part of him that was intrigued, Gwen could tell. To Gwen, the changes smacked of an excruciating desperation, but perhaps college was, as people said, the time to experiment, to transform oneself into whatever type of person one fancied oneself, and it was only her own small-mindedness that kept her locked into jeans and running shoes and made her refuse to cut her long, lank hair despite the fact, she had admitted to Ryan, it was a royal pain to take care of "even though I don't even blow-dry it. It's supposed to be healthier for it not to."

One morning when Curtis slouched into class, the tails of his shirt flamboyantly long, the hem of his jeans as well, so that his loafers flattened the cuffs when he walked, which Gwen found particularly unappealing, Ryan shook his head. "You'd never believe I ran into him in the financial aid office yesterday, would you?" Too cool for a backpack or the old messenger bag he'd once carried, Curtis held a sole notebook in one hand, like an afterthought, the stub of a pencil tucked behind his ear. His hair fell foppishly into his face so that he was forced to keep pushing it back. The look in his eyes of hurt defiance remained, and it reminded Gwen of a kid she had babysat for a few times back at home whose mother spoiled him rotten.

Ryan, who was from western Pennsylvania, talked all the time of how much he hated his job busing trays in the dining hall and how his single mother couldn't afford Yale on her salary as a secretary at a lumber company. Gwen squirmed each time the subject came up. She hadn't been raised to share details about her family's income or to unload her problems or complain. She had missed her couple chances to respond in kind, make the financial aid connection, and now it was too late.

In the few seconds that she was paralyzed thinking how to reply, Curtis twisted in his seat and whacked Ryan on the knee. "The fuck?"

Gwen felt such a sharp sickening jolt she couldn't speak, thinking their running joke about him had been discovered, but Ryan—Ryan was composed.

He stared down at the place where the hand had whacked his knee. "Excuse me?"

"Is that English the guy's speaking or what? Where the hell's he from, anyway?"

Ryan looked at Curtis. "Yes, that is English the guy is speaking," he said primly. "I believe he's from Taiwan." His eyes locked with Curtis's in some kind of challenge, and Gwen, who blushed easily, looked away.

She hadn't thought about Ryan Caughlin in years, but claiming a cold bench in Carl Schurz Park as Mary ran off to kick at a frozen puddle, Gwen was seized by the idea that he would suddenly appear. Today, this Tuesday afternoon in February. He would happen to be in Yorkville—there was a good chance, after all, that he had ended up in New York—he would be hurrying by and would glimpse her sitting there. She craned her neck toward the park entrance, some part of her truly expecting to see him. *Gwen Babineau?* he'd say, letting himself into the park with a look of astonishment. *Oh my gosh! Ryan!* She'd stand up to greet him — give him a hug. *This is crazy! It's karma! You'll never guess who I ran into today. And oh my God, get this: Now he's in pinstripes and European collars and these awful cuff links. No more blond, but his hair is slicked straight back with lots of product. His cheeks are sort of thin but he looks bloated, you know what I mean?*

Maybe he's had work done! Ryan would say.

You think so?

Wouldn't put it past him.

"Mom! Did you bring snacks?"

Gwen was so far down the road of the fantasy that Mary had to drum her knee to get her attention.

"Did you bring snacks, Mom? Mom!"

Gwen looked at the round brown eyes, tried to regroup. "Yes," she said at last. "Yes, Mary." She rummaged in her bag. "I've got goldfish in here."

"No cheese sticks?"

"No," Gwen said. "No cheese sticks today."

Final exams were before Christmas, and late in the term Gwen got wind of the fact that some students were developing a plan to cheat. She knew none of the details and had heard of the plan's existence only because someone had mentioned it to her, thinking she was in on it because Ryan was. Gwen was not, and she felt out of it with Ryan now too. Some days he was subdued, doodling in his notebook; others he was more upbeat but anxious and preoccupied, biting his nails incessantly. He and Curtis were friendly now, she gathered, for they would exchange a word or two for which neither needed to give any context. "You heard about Michael's?" "I'll be there." Gwen didn't want to pin him down, but the rumor was so persistent that after the last review session before the exam, she followed Ryan out of the building, tapped his shoulder, and said awkwardly, "You know what you're doing, I guess." Later she realized it was the closest thing to a statement of friendship she ever made.

Ryan turned around and seemed to really see her for the first time in a long while. In the wake of her agitation, perhaps, the troubled look in his eyes cleared. He gave her a quick hug as if they both knew it was good-bye. "You better get an A, smart girl!"

Long after they went their separate ways, as if they'd both woken up one morning and realized the impossibility of their friendship, and after Ryan had dropped math to, as he told her, "do more drugs," and after a kid she had never heard of got kicked out for cheating but John Curtis walked away with the only A, she remembered Ryan's quiet, composed response to Curtis, the implicit correction of his rudeness and racism: "Yes, that is English the guy is speaking. I believe he's from Taiwan."

Chapter Six

Dan had started making a point lately of coming home in time to read Mary a story and tuck her in. Previously, this had been Gwen's favorite task of the day. She enjoyed reading the picture books aloud—most of them, even the classics, were new to her, Camilla not having fostered reading in a big way when Gwen was growing up; that had been Gwen's own odd pursuit. And she had found, unexpectedly, that she was good at it. She did all of the voices of the characters and made Mary laugh. "Do it again, Mom!" the little girl would often cry, and, secretly, Gwen tried for an encore every night. But of course, this was what men did now and you couldn't argue with the logic. It was better, after all, for Mary to see her father more often, never mind that when Gwen happened to walk by her daughter's room, she would find Dan checking his BlackBerry and messing up the words to the story—not that Mary let him get away with it.

"'Where is Brown? There is Brown! Mr. Brown just...went to town!'"

"'Is *out* of town,' Daddy! Out of town!"

After Mary went to bed, Dan would sit on the couch and thumb his BlackBerry vigorously while Gwen put out his supper. He ate whatever Mary ate but Mary's suppertime was early—five thirty—so Gwen reheated the sides or cooked fresh pasta or rice. "Don't bother! I'll eat it cold!" Dan would protest but Gwen had her standards, after all. Occasionally, as she diced onions, chopped broccoli into florets, or creamed butter and sugar together for cookies for some school function, Gwen would recall that people in Nautauqua—teachers; her boss at the department store, Mrs. Nelson; the town librarian Mrs. Perette—had thought she would be an astronaut, a curer of cancer. When Gwen was in the fourth grade, Mrs. Perette had slipped her books about Marie Curie, Indira Gandhi, Margaret Thatcher—all the greatest hits, with no quibble as to the nature of their achievements; they might have included Boudicca and Catherine the Great. *Women Who Led*—had the trim, hardcover but cheaply bound, glossy-photo series perhaps been called just that?

Gwen doled out Dan's portion of chicken stew, got a serving spoon for the rice. Hell, she thought, slicing off a lump of butter to put on the microwaved green beans, old Mrs. Nelson had even suggested that one day she might be *running* Nelson's.

"You'll never guess who I ran into at school today," Gwen said, bringing the dishes to the table as Dan appeared from Mary's bedroom, clutching the BlackBerry, his face a mask of distractions.

"Mm."

He sat down and began to shovel in the chicken and rice. Having grown up with four brothers, Dan still hadn't relaxed about getting his share. He was not above standing in front of the fridge with the door open and calling out, "Who ate the last pork chop? I thought there was one more left!"

"Come on—aren't you gonna guess?" Gwen perched on a chair opposite her husband to give him some company while he ate. "You're never gonna get it, but try." It was rare she had something to share beyond a quirky comment of Mary's, an observation about the lack of playground maintenance in the park.

"Yeah?" Dan said finally, slowing the pace of his fork-to-mouth action a hair and sitting back a bit. "Gimme a hint."

"Okay..." Gwen thought, wanting to hold on to the leverage the suspense gave her, if only for a minute or two. "I think he's some billionaire now. Or works for a billionaire." She glanced at Dan. She couldn't tell whether he was concentrating on what she was saying or simply looking at her and thinking of other matters. "He's married to this new mother at school who's actually having us over for a playdate. Everyone gets the invitation, apparently—they say she's going alphabetically. I notice she mentions her husband all the time. 'My husband' this, 'My husband' that. Sort of—old-fashioned. Like she's just the little woman. Of course I have no idea who her husband is. Then today—"

Gwen stopped as Dan's BlackBerry buzzed. He eyed the message, snickered, answered it with rapid-fire thumbing, and laid the thing down, looking at it lovingly.

"Sorry."

"Are you gonna guess?"

"Wait, what was the story?"

Gwen rolled her eyes. "Never mind. I'll tell you, okay? John Curtis! John Curtis is a father at our school. You remember him?" She mimed pushing the hair back, the arrogant, pouty expression. "From freshman year? See, I was in math with him—"

"What?" Before she even clarified the reference, Dan was all attention, his eyes sharp and acquisitive behind the wire-rims. "At school? What do you mean? What school?"

Gwen gave him a look. "St. Timothy's."

"St. Tim's?" Dan repeated with an obtuseness so uncharacteristic, Gwen felt a pang of fear.

"Yeah. His kid's there. Well," she amended, "it's not his kid. His stepkid."

"Oh."

"They were living in London, just moved back. He definitely augmented his pretensions 'whilst' there—heh. He's all decked out in those contrast shirts with the white collar and cuffs—leather driving gloves." Gwen shuddered. Men's luxury goods repulsed her more than filth or obscenity did, as if true evil lurked amid the leather backgammon sets, the monogrammed humidors and haute shaving kits. Curtis, in his new iteration, seemed the embodiment of all that. Gwen could picture Minnie Curtis presenting her husband with such gifts, knowing they would go over well. Unconsciously he must have known when he married her that she would get how to do all that—that she would give him that kind of socially sanctioned present and, God knows, not something homemade and heartfelt...and shameful. It was the sort of thing couples agreed on without necessarily knowing they agreed. A certain type of man needed a wife to help keep things impersonal, as if marriage were a barracks, and inspection from the outside could come at any time. "They somehow managed to muscle in midyear," she mused. "It's funny because I would've predicted just this trajectory for him—the Teflon ascension to the marble halls of power. Though he's not actually the big dude," Gwen conceded. "To be fair. He only works for the big dude."

Silent and statue-still, Dan waited.

"He's not, you know, the dude collecting the modern art. That's Martin Kerr himself, apparently. Martin Kerr of Invictus Capital." Gwen's voice dripped sarcasm. "Invictus Capital! Gimme a break!"

Dan took a paper napkin from the plastic holder in the middle of the table and wiped his mouth. "You guys talk?" he said drily.

Gwen shrugged. "Please. He's so arrogant. And what can you

say to someone like that?" *I was just lying there and he . . .* The words came into her head again, unbidden. Gwen swallowed, and, feeling as if she were prevaricating, she said offhandedly, "So you do remember him, right?"

"Vaguely . . ." His food forgotten, Dan seemed to be sizing her up. He was watching her with an intent, considering expression, as if he had only just noticed whom he was married to.

He had never told Gwen about the Tamco investigation into Curtis three years ago. He had never mentioned it. It was the year they lost the baby, a year in which saying good morning when they passed each other in the kitchen—keeping up a front of normalcy for Mary—seemed to take all he had. Maybe he'd had some notion of presenting her with a triumph: *Take one guess who your husband is putting on trial this week!* When the investigation foundered, he saw no reason to mention it—they didn't need more disappointment.

To deflect Dan's strange scrutiny, Gwen said lightly, "Always was such a piece of work, wasn't he? He was in math with me. Started out so uncool, black sneakers, black jeans, reinvented himself as some Eurotrash preppie . . . boy, was that a crock. Tried to make the crew team at some point—failed. Those guys used to make fun of him, remember? Tom Wilmerding and Vint Prince . . . but then—then," she said, "he started investing money for them and he was their new best friend."

Embarrassing, that she could recall details like that, as if she'd had a Robin Leach–type role in college: "*Lifestyles of the Cool and Legacied,* with your host, Gwen Babineau!"

She was distracted for a second, thinking of Ryan Caughlin, and when she came back to the conversation, she realized that Dan's eyes hadn't moved from her face. A bit self-consciously, she filled him in. "As I say, we're having a playdate there. Oh, Dan, the kid is awful. Mary, of course, doesn't notice. Happy to play with anyone! I should be grateful, I guess. *This* girl—she's one of those kids who wear designer clothing? They say she's redshirting in the Fours. Past eligibility, no doubt. She's five feet tall! Six if she's a day, I swear. Really striking-looking—these blue, blue eyes and this tan complexion. Not Curtis's. Did I say that? He's the stepdad. I don't know at what point he came into the picture. Crazy to see him after all these years . . . not that we were friends!"

"Puerto Rican?" Dan's voice was devoid of all emotion, all nuance. Gwen looked curiously at him. He had never sounded so flat, so bored. He cleared his throat and repeated the question, peering into the Pyrex bowl as he scraped out the last spoonful of Uncle Ben's. "The wife?"

Gwen squinted. "Yeah . . . maybe. She did grow up in Spanish Harlem." She went on, though she had no idea why Dan was asking—or perhaps now she did have, knew just whence this utterly atypical interest in school gossip sprang, but wanted to keep up the pretense that this was just chatter, help him get whatever he needed out of it. "Or at least started there. I got the whole story. Didn't ask for it, but I got it. She offered me a ride home the other day. She doesn't even know me—maybe took pity on me? She was telling me about her husband, how they met and everything—it's unbelievable to me that the whole time it was John Curtis she was talking about—and when I said Mary and I had to get going, she said to hop in, we could go with her. Her driver came all the way over here."

"What was the story?" Dan said tersely.

Gwen tried to remember the facts, which had blurred even in the moment, obscured by the titillating frankness of Minnie Curtis's delivery. Gwen had marveled at the woman's openness before a perfect stranger. "Spanish Harlem . . . then the stepfather moved them out to Long Island. Put her in Catholic school . . . she never knew her father. Mother was an alcoholic."

"This all came out on one car ride?" Dan was skeptical.

"I'm telling you—she'll tell you anything!"

"Like what else? What else did she say?"

"Well...*she* never went to college. She was a paralegal when she met her first husband. She's..." Gwen searched for the right word—was surprised when it turned out to be so simple: "She's proud of it. She radiates pride. When she was telling me about her mother's drinking, I tried to change the subject—figured, you know, she might not want to get into it—but no. You know what she said? She said, 'Lots of people say their parents drink, but my mother—she was a falling-down drunk. She'd go through a quart before breakfast.'" Minnie had actually slapped her thigh when she said this. It was one of many gestures that seemed more suited to vaudeville than the backseat of a chauffeured SUV.

"There's more on the stove," Gwen added as Dan continued to scrape absently at the empty bowl. "I'll get it."

"Sure."

As she rose, Dan gripped his fork overhand and drilled his plate with it.

"How long, by the way?" he said impatiently.

"What?"

"How long has John Curtis been a parent at St. Tim's?"

"Oh. A couple weeks. The girl just started—right after the break." Gwen went to get the rice.

"Huh."

Gwen turned from the counter and gave Dan a sharp look that he unabashedly stonewalled, not even grabbing the BlackBerry for an excuse.

"Here we go!" She set the bowl down in front of him.

Dan looked up at her as if he had no idea what was going on. "What?"

"More rice."

"Oh. Yeah." After a minute he served himself some.

Gwen stood at the counter, slicing into squares the pan of chocolate chip blondies she and Mary had made that afternoon, cutting off a big rectangular chunk for Dan, who had a major sweet tooth. She sometimes wondered if the sweet tooth had come first, and the drinking was only an extension of it, not the other way around. Not that she was complaining. He kept it under control. It was his business.

"Must have written a big check, huh? To get in."

Gwen wasn't convinced. "Well, if *that* were all it took..."

"What do you mean?"

"Oh, come on." She started to spatula the blondies into a tin left over from Christmas. "There must be hundreds of people who could write a check. Plenty on the Upper East Side alone who could fork over, what, fifty grand for a spot without even thinking about it." She thought she was just stating the obvious but Dan said quickly, "You think? In this environment? Because last year decimated people, you know. Guys lost their jobs all over the place."

Gwen shrugged. "People say they 'knew someone.'"

"Curtis? John Curtis knew someone?" Dan sounded personally affronted. "*That* guy with a friend at St. Tim's? I find that hard to believe."

"Yeah?" she said lightly, pushing the top down on the tin. Her husband's relative innocence about how the world worked, his funny persistent blind spots given what he did for a living, could be touching but worried her a little too. The big prosecutor, yet she felt that he could be taken advantage of more easily than she could and that she—and maybe Mary too—had to protect him from the harsh realities. Maybe all women felt that way about their men. "He's in that world now—you know."

"I *guess*..." She brought him his blondie on a plate. "I mean, I get that he has the *money* now," Dan said. "But the connection? Even Kerr...Kerr with his billions—St. Tim's could give a shit about people like Martin Kerr."

Gwen let it pass. She was just happy that they were nearly done with the fancy nursery school. Mary had last month taken the Gifted and Talented test to get into one of the city's better public kindergartens. Gwen was counting on Mary making the cut—and she was counting the days.

"Invictus!" She took the plastic broom out of the little vertical pantry at the end of the kitchen. "Isn't that classic? A bunch of white guys identifying themselves with Mandela's struggle. I couldn't remember the exact connection so I looked it up. He had it hanging on the wall of his prison cell on Robben Island—the poem, I mean. But I'm sure trying to find the next stock to short is akin to overthrowing apartheid when you think about it, right? Invictus Capital." She sniggered. "What an ass-wipe."

Dan watched his wife working. He found her efficient, unshowy movements soothing. She began to sweep the strip of linoleum. The smart *swish, swish, swish* of the broom seemed to focus his thoughts...

He came to, wolfing the dessert he'd been handed. "This is good—thanks."

"Mary did all the mixing. She's so good at it now." Gwen dumped the contents of the dustpan into the plastic trash can underneath the sink.

"So, you're having a playdate with them?" Dan was suddenly in possession of the facts. "With the Curtis kid?"

"Next week."

"Just the one?"

Gwen hung up the broom and dustpan and closed the cupboard. "I'll invite her back but I'm sure she won't come."

"Right." Dan drummed his fingers, looked away, looked back at Gwen. "I don't know if I'd, like, become best friends with the Curtises."

Wiping her hands on her jeans, Gwen glanced up, a question in her eyes. She gave a brief nod. " 'Kay."

His proposal of marriage had not been dissimilar. A question floated; presently, her answer. And while it pained her at times to realize how many deviations they were from the norm—she never missed him when they were apart (nor, she assumed, did he her), for missing someone seemed narcissistic; they never spoke the words *I love you* to each other, for if you had to say it, you must not mean it—she was thankful for this about them, anyway: they didn't need to talk about every little thing.

After Gwen went to get ready for bed, Dan stayed sitting at the table to digest, not the meal, but the information. *Curtis.* Dropping the fuck into the parent body of St. Timothy's. He'd had no idea. The FBI, of course, had been looking at Curtis's banking records; credit reports; work e-mails. His personal life wasn't all that relevant to the case—no reason why Frank DiNapoli would have uncovered the connection with Dan's. But when Gwen said the name, Dan felt as he had on this morning's commute when he'd nearly been sideswiped by a delivery truck and had to jump back onto the curb, yelling and flailing his arms. Thank God she *had* mentioned it. Thank God she had run into the scumbag, recognized him, and passed it on to Dan. It wasn't that Curtis's being at the nursery school necessarily affected the case, but there was nothing Dan disliked more than being caught out. He wouldn't have enjoyed showing up at some parent event and running into the man he was pursuing without a little mental prep. Jeez, no.

Chapter Seven

Minnie Curtis didn't let a trifle insult her. The point was to fix the problem, not *dwell* on it. She had broad reasons for wanting to meet with Philippa (curiosity; "friendship") and one very specific one as well, and she didn't want their meeting to take so long to pull off that she would have to sacrifice the former in service of the latter.

So after being stood up a second time for morning coffee—Philippa had called and said peevishly, "It's just not going to work!" as if Minnie were at fault—Minnie had an idea: she switched up the invitation to an early drink one weekday evening. "And, Philippa, where would you—"

"Le Chien Rouge on Seventy-Fourth."

"Great! I'll see you there!"

It was a relief to Minnie that Philippa Lye bypassed the aggressive niceties the other New York mothers relied on and that she, Minnie, was fast learning to mimic: the competitive one-upmanship of both parties having no opinions or desires whatsoever could go on for ten minutes, for multiple e-mails: *You decide! I don't care. No, really—I'll go anywhere! We could go somewhere up here... but not if that's inconvenient for you! Are you sure? You're really sure? Because I don't mind.* It hadn't been like that when they lived in London. Minnie, who had a good ear (you didn't get from a San Juan *caserío* to Park Avenue without one), was picking up the New York conventions as if learning a language again—her lips forming expressions that were not her own and would never be, forcing herself to practice them in order to gain fluency: "I'm fine with anywhere." "Whatever you think—really." "Honestly, you choose."

Philippa, apparently, operated under no such head-ducking compunctions, and so Minnie found herself in the kind of shopworn, velvet-banquettes-and-mirrors French restaurant that women a little older than she—Emily Lewin, to name one—pass in the daytime with ironic looks, recalling the weeks in the summer of '95 that they hung out with those French boys who were getting their LLMs at Columbia...

She wouldn't have entered the place on her own, although not for the obvious reason that it was past its prime. Minnie didn't give a hoot about eating out. She was perfectly happy having cheese and crackers at home. When she and her husband did have dinner at a restaurant, John liked to go to the famous, top-tier places—21 Club and Le Bernardin, Café des Artistes and Nobu—places Marty Kerr recommended, as if (Minnie noted a little skeptically) they were great finds. Just as well. The more modest establishments made her husband uneasy. He would look nervously around as if he were missing a better party somewhere. He'd been similarly impatient when they looked at apartments that had fewer than ten rooms or were east of Park. Minnie had to talk him into buying the two estate-condition classic-sixes, one on top of the other, and taking on the job of combining them; he'd wanted turnkey, not a project. "Think of the value it'll create!" she insisted. She had learned to speak his language as well.

*   *   *

In a corner of the dark, sparkly room, a gray-haired couple dined with quiet determination. Their age would have made them incongruous in a place such as this, except that no one was incongruous anymore. Minnie had ordered a manhattan, which she wasn't drinking. Minnie was a teetotaler. Scarred by her mother's alcoholism would have been the knee-jerk analysis, but in fact she had never liked the taste of booze. It simply wasn't tempting. A cherry Coke was her favorite drink if she could find it. Or a Shirley Temple. She kept grenadine and ginger ale on hand at home and in lieu of supper often arranged "cocktail parties" for herself and Arabella, replete with Swedish meatballs and scallops wrapped in bacon. But it was the lowest of the low, she felt (and this did come from her mother's tutelage), not to *order* a drink.

The place—and waiting for Philippa in it—reminded her of the Fordyce, Crandall girls. She could picture them here a decade ago, the moment when the bar had no doubt peaked—hear their constant ironic laughter...Minnie sighed. The problem with those girls—with most American girls—was that they tried to punch above their weight. Thinking of their aggrieved plaint ("Philippa Lye!" "Philippa Lye!" "Philippa Lye!"), Minnie recalled rather sadly that they had all seemed to think that, given a break here or there, they, too, with their wide faces, their pug noses, their strong jaws, their athletic or disproportionate builds, might have been models.

Silly girls.

But that was America for you, Minnie thought, swirling the dark liquid in the glass but still not drinking. She had gone to New York from Puerto Rico at age nine, ostensibly because her mother was in search of her father, who was white, but really because the woman was bored and wanted to be poor and drink somewhere else. To become a movie star was every teenage girl's right—indeed, her burden. (Minnie had known she would never be a movie star, not in a million years, but, drunk or sober, her mother had loved old movies, she had started Minnie on them, and Minnie tried to comport herself at all times like Grace Kelly in *Rear Window.*) Philippa Lye, of course, *had* been a model. She had—so the story circulated at the law firm—been big in Japan until some murky incident there had derailed her career for good. But why did this rankle so with the other girls? Minnie had been truly puzzled by their jealousy. The career had run its course years before any of them had ever even met Philippa, yet it still entered into the bitterness they expressed at the trajectory of the woman's life.

At last, watching them carefully, as if she were an anthropologist set down on the fortieth floor of the Citicorp Center to observe the indigenous culture, she had grasped a truth that seemed to illuminate the whole culture of entitlement for her:

They felt that they deserved what Philippa had gotten.

Despite the wide faces, the long torsos, they thought Philippa's marriage to Jed Skinker "unfair."

Silly benighted American girls.

An incident from the firm that had disconcerted Minnie came suddenly to mind as she sat waiting happily enough at the bar, rehearsing what she would say to Philippa, how she would broach the important subject of the night. It was something trivial but she'd never forgotten it, probably because it encapsulated who she, Minnie Colón, was, and who the rest of them were. Of an overweight but stylish female partner, Minnie had remarked appreciatively, "She does very well with what she's been given." The other girls had laughed, a little scandalized, as they circled the table in the conference room doing document collation. At first she thought it was the implied reference to God she'd made that had set them off, though she'd purposely not mentioned Him by name. (She was learning day by day to survive in corporate Manhattan.) But no; it was something else. What became clear from their responses was that, while she considered the remark a compliment, they considered it an insult. "Oh, Minnie." "Oh God, Minnie, you really are a piece of work." "I'll tell Renata you said that." "'With what she's been given'—I love it!" It was against their code—their creed—to acknowledge that some were more blessed than others. That some were more beautiful than others. That some had to work harder for things that others were given at birth. A most basic fact that Minnie had known in her bones since she was three or four and her mother had taken her to look at the massive motor yachts moored in the San Juan harbor but that they didn't seem to teach in American schools; here, *they* were all *equal.*

"Let's take a table, shall we? I hate sitting at a bar." Thirty-five minutes late, Philippa gave Minnie a kiss on each cheek. "So affected, I know. But I lived in Paris for a year and I never got out of the habit." She preceded Minnie to a booth whose royal-blue velvet seat was patched with duct tape.

On her spiky heels, Minnie teetered into the other side of it and carefully set down the manhattan. "That must have been fun," she ventured.

"Oh, I don't know...the French can be so..."

"Mrs. Skinker?" The waiter appeared. "Something to drink?" It was an unlikely hour for two mothers to meet, the rest of their ilk home coping with baths and bedtimes, but if either woman felt self-conscious, she didn't show it.

Philippa eyed Minnie's glass mistrustfully. "What's that *you're* drinking?"

"Oh—just a manhattan."

"Really? That's a strong drink!" She herself ordered straight vodka. "Just one or two ice cubes, René."

"And some water for me, please?" Minnie added. It was all right, she felt, to have some on the side, though her mother had never touched the stuff.

"Do you always order manhattans?" Philippa asked. This very specific curiosity was something Minnie never would have expected from her.

"Pretty much. Since—well—way back. Since Fordyce, Crandall!" She made the conversational leap easily. "I told you I worked there, right?"

"No! Really? Or, wait—did you? So we overlapped?"

Minnie found it unpleasant that Philippa sat across from her without removing, or even untying, her coat or taking her handbag from her arm. She had to fight an instinct to admonish her.

"No, I started right after you left. "

"Did you replace me?"

"No," Minnie admitted. "I wasn't a legal assistant, you see. I was a trained paralegal."

"Oh—you . . . did one of those courses and everything?"

"Correct. I went to school for it."

"So those girls started drinking manhattans after I left? When I was there, it was all cosmopolitans. Megan and Jen—and the rest."

Philippa's focus on the point confused Minnie. "Oh, I wouldn't know what they drank. I didn't really socialize with them."

"No?"

"No, almost never." She added genially, "But I *do* know they were very jealous that you'd left to get married. It was all they talked about."

"Really?" Philippa sounded irritated.

"Very jealous." Minnie could still hear the teeth gnashing nine years later.

"How odd! Why should they care if *I* got married?"

Most unfair of all, Minnie had gathered, Jedediah Skinker had seemed to materialize out of Philippa's vision of herself. There had been an air of inevitability about the union—of its having been arranged offstage without anyone's having been consulted or having had a crack herself—that, too, had driven the girls mad.

"They didn't even *like* me. Of course, I tried to be friendly to all of them. I was friendly—"

"Ah, so you socialized with them?" Minnie interrupted. She couldn't picture Philippa at one of those midtown lunches, finishing off the shared dessert.

"Well, no," Philippa said. "But *in* the office. In the office, I mean. I was as friendly as could be."

Minnie said firmly in her rather formal English, hoping to clear up the matter so she could move on, "Anyway, it was not the Fordyce girls but a man who introduced me to manhattans." The real purpose of this conversation Minnie would reveal as soon as she was able to do so decorously: she wanted to get onto the landmarks board that the Skinkers were all over. She would have to introduce the topic subtly, skillfully. John had put her onto it—said he thought it would be nice for her. She knew what he meant was that it would be nice for him, but that was all right. He made the money, after all. She had no illusions.

"Old boyfriend?" Philippa guessed.

Minnie made a face. "I wouldn't say that. He was a blind date.

One of the secretaries set me up. Carlie—remember her? The one who sat at the end, with the permed hair?"

Philippa's eyes went large. "Yes! Yes, I do! Gosh, *she* set you up?"

"Yes," said Minnie, not understanding the outsize reaction. "On a blind date."

"No!" Philippa gave a laugh. "That's amazing! I thought people only went on blind dates in movies."

Minnie looked blank. "I went on dozens." She frowned. "You have to meet people somehow."

"Well—I guess so. Yes. *Yes.* Of course you do."

"He hired a car...he took me out to Peter Luger's." She gave a tight-lipped little smile. "I was very young. I didn't know it was fancy. I was really mad at first that I had gotten dressed up and had my hair blown out—and I was wearing these incredible shoes—and then he tells the driver we're going to Brooklyn. But when we got there, I saw one of the partners. A whole table of them, probably, but I recognized only the one."

"Luger's, God. I haven't been there in ages. The creamed spinach..."

Minnie found interruptions impertinent, so rather than engage with them, she simply waited for the interrupters to stop talking.

"...the consistency of pudding! Sorry—sorry. Go on."

"My date ordered for us," Minnie recalled fondly. "Of course I let him choose. And he ordered manhattans. I liked the sound of it. Just liked the name! And ever since then..." She picked up her drink and gestured with it.

"Limo to Luger's." Philippa tutted. "Probably hoping he'd get you into bed."

"Oh, well, he did!" Minnie had finally found a comment she

could warm to, girl to girl. The exchange so far had felt stilted, but she was relieved that Philippa—someone—had at last alluded to sex. She was beginning to think it was never spoken of on the Upper East Side.

"*Did* he?" Philippa looked taken aback. "Did he, now?"

"Oh, yes. Please! I figured—well, I supposed he deserved it. He ordered a very expensive bottle of wine. It cost four hundred dollars! And some champagne...I don't remember the name of it, but he said it was better than Dom Pérignon."

"I'll bet he did!"

Minnie didn't know what Philippa was implying by that so she said nothing.

"So—so why didn't you see him again? I mean, if you liked him enough to..."

"Oh, I didn't like him," Minnie corrected her gently. "Though he was a very nice man." Minnie had nothing to hide, but she hadn't the faintest idea why Philippa was interested in one of dozens of blind dates she'd gone on a decade ago. She had met so many men then, gone on so many dates—had had quite a run, if she did say so herself. She had settled for her first husband, Tony, and Tony had led her to John. But that was then. She wanted to steer the conversation toward the request that she was going to make, to at least get Philippa started talking about Landmarks Protection...

"Did he not call you afterward?"

Minnie gave a short sigh, the closest she got to audible impatience with a topic. "Yes, he called me. He called me two or three times." Philippa seemed to be waiting for her to elaborate, so she said succinctly, "I declined the invitations."

"But why?" Philippa leaned across the table. She dropped her voice. "Were you embarrassed to see him again?"

"Embarrassed?" Minnie said. "Why would I be embarrassed?"

"Well, *I* don't know. I mean, after you slept with him...So—"

Minnie was tittering, a hand to her mouth. "Well." She breathed through her nose, trying not to laugh. "The fact was, he was obese."

"What?" Philippa's astonishment carried. The gray-haired woman looked up reprovingly from her table, and the bartender and waiter glanced over from the bar, but she didn't mute her voice as she went on, "You mean, like...hugely obese?"

Minnie paused. "I don't know what qualifies as hugely, but...he probably weighed three hundred pounds? Or maybe four hundred? It's hard to tell, isn't it? After they reach a certain point. At the restaurant, he had to take the banquette, I remember that, and I had to take the chair because he told me he had broken too many chairs." She added placidly, "His physical appearance was quite different, actually, from how he had been described to me."

Philippa seized her vodka as it arrived. "So you slept with him, even though he was obese because you felt he deserved it?"

"He was a very nice man," Minnie hastened to say. She didn't want to give the impression that she was spoiled and ungrateful. "He was an industrialist," she said, taking pleasure in the memory, as she did in the memory of most of her dates, blind or otherwise, from the years when she had been on the make. Those had been fun, exciting days, of newness and expectation, of at last putting to use everything one had learned. "I learned that word that night, *industrialist.*"

"As well as to order manhattans," Philippa said in a marveling tone.

"That's right." Minnie raised her glass. "Cheers!"

"Oh! Cheers!"

"I have a confession to make," Minnie announced after putting her mouth on the glass but not really sipping from the drink. She set it down deliberately and clasped her hands on the tabletop, raising her eyebrows mischievously. "*You're* the reason I'm here." She giggled and waved her hand around. "Everything! All of it! It's all because of you."

"Oh, dear." Philippa grimaced. "That doesn't sound good."

"I was living in London, you see. I was married to a person I met at Fordyce, actually—Tony Barrow? Did you know him? He was English—he worked in tech—"

Philippa gave a little shriek. "Weird Tony?" she cried. "Weird Tony from tech? You've got to be kidding!"

"Yes," Minnie said after a minute pause. She hadn't flinched. "Anthony Barrow was my first husband. He is Arabella's father."

"But—this is brilliant! It's all coming back to me! I remember Tony! He was my savior when my laptop was on the fritz." She sat back in the booth, expansive. "God, what a fantastic place to work that was. I wish I were still there, I tell you. It gave me a sense of purpose, going in there every day. I'm not sure I've ever been happier!"

Minnie waited with a pleasant expression on her face.

"Weird Tony. Who would have thought?" Philippa seemed suddenly to remember herself. "I'm sorry." She looked as if she'd been rebuked, though Minnie had said nothing. "What were you saying?"

Minnie unzipped her purse, flashing her beautifully manicured nails, and withdrew a newspaper clipping. She handed it to Philippa, who took it and frowned. "As I say, I was living in London and I came across this photograph of you and your husband. You see, I always had to have my *New York Times*. I had to have the Styles section. I'd go down to the newsstand in Knightsbridge, and I'd turn right to Styles, and one day I opened it up—I was at work at the time. Arabella was in preschool and I was getting bored sitting around at home so I'd started a temp job just that week in Mayfair at a hedge fund, because the regular secretary was having a baby, and I must have gasped or something because I was so thrilled to see this photograph—*the* Philippa Lye, whom I'd heard so, so much about from the other girls—and the absolute boss of the whole place happens to be walking by. He gives me a grin and says, 'Something good in the news?' He comes over to see, and he's got one hand on either side of me on my desk—I'm quaking, I'm so nervous, here I am this little temp...and I say, 'You see *them?*' And I point and I say, 'I know her! We used to work together.'"

Before Philippa could react, Minnie said hurriedly, "I know I didn't really know you. But it seemed like I did. I'd heard so much about you from Jen and Megan and Marnie. They talked about you constantly. I knew about your modeling career...it really felt as if we'd met. I'd always look to see if I knew anyone in Styles. I figured one of *them* would make it into the weddings section...and instead, there *you* were! 'Mr. and Mrs. Jedediah Skinker arriving at the winter ball.'" The Landmarks Protection Society. She could recite the caption by heart. "The next day, John—he was Mr. Curtis to me then—started asking me all of these questions about you. Well, and about—about Jed—John knew about the bank, of course. Everyone knows Skinker, Farr! And I told him what I knew—that you'd been a model and left the law firm when you got married—" Minnie eyed her companion to see how her flattering rendition of the story was going over.

Philippa was still looking across the table in Minnie's direction, but she had gone blank. Minnie's story seemed to be having no effect on her whatsoever. She sipped her vodka.

"—swept off your feet by Jed Skinker…" Minnie hesitated, suddenly unsure of herself. Usually, there was nothing a woman liked better than having the story of how she met her husband recounted. "How is Jed?" she said as perkily as she could manage in an attempt to bring Philippa back in, adding, with the kind of performative little flourish she liked, "How is *Mr.* Skinker?" She raised her glass to her lips and this time took one real distasteful-but-necessary sip of her drink. "He's never at school, is he? Jed? I don't know why he would be. But it would be fun to meet him one day."

Even René, the waiter, appearing at Philippa's quick signal for another, must have noticed that for Mrs. Skinker, the name had the quality of a taboo. She turned her head away. "He's fine."

"How are his hours?" Minnie said sympathetically, feeling she had found firmer ground. "Are they terrible? He must work a *ton*. Family bank and all. John's are the worst! Weekends…he travels a lot too. I don't mind, though. I figure it takes what it takes. And I don't mind a night off, you know? I know they really value him. I mean Marty, obviously—Marty really values him. When we wanted to move back from London—just to, I don't know, start over, you know? Newly married couple? I didn't want to live in Tony's country forever. It seemed depressing. England is depressing. It's not the weather; it's the darkness. Nobody tells you that. Anyway, John wanted to move too. The next thing you know, we're moving back. He just sorted the custody right out with Tony. 'How'd you do it?' I asked him. 'How'd you get him to agree to it?' I can be so naive. 'How the'"—Minnie lowered her voice—"'eff do you think I did it?' he says. 'Money! Can't you get it through your head? *Money.* You just have to spend the money.'"

Self-conscious about hogging the airspace, Minnie made another attempt to draw Philippa out. "How about your Jed?

What's his view on all that?" When Philippa didn't answer, now gazing into the middle of the room, her hand clasped around the stem of her glass as if to anchor it to the table, Minnie said warmly, "It must be strange! Having your name on a bank!"

Now Philippa spoke up, to demur. "Oh, my name's not on the bank! I never changed it. I'm still Lye."

Minnie gave a cozy little scoff, thinking to flatter Philippa. "That's pretty literal, isn't it?"

"What?"

"I mean, for all intents and purposes, you are Mrs. Jed— excuse me, Mrs. Jedediah Skinker." Minnie signaled to the departing waiter, who had just brought Philippa's second vodka. "I'll have another as well!"

The man looked in a noncomprehending way at Minnie's full glass.

Minnie laughed. "No, I know—but this'll go. And I want to keep Philippa company! I don't want to leave her on her own, stranded!"

This gesture did not seem to affect Philippa one way or the other. She had withdrawn a matchbook from a coat pocket and was turning it over in her long fingers.

"And my point—what was I saying? Oh, yes, you are Mrs. Jedediah Skinker. And Skinker is the family bank."

"But I'm not involved," Philippa said in a small voice.

"Well, perhaps, but—"

"I've never paid any attention to it at all."

"You shouldn't admit that!" Minnie laughed nervously. "Why, Philippa! Tsk-tsk! You should never admit that! It's like saying your husband isn't worth anything to you! My God, I would never say something like that about John. These guys—they're out there every day fighting. We have to appreciate them or who else will, right?"

Philippa started to rummage in her bag. It was an oversize hobo-type sack, the gray leather aged smooth and mottled with stains.

"Well, anyway," Minnie said in a placating tone, "technically, your name may not be on the bank, but your children's names are. Your children—what is it—Ruth, yes? She is so adorable! Arabella just loves her. Wants a playdate ASAP. 'Please, Mommy, when can we have the little Skinker girl over?' Ruth and… Sebastian is the boy, I know, and—what's your older girl? Laura? Laura, isn't it? They're Skinkers, after all. Their names are on the bank anyway. Their names—"

Philippa rummaged at length, with increasing agitation, coming up at last, to Minnie's surprise, with a prescription bottle. She pressed the top down with her palm, opened it, and tipped out two pills.

Dismayed, Minnie said hurriedly, "The building is so beautiful. The most beautiful bank in New York. Wow. But of course that makes sense, doesn't it? I mean, I've noticed the Skinkers are very involved in the Landmarks Protection Society. It seems like such a good cause." She stopped. Philippa's eyes watered as she raised her chin and choked down the pills.

"I'm sorry!"

"Oh my gosh," Minnie said. "Don't worry about it!"

"One of those days, I'm afraid." Philippa seemed to attempt a smile. "I—I was late for pickup…" She reached for a water glass, her hand hesitating above Minnie's. "Again."

"Help yourself! Of course! Finish it!"

Philippa drank and her eyes flashed up to Minnie. "I'm a terrible mother."

"What? Don't be silly!" Minnie made the obvious rebuttal: "You have three children!"

"I thought—" There was a funny catch in Philippa's voice as she said, "Safety in numbers. You know?"

"Oh my God, are you crying?" Minnie could have kicked herself for letting the conversation descend to this. She had mismanaged it, but she couldn't think how. Usually people liked to talk about themselves.

Shielding her eyes with a long, slender hand, Philippa said, "We had a fight, you see. And then he had to go..."

Minnie reached out and patted Philippa's equally long, slender forearm, which lay lifelessly on the table. "It's going to be fine. Don't even think about it. Just put it out of your head. Hey—all couples fight, right? John can be an absolute dick to me! He can be an asshole!" She looked around and raised her hand for the waiter. *Coffee?* she mouthed. Then she gave a forced titter. "Sometimes I think John loves his boss more than me! Never mind that his boss practically propositions me every time he sees me."

Philippa said nothing, her eyes downcast. When the coffee came, she drank it without seeming to notice it.

Gently—but firmly—Minnie brought her back to the subject of the landmark society board. It had taken too many attempts to arrange this meeting to let it pass by without getting at least partway to her goal. She spoke again of the beauty of the Skinker building on Fifty-Fourth Street. "It must have been in your family for, what, a century? Since it was built, no? How cool is that?"

"Oh, no. They bought in the seventies. When things were going cheap."

Minnie could have screamed. Nothing was ever as it should be! The Skinkers had just gone and bought it when it was cheap? Everyone had told her they had built it! Everyone was always wrong. She managed to press on. "Well...that's even better! A real New York real estate tale. My husband would love that! Just love it. He always says he got me on the cheap, ha ha!"

"I'm sorry," Philippa said abruptly. "I've just realized I've got to go."

"You do?" Half in shock, Minnie mentioned the board straight out. She was going on, trying to smooth over the request, when Philippa interrupted.

"Oh, okay. Sure. There's a donation you have to make."

Minnie blinked. She felt as if she'd had the wind knocked out of her.

"Think it's twenty thousand. It might be fifty. Fuck, it might be a hundred. I'll find out for you."

"Well, I can't thank you enough. I—"

But Philippa was rising—had never taken off her coat. She was halfway to the door, the bag bumping against her leg; she was flapping slowly out, like a huge gray bird of prey.

Alone, Minnie wanted to cry. She took an actual real gulp of the manhattan but it was so disgusting it only made her want to cry more. The waiter appeared, though she hadn't summoned him, and, forcing her lips into a smile, she realized she had been stuck with the check.

Chapter Eight

In the big field at the farm, there was an oval-shaped depression surrounding the two great sycamores, as if, growing to their massive size these past two hundred years, the elegant giants had tamped down the earth between them. After more than a day's rain, water ponded there. What had been a pleasure as a child (it wasn't mere puddle-stomping Jed remembered but wading and splashing in the shallow water, lying down in it—egged on by his sister, Sallie, and his cousins—to approximate a forward crawl) now bothered him a little, for he saw it as a fault in the farm's drainage. How to solve it, though? Soil removal and relocation wasn't his thing. Too much like the 'burbs. The junior bankers, always talking of landscaping with an avaricious glint in their eyes, as if they couldn't wait to power-plant half a dozen nonindigenous saplings, get their hands on their semiannual dump of bark mulch. *Landscaping in the Hamptons*—Jed chuckled to himself; nobody had found his idea for a reality show all that funny.

He glanced at the row of casement windows that made up the southern side—the street side—of his office. It was a day for staying in, for keeping one's head down and doing the work, for giving the city its due. Rendering unto Caesar. February gray with a cold rain falling.

His eye, shrewd and bulging, fell to the paper he was reviewing, a prospectus for an upcoming stock offering, to the section entitled "Risk Factors." In this particular post-crash winter, the phrase had the ring of pathos. Closing the barn door after the horses had escaped...They were all thinking about risk factors now. He himself thought of nothing but. (He himself was nothing but.) He turned the page of the document. He'd always liked that metaphor. Oddly, one did run to close the door of an empty stall.

A very large, fair man with a high color and tufts of darkening blond hair, he sat hunched over the Regency partners' desk. The desk seemed to be lodged into his bulk rather than the other way around. As a young man, Jed had outgrown his father by four inches—the height more from his mother's side—and after college when he quit rowing, he had put on thirty pounds. Hugh Skinker had been scrappier, with the impatient clear conviction you expected from men of his era. A quick man, his father, but not a contemplative one, from a generation that had tipped but not overtipped. Nothing to feel guilty about.

Jed glanced toward the windows again but he couldn't actually make out the rain, only the suggestion of rain, a flicker in the light that alerted you to the fact that it was coming down.

Skinker, Farr was housed in an ornate, midblock mansion on Fifty-Fourth Street between Fifth and Sixth. Jed's office was on the fifth floor, the top floor but one. Six, with its pitched roof, housed the presentations department—the running joke that you had to be under five foot four to work in presentations. It would have made for a neater story if, as rumor had it, the Skinkers had built the Beaux-Arts edifice themselves. It had gone up in 1907—a year when Ionic columns, wrought-iron balconies, and carved grotesques served the same purpose as Sub-Zeros and Viking ranges today. When Jed disabused clients of the notion that his family had commissioned it and explained that his grandfather had shelled out a hundred grand in 1973 for the thing, they looked a little green before they swallowed and congratulated him on Grandfather Reg's foresight. Eventually, he stopped telling the story. The truth was, people didn't want to go back in time to stop Hitler; they wanted to scoop up Manhattan real estate on the crazy cheap, see Dylan in a café, maybe.

A Beaux-Arts example of the Renaissance Baroque—his father had been determined he should know the provenance. (Hugh had also collected all the art on the walls, starting with the vast—Jed could tell you obsessive—collection of works on paper, most of which now adorned the basement, home to the IT department and the print shop/mail room.) More of a Georgian man himself, Jed would no doubt have missed the opportunity. Reg's Folly, the family had called the building in the first decade, before the investment came up trumps. Jed still called it that: "Going down to the Folly of a morning." Hugh had worked tirelessly to have the thing landmarked, even joining the board of the preservation society to push the status through; it could never be razed. A son's mandate and also, perhaps, his limitation: to preserve. What, then, was *his* son's mandate? To "flourish in the new millennium," as websites for everything from Harvard to health clubs were fixating on these days?

Millennium—hell, he'd take a decade; 2010 seemed a long way off today. Melancholy mood he was in. Blame the rain.

There was a muted knock on the door and Carol Ann came in. She had a shy habit of never quite meeting one's eye. "That research you wanted, Mr. Skinker."

"Thank you, Carol Ann." He watched her close the door behind her—a tall woman, statuesque, with the old-fashioned grace that comes of adolescent instruction in posture. She had started with his father straight out of secretarial school and never married—Miss Ritchek then and now. It wasn't the kind of thing Hugh would have thought about, but Jed had surmised there was poverty in her background, and some amount of chaos; an adolescent vow fulfilled, perhaps: to make one's own money and keep to oneself.

He found his place in the document again. *The risk factors stated herein*...

(Good name for a horse, Risk Factor.... Risk Factor by Something-or-Other out of Genuine Risk. The filly that won the Derby in 1980. They'd watched it on the tube set up in Billy Flood's apartment above the barn, his mother cheering full throttle—a little frightening when she got like that. Wanted the girl to win. Ice cubes rattling in a tumbler of Billy's whiskey. "Go! Go! Go! Go!" He cheering too but twelve-year-old Sallie covering her eyes—afraid there'd be a broken leg, a horse destroyed. He did a Howard Cosell imitation and made them all laugh.)

He finished the paragraph, moved on to "Use of Proceeds." It was a coup, that's all he could call it, that Chip Noyes had managed to get a firm of this size awarded this mandate in the worst market they'd seen since Grandfather Reg came to work in November of '29. No question Noyes was his biggest talent. No rainmaker, Jed. No pretense of being one. The men relieved when he took the helm thirteen years ago after Hugh died and switched them over to straight commissions, 25 to 30 percent, and it hit their accounts the day a deal was done. He'd gotten a few things right, before he made one very specific wrong turn.

Rainmaker. It appealed to Jed as an accolade, for he didn't believe so much in a God as in Nature. Hard to remember Her in the city.

Seemed immaterial, what passed for seasons here. Hollywood set with the Rain switch turned on outside his window.

Rain would have stopped in Danforth by now. The sky over the big field would be lifting. Drizzle petering out, chased along by a new front from the east—only spatters blown from trees now. Not sure how he knew, but he knew. The weather vane on the barn, a horse and sulky, the horse trotting due west, mane flying—mane always flying.

He glanced back to the risk factors. He was turning obsessive-compulsive in his forty-fourth year.

...volatility in our revenues and profits...could fluctuate materially...

I'll say.

He exhaled with a fed-up noise. There was nothing to be done about that.

He wore no watch and eyed the French clock that sat on the carved-wood mantelpiece above the room's fireplace. Jed loved the building with the ironic love a man has for a mistress. Conscious it didn't represent him, he loved it all the more, the way Philippa secretly loved the mod cons she'd been deprived of as a kid in Dunning—color televisions with remote controls, ice makers, heat in cars that actually worked. But he loathed the clock. He mistrusted anything gilt or fanciful, possibly anything French—he loathed *objets* period—but kept it as a sort of caution against excess. The desk he cherished—its ink-stained serge top where both Hugh and Reg had scribbled and that he refused to replace despite Carol Ann's yearly exhortations.

Genuine Risk. Genuine risk...

Phil like a loose horse the night he met her.

A loose horse that knows its freedom won't last and so doesn't know what to do with it, stopping to tear mouthfuls of grass here and there but not settling to graze. The whites of her eyes showing, the quick skitter away—the deflection when people crowded in, fake right, fake left. A fine, nervy creature. Not delicate. Nor overfed. Rangy, like a point-to-pointer. When he spied her walking out of the bar, she tried to pretend she didn't see him—breedy creature giving the horse van the miss. *What horse van?*—circling around. *Where?* Took handling, the type did, to get them up the ramp without balking…

His mind *would* wander. Defense mechanism, no doubt.

Bank and farm. Farm and bank. The two strains in his life. Skinkers the bank and Husseys the farm. His grandfather Reg Skinker the New York banker who had married Charlotte Hussey, of Danforth, New York, the only child and a girl. (People who didn't know better said that Charlotte had married into the bank. The Husseys knew that it was the Skinkers who had married into the farm.)

Jed and Sallie, as Hugh's children, had grown up in the city, their childhood tied to the bank; Jed's cousins—his uncle Reg's daughters—on the farm. Going up to Danforth on weekends, Jed had never wanted to leave. His earliest memories from the barn: the intoxicating smell of the timothy bales in the hayloft; the hollow, ringing sound of a horse being led out onto the high wooden floor—one two *three* four, one two *three* four. When you looked up, as he always had as a boy, you saw a thousand motes in the weak light that streamed from the air-giving cupola above.

At the turn of the century, his great-grandfather Thomas Hussey had made improvements to the farm—added the so-called French drains to the barn, cemented the cellar of the main house. Jed knew all this. He had been weaned on it, tutored in the farm's history by Reg Senior and Junior—grandfather and uncle—knew the year the New Barn had been built over the old (1848). But when he recalled this fondly, coming home from Exeter to speak at his grandfather's funeral, Sallie was full of questions for him: "What did you mean, New Barn? It's really old, isn't it?" And "Why did Grandfather have French everything? Why not use American drains? That seems strange!" It was a shock to Jed—one of those moments when the present begins to shade the past for you. *Sexist;* there was no other word for it. Grandfather Reg and Uncle Reg hadn't taught the girls how to run the place. Oh, Sallie and his cousins drove the tractor and heaved bales up onto the truck, same as Jed. They had milked the cows as children, before Grandfather, with a banker's impatience for the bottom line, had thrown up his hands at the relentless demands of dairy and converted to beef, buying the thirty head of Belted Galloways the townspeople knew the farm by. But Grandfather and Uncle Reg hadn't bothered to teach the girls how things really worked.

"No, Sal," Jed explained, "not French drains from France. Henry Flagg French—he knew our great-grandfather."

The gilt clock ticked and whirred—foolish thing kept perfect time.

Anyone who knew what was going on would have assumed Jed was avoiding, with his line of thought about the farm, the appointment he had to keep this afternoon. If only the information the man wanted could have been supplied over e-mail. (Subject line, Jed thought crudely: *Next Week's Big Acquisition.*) Meeting John Curtis of Invictus Capital in person, which Jed had done twice in the course of their yearlong association, required him to be reminded of the ignominious fact that a man who chewed gum and played with his hair had so decisively gained the upper hand.

This was the third time he would meet him. Ironically, Skinker, Farr had been audited a couple months ago. Mostly the SEC left them alone, blue-chip reputation and all. First time in three years they'd come in. Of course the guy hadn't found a thing. Skinker kept its paperwork in perfect order. Hugh had been obsessive about that. The auditor had been very thorough, checking to make sure they had, oh, five copies of every prospectus for each deal they underwrote.

Corporate malfeasance hadn't occurred to the man.

Contemplating the meeting this afternoon with a mixture of dread and intense boredom, Jed half wished it had.

But it wasn't, thank God, Curtis who had started Jed obsessing about the farm's drainage today. The habit of thinking about the farm's problems preceded Jed's encountering that man by a decade. The truth was, Jed could think about the farm only by way of its problems—more or less troublesome issues that needed to be addressed (the shed that needed reroofing, his foreman Billy Flood's desire for an upgrade to an air-conditioned tractor before next summer). It had long been his way of avoiding confronting head-on his grossly unfair good luck: the girls had turned out not to want the place. When Uncle Reg died (his end the shock to them all that he had contrived to make it), they'd let Jed buy them out—begged him to buy them out. His sister, Sallie, was an Episcopal priest in Danforth, her congregation made up mostly of weekending New Yorkers whose faltering little church she had saved with her no-nonsense rhetoric from the pulpit ("Well, Jeddie, they should be tithing ten percent of their income—they want for *nothing*"). The meth-heads from the dying industrial town upriver kept her busy with something beyond the diocesan politics of New York State. As for his cousins—Reg's girls—they had disliked growing up on the farm, vocally envying Jed's and Sallie's childhood in New York. Maria, the beauty, was married now, in Paris; Pam lived ten blocks down from him, on Seventy-Eighth Street—spent summers on Nantucket with her husband and stepchildren.

Sallie, with her ear for injustice, had sensed her uncle's baseless repudiation of his own daughters as girls, observed his turning to Jed as the latter approached adolescence: "Jed says he'll take a weekend from his summer job to help with the haying! Says he misses it." "Soon as he gets out of Harvard, Jed says he's going to move up to the farm permanently!" Jed, who loved the place, was tickled to be tapped. It was only years later that it occurred to him that perhaps his uncle had claimed him for the farm only in order to settle a score. Jed's father, Hugh, had been claimed by Grandfather Skinker for the bank, Uncle Reg frankly overlooked, though he was the older son; he didn't have the quantitative skills, Grandfather said.

The old man had been right about that. Reg had very nearly leveraged the place into nonexistence, an angry, almost willful heedlessness in the debts he had taken on, the schemes he had invested in, as if, like most denigrated children, he'd been determined to prove his father right. Jed discovered all this when, as a single man in his mid-twenties, he drove up one wintry morning to the town lawyer's office in Danforth and took possession of two houses, a barn, and five hundred acres in Ulster County. The week before, his uncle's hunter had colicked after getting into the grain bin. Selfishly, Reg had kept the gelding alive, suffering, for twenty-four hours till the local vet, getting wind of the fact, drove over, reprimanded him, and put the horse down on the spot. In response, Reg had gotten their father's pistol from the study in the main house and shot himself in the horse's stall.

A suicide, his uncle.

An aberration, in their family.

All the things that Jed loathed: selfishness, drama—pretension.

(Although: There was suicide and there was suicide. The act could serve a purpose, if it came to that.)

A joke that year in the alumni magazine: *Is it true that Jed Skinker, the most eligible bachelor of the class of '86, is living in the sticks where the only women are his cows?*

It was true for two years anyway, during which Jed rose at dawn, tucked himself in at night with a glass of whiskey and back copies of *American Farmer.* And would be true still, Jed thought, bestirring himself to read the last paragraph of the prospectus. Except that Hugh—Hugh, who rode his bicycle to the bank and played squash four mornings a week at the Racquet Club—had dropped dead on the sidewalk outside of Skinker at age sixty-five. Jed's mother had called him at the farm to tell him. He remembered the moment perfectly because they'd had an early spring and a warm May, and the hay would be good. It was mid-June and he and Billy agreed they were about two weeks away from cutting. As he packed for the city, he thought of the buyout offers that he knew would come rolling in—clung to them, maybe.

In the event, though, his mother didn't want to sell.

"Mr. Skinker?"

Belatedly, Jed was aware of laughter in the outer office—women's laughter. "Carol Ann? Come in—*Sal?*" He rose from his desk. "Is that you?"

"I know you said no calls, Mr. Skinker," said Carol Ann when Jed threw open the door, "but I figured your sister—"

"Sallie! In New York?"

"'Tis I, Jeddie!' said Sallie. "Aww..." —as Jed crushed her in a hug, getting a noseful of the cheap shampoo she used on her blunt-cut blond bowl. "Big brother."

"Why didn't you call?"

"You see?" Sallie said to Carol Ann, who was watching the pair with merriment—Carol Ann was as fond of Sallie as anyone. "I've just been telling Carol Ann: because I didn't want you to make a reservation at a nice restaurant! You know how I loathe them. So theatrical! 'Would you like still or sparkling?' And such a grand waste of time. Of *course* I don't want bottled water." Sallie shook herself like a dog after a swim.

Jed took her in—the solidity of her in her clerical collar and black skirt and blouse. Despite having grown up here, his sister had little use for the city, looking on its basic assumptions with the alert, unconvinced mien of an outsider; she came down from Danforth as little as possible.

"We'll have something in the office. Carol Ann, could you—"

"No, no." Sallie was shaking her head. "I didn't want to trouble Carol Ann either, so you see—" She held up a paper bag from one of the sandwich places nearby. "BLTs on whole wheat. You eat too much white bread, Jed. You need to lose thirty pounds, and you know it."

"She brought drinks too, Mr. Skinker."

With mock severity, Sallie said, "Now, Carol Ann, we talked about this last time I was here! You were going to work on giving up the 'Mr. Skinker,' weren't you?"

Carol Ann smiled sideways. "I guess I got in the habit with Mr. Skinker"—by this, both Sallie and Jed knew, she meant their father—"and I can't get out."

"Well, at least you'll call me Sallie. And I grant"—she stepped back and cocked an eyebrow at her brother—"he's *rather* impressive in this context. I usually see him in overalls in a cowshed, you know."

"It's good to see you, Sallie," said Carol Ann. Jed's assistant made his sister seem young and brash—a crusader; raw. Jed *had* tried for a while to get Carol Ann to call him by his first name until he realized he was doing her no favors—the idea rattled her, upset her, even; it would have been taking something away. She bought her suits and shoes at the department stores and always dressed appropriately for the season and the weather. On rainy days like today, Jed looked forward to seeing the galoshes; in snow, the fur-trimmed boots and hat came out. She was girlish in that way, but a serious girl. On her lunch break, she slipped out to Saks to make a small purchase, a lipstick or a pair of stockings, or to review a sale or exchange an item. She lived up in Yonkers and had lost her little sister to cancer.

"It's good to see you, Carol Ann," said Jed's sister and gave the woman a hug before she retreated. Only Sallie would take such liberties, Jed thought. Sallie had never gone through the post-childhood rejection of spontaneous contact—she was free with her hugs, her cuddles, her handclasps.

"What are you doing in town, sis?"

With a concerned look around, as if her brother's office were somehow different than what she'd remembered from her last visit, Sallie settled herself on the grommeted leather sofa. Jed took one of the upholstered armchairs opposite and watched her deftly sort out the sandwiches and drinks.

"A Fresh Start, of course." This was Sallie's drug-rehabilitation charity upstate, a residency program for women in recovery. Other things came with the drug use: battery, sexual abuse. She raised her intense round blue eyes to his. "I need a better name. Two friends from seminary—Nancy and Bill, do you remember

109

them? They're helping me fund-raise. I'm terrible at it. I just sort of assume the money will come flooding in if the cause is worthy." She handed him a paper plate with a sandwich and a napkin; a can of seltzer water. "It's like, well, *I'd* give..." Her mouth full of sandwich, she asked, "You gave that man they sent you from St. Thomas's a job, didn't you? Carlos Florez? They've helped me so much, it's the least I can do...and he did seem to be the cream of the recovery crop down here."

"Yeah—he's in the print shop." Jed paused. "When he's not hooking up the junior bankers with all the blow they can handle."

Sallie looked shocked. "He's back dealing?"

Jed turned his palms over: *What can you do.*

"Dear God. I'll have to tell Nancy."

"At least now he's got a salary—capital to lay in some good product, right?"

Sallie stared at him for a second. Then her expression cleared. "Jed Skinker! You are so bad!"

Jed laughed. "Sorry. From what I hear, he's a good employee!"

"It's not funny." But after a moment she relented with a snort.

"It's good seeing you out of context," he said.

Sallie tried to glower but he could see the comment pleased her. Up at the farm, brother and sister had lived side by side for a decade. She'd been renting when he inherited the place and for years he'd been on her to take what they called the Little House—the house where they had spent weekends as kids. It was twenty minutes closer to her church, and the parishioners liked the idea of her living in the community—"by which they mean 'the richer community,'" she said when she wasn't feeling charitable. But having the house, and her whereabouts permanently settled, she admitted, freed her for other work, and finally she'd conceded. She loved her goddaughter,

Laura—the more, Jed felt, as Laura got older and was better company. Gay, Sallie had never come out in a big way. Jed had gathered there had been some disappointment in her romantic life a while back that precipitated her two years' sabbatical from her church building schools and teaching in Kenya. When she got home she seemed different, not exactly resigned but as if she had accepted something. But he was preoccupied—with the bank, Philippa, Laura's birth—and "Are you happy?" was not the sort of thing they asked each other; it would only make her scoff. Lest the housing arrangement fail—each understanding that siblings generally went their own ways in life—it had been from the start dogma that neither interfered in the other's plans or ever staked claims to the other's coming and going, so they frequently went a couple of weeks without a real conversation, even when Jed's family was up at the farm on the weekends.

"I need to come down more often," Sallie said soberly.

"Why?"

She raised her eyebrows as she ate her sandwich, as if it were obvious. "I'm becoming insulated up there, Jed. I'm becoming the kind of person—the kind of priest—whose focus is so local and so narrow that I'm losing touch with how the world works. I'm sitting on my stool at the Danforth Diner, chatting with Arlene and Jo, and I'm taking too much pleasure in being isolated from...all this." She gestured at the room and glanced uncertainly around at the ancestor portraits on the walls, the triple-monitor flat-screen on the partner desk. "You're the one who's really in the world. I've retreated." She took an emphatic bite of her sandwich and said, with her mouth full, "That's dangerous."

"And the fund-raising? Are you really having trouble? No one to tap in your parish?"

Sallie's shoulders went up and down. "Everyone cites the crisis, of course."

Jed said, "Why not let me chip in again? Us, I mean. We need more charitable donations."

"I defend you, you know!" Sallie said, as if Jed had made a different statement entirely. "Bill and Nancy," she went on diffidently, with a glance at him, "they'd like to burn all you bankers at the stake. I told them, 'The world needs banks, but they've got to be properly run.'"

"Not bad," Jed granted. "I may have to use that myself. So I can't write you another check? It's all I can do."

"Thank you," Sallie said soberly, "but we still have some of the founding donation Skinker made. And I'm determined it will be more than that. I don't want it to be a pet charity—like one of Ma's, you know?" She sat back, wiped her hands on a paper napkin and then on her thighs, and said curiously, "Have you seen her?"

"Ma?" Jed finished his BLT—he'd been hungrier than he realized. Sallie always seemed to be providing nourishment, dropping off soup at some neighbor's whose husband had been injured on the job; a pan of lasagna for a GED graduation party. The maternal basics came easily to her—regular meals, bedtimes. His mother, who had been known to call him at seven thirty on a weekday morning to ask if he knew whether his sister had considered "a new procedure I've been reading about, much better than IVF, where a man is not involved in any way!," failed to consider that Sallie's children were the addicts, the victims of domestic abuse she tended—the middle-aged parishioners whose money couldn't save their souls...

"She always seems to be in East Hampton when I call. Has she got a boyfriend out there?"

Jed chuckled. "No doubt."

The moment their father died, Winnie had stopped her visits to the farm. She had spent her childhood in East Hampton, and giving it up for Danforth when she married had been a bitter pill to swallow.

"Phil would know," Jed said. "Ma still tries to convince her we'd be happier out at the beach."

"When does she do that? When do you see her?"

"We have her over for dinner once a week."

"Philippa cooks?" Sallie looked incredulous.

"No, Ma cooks! Or they'll order in steaks from Melon's! Ma peppers Phil with questions—"

"I'll bet."

"Phil doesn't seem to mind."

It was strange. In the middle of replying to his sister, Jed glanced at the gold clock on the mantelpiece and felt dizzy, though he was seated. He must have closed his eyes for a second.

The next thing he knew, he heard, "Jed? Are you all right?" Sallie had come to his chair—was kneeling down beside it. "You're not well, are you? You're tired, Jed. You don't look well. Are you ill?" Only Sallie could look urgently steady, urgently kind.

"I'm fine," he said automatically. "I just remembered something I have to do." When he didn't elaborate, she knew not to ask. Wordlessly, though, she scrutinized him. "It's a hassle," he assured her lightly. "But it's not important."

Sallie was not one to rush to fill a silence. He could feel those probing blue eyes of hers on his face. Still kneeling, she placed her hand on his arm and said quietly, "There's a man in Danforth, Jed. He's had great success with addiction. I've sent a couple of my direst girls to him—hard cases. What I'm saying is that they could simply meet. And talk. *I* could suggest it. Woman to woman, you know? 'I've noticed, Phil, that sometimes when you drink you…' That kind of thing. Leave you out."

"Oh." Jed gave his sister's shoulder a pat. "It's not that. But thanks."

Her brow furrowed, Sallie observed him a moment longer. "Okay." She accepted his response, he knew. One early morning after an evening at the farm that had gone bad a couple of years ago, she had come upon him sweeping up broken glass from the kitchen floor. He'd felt he ought to say something, but before he could find the words, she'd let him off the hook, speaking first. "People have to come to things in their own time, don't they?" she'd remarked.

"It's what I believe," he'd said.

She got herself up off the safe now, walked to the casement windows, and looked out, first horizontally at the parking garage that had gone up a few years ago, across the way, then cocking her head to gaze down to the street, as everyone did. "I'd never get any work done here. I'd be staring down at the street all day. Watching the comings and goings. Making up stories about people."

"I did," he said. "At first."

She turned, with a half smile. "You were twenty-nine."

"Yes."

A worry came into her face. "This year's been terrible, hasn't it, Jed? I know you haven't even let on how terrible…There's a man in my congregation who was apparently quite high up at Lehman Brothers. He used to put a hundred-dollar bill in the plate every week…a victim of the crisis, I guess you'd say." Sallie spoke as if she were putting the term *victim* in quotes—it was no doubt difficult for her to get her tongue around the word when it applied to finance types, for whom, despite her family name, she had little use. With a shake of her head, she crossed to the sofa, sat, and slowly finished the sandwich, a ruminative frown on her face. "He's a good man. They say he'll have to sell his place up-state."

"I'd never do that!" Jed said. "I'd sell in the city. Move to Danforth."

"You sound as if you've got it all planned out," Sallie said speculatively. She studied his face before balling up her trash. "I wish you would, you know!"

Jed nodded. "One day…"

"Jed?" She moved herself forward till she sat perched at the very edge of the leather sofa. Her eyes searched his. "She'll sacrifice you. You know that, don't you?"

Jed demurred. "You have been at the farm too long. There's nothing so dramatic as all that going on." When she didn't respond, only kept her serious, steady gaze on him, he looked away and said offhandedly, "Skinker's all right, you know. So far we've come through all right."

His sister had an admirable capacity for staying on message; it must have served her well in the parish when people tried to squirm out of obligations.

"Jed?" she repeated. "She will sacrifice you if you let her."

"There was a moment, maybe…" An odd gratitude for his only sibling stole over him—she was the one person on earth who he could know for certain was not referring to Philippa.

His sister in fact quite liked Philippa. They shared some baseline of humor, some appreciation for the absurd, that he understood intellectually but not viscerally; it was their—perhaps a woman's—thing. Their relationship would come in handy if he ever had to—he stopped himself. My God. The fatalism. Distress, however much you tried to compartmentalize it, put you in an illogical frame of mind.

The gilt clock chimed the hour. "Ack! Is that right? I've got to be going!" Sallie wanted to make sure she caught the express, not the local. "As much as I love you, brother, I can't stand that slow train." He walked her down the three curving marble flights, mindful of the time, glad he could show her out without having to make up an excuse. The meeting was still forty-five minutes away—unless of course he canceled. Curtis had canceled before. That was almost worse. The emptiness of the afternoon afterward. Left with his thoughts. But somehow unable to go home early to Phil and the children.

They stood briefly in the elegant black-and-white-marble foyer, Jed's favorite spot in the building.

"You're up this weekend, right? Phil's supposed to come to the center with me Saturday."

"Is she?" Jed was surprised.

"Yes, Jed! They *loved* her. The time we went before?" Sallie dug in her handbag and took out a cheap black umbrella. "You see, they look at me," Sallie said, "and they think, *Well, of course this chubby middle-aged woman* priest *is going to be doing our laundry and making us tea and buying us books we'll never read.* She *never had any options—no wonder she became a Christer.*"

"Now, Sall—"

"*Doesn't* understand *temptation! Never had any.* Whereas Philippa! Beautiful, sophisticated married woman, big rock on her hand—well, it is big, Jed—who can't dress down if she tries, who's volunteering her time to be with *them.* Well, it's flattering—that's what it is! They know Philippa could be elsewhere. Me, they take for granted. As they should!" she said when Jed made to interrupt again. "As they should. I wouldn't have it any different."

"And how do you handle..." Jed stopped, but not out of delicacy. He only wanted to understand how, in a rehabilitation center, his wife—

"Oh, I don't get into it," Sallie said simply. She added neutrally, as if she had no great expectation about it, "Perhaps she'll learn from them."

Sallie stood on tiptoes to give him a kiss. "Coming up tomorrow or Saturday?"

"Tomorrow. Late."

"How late?"

"Nine? Ten? I've got some stuff to take care of today that'll keep me out of the office," Jed said vaguely. He would never have told her, and anyway, he didn't want to. The only person he wished he could tell was Phil. Because she would understand the type of person he was up against—the weak-eyed devil. Oh, she knew the type well. And she would have been able to help him, console him—she alone could always console him.

"Do not speed!" Sallie was saying. "I don't care if *you* go and break your neck, but not with your precious cargo..." She shook her head balefully. Jed's driving was something they'd fought about since adolescence. She had gone the other way—two hands on the wheel, pedantically signaling to change lanes even when there were no other cars in sight. "The thing about it is," she'd said once, "it doesn't suit you. You're not the type to speed. It's beneath you. It's the one thing Ma and I agree on."

And it's the one thing Ma doesn't control, Jed had thought. Rounding the first bend in the road as he left the farm as a sixteen-year-old, he'd felt free—high. Even Hugh had nothing to do with cars.

Found them irritating necessities. Whereas Jed was a tinkerer. Better at getting Billy Flood's tractor restarted than Billy was.

"I never speed with the kids!" he protested. "And anyway, you can't speed. Too many cops now."

Sallie wasn't having any of it. "Right. And they're about as likely to arrest Jed Skinker as their own mothers."

Jed held the door for her and she went out into the rain, opening the cheap umbrella, half the prongs of which were bent or detached from the fabric. She hadn't gone five yards before she turned and yelled, "I forgot to tell you! Roxie's gotten herself pregnant!" Roxie was the farm's German shepherd.

"What? I thought she was too old!"

"Spoken like a typical man! She's due in April!"

Jed had an immediate thought. "Can we keep them a secret?" he yelled. "For Ruth's birthday? I'll only tell Phil—well, maybe Lolo too!"

She grinned and held up two thumbs, the ridiculous excuse for an umbrella waving wildly overhead.

To repeat, we had nothing against her. In fact, we all really liked her. It was common when we were sitting around murmuring about the latest affront for one of us to say self-righteously, lest there be some mistake, "I mean, I actually like her." The rest of us, not to be outdone, would cry, "Well, so do I!" "So do I!" And the one of us who had passed on the particular complaint that had captivated us moments before would say defensively, "I wasn't saying I didn't like her." So it was established that we all, every one of us, really liked her.

At the same time, you have to admit that she was an anomaly. She was an anomaly and, at times, almost an affront. Perhaps that sounds self-involved and silly on our part. What did the problems of one former fashion model have to do with us, after all? But once in a while, in a quiet moment at pickup or drop-off, you might see one of us glance at her in a rather irritated way. Again, it wasn't that we didn't like her. It's just that our world turned on the cogs of certain accepted middle-class expectations—call them upper-middle, if you must—that she failed to meet. I don't mean anything so lofty as moral *expectations . . . We—we slotted in the vacations. We ran our children through the necessary extracurricular activities so they would never have to suffer the ignominies we suffered in any popular sport or pastime. We exercised—we at least did yoga. We carefully chose foyer sconces, backsplashes, accent pillows. It was known that these were things that one did.*

And the playdates — the playdates, the playdates. We hosted playdates for one another's children for our mutual benefit. Of course we knew that in the case of the working moms, they would not be home, it would be the nannies. This was no issue at all to accommodate. But she — Philippa Lye —

In the fall of the Threes class when her daughter Laura, the elder one, was at St. Tim's, we'd e-mail Philippa to see if Laura was free, throwing out a date — This Thursday any good? *As the days elapsed and we didn't hear from her, we found ourselves growing frustrated with that sense of powerlessness we hadn't experienced since we got out of the dating market. We'd remind ourselves that she hadn't asked us to ask her — it was of course our own problem if her rudeness ("I'm sorry, but at this point that's all I can call it!") got to us. But the knowledge only incensed us, for we had thought we were done with game-playing and one-upmanship. What — were we supposed to employ the old dating strategies on her? Such as never call her first, wait three days to return the call if she called us, never assume a date was a date? The worst part was that we suspected, as we had with those young men who took so much strategizing to manage in our twenties, that her failures in communication had nothing whatsoever to do with us. Pretending that she was guilty of social manipulation was our way of telling ourselves that we did matter, we did count. "It's not that I don't like her, I just don't have time for this!" said we to one another in exasperation. And: "It's sad because it's the little girl who suffers," watching the child wait with that forbearing look when her mother failed to make pickup again. Once, one late-fall afternoon near Thanksgiving, oh, years ago now, she never came at all. The father — let's not be coy, Jedediah Skinker — was traveling for the bank and they didn't have anything like a proper nanny, only some old family retainer who lurked about the apartment but didn't schlep, the number one requirement of a school-age child's babysitter. Eventually, so we heard, at the tail end of the day, Philippa's mother-in-law, Winifred Skinker, came to collect the girl in a cab — she was an old classmate from Smith of Mrs. Davidson, the head of St. Tim's. I would have liked to be a fly on the wall when the old chums had a word that afternoon...except that, given the almost pathological circumspection of their generation, it was unlikely that either would have referred to the elephant in the room.*

Then, like the very worst of the men we dated in our twenties, just when we were ready to escalate the situation publicly because we had been pushed to the limit, she'd come over to one of us and say, in that uncomfortably intent way of hers that made you feel she was looking directly into the most shameful part of your soul, "You're Teddy's mom, aren't you? You e-mailed me! I'm sure you e-mailed me! Laura would adore *a playdate. Just adore one. Could you come to us?" As we sputtered to get our bearings, she'd say, "What about this afternoon? Could you have lunch with us? Lolo, wouldn't it be a blast if Teddy and his mom had lunch at our house today?"*

In our little group, it was Marnie Pete who first had the "privilege" of going over to Philippa's for a playdate. This was a few years ago, when Laura Skinker was still at preschool and the boy, Sebastian, was a baby. It happened about six months before Marnie and James left for Hong Kong, when she was pregnant with number two. We all wanted to know what the apartment was like, but Marnie wasn't very observant in that way. Her own place was floor-to-ceiling Pottery Barn—giant clocks, lobster traps for coffee tables, apothecary shop for a kitchen—so all we got was "It wasn't very renovated" and the fact that Laura's unframed school pictures were tacked directly to the wall in her room. A graying African American woman in a uniform *fixed them lunch and it was this sort of gelatinous beef stew. A proper sit-down hot lunch—the very idea made us squirm. Marnie almost died because Teddy wouldn't eat a bite and made increasingly appalling comments—"Gross!" "What* is *this?" "Take it away, Mommy!" while Laura Skinker sat soberly working her way through the whole bowl.* Philippa *ate the whole bowl—that was remarkable because everyone assumed she didn't eat. "No," Marnie insisted. "Not at all. She ate like a horse!" Stew, potatoes, an unrecognizable green vegetable...Marnie said she became self-*

121

conscious about how she was holding her silverware, wondered whether she ought to cross, American-style, or keep her fork facing down, European-style, which had always seemed more natural to her. There was a lot of art; she remembered that much. She said some of it was "old" but some of it was "modern—you know, shapes, but faded" (love Marnie), and there were lighter things as well—she recalled a watercolor of a Jersey cow in the powder room. There were photographs in silver frames on a beaten-up grand piano. A fireplace, she recalled vaguely. No, fireplaces. A claustrophobic back kitchen painted yellow with a swinging restaurant door. Some dying houseplants. Ferns? Aloe plants? We asked her for more specifics—what sort of a sofa did she have? Did she own a television?—asked her to describe the furniture, the rugs, the layout of the place, but Marnie simply couldn't remember. "Nothing really stood out!" she claimed. About halfway through the meal, Philippa got a call on the home phone. She excused herself and took the call in her bedroom. Marnie had to sit there talking to the children and making conversation with the maid, who was not unpleasant but slow-moving and reticent. Then the children started asking her what they could do. Laura Skinker asked if Teddy wanted to watch television. (Ah! So Philippa Lye did have a television!) "Oh, no," Marnie said. "No TV on a playdate, Teddy." Eventually she got them playing an ancient game of Chutes and Ladders she dug out of some cupboard. She had to get down on the floor and play too, to make it stick, and she felt heavy and awkward not only because she was pregnant but because she didn't like taking charge in another woman's house, and she despaired of Philippa's ever coming back. After a prolonged absence, when Marnie was considering simply packing up and going, Philippa reappeared. She apologized but explained nothing, said only, "I'm so sorry, I had to take that call." She looked a little shell-shocked and then, to Marnie's surprise, she said vehemently, "God damn it to hell!" Marnie tried to pacify her—by that point she was thrilled just to have another adult in the room. She said the usual things that one says when one has no specifics ("I hope everything's okay"). Philippa looked at her very closely, very intently, and said something *like, "I can tell you really understand!" and embraced her, which Marnie found bizarre. Eventually she noticed the children, who were being good and playing their game, and Marnie said Philippa absolutely beamed. "They're getting along really, really well, aren't they?" she cried. "We'll have to do this again! You must come over more often." Marnie was frankly embarrassed now. She'd thought Philippa would be sort of remote and hard to get to know and that they'd keep it safe and discuss St. Tim's and holiday plans—that was Marnie's idea, anyway, she was ready to talk tidily of the condo they'd rented at Steamboat—and instead she was being embraced like an old, intimate friend. Philippa asked her, very seriously, "Did you eat lunch?" And then, "Did your son finish his stew?" And the—by all counts—worst mother in New York City actually gave Marnie a lecture on nutrition in which she emphasized—get this—*the evils of prepackaged food! *By now Marnie felt like breaking the fourth wall and just looking out at the audience and saying,* Where the fuck does she get off?

But it got better. For Marnie noticed the oddest thing: Philippa was drinking. Marnie kept this from us till the very end of her recounting. But yes, when Philippa came out of the bedroom, she was drinking red wine out of a water glass that she periodically refilled from a bottle on the sideboard in the dining room. She was matter-of-fact about it in the extreme—so matter-of-fact that she never even offered Marnie a glass! Marnie drank very little generally, even when she wasn't pregnant, but something about the encounter was so distressing, she would have accepted a glass had she been offered one—she emphasized this. "And I would've downed it in one gulp!"

It all went downhill from there—if you can imagine that there was still any vertical distance to descend. The children tired of the game. Teddy started wandering around looking for things to destroy while Marnie chased after him, feeling increasingly enraged and idiotic. The girl, Laura, went and sat on the sofa on her mother's lap and put her cheek on her mother's chest and they stayed in this silent embrace so long that Marnie became flustered and said she had to go "before he wrecks something, heh!" Philippa gave no sign of appreciating her good humor and didn't even get up to see poor Marnie to the door. Marnie kept thanking her and thanking her and saying she really had to go, and from the sofa Philippa gave her a distant look and said, "Do you?," as if Marnie had invited herself over. Then she said, out of the blue, "My mother's dying. I just found out. That was my sister on the phone."

Well, that was it. Marnie gave a groan of protest—it was simply too much. "I'm very sorry to hear that, Philippa," she said and walked straight out the door, collecting stroller toys and jackets and mittens and shepherding her child as she went. In the mirror in the elevator she saw that she looked like a harridan. Her face was red and her hair was sticking out all over and whatever makeup she'd put on was long gone. She overthanked the doorman who showed her out, as if to preserve some connection or make up for some failure on her part. She got out onto the street and she cried.

I cannot explain the effect Marnie's recounting of the playdate had on us except to say that while we thought we would be happy to get the details, we were not. All the fun had gone out of it—not just out of gossiping but out of getting and spending. Perhaps a better way to put it is that for a couple of weeks, we all stopped Googling Hamptons real estate.

How could you live like that? How could you...get away with it? How could you not enroll your children in extracurricular activities? Ought our *help to be uniformed? We liked to organize, to run a tight ship, to laugh among ourselves and be satisfied in small things—closet reorganizations, baking feats. Hell, we loved* one another *but would never have said it. Our children we did tell we loved but as a perfunctory bedtime sign-off that expressed less than saying nothing at all. We deflected compliments. We made deprecating comments about how much we had eaten at the last meal and how lazy we were and how badly we sucked at tennis when in fact we were not at all lazy and we were very good tennis players.*

Needless to say, poor Marnie never got another invitation. As a child would, instead of blaming Philippa, she seemed to internalize the shame—looking glum when the Skinkers came up in conversation, no longer enjoying the speculation about them. When Philippa saw Marnie at school, she didn't acknowledge her except for the same distracted nod we all got if we even got that. Until they moved to Hong Kong—and there are those who say Marnie urged James to take the job in part to get away from Philippa Lye—Marnie would have to stand there watching Philippa pick up Laura. And while the rest of us gave an appropriate, tight-lipped little smile to our own children so as not to display the favoritism that we all felt, Philippa would swoop down on her daughter and envelop her in a massive hug, crying, "Hello, my gorgeous girl! Did you have a wonderful day?" and each one of us remembered, in a depth of bumming-out, the moment, in preadolescence, when we had learned from either our parents or our peers that one had to pretend not to care.

But to be clear, we had nothing against her.

We actually really liked her.

We really, really liked Philippa Lye.

Chapter Nine

Minnie Curtis spoke in a bright, inflectionless tone as the elevator doors opened, depositing them directly into the vestibule of 7/8A.

"Welcome to my humble abode!"

The remark was so off-key that Gwen simply failed to respond. She wasn't sure what she had been expecting—a flashy postwar with a surfeit of bathrooms?—but it wasn't this. Stepping into the outsize chandeliered foyer, she wasn't immediately sure, in fact, what "this" was. From the foyer she could see through French doors into an immense dining room in which a dozen Queen Anne chairs were pulled up to a mahogany pedestal table; hunting prints hung on red walls. To her right, an imposing staircase led to the second floor, its Oriental runner tacked to the treads with brass rods. The apartment seemed to have been done to an opulent yet oddly corporate effect. In front of her, atop a round library table, a massive flower arrangement strained menacingly from an oversize Chinese vase that might have been priceless or might have been Pier One.

Or, rather, the apartment had not "been done," Gwen reminded herself, looking back belatedly to check on Mary, grateful to see that she had plopped down in the elevator vestibule to remove her shoes. Minnie had decorated it herself, mistrusting professions such as interior design, she'd made clear on the car ride up, for which the fees were high and the services aesthetically based.

"Who would pay someone for that?" she'd demanded of Gwen. "I mean, honestly! I know what I want!"

Allowing this with a nod, for she had no basis on which to refute it, Gwen had another insight into why John Curtis had married Minnie, child and all, besides the obvious, oft-cited one of her being hot. Curtis clearly had ambitions to social status (or Gwen assumed he did—those multicolored polo shirts and madras shorts, she felt, would not have been lightly jettisoned), but he wouldn't have put up with that same type of vulnerability in a wife. Minnie had ambitions, yes, but like many successful people in New York, she was extra-societal. If she'd wanted her kid at St. Tim's, the reason no doubt was that she'd heard it was the best—the same as she'd want the best range, the biggest diamond—and not that she felt, like the true social climber, that it would mean anything or say something thematic about where she had gotten in life. It was just that the best was the best was the best.

She did seem to take pride in her economies, arbitrary as they were. Her opining on the worthlessness of the decorating profession had occurred in the backseat of Minnie's Cadillac Escalade, driven by Minnie's driver—his and hers, she explained to Gwen, they had found to be a better arrangement than sharing a car. In the middle-seat row of the black leather interior, Mary Hogan had gone silent before Arabella Curtis and the aura, not exactly of privilege but of stuff—lots and lots of stuff having been gotten in her name—that emanated from Minnie's only child. Mary hadn't so much as looked at Arabella, instead staring down at the footwell with an expression of alarm, as if the unseen forces that had placed her in the older girl's proximity could at any moment cast her out again. When Gwen tried to break the spell with a word to her daughter, Mary shook her head briefly, concentrating. "My God!" said Minnie. "She looks so serious!" Gwen let the comment pass. For a certain kind of adult, she had learned, her daughter's presence seemed to constitute a rebuke.

Arabella was watching Mary laboring over the buckles of her shoes. The older girl had a look of amusement on her face, as if this were a revelation, how the little people lived—obeying commands, respecting property. She was wearing a smart houndstooth coat with a black patent-leather belt by one of the high-end fashion designers now producing children's clothing lines. She yanked the coat off as she came into the foyer, tossed it in the direction of the banister—and looked the other way when she missed.

Gwen gave a loud one-syllable laugh at this spoiled performance and then, to cover it up, bent to pick up the coat herself.

"Oh, Gwen, you don't have to do that!" said Minnie, busy with the elaborate closures on her own designer coat—toggles and zippers and interior buttons—but her tone suggested that servility never hurt.

There were too many rich people—that was the problem. The audience had been thinning for a long time. Everybody needed a Gwen, but there weren't enough Gwens to go around—someone to whom a ride in one's private car, a visit to one's McMansion of an apartment, was pure touristing diversion. *Bring it on,* Gwen thought, tilting her head back to examine the elaborate inlay of the ceiling.

"I'm playing with my Wii, Mom!" Arabella announced.

"I forgot to tell you"—Minnie eyed herself in a heavy gilt mirror opposite the door, turning her sleek head this way and that—"I invited Philippa as well. Your childhood friend, right?"

"Oh, did you?" Gwen felt an immediate sense of misgiving that she had ever mentioned the connection. "As I said, *we* weren't really friends," she hastened to say. "It was more her sister and I—"

"Mo-om, I'm playing with my Wii!"

"*Hola,* Arabella!" A broad-faced Hispanic housekeeper hustled in, laughing and ducking her head. *"Hola, princesita!"*

"Say hello to Lupe, Arabella!"

Keeping up a stream of giggles, Lupe collected the coats and ferried them off to a closet that had one of those false, knobless doors Gwen could never see the point of.

"I'm playing with my Wii, Mom, and they're not to touch the karaoke!" The girl retained a trace of the English accent she'd picked up in preschool, a trace of the English diction. It enhanced the imperious quality she projected. Gwen stifled an urge to laugh again. She rarely thought of her husband during the day but now she couldn't *not* think of him—of Dan Hogan's reaction to this Richie Rich episode she'd landed herself in. In the past they had laughed so often and so long about other people's follies…

"Are these real?" Mary said loudly, planting herself in front of the giant flowers. "They're not real. I don't think they're real."

"Now, Mare—"

"No one is to touch the Wii Karaoke except me!" Arabella called, running for the stairs.

Minnie was now applying lipstick in the mirror, as if she were about to go out.

"They are real, Mom!" exclaimed Mary, giving one of the petals a tug.

Gwen lunged and stopped the entire vase from toppling—just. "Yes, honey," she said shakily, "they are."

Oblivious, Minnie gave a dental patient's grin into the mirror, flashing her white teeth.

"Arabella, you lucky!" Lupe called, hustling back to the foot of the stairs. "You have nice friend to play!" She was the clanging, happy type of nanny some people went in for, Gwen saw, but whose tone-deafness always sort of alarmed her.

"Mom!" Arabella was lingering at the top of the stairs now. "You haven't answered me ... *Mom!*" The girl's eyes were screwed shut, her voice rose to a shriek on the last word. Mary stared frankly up at the girl, pleased and intrigued by this display.

"Arabella, *princesita*, don't talk to Mami like that. Arabella, your friend—"

"*Mom!*"

Gwen blushed and was mumbling something to Mary when Minnie said, "Have you ever seen such a naughty, ungrateful girl, Gwen?"

"I, um—"

"I'm throwing the Wii in the trash!" Minnie yelled disgustedly up the stairs. "You're a rude, spoiled girl, Arabella! Daddy spoils you! You deserve a spanking! And you'll get one later, do you hear me?"

At the top of the stairs Arabella put her hands over her ears and began to shout-sing, "Happy birthday to me! Happy birthday to me!"

Mary guffawed at this performance, which seemed to incense Arabella. She gave a murderous frown, stomped her foot, and sang louder, which made Mary laugh louder. "Mom, she's singing, 'Happy Birthday'! And it's not her birthday!"

"Um, yes, she is—"

"Nobody believes in spanking anymore, do they?" Minnie said

plaintively to Gwen or, rather, to the mirror, into which she was still gazing, now with a pouty expression.

"It's not her birthday, is it, Mom?"

"Um, I don't *think* so—"

"Well, I was spanked as a child!"

The pronouncement stilled the room, adults and children alike.

Quivering in her pride, Minnie at last turned her face from the mirror. "Spanked and, I mean, beaten! With my mother's hairbrush! Or a wooden spoon—a belt! Anything she could get her hands on."

Gwen hesitated, her hand on Mary's shoulder. She had been spanked, of course, but somehow she felt it wasn't validation that Minnie was after.

Upstairs, Arabella cackled and ran off.

"Oh, miss!" Lupe laughed and shook her head, toiling up the stairs after the girl, pausing to hold out her hand for Mary, who couldn't be invited fast enough. Gwen guessed that two or three less sycophantic women had come before Lupe and "not worked out"—the middle-aged white woman, for instance, who had suddenly stopped appearing at school. Lupe wouldn't work out ultimately either. Minnie, Gwen was certain, would burn through help like brands of detergent, congratulating herself on each capricious replacement.

"Come on!" Minnie said with a disconcertingly warm smile at Gwen. "I need a drink!"

The kitchen was vast, suburban-size, as even city kitchens must be nowadays. It glistened like an operating theater with menacing, hyperclean appliances. Minnie gestured to a row of backless stools pulled up to a dark, speckled-marble counter. "Have a seat at our breakfast bar, Gwen."

After hesitating a second to see if this moment was meant ironically, Gwen did as she was told while, from a double-wide, steel-doored refrigerator, Minnie removed an open bottle of white wine and yanked out the cork. "John is so into wine and I could give a crap! He's all Opus One this, Romanée-Conti that. He gets it from his boss—from Martin Kerr. Real wine snob, Marty. I'll tell you a secret, Gwen."

"Yes?" Gwen tried to smile to soften how deathly serious she sounded.

In a stage-whisper, Minnie said, "Sometimes I doubt if he can tell the difference between the ten-dollar stuff I drink and his two-hundred-dollar bottles!" From a cupboard she got down two crystal balloon-type glasses that seemed to have been fabricated on the same scale as the kitchen. After filling them nearly all the way, she handed one to Gwen. "Big cheers!"

"Oh," said Gwen, "cheers!" There was a natural pause after the toast, which Gwen ought to have filled by telling Minnie that she had gone to college with Minnie's husband—knew who he was—knew him, a little. It would have been natural to do so. Instead, she kept silent. She was unable to think of what she could add. *What a great guy?* Yet it occurred to her that from here on in, she was operating under false pretenses.

"John loves going to the auctions—just loves it. Do you know we've got eight hundred bottles in storage?"

I was just lying there and he . . .

"Eight hundred? Wow," Gwen said hastily.

Minnie clicked around the kitchen in today's ferocious stilettos, fixing a tray of snacks for the children. "I say, give me my mommy's chardonnay and a couple of ice cubes and I'm good!"

"Sure." Gwen said vaguely. There was a fascinating falseness to almost everything Minnie said. Even when Gwen had gotten the ride home from school with her that one time, and Minnie had filled Gwen in, unprompted, on her disadvantaged childhood, the narrative had been filled with hesitations and false starts that ended in non sequiturs, as if she were making up the disadvantaged part and in reality came from money—the colonial sugar fortune, say, that people sometimes still linked to her name. "She was an—she drank too much. You could call her...well, nowadays everyone's an alcoholic, but she...well, I mean, I—we kids—we really had to behave!" When Gwen, feeling obliged to continue the conversation, had asked a neutral question as to whether Minnie had any brothers or sisters, that, too, provoked switchbacks so bizarre Gwen wondered if the whole story was a sham. "Yes. Well, no, actually! I've got a half brother! I mean, I've got two half brothers. But one doesn't count because he's in jail. I mean, not *jail*-jail, but...well, he is locked up..." But her falseness didn't have the quality of dread, of covering up and defensiveness one typically associated with people who lied. It was as if she was always attempting to charm, even people like Gwen, which was flattering in its way. She was like a woman at a speed-dating event, Gwen thought, who tries on a slightly different personality with every suitor. Arriving at school this afternoon, she had been "knackered beyond belief, Gwen! You wouldn't believe the hours I've been keeping!"

On the tray, Minnie had placed bags of Oreos, Cheetos, M&M's, and a liter of Coke. Gwen fairly stared. She was used to the usual disclaimer of the knowledge-economy parent: "We have one sweet a week, except on a playdate..."

"Can I help?" she said belatedly as Minnie added a handful of Tootsie Rolls.

"Please! You sit there and enjoy! Make yourself at home!" To Gwen's surprise, Minnie hoisted the tray up on her shoulder. "I used to waitress!" She laughed. "I mean, not really waitress...but I worked in a restaurant!" Her body flashed with authority as she carried the tray off, her heels clicking as she went. A distinction Gwen had picked up in an anthropology class she'd taken years ago came to mind, that there were two kinds of cultures, shame cultures and guilt cultures.

She took a cautious sip of the wine. It was so oaky and medicinal-tasting she almost gagged—forced herself to swallow it. She looked around for something of interest but the kitchen was without personal effects, as if the Curtises never received mail or made a list on a Post-it or consulted a recipe in a cookbook. What did they do for food? Gwen wondered. She found herself gazing at the hood of the eight-burner, restaurant-size stove. It was like a chrome dragon descending, mouth open, to devour the kitchen.

After a couple of minutes, the doorbell rang. Gwen didn't move, praying that the nanny would answer it, but when it sounded again, she got down off the stool reluctantly. Walking through the large, dust-free, heavily furnished rooms, she felt as if she had wandered off from a school field trip to a government building—a treasury or a courthouse—and had ducked under the velvet ropes. Or as if the whole thing was set up as a massive scam, and the hunting prints and Oriental rugs could be packed up in twenty minutes flat.

She opened the door to Philippa Lye and her two younger children. Philippa had a finger to her chin and looked stricken.

"I've been here before," she said to Gwen, coming proprietorially into the apartment, trailed by the little boy and girl. "It didn't used to have two floors..."

"Apparently—"

"No, but I'm sure of it! I'm having the most violent sense of déjà vu." She went on in her peculiar, vacant yet intent way. "I recognized the doorman! It's the same man! I swear I recognized him."

Gwen fell to helping the children, getting their coats off and hung up in the closet.

"When Nan's grandmother lived here, the powder room was right there—where the stairs are. It had this faded striped wallpaper..."

The little girl was a blond sausage, her hair cut blunt across, a real towhead. The boy was more like his mother, angles and bones, tall for his age, with a wary frown on his face. He caught sight of the vase of flowers and drew back with an accusatory stare. "I want to go home!"

"My roommate from Dunning—we spent a weekend here," Philippa went on. She was staring through to the dining room now. "I can absolutely *see* the living room, all the needlework and the chintz and the stacks of manuscripts. Donald Fessenden was in publishing...he started the paperback, as I recall. You know, before it had been only hardcovers. Books weren't accessible to the masses," she clarified, apparently for Gwen's benefit. She stepped slowly back until she was standing right beside Gwen. The physical proximity was as disconcerting as always, given Philippa's holistic self-absorption. "It was so funny; we bought a bottle of vodka and we were going to sneak it in our rooms, you know, drink it out of the bottle before we went out, and Mrs. Fessenden, Buzzy, Nan's granny, has her maid come and knock on our door—Joy was her name, lovely woman, been with them for years—and *invite us to join her* for a gin and tonic! She invited us to come and have a drink with her! We were fifteen. Maybe she thought we were in college—I don't know. I remember Nan's saying, 'Well, I guess I could have one more, Granny,' as if she had to be persuaded."

Lupe appeared, chuckling as she trundled out from the kitchen with a stack of plastic cups. Philippa gave the woman the same stare her son had given the flowers.

"Mami forget the cups! I get it. Up and down! Up and down! The Wii is broken! She fix it." Catching sight of Philippa's children, she stopped and mugged an exaggerated happy face. "*¡Ven! ¡Ven conmigo!*" She clapped her free hand on her thigh. "Come! What you waiting for? Arabella is upstairs!" The two children stared neutrally, as if not knowing what to make of this apparition, not understanding what it had to do with them. When Lupe repeated her exhortations, Philippa seemed to snap out of her reverie. "Go ahead, you two!" she said airily. "Run along!" The little girl took the woman's hand after a moment, gazing up at her, but the boy, who had gripped Philippa's thigh as Lupe advanced, began to whine. "No, Mummy, I don't want to—". Gwen was about to volunteer to take him upstairs to join the others when Philippa forcibly pulled the little hands apart. "Don't *cling*, Sebastian!" He opened his mouth to cry but before he could, Philippa yanked him forward.

"Ow!" howled the boy. "You hurt me!"

For that, he got a mean little push toward the nanny.

"Have fun!"

Yet she stood perfectly still as she watched the party of three ascend the stairs, Sebastian scowling and protesting as Lupe dragged him along. "You're jerking me! You're *jerking* me!"

"*¡Veeeeen! ¡Ven!*"

"It's sad, isn't it?" Philippa said reflectively. "Watching some nanny take your children up the stairs of some hideous apartment—I mean, as if they were any old children?" She turned to Gwen and seemed to actually take note of her presence suddenly, as if she had gone into a different mode of being altogether. Searching Gwen's eyes, looking from one to the other, she said, "How many do you have, Gwen?"

"Me? Oh, I just have the one. Just one."

"Oh, really?" Philippa said, though not unkindly. "She's an only?"

"Yes."

Unaccountably, Gwen felt she might start to cry. It was as if the question had short-circuited her system, which was wired for making do, not for bounty. No one ever asked a follow-up question in this town. Questions were proffered only as segues into bragging about oneself or one's children. "Do your children...? Because *we*..." Tears sprang to her eyes; Gwen batted the air and smiled manically to get her breath.

"I'm sorry."

"Oh, it's okay." Gwen cleared her throat. "One's good. One's fine. You know."

Philippa went on observing her until Gwen said, "Come on!," trying to channel Minnie's peppiness, and led her out of the foyer.

In the kitchen Gwen offered Philippa her own glass of wine. "You take it."

Philippa accepted it, sipped absently.

"It's not very good," Gwen said apologetically, as if it were her fault. "I—"

"I'm getting shivers! I remember the little pull-door fridge was over there, with one of those internal iceboxes...and there was a—a machine for warming bread, or plates—although I don't understand..." Philippa's voice trailed off as she turned slowly around with a hesitantly pointed finger. "Oh! They've sacrificed the maid's rooms! Of course. There'd be no room for dear Joy now. Nan and I wouldn't get our gin and tonics. Just as well, considering how that night ended up." She looked at the wine in her hand. "What the hell is this?"

"I'm not too sure."

Philippa drank again from the glass. "For God's sake! Wouldn't you think—I mean, with all this money—couldn't she open something nicer?" She gave an irritated look around. "Where's the bottle?"

When Gwen looked at her blankly, Philippa said, in the quiet but urgent tone of voice one uses in an emergency, "The bottle of wine? Where's she keeping it?"

"Oh!" Gwen said. "She put it back in the fridge." Philippa located the bottle in the refrigerator door and refilled her glass. There was a deft economy to her movements, like those of a practiced thief.

"You're not going to tell on me, are you, Gwen?" she asked as she jammed the cork back into the neck.

Gwen flushed. "Of course not!" It pained her that from her own abstention, others inferred censure. She didn't really care if people drank or caroused or kept their children up till all hours and left their houses a mess and fed them chicken nuggets every night. She fell silent because she could never think of anything to say. She was embarrassed by her own lack of vices, her plain-vanilla competence, the implied aridity of her days. She climbed back onto her stool and pointed at the bottle. "You'd better put it back, though, if you don't want her to know."

"Oh yes—I certainly had better," Philippa said archly, but she did return it to the door.

The casement window above the sink was an anomaly in the kitchen: small and rectangular, human-scaled, as if the renovators had missed it. The view, Gwen noticed, was pleasant for a back view—town houses, back gardens, a church spire.

"I wonder," Philippa said, leaning over the sink and peering out, "whether it was Minnie who bought it from the Fessenden estate." She added defiantly, as if someone had told her she shouldn't: "I'll have to ask."

Gwen would have advised against it. Minnie didn't seem to like it when people had pasts—backgrounds, family—that informed their presents. But Gwen grasped that this was habit or even a pleasure for Philippa—that whenever she knew she had to behave, she would fly in the face of it.

Philippa moved with her glass over to the island. Gwen could feel Philippa's eyes on her face, going speculatively over it. "I remember you perfectly!" Philippa said. "The dress-up games you and Rose and I used to play!"

"You do?" Gwen tried not to be flattered, failed utterly, and broke into an idiotic grin. They had never actually spoken about their childhood beyond Gwen's hurried, mumbled explanation when she first saw Philippa at school. She had occasionally wondered if Philippa even remembered how they knew each other.

"You and Rose—always playing school. You were nice to her—you let her be the teacher."

"Oh, I didn't care." Truth be told, Gwen had enjoyed simply being in the Lye sisters' house. It was large, yes, and according to Gwen's dad, it was falling down—"You see that curling on the shingles? All the missing ones? Needs a new roof. Cedar's nice but it doesn't last." Inside, the rooms were underfurnished—the bedrooms on the third floor where they played empty save for a lamp, a bedstead. But they had a grandness; they felt properly proportioned. There was something about the halls, too, about the flow of one room to another. Gwen could intuit as children can the correctness in its design. The Lyes' was the only nice house she ever visited. When she went home, her own 1970s Cape felt small and cheaply made, the wall-to-wall carpeting the most modest of comforts compared to those echoing wood floors and fraying rugs and hallways. She couldn't picture playing dress-up at her house, even if they had had a costume box.

"Remind me, how did you know each other?" Philippa said curiously. "From tennis?"

"No, no—Brownies. Girl Scouts."

"Girl Scouts! Oh, my word. I'd forgotten Rose did all that. Poor thing. She tried so hard to be normal." She looked hard at Gwen, interest and approval mingling in her expression. "And where in Dunning did you live?"

"Nautauqua," Gwen corrected her. "I'm from Nautauqua," she said hurriedly. She wanted no mistake of what she claimed. Dunning had the boarding school and the two white-steepled churches on Main. Nautauqua was the next town over, with the commuter rail station and a sports bar next to it; a traffic circle with a McDonald's and a Burger King and, off one of its tentacles, an army base that was slowly being decommissioned. The two towns combined for high school and a few other things—Girl Scouts; a 10K race Thanksgiving weekend at which Gwen's dad, Robert, had officiated before he had the stroke. Not that Philippa or Rosemary Lye had attended the public high school. There was a world of difference in having been a day student at Dunning, as the Lyes had been, and having gone to Dun-Naut, as the kids called it—Dunning-Nautauqua Regional Secondary School whence Gwen Babineau had been among the few students her year to matriculate to a four-year college, the Ivy League gloss beside the point—gilding the lily.

Philippa came around the island to the stools. "Are your parents still there?" She climbed up on the one right beside Gwen, her wine sloshing out on the counter as she did.

"Yup." With pride Gwen added, "Same house."

There was something foolish about the two of them, two grown women, sitting so close together. Gwen would've made a distancing remark—"This is cozy, isn't it?"—but Philippa's presence seemed to shame her away from that sort of conventional thinking. After a moment she volunteered, "My brother tried to get them to move to Florida because the winters are so tough, but my mother won't leave Nautauqua. She'll be there till the day she dies," Gwen predicted.

"Oh, that's funny." Philippa nodded appreciatively. "Because my father wouldn't leave Dunning. All his life. He was born and died in the same house."

"Oh—well: the Lye house," Gwen said. "I get that. The best house in the whole town!" As soon as she said it, she was mortified at having sounded the sycophantic note.

Philippa eyed Gwen and seemed to go on carefully. "It's been razed now. My mother sold it when my father died. They put in condominiums."

"What?" Gwen gaped at her. "You're kidding me!" She forgot herself entirely. "The big Lye house is gone? Since when? That can't be! It was there forever! It was like—the anchor of that part of town, the green and everything!" She stopped abruptly, realizing how rude she was being.

"Yeah, it was there a while. My father's family. Or at least," Philippa said lightly, holding up her wineglass and scrutinizing it, "the man I believed was my father for twenty years."

Gwen's expression went dunce-like. The outlines of the story were known to her, as they were to everyone local. The Lyes were the one name in Dunning; there was Lye Hill, which accounted for half the open acreage of the town; the Lye Bird Sanctuary; Lye Cottage, where the Nautauqua Valley Hunt used to stop to refuel; Lye Hall at the Dunning School...and in contrast to those bucolic touchstones, Lye was the name on the textile mill upriver in Nautauqua. There had been a scandal when Philip Lye remarried a few weeks after his first wife died. Their cleaning woman. Their cleaning woman, whom the couple had come to depend on more and more as Nessie Lye's cancer advanced. And then in seven or eight months, the child: Philippa.

It was the kind of story about which Camilla Babineau would say—no doubt had said—"What goes around comes around." Enjoying the sentiment. Taking pleasure in the fact that you couldn't get away with things—the truth would get you in the end.

Sheila. With an odd, emotionally incorrect satisfaction, Gwen recalled the woman's name. Besides the cleaning jobs she'd worked nights as a cocktail waitress at Kelly's, the bar on Route 27, just over the Nautauqua line...

What might Camilla have said, exactly? How would she have phrased it? "The older girl, you know..." Or "People say..." Her lips tight like a ventriloquist's. " 'Course, the younger girl looks just like her father. No proof needed there."

What comes around goes around.

"He *was* Rose's father!" Philippa assured Gwen. She slipped down off the stool, still clutching her wineglass, and went to the sink, where she peered intently out the small window again.

The day, already an oddball, took on a surreal quality. Yet instead of Philippa's private tragedy ushering in some excruciatingly awkward state, Gwen had the strangest feeling—a feeling she hardly ever had in New York—of an ethereal calm. Philippa was from Dunning. The next town over. Rose Lye's older sister.

People—Minnie—might have turned this into "We grew up to-gether," but it was nothing so proprietary as that she would have claimed. It was the most basic of connections they had, that was all—coming from the same place; ending up here. It was simply that she recognized Philippa. She had known her forever. Knew that there were certain knolls, certain elms and certain oaks along certain roads, certain bends in those roads, certain graveyards and plays of light Philippa had known as well. That's all she would've claimed. If anyone had asked her what growing up there was like in the '70s and '80s, she would have said that the overarching principle, which she had been able to see only lately, in reflection, was a randomness. A randomness that had vanished, that this town, with its strivy parents—slotting in the schools and the lessons and the vacations and the camps; this kitchen; gut jobs; chain stores; the Internet—seemed determined to eliminate. Not to root out, that was impossible, but to pave over and over until you could only regain it now by trying to insert it artificially into one's own child's life. Then, there had been a randomness to how things turned out. You might become a model. You might never leave.

"Our father *was* Rosemary's father," Phil repeated. "I didn't mean to imply—"

"Oh, no—I know." Gwen cut her off awkwardly. "Where is Rose these days? I've been meaning to ask."

"Rosemary?" Philippa looked surprised. "Oh, she's still in Dunning. In one of the condos they built on our land, actually. They're the only affordable housing in Dunning. She said, 'Why cut off my nose to spite my face?'"

In the quotation, Gwen had a fleeting but vivid flash of Rosemary Lye, who even as a girl had been bent on making pain kneel to practicality. Gwen could remember Rose's saying, over some

143

disappointment visited on the Dunning-Nautauqua Girl Scouts, "It wouldn't have mattered anyway. We wouldn't have been able to stay for long," and then giving some hardworking reason for why the treat could never have been enjoyed—Camilla-like in her will to resignation. Gwen nodded. "I could see her doing that."

"She's enormous," Philippa said, with no modulation in her voice Gwen could discern. "Morbidly obese." She walked to the kitchen doorway and glanced down the hall. "She chose it, almost." She turned back into the kitchen, her watchful eyes on Gwen. "She didn't want my vice, you know?" She held up the empty wineglass and shook it. "Anything but! Anything but me." Then in a hushed tone she said, "Get me one more, will you, Gwen?" and placed her glass on the island in front of Gwen. "I'll keep watch."

"Sure." Gwen felt stiff getting down and taking the wine out. She filled the glass way up to the top and carried it carefully to Philippa. She was fumbling to put the cork back in the bottle when Philippa stopped her.

"Just leave it." And when Gwen hesitated—"Leave it," she ordered. "I don't know why I bother."

"My brother's still there!" Gwen said. "In Nautauqua." She went on with her awkward segue: "He's a cop in Dunning, as a matter of fact!"

"Is he?" Philippa said absently, but Gwen could tell the connection no longer interested her—not really. Philippa leaned against the breakfast counter. "I always thought I'd move back to Dunning. Take up the Lye homestead. I always suspected that leaving was just an interim state—a purgatory I was being forced to endure before I could go home. I mean, really: New York City? *Tokyo*? Can you imagine? Please! None of that had anything to do with me." She gave an exaggerated comic shudder. "I think knowing I was always planning to go home, that there was nowhere nicer than my own home, made me reckless. The security, ironically. If I hadn't had that to rely on, I'd have had to have been a hell of a lot more careful."

"Yes, you would have," Gwen said.

"But as I say, Sheila sold it." All at once Philippa sounded drunk. "They razed it that week. She'd let it fall into disrepair and nobody wanted to restore it. It wasn't quite the right moment. A little early for that. Nowadays...I was in Tokyo. I got fired from a job and my agent dumped me and I called home to tell her and she said, 'Well, don't think of coming home because home's gone.'"

"I'm sorry," Gwen said automatically.

"Don't be!" countered Philippa. "After all, I'm not a Lye. Not really. It was a 'bit of a shock,' that's all I'm saying, because I always felt it was the one authentic thing about me—my 'lineage.' Let's say I enjoyed it, even though nobody's ever heard of Lyes in New York. Isn't that silly? How pathetic! To cling to a name in this day and age."

Standing with her back to the sink, Gwen felt weary suddenly, tired to her bones. Minnie's vast kitchen, with its glaring appliances, its sterile surfaces, its imported marble and aggressive, obstructionist island, seemed to have itself razed Philippa's childhood house; put up the condos that took its place.

There was a silence in which Philippa again examined her glass, tilting the little wine that was left in it back and forth. Gwen turned and busied herself getting a glass of water, remaining at the sink and primly drinking it in gulps, refilling it, wiping with her sleeve at a single drop that fell on the counter.

Philippa came over and stood beside her. She set down her

wineglass in the sink, and they both looked momentarily out the small window. "Apparently my real father was a truck driver—you know, passing through."

Gwen nodded.

"There's that Boston–to–New Hampshire route. It goes through Dunning."

Gwen gave another stiff nod. "Makes sense."

At the same time, they both heard the clicking of Minnie's shoes across the marble in the foyer.

"And your mother?" Gwen asked.

"Oh, she's dead!" Philippa said. "She didn't get to enjoy the windfall after all."

"I am so sorry!" called their hostess before appearing in the doorway. "Lupe is completely useless when it comes to anything technological!"

Chapter Ten

When Dan Hogan was growing up, his father had planned many vacations. On his small-town lawyer's salary, Perry Hogan wanted to take his wife and five sons to Disney World. "We've got to do it while they're still young enough to believe," he said. That trip didn't happen, but a few years later, Perry felt their taste as a family—with the boys now between five and twelve—had grown more sophisticated, and he set his sights on the Caribbean. "It won't be fancy," he admitted freely, but there was an inn on a beach he had read about in a travel magazine he'd been thumbing through in the dentist's office, an inn on one of the less popular islands, apparently. Dan remembered looking up the funny name in the family atlas: Jost Van Dyke. Dan and his brother Tim, the older by thirteen months, would lie awake at night bargaining. "I'd be fine with going to one of the lame Caribbean islands," Dan would say, "if not the lamest," and Tim would respond, "I don't even care if the hotel is nice. I don't care if it's a dump, if we're on the beach." One quixotic summer when Perry had been captivated by the geography of the Iberian Peninsula, he announced they were going to go to Portugal for Christmas. Yes, it was a little out there, to just up and take the whole gang to Europe, to cross the Atlantic the first time not for London or Paris, but he'd become fascinated by the idea of staying in one of the old monasteries. They all learned the word *pousada* that summer, though by Christmas the trip was no longer mentioned. Stunned, when he awakened at last to the pattern, Dan realized his father had been playing the same game he and Tim played—he was trying to placate the gods by the modesty of his hopes, by the broad and unexacting range of what he would be happy with. When Dan at last made it to Disney World, the summer after his first year of law school at the end of an August that was sweltering in New Jersey let alone in Orlando, he'd sent his father a postcard that he'd meant to be funny but that he realized afterward might have been cruel: *Next year, Portugal!*

In the elevator, coming down impatiently from his office, Dan clenched and unclenched his hands. He had been contemplating a takeout salad when Brenda Purzinski, the SEC staff attorney on the Invictus case, had phoned. "Hey, Hogan. I'm coming out of court right now, and I got something for you guys on our favorite once-and-future perp. You wanna meet me at the Stands for a low-carb salad?"

"Wow, that's appetizing. And in February, no less."

"I know, but it's not that bad out and I've only got ten minutes."

He emerged into the bright winter day. The fist-clenching had nothing to do with Brenda. Whenever Dan got a promising piece of information on a case, he felt a surge of combativeness, as if the good news couldn't last: someone would fuck something up and Dan would be deprived of something. They'd subpoenaed John Curtis's cell phone records a couple weeks ago. As usual, the information was coming in in dribs and drabs. And Dan had good reason to be paranoid. For how many years had Martin Kerr's firm stood impervious—vexingly impervious—to a swelling stream of accusations? The two companies that had actually been ticked off enough to sue Kerr for stock manipulation had seen their lawsuits overturned; one, a microchip company, had found itself owing fines to Invictus when Invictus countersued. From all accounts Kerr was like that—he wouldn't settle for just getting off. He had to go the extra mile to fuck the entity that had crossed him.

But Dan had hope this Tuesday afternoon. *Ah, but I do, lad!* he thought, channeling his youngest brother, Andrew, who could do the brogue. The two lawsuits had occurred in the prelapsarian world of a few years ago. February 2009 was a different universe. Across the floor from him, Diane Costa was buried up to her practical, gold-stud earrings in the machinations of Bernard L. Madoff. Was it too much to ask that the crisis machine spit out Invictus as well?

"I'd be happy with a single incriminating call," Dan said to himself in case the gods were still listening—if they ever had been. "A single call." The winter sun blinded him and he squinted at the little food huts on St. Andrew's Plaza.

"What do you want, Danny? Hurry up!" Brenda called to him from her place at the front of the line of the Mexican one.

"Quesadilla, Diet Coke!" It calmed him that she thought the same way he would have, sneaking his order in at the last minute with hers so he wouldn't have to wait on line, yelling at him to save him the hassle.

The picnic tables on the plaza were empty, given the time of year, though Brenda was right—it wasn't that bad out. If Dan hadn't been so persistently underdressed, he wouldn't even have been cold. At least there was no wind. They chose the table that had the most direct sun, and Brenda took the plastic top off some kind of chicken-and-shredded-lettuce salad, and grimaced. "Ugh. Yours looks better."

"Have to agree there."

She'd been dieting for as long as he'd known her. He wondered if their friendship had reached a level where he could tell her straight that her appeal was her red hair and her sun-weathered face and her warmth. That even if she killed herself to lose the ten pounds, she'd still have the body type of a plump person, so it just wasn't worth the struggle.

Probably not. Over his quesadilla he glanced at her doggedly spearing a bite of lettuce with a plastic fork. Definitely not. Everybody had to have some stupid goal that kept them going.

Perhaps it was vanity but Dan sensed from her silences and roundabout questions and from the way she looked at him that she felt she might have married him, or someone like him, or even, specifically, one of his brothers; that she felt, with respect to him, that she had been cheated out of her heritage dibs, as it were. Purzinski was her married—and now divorced—name; she was born a Murray. He never mentioned Gwen to her out of delicacy for her feelings, even when avoiding it was inconvenient and involved circumlocutions, and she never asked, but from some early conversation, she knew that Gwen wasn't Irish, wasn't from New Jersey out of New York—Woodlawn—as both Dan's and her grandparents were. She brought up the Irish connection a little too often and that embarrassed Dan because she had the wrong Hogan brother. David was the one who'd gone to Notre Dame and stayed overtly Catholic, whose daughter Katie did the Irish dancing and whose wife made Irish coffee in glasses purchased specially. Dan was too one-note for all of that; he'd just wanted to get out.

Then again, he went right along with her when she mentioned it. He didn't want to crush her moments of joy and connection—so sue him.

"So…" He took a bite of his quesadilla. "Phone records proving interesting?"

To his infinite relief, she nodded. "Oh yeah." Sounding like one of Mary's preschool teachers, she said, "We've got not *one* but *two* suspicious trades!"

The two of them had worked together on Curtis the first time around, on the Tamco investigation, when the guy was merely cherry-picking trades to make himself look good. While she'd want to make sure the SEC got their fines or industry ban or whatever they could, he sensed she would positively relish seeing Curtis fuck up on a criminal level.

"Yeah?" He cracked open his soda, held the plastic bottle away from himself while it fizzed out. "Another pharmaceutical?"

Because, you know, I'd be happy with just another pharmaceutical. That would be totally fine with me.

"Nope." Brenda grinned. She was having fun building up to the reveal. *Well, let her,* Dan thought, steadying himself so as not to steamroll her with his impatience. She deserved a little fun—she had a thankless job, in Dan's opinion, the stultifying effects of the government salary without the galvanizing cachet his office had of putting the true bad guys behind bars. And a shitty divorce to boot—her husband had just walked out one day, he'd heard. She never mentioned it. "Slightly different scenario this time. Ya ready?"

She laid the plastic fork down, wiped her hands on a paper napkin. "So, he calls an investment bank a bunch of times in a week."

" 'Kay."

"This is in April of last year. Places a huge bet at the end of the week—on a Friday. Huge bet on Nanotech." She paused before she delivered the punch line: "The Friday before they're acquired by ATG."

Dan absorbed it. "Got it."

"Turns out, of course, that the investment bank he was in touch with was advising ATG."

"Okay." He was loving this but answered tersely because he didn't want to encourage her to drag it out. "And the other?" he prompted as soon as he dared.

She drank from her Diet Coke, and Dan did as well, to have something to do. "Same deal, three months later. Now we're up to last summer. The calls. Followed by a purchase of a *remarkable* amount of Eulalia stock. Only difference is now it's Eulalia and Dax."

"Uh-huh—'kay." Dan shifted on the bench. He felt hope tentatively stirring as well as an overwhelming, potentially scuttling impatience to go and arrest John Curtis the fucking fuck this very minute. He could see 26 Fed—the FBI building—across the way, looming large and glittery in the winter sun. He had never been more conscious that he belonged on the other side, out with Frank DiNapoli, making arrests, the face-to-face contact with the shitheads, which Dan only got in court, this white-collar position a life he'd jury-rigged... "And who, pray tell, might the bank be?"

"It's funny..." Brenda wrinkled up her face. "It's a small bank. Family-owned." She hesitated—met his eyes. "I was surprised, Dan."

"Yeah, well, these days—" He didn't want to sound dismissive, tried to put it another way: "I mean, we're in the eye of the hurricane here, right? Madoff—"

"Skinker, Farr. There's never been a whiff of anything."

The psychological flood of true surprise.

"Conservative place—you know what I mean? A reputation for being conservative."

"Skinker?" Dan said. For a moment he was aware only of the mental gear-grinding of trying to catch up. *Skinker?*

"You heard of them, right?"

"I mean..."

"On Nanotech, twenty minutes after the last call, we get the trade."

"Twenty minutes," he repeated.

"Yup."

"Jeez. I know the guy," he said shakily, wiping his mouth.

"You know what guy?" asked Brenda, all business. "Is this—is this gonna be a problem?"

"Oh, no. No, no." He pulled his glasses forward on his nose and rubbed inside one lens with a thumb. "I don't *know* him. I've met him a couple times. Socially. My kid's school. We're parents at the same school. Jedediah Skinker."

"Ah. The big guy—the scion. Well, with any luck, he's got nothing to do with it. This is a trunk line."

He wasn't thinking clearly. A second too late, he chimed in, "Right—right. Of course." She didn't know. The fact loomed up in front of him like a giant boulder but Brenda didn't know, hadn't put it together: John Curtis and "the big guy, the scion" were fathers at the same school.

"In fact," Brenda went on chattily, "he probably doesn't have anything to do with it. Listen to this: Drew, newest kid who works for me, has found a guy in the back office...you'll like this, Danny"—she gave his hand a little pat—"a rehabilitated guy who had a couple drug misdemeanors."

"Yeah? Huh. I see. Okay." Dan wondered if he sounded as odd as he felt.

"In the print shop. He was a charity hire of some sort. Some group—I'm forgetting the name—you know the one I mean, they help guys coming out of rehab find gainful employment? Outfit them, train them how to interview, provide references…In fact, wait a minute, where is it?" She pulled out her BlackBerry and held it at arm's length, squinting. "I just had it. Bear with me here…Yeah, yeah, here it is. Just what I thought: Your man Skinker is on the board. Fresh Start—that's the name. Sounds like a laundry detergent."

"Huh."

"Or a cat litter."

"Figures," Dan said hollowly.

"Yeah? What kind of a guy is he? I mean, other than Phillips Exeter, Harvard."

"I believe you just say Exeter."

"I'd never pass in high society, Danny." Brenda was juiced up, invigorated, the way Dan should have been. She must have picked up on the oddness of his reaction, for she said, "But, I mean, you like the guy?"

Dumbfounded, Dan didn't answer at once. Then he said, querulously, as if they were arguing, "Bank doesn't even have a website!" Brenda looked at him. He pushed the last bite of quesadilla away. The smell was suddenly nauseating. "He's got a place upstate somewhere," he added vaguely, knowing it was irrelevant but wanting to say something that sounded reasonable. "Danfork? Danforth?"

"Oh yeah? That didn't come up, I don't think. Anyway, too bad." Brenda clicked her tongue. "This *is* gonna suck for them, you're right." She stuffed her garbage into the paper bag, the salad only half eaten. "Suck big-time. Even if he himself is unstained. Although if it's just the one bad egg"—she shrugged—"they'll probably roll on down the road for another century or so."

"You guys already getting Skinker's phone records?"

He found that some part of him hoped they were not.

"Yup. We should know by the end of the week. Who was on the other side of the plethora of calls from Mr. John D. Curtis the Fourth of Invictus Capital Management."

"The Fourth?"

"Naw, I'm kidding." Brenda gave a laugh and stood up to go. Wanting to detain her, but with no reason to, Dan rose too. *Do what she's doing; don't look weird.* "But he added the *D.*, right? I'm betting he'll tack on a *Fourth* next."

"Right," Dan said, too loudly. "Wouldn't put it past him!" It was even more disconcerting that he had missed the joke.

"In the meantime, watch yourself at those preschool events!" Brenda urged.

"Will do!"

They threw out their trash and paused on the plaza before heading in their separate directions.

"It's a small world these days," Brenda allowed. She looked at him with kindness. "A small world getting smaller. How crazy is this—you know my ex-nanny works for your boss?" She named the current head of the criminal division.

"I hope she likes overtime!" Dan let the banter go on a little long, leaning on the jocular tone. He had to prove everything was normal, prove he wasn't an emotional liability. The Skinker mystique was an article of faith on Wall Street. But for Christ's sake, he of all people should have been immune to it.

*   *   *

Back in his office, Dan sat staring at the shelves of law books, at the congratulatory plaques on the wall the FBI had given him to commemorate his victories over the years. He tried to get his head around it. *Get a grip, guy. Get a grip right now!*

Brenda had said it: They were a highly conservative boutique, Skinker. Underleveraged, overcapitalized, one of the only, if not *the* only, advisory firms still in private hands—in the founding family's hands, no less. As far as he knew, both the front-office and the support staff rarely turned over. As to the lack of a website, it was known Skinker, Farr executives felt they weren't the right hire for any client who would find them on the Internet. So, yes, the news was just a wee bit surprising...

Dan pulled out a yellow pad and began to scribble notes on it. *ATG & Nanotech. Eulalia & Dax. Invictus &*...His hand hovered over the page. Here was where he needed to add *Skinker, Farr*. He laid the pen down and ripped at his cuticles.

The truth was, it hurt to go there. It hurt Dan to go there. Get a grip, guy. Get a grip right now.

Jedediah Skinker was a man who hadn't had to make the money he lived on but had been handed it at birth, a fact that normally meant an automatic write-off for Dan but that, in the case of Skinker, seemed to take on a possibility beyond his being lazy and undeserving. The money seemed to have given the man the freedom to choose, to have put him—as one hoped it would in one's own case—beyond all that. From everything Dan had heard and infrequently, though significantly, observed (one seminal conversation at an otherwise aggressively boring and pretentious St. Tim's parents night having formed his main impression) the money had made the man rational, disinterested. He was the almost *a*-capitalistic head of a family bank. Stories abounded: The subway rides to work. The shirts with frayed collars and the twenty-year-old trousers that ripped in the seat during some important pitch meeting. The money itself he seemed bent on giving away. The one time when Dan himself had spoken to the man, on that fateful parents night, Skinker had never said in the entire conversation what he did or who he was; nor had he raised the sad, limp status flag so doggedly flown by their generation: where he went to college. He'd not so much as alluded to where he lived in town or where he went on the weekends; Dan had to drag the latter out of him. In fact, after inquiring politely about what class Dan's child was in, the man had initiated a conversation on the topic of—"I'm not making it up, I swear!" Dan had assured Gwen afterward—*farm drainage*. He was going on about the efficacy of some type of drain…and in the middle of this, the guy's wife came over—a beautiful brunette who had the kind of looks that made Dan feel sheepish because they were so beyond his ken. In the first place, she was half a foot taller than he was. Her remarkable face seemed to give the lie to America's conceit of being a classless society; some tenacious claim in her bone structure, in the length and shape of her bare arms and fingers, that all of the old distinctions were still in play, for those who knew enough to recognize them, whereas people like Dan and the rest of the pretentious Ivy League bozos standing around the preschool classrooms—well, they were just kidding themselves. They should take their flat-screens and their flashy-label wine and their souped-up cars and go home.

Then the woman spoke to her husband. At the first slurred phrase, Dan did a double take. Nobody got drunk at these school functions. Ever. Hell, nobody even got tipsy! That was the prerogative of another generation. Today's parent body was founded on control, control, control. Dan himself would never have made the mistake. Much as he craved a second red wine, he had stood cracking and peeling apart his plastic cup and finally ripping it into little pieces for the better part of an hour. In Skinker's situation, most men would have given in to embarrassment—made a crack or drawn their spouses aside for hot, terse words. Skinker was neither embarrassed nor jocular. Skinker was...stolid. The man's face reflected no emotion, yet oddly, overhearing his wife's request that he put her into a taxi made Dan feel acutely supernumerary.

"I'd better go home. Will you put me in a taxi?"

"Of course."

No more than a dozen words between them and Dan found himself staring at the floor as if trying to avoid ogling blatant PDA. The low tones—the intimacy of the request—was that *darling* she'd called him? It made him squirm just remembering.

Skinker excused himself and saw her out, then returned cheerfully a few minutes later to resume the drainage conversation! So, yes, these particular drains—French drains, made of some type of perforated pipe, was it? There was some issue with standing water near his barn—upstate, Dan gathered, in Danfork, or Danforth. When Skinker got into the details, Dan lost the thread and found himself barely looking at the man but inwardly studying him—not so much a trick from the office as an innate habit his job in the U.S. Attorney's Office had made use of. Rumor had it he had been farming, had been living upstate as a farmer, when Hugh Skinker, the father, dropped dead of a heart attack and he had to come back from—what was the actual name of the town? Dan needed to check on that—and, at his mother's request, take over the bank.

He could find out the name of the town and then—With a jolt, Dan realized that he had already put Skinker into the category of a person of interest. With misgivings, he wrote *Jedediah Skinker* across the top of a new page of the legal pad, then took his pen and perversely blacked the name out so thoroughly that no one would have been able to make out what it said.

It wasn't until he was heading home on the subway that Dan's thoughts finally caught up with the facts. He was sitting on the hard seat, his eyes scanning the ads, mentally rejecting their claims one by one, when it hit him. It was all backward. It made no sense. There was nothing in it for Skinker.

He sat back carefully against the seat, trying to look relaxed, as his mind raced: it was all backward.

It was a fundamental element of insider trading: the tipper had to get something for the information, even if that something was intangible—social connections, social standing, an implied "in" into an elite club. He watched people file out and others press in at the next stop. Of course—it ought to have been the other way around. Skinker ought to be *getting* something, not giving; a guy like him would never be tipping a fuckhead like Curtis. Skinker was the scion of the bank his great-grandfather had founded. Skinker was the son of a socialite who was on the board of one of the uptown girls' schools, the names and nuances of which Dan prided himself on not keeping straight. John Curtis was the bottom-feeder, the benthic organism trying to transform himself into a top-level carnivore.

Dan gave a paranoid grin around the car. In all probability, the St. Timothy's connection meant nothing. No doubt it was a big, fat red herring dragged right across his particular path to throw him off, because, sure, the old Dan Hogan would have found it a wildly implicating coincidence. Yet the fact that Curtis and Jed Skinker were both fathers at an uptown preschool didn't mean that either one even knew who the other one was. Men didn't *hang out* at the school. (Although, according to Gwen, a certain kind of man did exactly that, ostentatiously chaperoning a field trip to make it clear he didn't *work* for the Man, he *was* the Man—but also according to Gwen, there was a lot less of that after Lehman.) Gwen had said the Curtis kid had started just now—in January. The incriminating calls predated her arrival by months and months.

Brenda was right to give him funny looks when he'd jumped— long-jumped—to the conclusion that Jed Skinker was involved. It was a type of megalomania, thinking that the guy you knew was *the* guy. Even a storied old firm could have one bad apple. The druggie in the print shop Brenda had mentioned, for instance, if you wanted to start, oh, just anywhere. Or some trustworthy senior banker who had recently turned fifty-five and had had the jarring realization that he was going to die one day. That was the moment the reliable, straight-ahead income generators acquired mistresses named Destiny whom they met in Florida strip clubs. Dan had seen it many times before. A man couldn't simply write checks to his Destiny—the wife would see them. Instead, a tip on a stock that just might go up...Destiny, rather than confronting one's destiny. Dan's mother-in-law had a saying she repeated like a tic: *You're dead a long time.* Anything worth a night to forget that.

It was only the paranoid part of Dan, the jumpy, compulsive part, that could hear Gwen's saying, of the Curtises' admission to St. Tim's: "Oh, come on. There must be hundreds of people who could write a check."

"Curtis wasn't *there* when you went over, was he?" Dan said as they finished supper.

"John Curtis?" Gwen shot her husband a look. "A dad at a playdate?" Sometimes it seemed the men really didn't understand how things worked.

160

"No, no—I figured. Just thought maybe he made an appearance or something."

"Nope. It was just the girls." Gwen felt a tremor as she said "the girls" for she had purposely left out Philippa when Dan asked her about the playdate, some protective instinct kicking in—though whether she was protecting herself or Philippa, she couldn't have said.

Dan had met Philippa only once, but he had taken against her. At a parents night at the school nearly a year ago, Dan had spent the evening talking to the Skinkers. Gwen had pressed him afterward about her old acquaintance. "You must have said *some*thing to her!"

"Not really. She left early."

"But, I mean, how did she strike you?"

"Fine. Attractive, obviously. If you like that emaciated, I'm-an-alien-from-Mars type."

"*Dan.*" Later she brought it up again, marveling: "Everyone said she would be a model, but to me it's still crazy that she actually managed to go from Dunning—"

"She was wasted!" Dan practically shouted. "She was drunk off her ass, okay? What am I supposed to say?"

Gwen blinked. "Nothing."

It was like her school days, when Camilla hadn't cared for some girl Gwen had started to go around with. Gwen learned to keep those friendships to herself. Even now, when she went home to Nautauqua, she'd tell Camilla she was "meeting some high-school people downtown" when what she really meant was that she was getting a coffee at McDonald's with Karen Coon, who'd had an abortion in eleventh grade.

It put Gwen on edge to have Dan grilling her again when there was so little she could tell him beyond describing the gargantuan apartment for the third time, how it had felt like being inside a bank. "Corporate, you know—no personal touches. As if it all might vanish tomorrow. Rented paintings—that kind of feeling."

"*Were* they rented?"

"How would I know?"

Earlier in the evening, as she passed Mary's bedroom door, she'd heard Dan asking Mary what "the Curtis child" was like. Mary had thought about it for a moment and then said soberly, "She has lots and lots and lots and lots and lots and lots of toys. She has Wii Karaoke."

"Oh yeah?" Dan sounded sycophantic and not himself in a way that faintly repulsed Gwen.

"People don't need that many toys," Mary said. And because she was quoting her mother, Gwen had hurried away toward the kitchen, ashamed of spying.

Now Dan said absently, "Right, right...and so...I mean... what about the Skinkers? They're not friends with them, are they? With the Curtises."

Gwen was startled. "What—the two couples, you mean?"

Dan shrugged. "Yeah. Or the moms, maybe? I don't know." He scratched his temple, shifted in his chair. What a brilliant prosecutor her husband must be, Gwen thought. All the tics and gestures showing his diffidence, his distractedness, his bored impatience with whatever information she could provide...all while ruthlessly extracting it from her.

"She's very egalitarian, Minnie," she said brightly. "I think she's had everyone over once. She doesn't seem to have favorites or even really to care. She goes right through all the motions. You don't get the feeling that forming a real connection with anyone is part of the plan. But she does go through the motions..."

Gwen knew she was talking too much, the way a liar does, to cover an omission, but Dan didn't say anything. She had the uncomfortable feeling he knew she wasn't telling the whole truth. But she believed in keeping some things to herself. Men didn't need to know the details of their wives' female friendships. They irritated them—made them jealous, maybe. Because they didn't have those kinds of friendships. They flew solo. Dan did anyway.

"What a creep, huh?" Dan snickered and went on as if John Curtis were suddenly back to being just a name he'd known in college. "Didn't he attack some girl freshman year?"

"Who, Curtis? A few girls!" Glad of the change in subject, Gwen elaborated, "At least, according to the rumors. Who knows if they were true."

His BlackBerry buzzed, and Dan glanced at it hopefully. "Sorry!" he said, sounding relieved. "This'll be quick. They're doing an approach tomorrow—guy in Westchester." He held the device to his ear. "Frank? Yup—no, it's fine. It's fine. Shoot."

He moved the phone away from his mouth. "Just leave them," he said in an undertone as Gwen cleared his plate. "I'll put them in the dishwasher."

"There're hardly any!" she murmured. "I'll just do them."

"I'll be off in a sec!"

"It's fine!" Gwen insisted. "I'm just gonna do these because I want to go to bed early."

She was soaping the last couple of dishes while Dan issued instructions to his agent, not thinking of much of anything, when her hands seemed to slow of their own volition, then stop. Her face sagged. She felt flattened. She could not go on. It was as if she'd been given a piece of very bad news earlier in the week—as if someone had died—and she had managed not to think of it until now, to put it out of her head with some extreme, pathological form of denial. But now the news had come back and felled her with its force. *A few girls,* she heard herself saying. *According to the rumors.*

Didn't he attack some girl freshman year?

A few girls! At least, according to the rumors. Who knows if they were true.

She let the tap run on, wasting water, listening to the subtle variations in its steady gush.

Who knows if they were true.

Why had she introduced falsehood into the conversation? Why the undermining comment?

Gwen slowly sponged and rinsed, sponged and rinsed the sole remaining plate, noting—appreciating, even—its white plain-ness, and thought about college again, for the second time in a week, when she hadn't thought about it in any kind of depth for years, as if that time in her life, with its briefly intoxicating possi-bilities and its even more rapid curtailments of the same, still had power over her, a Yorkville housewife in her mid-thirties whose life, despite the notable geographical change, wasn't turning out so very different from her mother's after all.

Freshman year. Freshman year again. Gwen had found her crazy next-door neighbor Melinda in the bathroom crying, a mess, one morning very early, the girl just home from her night out when Gwen was getting up for a run before her required Spanish class. *¿Y a ti, te gusta también bailar?* A Chinese American girl from L.A., Melinda was dressed in her usual mélange of cutoffs, holey fishnet stockings, Converse high-tops, and a ripped sweatshirt. Her dark brown hair with its streaks of peroxide blond was a beehive mess; whether it was snarled or teased that way on purpose, Gwen had never worked out.

She and Gwen weren't friends—such an association would

have had to cross too large a campus social divide—but they knew each other from the entryway, and their encounters on the landing or in the bathroom had a pleasant, lingering quality to them. Melinda had confessed to Gwen that she was an erstwhile Group IV person (math and the hard sciences) who was pissing off her parents by doing anthropology instead. Gwen would rib her sometimes and tell her it wasn't too late to come back, get a real major. Melinda had come across Gwen in the college library late one night when she was tripping loudly through with drunken friends and told her afterward, "You remind me of my father, Gwen. You're so hardworking!" Gwen would sometimes catch Melinda looking at her with a funny expression of approval. "My father would love you," she had said.

But now—early on a weekday morning—Melinda was looking at her own wrecked, mascara-stained face in the mirror, as if seeing herself dismayed her. She was sobbing and wiping at her eyes with bits of toilet paper she was tearing off a roll on the sink. Gwen swallowed—felt herself stiffen. The Walk of Shame, girls called it, and they laughed—hollowly, Gwen thought. Gwen didn't really see the humor in it, just as she didn't really feel the compunction to Take Back the Night, another popular campus trope of women's empowerment she had been introduced to. She couldn't help it—she found the early '90s university brand of feminism shameful. She had been raised to think of the poor, the five-dollar bill she put in the plate on Sunday quite literally associated with the impoverished people who lived down the road from St. Agnes's people, like Patty McLean, whose clothes were sad and poor, or the Gagnons, who you knew never went to the dentist. "Women's issues"—she could imagine the look that would cross her mother's face at the mention of such a thing in a setting such as this.

Still, she said dutifully, "Hey, are you okay?" Melinda shook her head wordlessly, her eyes large and brimming with tears. "Oh no—what's wrong?" Gwen said quickly, though she had a pretty good idea.

"He—"

The girl started to cry in that hyperventilating way, her chest heaving. She stopped every few words so she could get enough air to go on. "He—he—he—"

Gwen squirmed inwardly at the naked display of emotion, the likes of which never occurred in her family. She felt an intense sense of distraction come over her and had to force herself not to look at her watch.

"I passed out. I was just...*lying there* and he—he—he was fucking me, Gwen. He raped me. He raped me. Oh my God! I was passed out and he raped me."

The frank description appalled Gwen, maybe more than the idea of the act itself. She managed to reach out and pat the girl's shoulder. "Oh, Melinda..."

To her surprise, Melinda embraced her, bawling, squeezing her tight, her mouth open on Gwen's shoulder. As awkward as she felt, Gwen was touched that Melinda would choose her for this confession, that she would consider Gwen Babineau worthy of physical contact.

When Melinda got control of her breathing, she leaned against the sink and cried it all out to Gwen. "I must have had ten beers. I did tequila shots, Jell-O shots—oh God!" Gwen nodded; Melinda's eyes searched Gwen's. "You know who I mean, right? John C-c-c—" Melinda's voice caught on the hard *C* and she couldn't go on. "From upstairs," she choked out. Gwen could have screamed at the absurdity of it, that this person could be back in her life only two months after the cheating scandal.

"I was just lying there! I passed out in their room and when I woke up he was... he was... he was—"

"It's okay."

"*—fucking me!*"

Despairingly, Gwen tried to hide how fidgety she felt. They were having a quiz in Spanish today. She had planned to go over the words in her head while she jogged up Science Hill.

"Oh God! I don't know where my underwear is." Helplessly, Gwen listened as she became even more distraught. "It's lost! I lost it there! It's still in their room. I didn't even say anything, I was flat on my back, and I didn't have time—when I left—I mean, I didn't even tell him to stop." Her voice broke. "I didn't tell him once. Not once."

"I'm sorry. I'm so sorry."

"What am I going to do?" She wept openly now. "What am I doing? Oh my God, what am I doing? What if I—" Melinda let out a harsh bark of a cry and stopped. She wiped her face on her sleeve and looked at Gwen. The piteous look in her eyes seemed to clear in the wake of something harder. "Do you think I should go to the police, Gwen?"

"Oh, I don't know about that."

It was like the time she dropped a piece of her mother's wedding china on the tiled kitchen floor at home. Gwen's remorse was instant, and total; she felt the shock of the irrevocable and desperately wanted to rewind, wanted Melinda to embrace her again, depend on her again. But Melinda suddenly seemed to withdraw inside herself and, with a shift in her body language, to reject Gwen, to release Gwen, though she no longer wanted to be released.

Panicked, Gwen tried to strike a jocular tone, say something that would comfort Melinda. In her misery, she punched the girl's upper arm and said the first thing that came into her head: "I mean, after all, you were pretty drunk, right?"

They were never friendly again. Melinda didn't snub her—it was worse. She was flatly courteous. Silenced, Gwen dreamed of getting her day in court. Three years later at graduation, when her parents got stuck in a buffet line with Melinda's parents and they were all four of them very friendly and pleasant, the two dads trading gripes about small-business ownership (Babineau's Garden and Lawn; a buffet-lunch restaurant in a strip mall), a hope for reconciliation had risen up in her—the warm embrace—but when Melinda quietly turned her back so as not to have to speak to her, Gwen wanted to scream the words she had long ago formulated: *Well, if it wasn't your fault you were so shitfaced you couldn't see, then whose was it, pray tell?*

Although by then the argument felt hollow even to Gwen. For, in a miserable, extended rebuke, she had found out there were others. An incident at a fraternity house sophomore year. An off-campus party one of Dan's roommates had attended...But John Curtis had reached a certain amount of celebrity at that point due to the investing he was doing out of his dorm room. They said he had made twenty thousand dollars for Vint Prince and that Vint Prince's uncle "wanted in."

Gwen put the plate heavily into the dish rack as if the weight of it were suddenly too much. She wiped her hands on the towel and spread it out across the plastic rack screwed to the door under the sink. She could hear Dan, still on the phone, pacing, making monosyllabic assents. He wouldn't notice the oddity of her standing there, standing motionless at the edge of the strip of kitchen, looking past her reflection to the windows of the former tenement building across the street. The single man who lived in the apartment opposite them was going through the exercise routine he followed nightly—jumping jacks and squat-thrusts—rigid self-discipline for some long-term pursuit. Well, she respected that. That, she understood. She would have done as many squat-thrusts as it took. They threw you in together at these colleges because you were smart, got good grades, took BC calc, got a 5 on the AP Chem exam. No one warned you. No one told you what the expectations of your views were going to be. You were just thrown into the teeming, high-achieving Ivy League mass and expected to pick up on all that. Or, rather, the college probably hoped the students would have intellectual debates, you representing your background and ideas, others representing theirs. They didn't count on the snowballing of the dominant opinions. You got left on the sidelines, unaware that you had the wrong views, then, when it was too late, years and years after, when you had spent college hanging out with Dan Hogan and his crowd because they could see the humor in the spelling of the Womyn's Center, you saw dimly that you might have said to Melinda, *Why not? If you think it would help.* Or, Gwen rebuked her former self, her nails against her palms, you might simply have said yes.

Yes, Melinda. You should go to the police.

Yes, Melinda.

And I'll go with you. I'll take you there.

Instead, she had gone on her run up Science Hill, rehearsing the tricky Spanish preterit in her head, not shirking from the irregular verbs—forcing herself, in fact, to repeat those a greater number of times than the easier ones to ensure that she would get an A.

Chapter Eleven

Heather Baird got out of her cab on Eightieth and Madison, waving madly and calling to Jeannie Haskell, whom she'd spied loitering on the corner, probably so as not to be early. Jeannie hated to be early. "Don't tell me you're alone again!"

"I am!" Jeannie cried. They seized each other's arms, beaming. "Doug's got his class tonight."

"Yes! Bert's in London!" The two women fell into stride as they walked up the block toward the Steins' town house. "We can hide in the corner again and gossip."

"Perfect. Perfect! Can't tell you how much I was hoping you'd be alone again too."

"Which one is it? Do you remember?" Heather and Jeannie slowed reluctantly in front of a triptych of town houses. Was it the brick Federalist one with the climbing vines? Or the Italianate one with the second- and third-story balconies? Or was it, perhaps, the one in the middle with the entrance down the stairs and the extra floor? Jeannie looked quickly back. Neither of them wished to be overtaken by other arriving parents who would authoritatively tell them which house it was. Extreme wealth had a quality of fame to it, making people hoard knowledge as if it were a direct line to insider status. Not that either Jeannie or Heather wanted to become an intimate of Lally or Ron Stein; they just didn't want to have to ask.

"That one, isn't it?" said Heather doubtfully, pointing toward number 9.

"I don't know..."

In Jeannie's hesitation, the massive front door of number 7 (extra floor) was drawn back. "The Steins?" inquired a blandly superior young man in a dark jacket.

"Yup!" said Heather angrily.

"Yes!"

"Yup, yup, yup!" They squeezed down the short stairs, falling over themselves to show that they had known all along which house it was. Jeannie was already pushing past the young man and into a low-ceilinged vestibule that led to the house proper. Heather scuttled after her, and together they passed through an iron security grille, left open for the evening, its keypad flashing minute green and yellow lights. Were they, Jeannie wondered as she cast an eye up to the vaultlike ceiling and noted a security camera, being recorded?

They paused inside, bewildered by the glut of marble that confronted them, though they had sworn to themselves that they would not allow any material thing tonight to take them aback. "So great Ron and Lally are hosting again, isn't it?" said Heather loudly, refusing to be intimidated by the five-foot-wide marble staircase that swept in an arc up to the second story, or by the expanse of white marble floor spilling toward the institutional-size kitchen, the latter bustling with an army of uniformed cater waiters, or by the marble walls hung with tapestries, but her voice sounded small. The room was denuded of furniture save for two massive sideboards made of some kind of petrified wood that faced each other across the vast stretch of cold white stone. Jeannie, too, snatched a few glances this way and that as a second tall, smooth-faced young man silently whisked their coats away. In their hesitation, a thirtyish blonde in a double-breasted red skirt-suit, her hair drawn up in a secretarial bun, came forward. "The Steins are happy to greet their guests upstairs," she announced and gave the pair of them the placating smile practiced by customer-service professionals on unruly clients. Though surely they had done nothing to alarm her! Heather thought, miffed by the authoritative gesture the young woman made, her open palm arcing out from her midriff, as she funneled the two of them toward the stairs.

Side by side, they trudged up them obediently, conversation stifled. That song...that song coming from the piano upstairs—Jeannie hummed a few bars under her breath, grasping at it; it was some 1930s show tune and the words escaped her. Perhaps they had played it at her and Doug's wedding? If it was up to her, she would have had a DJ, but her father had insisted on a band.

The stairs opened onto the—*What,* Heather wondered, glancing uncertainly around, *would you call it?* Not the parlor floor—that sounded kitschy, deep-Brooklyn Victorian. Make a million in a start-up and renovate a Fort Greene brownstone. The *piano nobile?* Bits of her required lit courses at Colgate would pop into her head at random, the gloss of the liberal education she had acquired before heading straight to the econ major (she was going to move to New York and make some fucking money). But that phrase conjured a palazzo warmed by ambient light; orchestral music swelling; French doors opening onto balconies; the pleasures that even Heather, who wasn't particularly well traveled, had grasped Europe alone could provide. This room was so chilly and abstract, its simplicity not soothing but ferocious...this was wealth not as comfort or enjoyment but as a cold corrective measure, as if some thousand-dollar-a-day decorator was having his vengeance on the inhabitants. There wasn't a book in sight, of course, or a work of figurative art to reassure one of one's own existence. What must have been seventeen-foot-high ceilings made the group of parents huddling in the corner behind the gray ultra-suede sectional sofa appear dumpy, as if the room had been made for a larger, more significant race, one that didn't have to stuff itself into panty hose or pay through the nose for monthly highlights in a condescending salon on Madison. It was no wonder Lally Stein (there she was, on the threshold with that Gwen woman's husband, of all people) wore stiffly angular dresses, cruel pumps, heavy gold. The house sought, perhaps, to put you in your place. You had to stand up to it—apparently even if you were its owner.

"White wine or mineral water?" A waiter rapidly circulating paused before Jeannie and Heather. "The Steins are happy to inform their guests that the wine this evening is their own."

Confused by the circumlocution, the two of them hesitated before seizing wine.

"Right!" Jeannie recalled with relief. "Ron's got a vanity vineyard in the Languedoc."

Heather raised her glass. "Cheers to Ron. Well done, Ron."

"Cheers!"

"Who's that Lally's greeting?" Jeannie asked, sotto voce, elbowing Heather.

"Oh—you know, what's-his-name. The husband of Gwen—what's-her-face."

"Oh, right." Jeannie frowned. "Was she new this year?"

By unspoken consent, they sidled up to their hostess. Each of them had independently promised herself she would not comment on the house, would not fall into the unsophisticated pitfall of gushing, but at the last minute, Lally's frozen smile, her oddly motionless posture, her stare just over their heads and toward the balcony seats in the offing, the knowledge that she had had so much work done reinforced by their close-up of the work itself—the plumped-up lips and frozen forehead—unnerved them. What, apart from her possessions, her stature in this town, could you talk about with a woman like Lally Stein? "Your place is looking great!" Jeannie opened, feeling as if the time allotted for her audience might soon expire and that she ought to toady in a hurry.

"I was just saying to Jeannie how nice everything looks!" Heather agreed.

"Thank you," Lally pronounced patiently, her tone indicating the endless trial in her life that sycophancy posed. Jeannie stole a glance directly at the woman's cheekbones. They lay in a pronounced steep diagonal from her mouth to her eyelids; when Lally spoke, she moved her lips slowly and mechanically, as if trying not to upset them.

"Ladies!" said Dan Hogan brightly, rising on his toes.

Heather stared at him; what had *he* got to look so cheerful about? According to her college pal Jen Kim, he had dumped a partner-track job at Buckland to go on pursuing white-collar criminals for $150,000 a year. Her hand tightened around the stem of her wineglass while her other elbow pressed her clutch purse defensively to her side. There had been an unpleasant moment last summer when Bert had had to retain counsel in connection with a patently trumped-up, hypertechnical SEC investigation...her life had flashed before her eyes! Oh, it had been awful. And now this little man, looking pleased with himself, probably jailing friends of theirs as they spoke...

"Is that a DeKwan?" Jeannie blurted out, pointing to a massive abstract painting on the far wall—aggressive black slashes on daubed off-white. At once, she reviled herself for the question. She'd given in to the fateful impulse—the desire to make sure that Lally knew that she knew! The desire to somehow, in some way, put herself on equal footing with Lally Stein. *I may not be able to buy contemporary art, but I do recognize it!* But rich people and celebrities didn't care if you knew! In fact, it was better if you didn't know. It wasn't *about* you, and that's what you must never forget.

Lally made a moment's frightened-yet-at-the-same-time-censorious eye contact, as if Jeannie, in some prompting role, had fed her the wrong line. "It i-i-i-is," she said, drawing out the word doubtfully. "It is a DeKwan."

Having blundered, Jeannie had no choice but to respond with the craven "Wow."

"Wow," Heather echoed loyally.

"We know him!" Lally remembered, suddenly looking cheerier. "We bought it right out of his studio in East New York. Ron and I both fell in love with it."

"*Did* you?" marveled Jeannie, feeling even more acutely that she had to smooth over some error she had made by dragging culture into the conversation.

"Wow," Heather repeated glumly. There was something lowering about a billionaire's wife playing an authenticity trump card. She drained her glass. At least the white wine was going down easily.

"East New York," interjected Dan Hogan. "Keepin' it real, huh? Did you take the Z Train out there?" All three women looked at him with shock, but he was grinning imperviously into the room through his silvery wire-rims.

"I'm sorry?" Lally said with distaste.

"You ladies want to hear my idea for a really expensive piece of contemporary art? One that probably only someone like you could afford, Mrs. Stein?" Lally frowned as the impertinent, badly dressed man pressed gauchely on. "An installation of neon letters simply flashing the words *No Negative Feedback*. Just flashing those three words on and off: *No Negative Feedback*. On and off." He reached out and gave his hostess a pat on her stiff wool epaulet before making a funny little bow and exiting the conversation.

Seemingly unsure of what to make of this outburst of uncowed behavior, Lally turned hastily to the two women. "Ron and I have a rule about buying art." She paused to let the suspense build before going on in a cozy, just-for-their-ears murmur: "We both have to love it."

"Really?" Jeannie said. "What a good rule!"

"It can't simply be that Ron loves it or—or that I love it."

"You both have to love it?" Heather was nodding manically.

"That's right!" Lally said emphatically. "We *both* have to love it."

Lally's moment for revealing inner truths suddenly seemed to have ended. Drawing herself up, she said, "Won't you have something more to drink?" and made the identical gesture the blond secretary downstairs had made—palm arcing robotically out from her midriff, in the direction of the bar that had been set up against the back wall—before walking on into her living room. She had the stilted peacock's gait Jeannie recalled from when she and her sister, Ali, as little girls used to pretend to be models, balancing Frankie Goes to Hollywood and Flock of Seagulls record albums on their heads as they walked across the linoleum kitchen floor in Ridgefield, New Jersey, pre their parents' divorce.

The piano shifted effortlessly into another show tune. The cater-waiter circulated past them and they traded in their empty glasses for fresh ones.

"He can't have just said that."

"Bless him—he did."

"What a freak!" Heather said delightedly.

"They're both total freaks. She cooks three meals a day, goes to the park when it's zero out..."

"Gwen—what's the last name?"

"I forget. Cheers!"

"Cheers!" A little buzzed now, Heather felt a rush of love for her friend, who, like her, was middle class in this town. Both women worked; Heather covered insurance companies and Jeannie was in equity sales at a rival bank. They had met back in the day in the training program at Merrill, years before husbands and children. The two of them also *made* it work. Jeannie, Heather knew, would never forgive her twice-divorced mother for selling the house on the shore; she rented now, the last two weeks of August only. Heather pretended that it was no bother to drive five hours to the lake in New Hampshire every other weekend; she shared the house with her grown brother. They were part of that unheralded breed of women, Jeannie and Heather, who had crow's-feet and faded freckles, who took a spin class in the mornings before work and showered at the gym, who got Thai takeout for dinner, and who had never seen the point of quitting. They loved their children, but they loved their jobs and perhaps their husbands more—their underperforming husbands. There was more than a whiff of that in both cases. Jeannie's Doug had been fired from trading, had started up an online custom-shirt business that no one had heard about in a little while, and was now in culinary school downtown. Jeannie kept it positive, maintaining that Doug had finally found himself, "and we're so happy!" Heather's Bert had ultimately held on to his job at Credit Suisse, though it was somewhat unclear what his role was; even Jeannie couldn't have said exactly. Heather preferred to talk of the volunteer work he did through their church, the real difference he was making in those kids' lives.

Not that they were bitter tonight—not at all. In fact, they realized simultaneously that they were having a wonderful time. The truth was, you *wanted* to go to the Gundersons' or the Steins' or the Lewin-Simons' for one of these parties. You needed the massive restaurant kitchen with a salamander and eight-burner stove for the catering staff; you needed the two-story entrance hall in case of rain. What would fifty-odd St. Tim's parents do crammed into Jeannie's classic-six in Carnegie Hill, having to avoid leaning against the one good oil painting as she pulled frozen pigs in a blanket out of the oven, as she did at her annual Christmas party? When you had the Steins' sort of spread, everyone could relax, everyone could retreat for one night from claustrophobia and compromise. Nobody outside of New York understood that—notably, Heather thought, feeling her blood pressure rise and reminding herself to breathe in through her nose slowly to a count of five and out through her mouth, her brother, Mitch, who, on an attorney's salary, had a big house in Lexington, Mass., with things like light and space and the out-of-doors, a place to hang your coat and hide the computer printer—storage for the frickin' ironing board, which, thank you very much, Heather herself still used in a pinch. She really had to replace the Bed, Bath, and Beyond metal drying rack she kept set up in the tub of the master bathroom, the one arm no longer—

"Oh God, look who's here." Jeannie nudged her.

"Oh no." Heather made a face. "Why?" she said plaintively.

Sipping their second wines, the two women watched Philippa Lye haltingly ascend the staircase. They were used to seeing her in her combat gear: her fuck-you winter shearling, the various standoffish hats. Tonight it seemed she had dressed carefully—with a fear, perhaps, of offending. She was wearing a black, cowl-necked crepe dress with three-quarter sleeves and the sort of beribboned low pumps Upper East Side old ladies favored; Mrs. Davidson, who was to speak later, would no doubt be wearing the same. Philippa's hair was pinned up, though somewhat ineffectually, as large tendrils of it were slipping down on both sides in just the sort of poor-helpless-me act that incensed practical-minded Heather and Jeannie, who had made a pact and shorn theirs before the last promotion. At the top of the stairs, Philippa hesitated and seemed to look through her eyes, rather than out of them, quite nakedly unsure of where to go next but, courteously, not pinning anyone down with a stare. Nevertheless, the vulnerability made the two women set their teeth and turn their backs on her.

"Why does she even bother to come?" The remark sounded harsher than Jeannie intended. But it had been a long week—a client pissed off about a bad IPO allocation; management revising sales targets upward again. She just wanted to enjoy herself tonight. Was that too much to ask?

"Why does *he* never come with her?" said Heather, opening herself up to the room again once Philippa had started to make her way purposefully toward the drinks table. There was a brittle edge to her voice, for Jed Skinker had come to her in a dream one night. Odd, because he was much too big, too large and unfit and far too fair for her. He had the expanding paunch of the former

179

athlete...had he rowed at Harvard? Or was it actually football he had played—"the last WASP walk-on." Hadn't someone referred to him that way? Or was that the father? Or the grandfather? What did it matter when Heather liked a dark, wiry man. Her boyfriends before she met Bert had been Southern European, South American—a string of Flavios and Pablos. There was something about Jed Skinker, though...his hands, perhaps—something intelligent in the large hands that, in a dream once, had caressed her. At the beginning of that dream he had shown up at the foot of Heather's girlhood canopy bed to make love to her. He had been wearing black tie with the tie loosened from his neck, as in a photograph she'd seen once on Philippa's bureau...wearing it casually, as if he'd been born in it. But you could tell by looking at him that he wouldn't be a sexy dancer, and this was a sine qua non for Heather. They said he had lived as a farmer in his single days. (Not artisanal goat cheese or anything mainstream, but a dairy farmer, in some godforsaken place upstate, not, say, Millbrook or anywhere people had heard of.) And that his sister was a priest who lived an ascetic life of Christian charity...Heather sloshed the wine in her glass in irritation.

Heather herself stuck to the rules—stuck to them with an aggrieved angry sigh, which, however, she alone was allowed to make. Let Bert or her older daughters hint that he or they might want to forgo Midnight Mass on Christmas Eve and she came down on them like concrete: "If we don't go to Mass, what's the point of the whole thing?" She and Bert had gone through Pre-Cana; her oldest girl, Maddie, had been in CCD prior to confirmation. But that was one thing. Displays of faith, of true seeking and questioning (yoga, Buddhism, vegans), enraged some shallowly buried part of Heather, a part that felt—though she could name but a few of the personal wrongs she had suffered—an immense, a global sense of deprivation.

Silently, she followed Philippa's progress toward the bar. "She'll get trashed and we'll have to help her into a cab. Mark my words."

"Wouldn't be the first time."

"Wouldn't you think she'd do something about it?" Heather said coldly.

"What, like join AA, you mean?" said Jeannie. "Or, like, check into Hazelden?"

"Or just, you know—*quit*. Would that be so hard to do?" Heather stared, disgusted at the woman as she fingered the gold necklace she never took off, the one that spelled the names of her three girls: *Maddie, Lily, Grace*. "Those poor kids."

From across the room came a sound like a sea lion gasping for air. "Oh, there's Emily! There they all are! Come on," said Jeannie, putting a propelling hand to Heather's back. "Let's go talk to her and Betsy. Oh, and Ann too. I never see them anymore."

Gwen Hogan lingered in the no-man's-land that surrounded the grand piano, trying to locate Dan without making it obvious. She found him, with his back to the starkly high windows, regaling Jim Truscott with stories from court. Jim was a partner at Weinrib, Lewis and Dan's sometime opposing counsel. While Gwen hung back, Jim's wife, Tanya, elegant in a belted, color-blocked wool dress and pumps, joined them and the three continued to talk and laugh, Dan occasionally tapping Tanya or Jim's arm to make a point. Tanya looked skeptically bemused, as if to say, *These men!*—as if, Gwen thought, worrying about cramping her husband's style had never crossed her mind. Ironically, Gwen always had to bribe and beg Dan to go with her to school events, Dan having made it clear that empty socializing with people not their friends was beneath him; he had white-collar criminals to jail. A year ago, at the Gundersons', he had spent the entire party huddled in a back hallway on the phone with DiNapoli and Gerry, arranging an early-morning approach in Rumson, while she blushed and kept excusing herself to no one in particular to go to the bathroom, eventually hiding in there, studying the wallpaper, which depicted Versailles, and marveling yet again at people who had paper hand towels printed with their initials on them for one-time use. But get him off his phone, and her husband loved a party. Only a sense of this not being his crowd, she felt, kept Dan in check at these functions, while she, feeling she should let him shine, clung to the walls and halls, marking the time in five-minute increments. Acutely self-conscious now, having already downed two club sodas, she eyed the pianist, who was just returning after a break, but he was scowling forbiddingly, as if the one thing he counted on at a party like this was that he wouldn't have to speak to the guests. Gwen instinctively drifted toward the waiters and bartenders, though, in striking up a conversation or two over the past few years at events such as these, she'd been reminded that she had no more in common with these young men and women than with the St. Timothy's parents; they were ambitious, vivacious, graceful creatures—dancers and actors, who, like uptown saleswomen, didn't tend to notice Gwen lingering hopefully in their presence. (She had a particularly hard time getting served in shops that catered to women. Department stores were such a trial that she had a repeated fantasy of raising a bullhorn to her lips and announcing, "I have money and am prepared to pay for purchases!" Minnie Curtis, Gwen felt, who had just arrived and was laughing on the stairs with Jessica Kaplan, the yoga teacher, and Jessica's husband, would know how to manage shopgirls.)

Their host, Ron Stein, led a group of parents away from the drinks table toward a painful-looking metal sculpture, all acute angles and rusting nails. As the now-healthy-size crowd parted to let them through, Gwen spotted Philippa Lye. She was standing next to the bar, a blank expression on her face, taking mechanical sips out of her wineglass, as if she had tuned out her surroundings completely. Nobody else Gwen knew could stand like that at a party—alone and beyond caring. Her detachment seemed so extreme that for a second, she looked like a crazy person to Gwen. It didn't help that when Gwen went over, she could hear Philippa humming an off-key tune between sips.

"Philippa?"

Philippa's eyes flickered cautiously to Gwen's face. "Hello."

"Hey."

"Are you enjoying yourself, Gwen?"

"Me? Not really! I dread these things. But I feel we've got to come, for Mary's sake."

"Me too," said Philippa. "Sebastian would be fine with our being utter recluses, but little Ruth—she's got a birthday coming up. She's very social—wants to invite the class! I need to make more of an effort," she added seriously, which was somehow touching, given her stature in this town.

"Me too," said Gwen. "Me too."

The groups shifted again and Minnie Curtis came into their line of vision—already standing in the central and largest group of parents—apparently giving focus to it. "*She* looks as if she's enjoying herself," Philippa remarked.

Minnie was animated, gesticulating when speaking, throwing her head back and laughing when someone else spoke. Presently, she turned, opening up the circle, to draw in Lally Stein— beckoning, insisting, even when the woman attempted to snob her out with a faux smile. Minnie's shoes tonight, Gwen noted, were glittering sandals, and bejeweled.

"I don't know how she walks in them," Gwen confessed.

She expected Philippa to ignore the comment but she took it up: "Oh, it's easy! If you don't care about comfort."

As if she had sensed their scrutiny from across the room, Minnie looked over at the pair of them. She waggled the fingers of her free hand in their direction and gave them an impish tee-hee-hee grin, then turned her attention back to Lally, who, a moment later, led Minnie past them with a proprietary air.

"I'm getting the tour," Minnie murmured as she went by, giving them an excited thumbs-up. She turned back to them. "John's running late but he's on his way! Be nice to him when he comes?"

"I knew Minnie's husband in college," Gwen said to Philippa. When Philippa didn't reply, humming her tune again, Gwen clarified, "Well, I didn't know him. Knew of him, I guess. Knew who he was."

"Uh-huh," Philippa said vaguely. "Was he nice?"

"No." Gwen laughed. "But I guess if you don't care about comfort…"

Mrs. Davidson turned away from a joke Ron Stein had made and cried to the voluble crowd: "Well, hello!" The room seemed to quiver—with an effort, like a rowdy classroom, to calm itself. The parents strained toward Mrs. Davidson as she took her place in front of the grand piano, as toward a revival preacher. She was short in stature and had the sort of preternaturally thin arms and legs that seemed to be a prerequisite to living in the "corridor" of the Upper East Side, so many of the parents could barely see the woman over the small eager crowd that immediately encircled her.

They could hear her, though.

"We are having a wonderful year with your children!" she announced, and they felt it, every one of them. Even Gwen Hogan looked up in surprise because she, too, could feel it: the benediction on them in the woman's voice.

Protectively flanking Mrs. D., Ron Stein beamed. He looked tickled, like a praised child. The modernist crystal chandelier overhead cast soft light on his round, tan head, which glowed with grooming and wealth and a blunt, cheerful sexuality that had kept him in women long before he'd thought to short-sell subprime mortgages. His frat brothers at MIT had called him *el maestro*—an allusion only in part to the summer he had spent backpacking around South America with a guitar on his back.

"It's so nice to see you all!" Mrs. Davidson said or, rather, projected in that voice of hers. "You know, when Ms. Babcock and I came back to meet the board of trustees at St. Timothy's a week before Labor Day…"

Ron was standing right beside her, so he had to look interested and appropriately serious, but he felt like closing his eyes and just letting the Voice run over him like some kind of aural gravy.

"…we spent a lot of time talking about character…"

Fuck the Times*!* Ron thought suddenly, his face contorting angrily.

"…because of course people think that character isn't something one can teach"—Mrs. Davidson mimed idiocy—"especially not to preschoolers!"

The *Times* had gotten it all wrong! Ron thought, filling with outrage. As they always did! The fucking liberal press, with their tiresome annual chestnut on the odds of getting into a Manhattan nursery school.

"Well, I'll give you *one guess* as to what I said about that!"

Ron closed his eyes and nodded appreciatively, far along his own tangent. People didn't prostrate themselves to get a spot at St. Tim's because they wanted their kids to go to Harvard. That was the view of some embittered middle-class reporter, some Bob wannabe making eighty K a year and colonizing some unsavory outer-borough enclave who never let anyone forget he was Kirkland House '91. No, whether people knew it or not, it was the Voice that drew them. Even he could hear it; even that forlorn, ponytailed girl-woman lurking like a dorky ghost in the corner by the granite block he'd paid a small fortune for could hear it; even the Truscotts could hear it, the preppie African American couple whom Lally had been falling all over herself to make friends with when everyone knew that race had never been the issue in New York, it was class, *class, class!* None of them could have traced the Voice's exact provenance; most of the parents could but guess at the things that the Voice alluded to in its inimical diphthongs and non-rhotic nouns (*charactah*): the spankings and the cigarettes and the gin and tonics you didn't waste the good gin on; the Mercedes 280 D with the matching hubcap plates, the sickly sweet smell of its perforated leather interior, Dick and the boys (now grown) joking about the "voodoo stick" on the long drive up to Maine, during which, out of principle, you never took a rest stop (and why would you, seeing as no one "hydrated" in those days). Mrs. Whitmer (née Martha Pingree) Davidson, the twenty-year head of St. Timothy's, whose *hello* alone seemed to dispense with the numbing, nullifying past fifteen years in New York.

"You know it, and I know it, and your children know it!"

It was a voice—this they did know—that was impressed by little (save perhaps a bright toddler's remark), a voice that one could imagine saying "Fiddlesticks!" to excessive executive compensation, to new construction and "concierge services," to the gyre, turn, and swag of the aughts. The Voice's tone and timbre, the ancient rhythms it owed to Dutch settlers—it reassured Ron in a way that Lally never could. He opened his eyes and looked right at Mrs. Davidson. He was in love with her! Seventy if she was a day. Their eyes met—hers a-twinkle—and he decided to give her another fifty thousand dollars. Chump change. He would write the check tonight—he couldn't wait to write it. If the real estate boys Herb and Stephen Simon could do it, then so could he. Stephen, he'd noted irritably, had even gotten himself onto the preschool's board. Maybe something to do with the gravitas his wife, Emily Lewin, provided—girl seemed serious, wore no makeup or jewelry; sexy though, funnily enough...as long as you could avoid the laugh. Ron crossed his arms abruptly over his chest as if someone had accused him of something. Screw Lally with her Central Park Conservancy! She didn't set foot inside the place but twice a year.

"Nevertheless," Mrs. Davidson was saying—"nevertheless, we ought to remember..."

Ron didn't even hear the rest of the sentence (which was a veiled prohibition against boasting about one's child's admission into grade school or complaining about one's failure therein), for he fixated on the word alone: *Nevertheless*. It seemed to reverberate around the walls of his enormous house. That word meaning "In spite of such and such." In spite of—well—everything that surrounded them! In spite of the static insulation of extreme wealth; in spite of the malling of Manhattan by chain stores; in spite of the black kids working at Best Buy (Ron's conscience pricked him uncomfortably) actually showing up for work to make $6.55 an hour; in spite of today's teenagers (thought Tommy Fleming, who had a thirteen-year-old from his first marriage), who would rather stare at their phones all day than drink vodka and lemonade in the Plaza Hotel after the Gold and Silver Ball; in spite of the feeling you'd have driving back from Quogue and sensing—thought Guy DeGroat, his prematurely silver hair a-glint under the chandelier—as you thundered down the Long Island Expressway past LeFrak City, catching glimpses of cartoon videos playing in the backs of minivans and SUVs, that the uglification of the world was near complete—*nevertheless*, the old, fine New York still existed. Perhaps it was being gutted and plastered over; perhaps it was sinking into the water. Perhaps there were no more limousines on Park Avenue (imagine it! no more limos on Park, Guy's wife, Ann, was thinking, remembering being groped in such a vehicle the winter she came out) and people wore acid-washed jeans to the Plaza, and they had moved the National Horse Show out to the Meadowlands years ago, Betsy Fleming thought, slurping the ice from her glass, so you no longer witnessed the sublime annual spectacle of amateur owner-hunters backing out of CAUTION: HORSES vans on Thirty-Fourth Street. But as long as you had this living specimen, this Mrs. Davidson, with her bang-cut brown bob, running a little church school on a side street on the Upper East Side of Manhattan, a school where they still let you sing Anglican hymns at Christmastime, it was not totally dead.

The speech, which had touched on raising money for financial aid, though Emily Lewin, who'd run the spring auction the past two years, happened to know that the school had trouble recruiting any families who needed aid, was coming to a close.

Girlishly charming, punchy, Mrs. D. was winding it down. "And we thank you for your time—we thank all of our parent volunteers especially! And for all who contributed to the annual fund..."

In that voice that seemed calibrated to elicit good behavior from adults as much as children, she was thanking them, thanking *them*. "And most of all," she said with the comic lightness but commanding presence of the old pro, her posture ever so slightly humpbacked, her gnarled right hand in the air, "for your generosity in giving us"—her timing perfect, she stretched out the final pause—"...your children!"

Exultant applause broke out, altogether too vehement for the setting.

As the party careened into its second half, parents crowded the bar. The volume in the room rose to a triumphant roar.

It was as if, Gwen Hogan thought—still hovering next to a tomblike sculpture, for she had nowhere else to go; Philippa had disappeared—the parents assembled here felt themselves oppressed in their daily lives, like members of a secret cult, and this gathering, at last, had given them rein to glory in their difference. Ron Stein was fox-trotting Mrs. Davidson around in a circle, spinning her out and reeling her back in, and Gwen, remembering seeing the man escape into his Escalade after some other parent function, recalled suddenly a bumper sticker that had adorned a neighbor's car when she was growing up—MY OTHER CAR IS A ROLLS-ROYCE! Mr. Luciano, the chemistry teacher at Dunning-Nautauqua High, with his beaten-up rust-colored Chevy Chevette, the backseat piled high with textbooks and papers to grade.

Dan was summoning her from across the room, giving her the *Let's go* signal. He rose on his toes to make sure she saw him and when she acknowledged him with a brief nod, he turned and walked quickly to the stairs, his impatience breaking out like the rash that had ended his career in corporate law. He'd had enough.

Now the parents were all seemingly caught up in a frenzy of agreement—"Yes!" Gwen could hear. "Yes!" "Yes!" "Yes!" "Yes!" coming from all sides as she made her way through them to the stairs.

You couldn't make that same kind of bumper-sticker joke anymore, not here, anyway, and not just because of the wealth. MY OTHER CAR IS A CHAUFFEURED SPORT-UTILITY VEHICLE! wasn't funny. A Rolls-Royce—a Rolls belonged to Hollywood, to the kind of Hollywood New York City Gwen might have imagined as a child. Perhaps there was no more Tinseltown version of New York. No screwball-comedy version with uniformed maids and dollar signs for door handles. The truth was money wasn't funny anymore. A hedge-fund manager did not a tycoon or a titan of industry make. Fund managers also weren't funny. She took a fleeting glance around the room; a few of the parents were making larger, more emphatic gestures with their hands than they would have an hour ago. The Big Apple that you, like some willing Eve, could take a bite of, opening up a world of pleasure...New York as a storied land for the crazy few...that was over too. Probably for those for whom the city was still an aspirational entity, cash was the inspiration, as well as the end—the capitalist magnet exerting its enormous pull...

Minnie appeared in her path, beaming, her teeth so perfect and bright white they were like the disembodied teeth of a dream. The smile disconcerted Gwen for a moment; she felt as if she were missing some critical meaning behind it.

"You're not going, are you, Gwen?" Minnie said with polite petulance.

"Yeah, I've got to go," Gwen said, unable to come up with even a sentence fragment of small talk. But Minnie had already moved on into the room.

"Yes!" she heard Pilar Fleming's dad, Tommy, say. "I could not agree more!"

Gwen peered over the balcony to see how far ahead of her Dan was, see if he was already outside, but instead, there *he* was. John Curtis, ascending the stairs at a staccato clip, as if, like some creature from the Sci-Fi Channel, he'd eaten her husband on his way in and kept going. The eyes bore into hers as he gained the landing. She heard someone mutter, "Gross"—realized the word had come out of her own mouth.

She was aware in her peripheral vision that Philippa was coming toward the stairs from the other side. Maybe Gwen could walk out with her. Curtis had hesitated, throwing all three of them together for a second, and so as not to shirk the introduction, Gwen said, "John Curtis, do you know Philippa Lye?"

Then Gwen's heart gave a horrible jolt because Philippa's face went dead with shock. Curtis looked at Philippa carefully. "Hey, hey, hey—how're you doing?" he said smoothly. He put a hand on Gwen's shoulder and moved her bodily to the side, pressing on into the party. "Ron? Ron, hey—think we met before."

Philippa's mouth was working. "You all right?" Gwen asked in dismay. What horrific faux pas had she committed?

"What the hell?" Philippa spat out, causing the parents standing closest to them to turn, their insouciant expressions dying on their faces.

"I'm so sorry!" Gwen said, mortified. "I didn't know—"

"What the hell is *he* doing here? Why did you bring him over to meet me?"

"No, no—It was a coincidence. I just—"

"Why is he here? What is he doing here? I don't understand it!"

"Philippa? Can I—do you want—"

191

"Going—I'm going! I've got to see—my bag—my way out..." She was incoherent, waving an arm around.

"Philippa? Let me go with you—"

A few parents were watching, concerned. They started to close in but at the last minute, Philippa recovered her mobility and shot through a hole to the staircase.

A man—Guy DeGroat—put a hand out to steady her, said her name—"Careful, Philippa!" But instead he made her trip. She flailed—"Ahh!"—her hand shot up as she crashed to the floor. Jessica Kaplan gasped—the last sound before that particularly pregnant silence that greets the spectacle of a drunk woman hitting the floor, the exposed underwear—it was too much. As one they cringed. They looked away. A woman's voice said, "Oh, my word!," followed by the wickedly hopeful, "Is she all *right?*" Fighting off all aid—"I'm fine! I'm fine! I'm fine!"—Philippa got to her knees. She scrambled to her feet, grabbing for the railing. Before Gwen could stop her, she was down the stairs, the heels of her shoes going *rat-a-tat* on the marble. In a blur of loose hair and dishevelment, she was gone.

A question had formed on the lips of everyone in the crowd. Their eyes searched one another's faces, looking for confirmation that it was not *their* fault...a touch of humor in the looks exchanged. A "Jeez!" Then someone said, "O*kay!*" and the talking resumed, in murmurs at first.

Gwen went after Philippa, slowly, carefully, putting one foot after another on the marble steps—she was still trembling. Dan was coming from the corner coatrack with their two coats. His eyebrows were way up—the cynical amusement that he took in the antics of the rich animated his face. *Is this chick crazy or what?* And it was alluring to have that, at least, with all that they had lost. Gwen knew about Diane Costa—had known the night it happened. A colleague had called the apartment looking for the two of them; it was as simple as that. And Dan. having previously talked about her all the time, never pronounced her name again in Gwen's presence. And it would have been good cozy fun to share the mutual high ground tonight. *Totally friggin' nuts!* her eyes might have answered. *What the—* But Gwen shut down the jocular question in his eyes. Philippa had not asked for her friendship; Gwen's loyalty was as much to an idea as to a person. But reaching the bottom of the stairs, Gwen said tightly to her husband, "All set?"

Upstairs, the pianist went on imperviously, "'Fly me to the moon...'" Those old exuberant standards that this crowd clung to for parties and weddings, as if the sound track alone could usher in a new bull market.

Chapter Twelve

Laura Skinker must've been the quietest seven-year-old on the Upper East Side. She was so quiet now no one could have realized she was awake, even though she had been for nearly nine minutes. The thought made her grin in her bed and shiver and press Flat Pig to her chest so as not to make noise and wake Ruthie, asleep and mouth-breathing a few feet away in her toddler bed. Laura had woken up a little while ago and had simply lain there, allowing only her eyes to rove, from the blue and yellow flowers on the wallpaper to the glass doorknob on the white door going in to the bathroom to the white light fixture on the ceiling above. Yes, only her eyes moved, as if her body were paralyzed from the neck down, like the man who sat in a wheelchair on the corner of the midtown block where Daddy's bank was except no—he was paralyzed only from the waist down because he could hold things, he could hold his change cup. She wished she hadn't thought of the man in the wheelchair. It made her writhe inwardly, as if there were a weight not on her body but on her mind because lately she understood without having been told that neither Mummy nor Daddy could remove the weight, it would always be there, even if Mummy put dollar bills in the cup and said people should give bills not change, people were disgusting and stingy, and to escape the feeling she looked quickly at her glowing alarm clock to see what time it was now: 7:19. She had been awake ten minutes and still no one in the apartment knew she was awake. When she had first opened her eyes, the clock said 7:09 and Laura had felt *flooded* with a sick, fighting feeling. No! No! Oh, no! She had to wake up by 6:45 to make the bus. She had allowed herself one little whimpery cry but mid-cry she had realized that not only was it Saturday but it was also March vacation—spring break was starting today!—so there was doubly, triply, quadruply no school today. She had giggled—actually giggled aloud, and felt such blissful relief about its being Saturday and vacation that she was much happier than she would've been if she'd never thought it was a weekday. It had happened before, oversleeping. Sometimes when Daddy had to go in early or was traveling, her mother slept right through her own alarm, and last year, when Laura was in first grade, she had missed the bus three times. But Daddy had bought her the Peter Rabbit alarm clock and now she could not only tell time but also set her own alarm so that she didn't have to depend on Mummy. "Between you and me, Mummy's not a morning person," Daddy had told her. He said it as if she were a grown-up and he were sharing a—not a joke with her, but an adult observation. Daddy's eyebrows raised—"Mummy's not much of a morning person, Lolo." If you weren't a morning person, Laura knew, it meant you were grouchy and slow-moving in the morning and little things going wrong—such as running out of milk—incensed you and made you yell and say, "Jesus Christ!" (They said "Jesus Christ" in church, and sometimes—oddly, Laura felt—"Jesus *the* Christ," but then it wasn't a swear, it was all right, though Mummy had other quibbles: the "culture of self-flagellation," for instance, the whole long litany starting "Although we are not worthy" et cetera, et cetera. "I just can't bring myself to say it. Protesting a bit much, isn't it? You'd think they'd modernize." "I agree, Phil"—Daddy, after a pause, when Mummy was done with her rant last Sunday. Mummy: "Then why are we here? Why are we coming? Are we just total and utter hypocrites? It's not as if I actually be*lieve*..." Daddy, not taking the bait, continuing, humming the closing hymn as they walked down Fifth.

And one was a doctor and one was a priest, and one was slain by a fierce, wild beast! They were all of them saints of God and I mean...

Mummy, looking miffed but keeping silent, perhaps enjoying Daddy's singing, the funny hymn that sounded like a fairy tale.)

Laura looked at the time again and clutched Flat Pig. She was so hungry she was shaky-weak, but she didn't feel like getting up—not quite yet...

It was worse to run out of coffee, of course. Bad to run out of milk but worse to run out of coffee. For one thing, Laura knew what to do if they ran out of milk: you got the Parmalat from the pantry. Parmalat was milk that didn't have to stay cold until it was opened. If you put Parmalat instead of milk on your cereal, you hardly noticed the difference. Sebastian would protest but Laura bet he wouldn't have been able to tell if he hadn't seen the carton, so if they ran out of milk she always poured the Parmalat into a pitcher. That was when Daddy was traveling that she helped with breakfast. If you ran out of coffee it was worse because there was no Parmalat coffee; you had to buy it outside at the deli on the way to drop off the younger ones at nursery school. If you ran out of coffee, it was bad—even Daddy grumbled—but if you ran out of coffee *and* you weren't a morning person, it was really terrible. You would swear and maybe slam a door and you might say something mean to Laura, such as "Why are you staring? Don't *stare!* It's rude to stare! Don't act spoiled, Laura! It's unbecoming!"

Now that she had the alarm, which told both digital and mechanical time (and mostly Laura cheated and looked at the digital numbers even though Daddy liked her to look at the clock face), some mornings it was *Laura* who woke *Mummy* and told her they had to get ready to go. She woke her very gently because Mummy could really yell if you woke her too quickly. The bus was three blocks away and they had to walk out the door by 7:25. Mummy really didn't like it when Daddy traveled because she had to be the one to take Laura to the bus, and she had to bring Ruth and Sebastian with her. That was an unbelievable fucking hassle. Ruth was easy and sweet but Sebastian was a living nightmare. He was a devil child. A couple times when Mummy had a splitting headache and failed to make Sebastian get dressed, she'd taken Ruth and left Sebastian downstairs in the lobby in his pajamas with Ray, the doorman, but the old biddy on the ninth floor had complained, Mrs. MacFarland, who could go screw herself I mean really go *fuck* herself.

But today was Saturday. Saturday. Tomorrow they were all four going up to the farm because Daddy was starting his vacation to coincide with *her* March vacation but today he had things to tidy up at work so today... today loomed with pleasant blankness. The blue and yellow flowers connected to the blue and yellow flowers connected to the blue and yellow flowers... stem into petal into stem into petal... Mummy wasn't into scheduling a million activities. Children like that would grow up to be little bores. Mummy also wasn't into traveling. Nor was Daddy. Mummy didn't like "touristing," and Daddy didn't seem to notice there were other places to go to apart from the farm. Vacations they went up to the farm. Laura had to pretend she didn't care when classmates said they were going to ski out west, they were going to St. Bart's, they were going to the Galápagos, they were going on safari in Kenya, because Laura was never going anywhere...Once she told her aunt Sallie, even though she knew it sounded spoiled, and Sallie said kindly, "All those places will be there when you grow up," and she hugged Laura and whispered in her ear, "You know what? I'll take you skiing out west some time—the snow's better." But today they might go to the park. Or they might go to the bank. If Mummy felt really hideous and had a splitting headache, Daddy would call Mrs. Sampson to watch Sebastian and Ruth and he would take Laura to the bank with him. The bank was a beautiful fancy building on Fifty-Fourth Street. It did not have columns outside such as Mr. Banks's bank did in *Mary Poppins,* and in a way it didn't look serious enough for a bank because of all the crazy gargoyles, but it was one. The best part about the bank was that it had their name on it: Skinker, on a brass plaque outside the doors. (Also Farr, but Laura didn't pay as much attention to the Farr part and, of course, Skinker came first.) It also said Skinker, Farr on the stationery and the pens, which Laura was allowed to use to write with if Daddy had to do some work. Her great-grandfather Thomas Hussey had started the bank and Daddy had—well, Daddy had continued it. You couldn't take money out of the bank, unfortunately. It was, Laura now understood, not that kind of bank. She never spoke of it at school because she was sure that her classmates would make the same assumption she had, and they would think that Laura could go to the bank any time she needed money and just take out as many dollar or twenty-dollar bills as she wanted and Laura did not want to have to correct that impression, though when Kate Kellogg told everyone, "It's not the same as a real bank!" Laura had felt ashamed and had said, "Yes, it is!" and had had to lie her way out of it. Laura's savings account wasn't even at the bank; it was at another bank, one without her name on it. Because, again, Skinker was a different kind of bank. "Maybe you'll work here someday," Daddy's assistant, beautiful Ms. Ritchek with her low, quiet voice that made shivers run up Laura's spine, would say to her when she visited. "Continue the family tradition." And although Laura recognized this as a compliment…she wasn't sure she would. Daddy looked nice in the morning when he shaved and went to the bank. But really, the only fun parts for her were seeing their name on the plaque and having Ms. Ritchek be nice to her and the occasional leftover tray of cookies you found wrapped up in the little kitchen where the coffee machine was. She told Ms. Ritchek, "Yes, maybe I will," to be polite, but she mentioned that she also wanted to be a ballet dancer or a veterinarian.

"Her father's daughter to a T…"

"Got the Skinker swayback and the stomach that sticks out…"

The mothers would talk sometimes when they thought Laura couldn't hear.

"The boy's got *her* height, doesn't he?"

"Girls are fair like Jed and built just like him…they even have the same walk!"

"Strong genes!"

"She's a mini–Jed Skinker! A mini-him!"

And from Miss Oliver herself, the ballet teacher: "Stretch, Laura! Stretch up! Make yourself longer! Taller! Stretch your head way, way up out of your shoulders!" when she was already stretching up as hard as she could and if she stretched any more her arms would pull out of her sockets.

Laura ignored comments such as these because she knew she was the best dancer in the class, no question, because Mummy said so. When Mummy told you something, you believed it, not like Deirdre's mother, who was always telling Deirdre how good she was at everything, how really amazing her pictures from art were, how beautifully she sang—all right, she did have a pretty voice—and thanking her for hanging up her coat and clearing her plate and brushing her hair and other things you were simply supposed to do and that Laura, at her house, was never thanked for or praised. In one way, Laura enjoyed going over to Deirdre's apartment (there was a pool in the building, for one thing, and a room for watching movies with seats in rows just like a movie theater) and being thanked and praised herself by Deirdre's mother for hanging up her coat and clearing her plate, but she also felt deflated and irritated when her really-amazing-kind-horse-monster collage from art was praised in the exact same tone and almost in the exact same words as Deirdre's pretty-bad turtle. Mummy was not like that. Mummy was able to tell the difference between a good picture and a bad one. Mummy was critical of many things—of all the goddamn construction; of honking; of people who didn't say please and thank you; of iPads; gum-chewers; solicitation by phone at the dinner hour—but Mummy had told her she had a beautiful body and that she looked like Daddy and that there was no one better in the world to look like or, actually to *be* like, than Daddy and that all the Skinkers had swaybacks and sticking-out stomachs and it was a mark of distinction. Mummy was funny. Funny-odd, not funny-ha-ha, though she did have a sense of humor. She got angry at Daddy and yelled all the time and cried and swore and the other night said, "I'm going into the bedroom, I'm going to close the door, and I'm not coming out!" only with lots of swears, but in private she told Laura nice things about Daddy almost as if they were secrets, as if she didn't want Daddy to know that she knew these nice things about Daddy. And sometimes when she spoke about Daddy, a look of pride came into her face, even of conceitedness that Daddy was her husband. "But Sebastian looks like you. He has your height," Laura had pointed out, trying out what she'd heard on Mummy. "Well, as long as he doesn't turn out like me," Mummy had said. Laura didn't say anything because of course her brother already was like Mummy. Sensitive and scowling and proud and snapping at people and picky about everything—the tags on his clothes and the light in his room and how far ajar his door was left at night. It could have been Sebastian who yelled, "I'm going into the bedroom and I'm not coming out!" *Had* it been Sebastian? Laura paused to consider, squeezing Flat Pig.

All at once she felt afraid with the treacherous fear again. In his bedroom, through the bathroom that connected their two rooms, Sebastian must still be asleep. But that was unheard of. Was she *mistaken* that she was the only one awake? Had her brother been up and woken Daddy and they'd gone out to buy croissants all while Laura slumbered? It had happened before. She cast the down comforter back and got quickly out of bed, listening intently, fearfully. It was so still she couldn't hear anything but little Ruth's breathing from the toddler bed in the corner. But then she remembered that Sebastian had been up in the night. Laura had heard Mummy go in, Daddy go in, an argument, wails...that must be why her brother was fast asleep now. Still, she tiptoed very carefully into the bathroom, the tiles cool beneath her slipperless feet, opened the door a fraction at a time, wincing when it creaked, and peered into Sebastian's room. Her brother had thrown off all the covers and was sleeping with his arm flung up over his head, as if he had collapsed midtantrum.

Presently, Laura found herself sitting on the braided rug on the floor of her room looking at *The Cat in the Hat Comes Back*. She enjoyed reading her old picture books though she felt there was something secretive about the habit, as she was technically outgrowing them. CHOOSE AN APPROPRIATE BOOK FOR YOUR READING LEVEL! said the sign above the book boxes in her classroom. "Appropriate," Mummy had said, glaring at the sign, on Parent Visiting Day. "God, how I loathe that word." "Mummy!" Laura had whisper-pleaded, tugging Mummy's hand. Then understanding softened Mummy's face, and when Ms. Karten appeared, she had nodded and said, "What a lovely book display!" and raised her eyebrows at Laura. Mummy did have a good sense of humor when she wasn't ready to kill someone or "firebomb the place."

When Laura got to the part where all the little Things keep popping out of the hat, she turned the book over and, leaving it splayed on the rug, left Ruth sleeping and went down the hall past all of the framed family photographs (going back to the funny colors of the '70s and past that to Gammy as a girl in black-and-white) to the kitchen. Mummy's plants caught her eye, a row of potted violets and cactuses and viny things, crowded into the counter near the only window. She got the plastic watering jug from underneath the sink and watered them and picked off the dead leaves.

She carefully poured herself an orange juice and got out all the things she could remember for pancakes, all the while willing Daddy to wake up and make them for her. Eggs, flour, butter...the kitchen was a peaceful room, the morning light streaming in over the little plants. A pegboard took up the far interior wall opposite the service elevator, where the pots and pans and strainers were hung, for Laura's grandmother was a top-notch cook. When Gampy died, Gammy had moved into a smaller apartment in the Sixties, to be closer to her club, and

Mummy and Daddy had taken over this apartment. Mummy was pregnant with her at the time. Laura had never met her grandfather because Gampy had died before she was born. On Mummy's side, she didn't have grandparents. Mummy's mother had died of cancer but it wasn't sad because Mummy didn't like her, and Laura didn't have a grandfather on that side. Not that Laura really believed there was an actual time before she was born. It was like when you rode the subway—she never thought about the fact that she was actually moving below the streets of Manhattan; she felt that she had entered a different, parallel world. The period before she was born was the same. She had been there—she just didn't know it yet. There was, after all, no possibility that there had been a time before she existed—it made no sense. And Daddy's bedroom when he was a boy was Sebastian's bedroom now and their aunt Sallie had had Laura and Ruth's bedroom and their dog growing up was called Barkie and he had slept in Daddy's room " 'cause he liked me better!" Daddy said with a twinkle in his eye but Aunt Sallie claimed it was because Daddy bribed him with treats.

The spice cabinet was up above and to the left of the big white stove and Laura liked to look inside it, which she did now, dragging over a kitchen chair. She liked to read the names on all of the ancient spices that they hardly ever used. Not cinnamon and nutmeg but turmeric, mace, whole cloves, allspice, sage. Bay leaves. She took them out and lined them up on the kitchen counter. The kitchen floor was black and white squares—"Very eighties," Mummy called it. The service elevator came right to the kitchen door. Sometimes Sebastian got to ride up with Ramón, the porter, who was Ray the morning doorman's son, if he had a grocery delivery but Laura didn't like the smell of trash that lingered, so she politely said, "No, thank you" when he asked. When she got bored with the spices, she got herself another glass of orange juice, but after a few minutes, she was tired of waiting, the excitement of waking up early had worn off, so she walked back down the hall and listened outside of her parents' door. Unbelievably, as she stood there, the knob began to turn. She stepped right back. Daddy looked down at her in his robe and they mugged and grinned at each other in total silence. As Laura was thinking how funny it was that you could make such absurd faces without any sound at all, she noticed, when he stopped to pull the door quietly shut behind him, how tired Daddy looked.

In the kitchen, to cheer him up, she said, "Isn't it nice that Sebastian slept in today?" It took Daddy a moment to hear her but when he did, he said, "Very nice. Unprecedented!" and he set about making pancakes, which made her feel she had cheered him up a little. Laura had remembered everything but the vanilla. They worked together silently and efficiently. *The Joy of Cooking* was propped open to Pancakes, Griddle Cakes, or Batter Cakes, which Laura thought was funny—imagining those weird people in pioneer times or some time like that who called pancakes "griddle cakes" or "flapjacks" or "johnnycakes." Laura helped by cracking the eggs, which she was known in the family to be good at (as well as separating eggs for desserts), and measuring the milk, and while Daddy got the coffee going, and then the bacon, she stirred the dry ingredients into the wet. Pancakes were the only thing Daddy could make besides fettuccine Alfredo. Mummy couldn't cook either. She could make only children's food—tuna melts and grilled cheese and baked potatoes and baked beans from a can. Gammy came over sometimes and cooked dinner and left extras, and sometimes Reina, the wife of Ray and the mother of Ramón, dropped off chicken Milanesa for them because she worried that Mummy didn't eat.

"Do you think I'll work at the bank when I'm older?" Laura said conversationally when the two of them were pouring out (she) and flipping (Daddy) the pancakes. A drop of hot oil sprang up at her and caught her in the arm. She winced and rubbed the arm against her nightgown but didn't say anything. She wanted to say something nice to take Daddy's mind off whatever it was that was bothering him. To her surprise, her father took her seriously—too seriously; she had just been making small talk. She squirmed under his attention.

"Would you like to?"

"Maybe," Laura said, feeling panicky.

"The bank may not be around forever."

"Yes, it will," said Laura, thinking Daddy was joking.

Daddy watched the pancakes cooking and didn't speak. Then he said, "The bank may take early retirement, Lolo."

She glanced at Daddy's profile but it was scrupulously neutral, like Ms. Karten's when she tried not to take sides in a classroom argument even though it was clear that Veronica L. was the one who started it by bragging. Of course she didn't jump four feet on her horse! Did she even have a horse?

"But the building will always be there," Laura said.

"You're right. The building will always be there. No one can ever tear it down. But one day there may be something else inside it."

"Would the plaque still be there?" said Laura.

"No," Daddy said after a minute, sliding two pancakes at once off the spatula and onto the platter. "The plaque would come down if the bank weren't there. Somebody else's plaque would go up."

Laura felt the cheer run away from her but she kept on smiling. There it was: the weight pressing on her—when she had thought to have an innocuous conversation to cheer Daddy up!

"Why?" Laura's voice broke but she managed to move and cough so it wasn't obvious to Daddy. "Why would the bank retire? It's been going so long."

Daddy looked at her. He was kind and wise, which reassured her a bit, and more than that, Daddy was patient. Daddy never told her to hurry up; Daddy had time, whereas Mummy— Mummy had no time. Mummy didn't have a job but she was always hassled and late and cross.

"Well," said Daddy, "if I had to choose between the bank and the family, I'd choose the family."

"But the bank *is* the family," Laura said automatically.

"You sound like someone I know."

"Mummy?"

Daddy smiled. "No. Gammy."

"But why would you have to choose?" Daddy wasn't making any sense.

"Oh," said Daddy casually, flipping the current batch of three pancakes just in time, "if I weren't smart enough not to have to choose."

"Maybe we could save the plaque," Laura said quickly. "We could bring it home and keep it here."

Daddy agreed. "We could—we could save the plaque."

"But what about Ms. Ritchek?" Laura asked. "Where would she go?"

"Oh, we'd save her too. Maybe," Daddy added, "we'd take her home too. She could share your room."

"Daddy!"

"No...I'd find her another job. Ms. Ritchek is so good at her job that that would be easy."

"At another bank, you mean?" Laura distinctly did not like the idea of Ms. Ritchek working at someone else's bank.

206

"If she wanted to."

Father and daughter waited for the bubbles to appear in the two cooking circles of batter. It was as if they were both thinking the same thing, for Laura didn't feel self-conscious when she protested suddenly: "But Mummy *likes* the bank."

"Yes."

"She has nothing against it. It's just I think life would be simpler at the farm."

At seven she already knew it was her job to keep a conversation with a man going, to suss out the right—the cordial—response. She could feel Daddy glancing at her but she stayed focused on the pancakes, embarrassed because she wasn't totally sure what she'd just said—she was only quoting, after all.

Ruth had woken up. She appeared in the kitchen in her nightgown with her blankie as Daddy and Laura were sitting down at the table to eat. Laura didn't feel like sharing Daddy but maybe Ruth would cheer him up.

"It's almost my birthday," her little sister said. Daddy and Laura laughed and Laura said, "It's not your birthday for two months, Ruthie!" She immediately thought of the secret—of the puppies who had been born up at the farm and were now being hidden away at Billy Flood's house so Ruthie wouldn't know. She thought of the puppies and she didn't say a word, though she glanced at Daddy and had to press her lips together and her face twitched when he raised his eyebrows at her.

"I'm inviting my whole class."

"Are you sure?" Laura asked skeptically, and with a pang, wondering if Mummy had allowed this. "Did you ask Mummy?"

"She said I could." Ruth climbed onto a chair.

"Did Mummy say Ruth could have the whole class?"

Daddy nodded, passing Ruth the plate of pancakes. "Oh, yes. The whole class and all the neighbors and all the kids from Jumping Gymnastics and—"

"Junior's Gym!" Ruth squealed. "It's Junior's Gym!"

"Everyone's invited to the Plaza for a seated dinner for two hundred. We'll have caviar and lobster bisque and champagne flowing out of ice sculptures—"

"Daddy!"

"That's what Mummy said!"

Ruth, knowing she was being teased, pursed her lips tolerantly. She poured far too much syrup on her pancakes in Laura's opinion and murmured: "I'm inviting the whole class plus Arabella."

"Who's Arabella?" Laura asked, suspicious again, for Mummy wasn't always so hot on the details. She might have said Ruth could invite some totally inappropriate person, like an older child whose mother would make her come and who would ridicule the younger kids and the younger-kid activities and be a liability.

"Arabella's my friend," Ruth said, frowning as she worked at using her knife and fork to cut her pancakes. "My new friend. Who I made. Arabella Curtis."

Then the weight pressed on Laura again, for Daddy spoke in the fake, fishing way that other, inferior parents spoke but never him or Mummy. He said, paying too much attention, "Is Arabella Curtis your friend, Ruthie?"—repeating, for no reason at all, what Ruth had just said. "Your new friend who you made?"

Chapter Thirteen

A charity function, the caption said. The New York Landmarks Protection Society. The *Times* photo showed Jed Skinker and his wife in evening dress "arriving at the Winter Ball" two years ago, their coats open, her dress long and glittering. Not only was Mrs. Skinker tall, she had that slouchless assurance in her height, as if—in Dan's opinion—she were exercising a right—her genetic privilege to be taller than you.

Dan had been looking at the picture for weeks now. He couldn't shake the unpleasant feeling that he was squinting through a peephole, ogling a world he could never enter. That wasn't saying much, but the fact was he wasn't talking about a socioeconomic barrier so much as...a genre divide. He felt as if he dwelled in some hackneyed network sitcom, whereas the Skinkers inhabited a public-television drama, a featured television "event." He pictured the parties in their world as more lavish; the marital fights uglier; every constituent a knight or a joker. It was neurotic, nowadays, when the meritocracy had never been more ascendant, to dwell on the accident of birth, but the Skinkers brought you up short, reminded you that the fancy restaurants and four-star hotels, the idea of which you preoccupied yourself with, were middle-class treats, candies on sticks to keep you quiet in the bleacher seats...Better, maybe, to be like Gwen and eschew all that—"One of those people who like to eat at fancy restaurants" she would say of some acquaintance she had consigned to terminal mediocrity.

A Thursday toward the end of March, the workday coming to a close. Four weeks into the Lenten regime: no sweets; no bread; no booze. And a run across the Brooklyn Bridge every day after work. Why? Because it was there. He was out of excuses. And any jerk could get through two miles, even a sad, out-of-shape desk jockey like himself.

Already dressed for the run, Dan put a foot up on the edge of his desk and tightened the laces of his worn-out running shoes. He had never been able to bring himself to join a gym. He would start his cross-examination of the poor benighted health-club employee during the tour of the machine room, maybe not even let him or her make it to the membership pitch, when his rejecting, obstructionist mind-set proclaimed it all bullshit: "If you really want to get in shape, all you need is a pair of sneakers." What would it be like, he wondered, to go through life saying, "Yes, please," and "Sure, why not?" and "Okay, I'll give it a try!" rather than "No, no, no, no," as if his mission here was to let nothing get past him? He noticed a growing hole on the little-toe side of the sneaker. *Don't whine; you'll get new ones when you get through this.*

This.

He zipped up his windbreaker and glanced at his watch, though there was nowhere he had to be. Gwen had taken Mary up to her parents' in Massachusetts for the two weeks of spring break. "Next year we'll go away," Dan promised, feeling panicked as he embraced her outside of Penn Station. "Okay—sure."

Gwen didn't seem to hang on the idea, and it was only when he had left them and was heading down to the office to put in a few weekend hours that Dan realized he'd pulled a Perry Hogan: he'd made a promise about a future trip that might never happen, not because, like his father, he couldn't afford it—he could, just—but because he simply wasn't all that interested in vacationing and assumed she wasn't either. He missed them now. The apartment felt deserted. Getting takeout every night and running the dishwasher with three plates in it, he didn't feel quite as rebellious as he used to—more sick of himself, for not living up to her standards.

It was very important that he focus on the *small* ways in which he wasn't living up to her standards. He still caved and bought the occasional six-pack of paper towels, a luxury that Gwen hadn't grown up with and had deemed unnecessary.

Dan eyed the photograph. There were several in the file by this point: clips from Skinker's wife's modeling days, her look then more mainstream pretty, less edgy than you'd expect; sober corporate-board profiles of CEO Jedediah Hussey Skinker. But the *Times* photo was the one he kept coming back to, seemingly unable to move on from the glam shot, though the case itself had moved on—had moved right along, the pieces falling into place, one sickening click after another. All the reasoning he had done—the painstaking reasoning of convincing himself that Skinker was in the clear—had to be in the clear—had been for naught. He almost still couldn't believe it, pathetic as that was.

In the photo you could see that something had disturbed her, though not the flash of the camera—she wasn't looking at it (nor was she looking at Dan himself, he had noted, though he'd positioned the clipping this way and that to see if he could catch her eye) but just past it, eyes open wide. With alarm, he'd thought initially. But he had studied the picture for so long that he could now detect nuances in the Skinkers' facial expressions he hadn't caught before. He suspected that hers wasn't a startled reaction to something specific so much as an everyday kind of thing—the unfocused intensity in which she habitually dwelled. He guessed that she was always being gripped by something, alarmed by something.

They said that about alcoholics, about addicts of all kinds— that they could think only one step ahead. Sometimes when he looked at it long enough, the photo would start to irritate Dan. He'd have an impulse to shake her, to shake the short-sightedness off her face, make her notice her husband, or him, maybe—something. But that was *his* thing: Jed Skinker himself didn't seem concerned. The man radiated largesse. He reminded Dan of a benevolent dictator, the tolerant-till-crossed demeanor. Or was Dan back in Biddeville High SAT prep, confusing *largesse* with actual *largeness?* Skinker's bulk harkened back to a time when rich people ate the most. Handsome couple. Even DiNapoli agreed. "Good-looking people, Danny," he'd said when Dan showed him the photograph. "Very attractive people."

Dan deliberated a second, then snatched the picture off his desk and folded it into the inner pocket of his windbreaker with his apartment keys and MetroCard. He gave the desk an exasperated, perfunctory tidy and turned out the light. His plan was to run over the bridge and back, then hop the train home. He had to get out, get some air—this thing was starting to suffocate him.

It was one of those days not long after the time change. The early-evening light when he came out onto St. Andrew's Plaza startled him. Dan glanced almost shyly at the sky. This time of year always made him feel as if he'd been given a personal reprieve—blessed in some way that didn't apply to everyone else. He darted across the traffic on Park Row and set off at a quick pace for the bridge.

He hated the start of every run, hated every step of it, thinking, *Jesus motherfucker fuck running,* but knowing it was only a matter of keeping going. Run it off. Run it off…

He's too caught up in the case, that's all. He needs to get his head straight—get some perspective.

Dan's hope that Jed Skinker had nothing whatever to do with John D. Curtis vanished for good a week after his lunch with Brenda Purzinski. The bank's phone records came in—incriminating as hell. He appealed nakedly to her sense of logic: "I'm telling you, though, Bren, it makes no sense! If you knew the guy—" "Sorry, Danny."

Where had he read that mourning had five phases, and the first was denial?

Dan feels a cramp in his side and accelerates onto the bridge, trying to contain his irritation at the slow-moving touritts who clog the first fifty yards even this late in the day.

For now there is no longer any question who Curtis's connection at Skinker, Farr is, whom he had spoken to—patched through each time by one Carol Ann Ritchek, Jed Skinker's personal assistant, Curtis not even bothering to call Skinker's cell phone, that same theme of flagrancy Dan recognized from the Tamco case. The secretary herself is coming in tomorrow morning at seven. Dan understands he will have to have the box of Kleenex ready. DiNapoli, doing his kinder, gentler approach, nevertheless reported that after he showed up at her apartment up in Yonkers the other night (modest, meticulously kept, plastic covers over the living-room furniture), she had gone into the bathroom, closed herself in while DiNapoli waited, and broken down—"wept most pathetically, Danny"—before she emerged, having redone her makeup, and agreed to come into the office and talk to them, "though you'll find I have almost nothing to say."

Dan alternately breathes into his side and tries to ignore the cramp. He'll never let himself get this out of shape again. "Swear to God!" He barks the words aloud over the noise of the traffic below in an effort to contain the pain, focuses on the American flag that flies from the top of the first tower, as if it could speed him along.

Despite the damning evidence of the phone records, Dan felt he had done an admirable job of keeping denial going at first. He had turned back twice to Carlos Florez, the drug offender in the print shop. He'd already told DiNapoli to consider him as a potential suspect. Now he ordered the full workup, the man's name plugged into a dozen federal databases.

He'd spent ninety minutes explaining to Matt Nast why a tipper/tippee relationship between Jed Skinker and John Curtis in which the former was beholden to the latter would never exist. " 'Cause it's all backward!" It bothered him. Then it angered him. All at once, denial was over and now, apparently, he had moved on to anger. Skinker had played him. Somehow he'd missed the hint when he'd met the guy at school that all was not as it seemed— some nefarious angle in the farm-drainage conversation. He'd been duped. He'd been taken in by the Skinker mystique, and he'd been duped.

His lungs are burning. For God's sake, he can barely move, he's so pathetically out of shape, can barely put one foot in front of the other, but somehow he does. He keeps going, slogging around the straggling packs of late-afternoon tourists; the well-adjusted souls who walk home to Brooklyn to enjoy some fresh air, to "stay active." He'll never be like that, taking a pleasant walk for exercise. As long as he can remember himself as a cognizant being, it's been all or nothing. Drink all night and run it off in the morning. Somehow he keeps going. Just keeps going.

And, like the glimpse of some tourist's fluorescent jacket he keeps seeing in front of him, the truth flashes before him as well.

Hadn't he, in fact, always known?

Hadn't his mind flitted to the truth the very moment Brenda pronounced the words *Skinker, Farr* that lunchtime a month ago on the plaza?

Her.

The man's wife.

His beautiful wife.

His beautiful wife who drank.

Dan glances to the right, south, to take in the harbor, the shipping containers and the cranes in Red Hook, as if his pointed observation of such things—Dan Hogan's bearing witness—can beef up the connection the city maintains, more tenuous every year, to an industrial past, to the ports and the trade and the working classes...The surface of the walkway beneath his feet has changed from metal to wooden slats, and surprise, surprise, he's suddenly in a rhythm—not exactly enjoying the run, that'll come later, but at least he knows he won't quit.

In the end he got lucky. Unbelievably, feel-bad-about-it lucky, given his reluctance to focus on Skinker. He doesn't like to dwell on that, either, as if the luck might diminish his competence, but he's standing there at the Steins' party two weeks ago, sober as an AA sponsor, giving Gwen the *Let's go* signal, when he gets handed it, handed the connection, like one of those flaky-pastry canapés Lally Stein had served that seemed to make Dan hungrier and hungrier the more of them he ate. *She* knew Curtis. Skinker's wife had recognized Curtis. Was, seemingly, shocked senseless by the unexpected presence of John Curtis at a St. Timothy's parents' event.

Whoa was the brilliant thought he remembers having. *Wait just a minute. Whoa, whoa, whoa.* But he couldn't catch up. Couldn't think that fast. That reaction . . . all out of proportion for a parent night. Maybe the reason it took him a while to process it was that *terror,* at an Upper East Side school gathering, isn't one's go-to emotional read.

"What the hell was that?" was Dan's opener when they had left the Steins' and were across Park, Gwen at her usual race-walk to get home and relieve the babysitter, Dan striding alongside.

"I saw Curtis come in—didn't really relish the idea of a chat—so I jumped behind the coatrack. I thought Miss Blond Cruise Director was going to have me arrested for disorderly conduct." He'd glanced at Gwen—he could usually get her with even a suggestion of the humor that had been so lacking in her childhood. He liked to make her laugh. "'Please, sir, allow me to get your coat for you.' 'Please, sir, un*hand* the plastic hanger. *I* will take down the garment—'"

Gwen, however, had gone white with affront. Surprised and not quite sure what to make of it, Dan was silent for a block or two, keeping pace with her, stealing looks at her profile, waiting for an opening. But she was practically twitching with disgust.

"I see Curtis go in," he tried again, affecting a puzzled tone. "I look up the stairs, see you trying to introduce them. The next thing you know I see *her* come tearing down like she's being chased." He paused. "They're not heading up the PTA together, I take it."

The early March night had been raw and damp. Dan had been glad to be walking at a pace that would warm him up, glad to be out of that mausoleum of a house, most particularly glad that his kid was going to public school next year. And yes, in the back of his mind, he knew that what was spurring all this gladness was the fact that *he had it,* whether Gwen or anyone liked it, whether it was unfair or cheating somehow—he had the connection between Skinker and Curtis. He had been handed it. Live.

And even if he had known intuitively where the one liability in the man's life of circumspection and duty lay, it wasn't the same as seeing that reaction of hers. Fleeing the man, she'd practically run Dan over.

He'd cleared his throat tentatively. "Was that about *Curtis,* do you think? Was that why she took off like that? Or was she just plastered? I did see her hitting the bar. Do they *know* each other? How would they know each other? Bizarre."

Gwen had stopped on the street and looked at him with the closest thing to dislike he'd ever seen on her face. "He must have raped her, Dan."

"What? Whoa!" He put up his palms as if dropping something. Okay, maybe he was playing dumb a little. "What did you say?"

Truth was, the idea had crossed his mind as well.

Tightly, with a threatening note now: "You heard me, Dan." Was that hysteria lurking? In Gwen Babineau's voice?

"Right, right, okay," Dan conceded quickly. He gave a solemn nod to show he was being serious—no more joking—and hurried after her as she started ferociously down the block again. And now he knew he'd really better not open his mouth because his main reaction to the word *rape* had always been reflexive denial. *It wasn't me!* he always wanted to say when women mentioned it in that pissy tone they used, as if (as an irritating piece of college graffiti had claimed) all heterosexual sex was rape.

"Right, right," he repeated. Fuck it. He would drop it—drop the topic for the night. Gwen rarely got angry. Her rational weighing of the pros and cons, her calm willingness to see the

217

other guy's side—"Maybe he just didn't realize..."—were the five-bar pens that corralled Dan's free-floating rage. Somehow he felt that if he pushed her on it, and she didn't want to be pushed, the whole thing would explode in his face.

As they waited to cross York, he considered telling her about it all. Why not come clean, make Gwen his ally? Lord knows he needed one. She must realize he was investigating Curtis, must have guessed the moment he told her not to start hanging around Minnie Curtis and her kid. He could come right out now and tell her Jed Skinker was on the other side, the husband of her childhood acquaintance; that he wasn't just gossiping tonight, he had to know the history between Curtis and Skinker's wife. Did she know anything? Could she help him out? But the light changed, and Dan balked at the idea. His wife was already uncomfortably close to the investigation. The only thing saving it from being an utter cluster-fuck was her ignorance as to the latest developments. If Dan were to inform her that he was investigating the Skinkers as well...Side by side, the two of them neared their building. Gwen was the stablest person he'd ever known. That was why her unpredictability on the subject of the Skinkers unnerved him. In the muted light of the elevator, he wished he could get a better look at her face. What was she thinking behind that forbidding—but also oddly forgiving—mien? She had taken a stand tonight. She cared. For some reason relating to her childhood maybe, she cared about Skinker's wife.

He gave her a lame smile as the elevator stopped on Five. No way was he going to tell her.

The quick pace as he gains the first tower is starting to feel unsustainable but Dan pushes on, annoyed now rather than agonizing that it's still so hard.

To be clear, as far as the Steins' party, Gwen's assumption was also his assumption—the only plausible explanation for *her* reaction. The guy is a known rapist, after all. Weird, how the jury is *not* still out on that. How you could *be* a rapist. Not some guy who'd had a few and had an aggressive streak but a guy who, given the opportunity, raped women. Or maybe looked for the opportunity! Found the opportunity and fucked them against their will. Overpowered them and fucked them...fucking disgusting.

He wondered when it had happened. In her twenties, maybe? Her modeling days? A lot of guys had a thing about models. Or more recently? A one-night stand after she was married? That would help explain the terror.

If Mrs. Skinker had cheated on her husband, she had picked the worst possible guy in the tristate area to do it with. It creeped Dan out thinking about the twistedness of the Curtis psyche. You get a man's wife into bed, an alcoholic, easy target; you rape her, 'cause that's your thing; and then, as a bonus, you force the husband to tip you off on material nonpublic information...The truth was it didn't make perfect sense to him. It didn't totally jell. But Dan could guess at the range of leverage that might be available to Curtis after only one night with that unhinged woman.

Skinker's beautiful wife.

Who drank.

Who'd apparently signed up for one night of indiscretion with a hundred-year-old bank as collateral. Played roulette with the livelihood of two hundred people, if this brought Skinker, Farr down. *Twenty minutes after the last call, we get the trade,* he hears Brenda saying.

Dan feels sick. "Fuck!"—as the cramp returns with a piercing jab.

One night of indiscretion.

One night!

Frequently what hits Dan the most about his own transgression is the unfairness of his not being able to make it go away.

One night!

One stupid night.

How could it be the case that he couldn't go back in time and erase it? Make it so that it never happened? From time to time he's thought of pulling Diane aside and asking her directly for her eternal silence: *Can we agree that this never happened?*

He grimaces as he makes it to the second tower. He raises his eyes to the plaque to the Roeblings. At some point he memorized the wording, just because he thought he should, that it might be a clever thing to trot out...John Roebling *who gave his life to the bridge;* Emily Roebling, *back of every great work we can find the self-sacrificing devotion of a woman*...Then he's past the tower and running downhill toward Brooklyn. He's gotten through the worst. The red capitals of the Watchtower sign weirdly majestic to his right—the crazy shit people get into during their time on earth...

"Skinker's wife."

That was a little game Dan was playing with himself. Pretending he didn't know her name. Not wanting to expose himself in that way, admit that he knew her name.

Mrs. Skinker.

The wife of Jedediah Skinker...

Before that, she'd had a couple McJobs—her only real job was as a legal assistant at the midtown firm Fordyce, Crandall; before that, modeling...Japan...and that funny fact that she came from Massachusetts, one town over from Gwen. "The nice town, with the boarding school, the Colonial houses, and when we were little, a hunt club still." Dunning—the town where Gwen's brother, Bobby, was now a sergeant in the six-man police force, catching teenagers partying by the Nautauqua River after graduation, driving the veterans in an open car for the Memorial Day parade. Gwen had shyly let it slip, half embarrassed, in Mary's first days of preschool that she couldn't believe it but there was a mother at the school whom she knew—or sort of knew—well, didn't exactly know, but had known...

"Did you say hi?" he'd asked impatiently—already annoyed by this woman who had some hold over his wife.

"I did! I said hi to her. Even though I really only knew her sister...gosh." She became atypically self-absorbed for a moment; smiled to herself, said softly, "She was a model. Can you believe it? Someone from Dunning? She went all the way. Not just magazines but magazine *covers*..."

Dan had promptly changed the subject. He didn't like to see his wife beholden. He didn't like to see her in awe of someone. Not Gwen. Shortly thereafter, of course, he met the woman himself, at the parents night when he had spoken to Skinker. *Why, she's just a drunk!* he remembers thinking. The great Mrs. Skinker—his wife's hallowed childhood pal—no more than a public drunk! He'd said as much to Gwen, but it didn't seem to register. "She's so incredibly poised," she'd said another day. "She'll stand there at school, not talking to anyone, with no self-consciousness at all about it. I could never do that. *I* always have to pretend to be doing something." Dan had coughed and excused himself—was it up to him to tell her that Skinker's wife was simply practicing the extreme conservation of movement of the wildly hungover?

He feels almost cheerful as he presses along now. The scope of it all, the boat traffic on the expansive river, the cool evening air and light. Perfect night for a run.

Why, he wonders, do people have so little self-control? He

doesn't get it. Why does she let herself go? Why not have just a shred of self-discipline? *He* could put her on a program, tell her what to do.

Six out of seven, his draconian rule.

When he isn't on the wagon, as he is now, Dan gets through the weeks ticking off the nights when he doesn't drink at all. Friday nights—sure, all bets are off. If he and Gwen stay in, he sometimes drinks nine beers. Or if they go out to dinner, which they don't do that often, because he sees through the allure of it—prefers Gwen's cooking and toggling between ESPN and the late-night talk shows—he'll have three or four vodka tonics and a bottle of wine: don't kid yourself that you're sharing it. But he *contains* it...Jesus, can't she at least contain it?

Gwen never judges Dan overtly. Gwen isn't judgmental; her message seems to be that she has better things to do than look down on people and criticize choices that have no earthly effect on her. His wife simply never acknowledges that weakness is a possibility. Many times in the past, Dan wished she would criticize him—wished she would at least say *some*thing. On their *wedding night,* just to choose a random example. When he got blind drunk at the bar of the Dunning Inn. For some reason he'd counted on a little wifely nagging out of the gate, a little preemptive guilt-tripping, maybe just a "Really, Dan? Tonight?" when she overheard him asking Bobby to bring him another, this time a double. None came. That was fourteen years ago. None has ever come. A few weeks ago, in anticipation of the Ash Wednesday cutoff looming, he insisted on opening a fresh bottle of white over dessert. She wouldn't even say, *Well, I'm done. I don't want any more,* put the onus on him for whatever happened next. She just watched him out of those pale blue eyes... "Okay." Yearly, he performed this ritual of giving it up altogether and though he dangled that fact repeatedly—"Feeling more well rested these days!"—she wouldn't comment on that either.

She whom he married because he felt alive under her disapproval now voices no disapproval. Long before the Steins' party, Gwen, he realizes now, with the sort of insight only cardiovascular exercise seems to afford him, went silent.

The darkness in his soul makes him afraid that her disgust with him is so total that lighthearted chastisement was off the table forever. But in the moments when he lies beside her before sleep cancels his thoughts, he feels that that is himself talking—"Saint!" and "Sinner!"—and that she, she is more simply...waiting. He curses himself, and sometimes he speaks to her sleeping body: "I promise—" or "I'm really going to—" and he places a hand as lightly as he can on her rib cage, shuts his eyes and prays, "Take me in, take me in, take me in..."

Dan forces himself to sprint the last fifty yards. He tags what he considers the Brooklyn end of the bridge—a lamppost where the walkway flutters out before its long stretch into the borough. Instead of turning around, he snatches the *Times* photo out of the pocket of his windbreaker and looks at it, obsessed bastard that he is. It fucking irks him that the woman's weakness is public knowledge—often, public display. Skinker ought to say something, do something—get after her for God's sake—or for the sake of his children. What sort of a mother doesn't keep herself in hand? Is she habitually drunk in front of her kids? Jesus. Dan scrutinizes the photo for another minute, the wind off the bridge rifling it so he has to hold it open with his two hands. He's furious at himself for not getting the second half of the run over with but he stands there, getting chilly in the breeze as the sweat dries on him. He glances at Skinker's profile—Christ, why doesn't he say anything? In a different way altogether from Gwen, the man looks as if he would consider it beneath himself to comment on his wife's drinking. Or not that, Dan thinks—it was not some prurience that holds him back. The man looks as if he came, long ago, to some constancy in vision of which his reserve on the topic of his wife's drinking is the merest footnote.

People like that, though...Dan shook his head. He crushs the clipping in his hand and starts back up the bridge. People like her...he won't say it aloud, but it's almost as if she needs a smart slap just to get her out of her own head for five minutes.

He runs along, lighter now, faster, the buildings on the other side rising up before him—Brutalist '70s eyesore; the courthouse and Municipal Building—and he pictures her, in her haughty vacancy, ignoring a slap—ignoring an actual slap in the face, impervious, like one of those inflatable dolls. Slap, slap, slap—no reaction. She seems like the kind of person one can't get through to, the kind of person experience will never change. Maybe the initial attraction to Curtis was some type of masochistic urge. Maybe she picked up on his nihilism and knew he'd be the right choice for a night away. Bizarrely, the thought starts to turn him on. It's twisted, but it turns him on—the idea of just fucking her and getting no reaction at all. Hell, he'll take anything that'll get him through this run. He runs faster and faster along the bridge till he's flying. He's the fittest man in this whole goddamned town. He races toward Manhattan, imagining himself giving it to Skinker's wife as she ignored the fuck out of him.

When he was done, he felt for his keys and his MetroCard in the pocket of his windbreaker, ran his fingers through his hair, but hesitated at the entrance to the subway, looking down the stairs to the train. He glanced back toward St. Andrew's Plaza, the building. The office would be mostly deserted by now. But Diane was working late on Madoff...

When he remembered that moment, that moment when, at the bottom of the subway stairs, he had pushed his face against hers and they had kissed and he had realized—*Oh my God*—what was going to happen. The thrill of realization, the anticipation so acute... he stood motionless, reliving it. It had been ecstasy, that moment. He knew that now.

MetroCard in hand, he limped a little going down the stairs to the train, had to grab the handrail like an old man; his muscles were starting to tighten on him. And the whole ride home he had that look on his face that old people sometimes get when they're alone and trying to remember something—half concentration, half confusion—as if someone was keeping them in the dark.

Chapter Fourteen

This guy I know from the training program tells me we're gonna go out to meet some girls at 5757. "You know that's where all the high-end prostitutes hang out," I tell him. "Ha-ha." "Don't laugh," he says. I give him a you-crazy look. He just waits. "Rob went the other night," he says. Now I'm waiting—about fifty yards out of my depth here. "I got a name." Derry takes a card out of his pocket with a big shit-eating grin: "Katya." I told him, no, there's no way—had the Series 7 exam in the morning and I had to spend the night cramming.

Right.

Derry and I get there, we're hanging out with these Russian chicks. Two of them. Katya wasn't there, though—she never showed up. Or maybe that was just a name, you know, like, ASBESTOS POISONING? CALL 1-800-MARGARITA! These two we're with—they both had American names, but they were stage names. "You think we're so dumb we can't pronounce Liubov?" Chris says. One of the girls takes him up on it. She's like, okay, starts going to town on what fucking idiots Americans are. "It's Ukraine, not *the* Ukraine—why you say 'the Ukraine'? You know

Soviet Union? *SSR*—what you think it means? What you think *R* means? It mean 'republic.' Ukraine was republic of Soviet Union." This is when he's asking her where she's from. When she's done, my man Chris lets out a torrent of Russian. Picked up from Sacha—a Muscovite on the desk. Probably said, "I want to have hot sex with your mother's dog." She's laughing, rolling her eyes—"Only Russian? You don't speak Ukrainian?" Well, after that, whenever we wanted to refer to the night we'd say, "Only Russian? You don't speak Ukrainian?" although let's say I wasn't all that hot on referring to the night. The other one's softer, more subservient...Chris is digging the bossy one but then this deeply, deeply unappetizing guy shows up—swarthy dude, gold bracelets, pinkie ring—and "Lisa" gets all excited and leaves us to go sit at his table or, rather, perch at his table, so now we're down to one Russian. Just like that, somebody else comes over to us. Only she's American. I start talking to her because the other one is freaking me out. Too slavish, you know? She was all, 'And how about you, Guy? Do you support any football team in particular?' I just can't do it. Too weird. I close my eyes and imagine getting it on with this girl and I got...nothing. No can do, even with my eyes closed. It's looking like it's gonna be a long night. Chris would never drop a thing once he got going. But this American girl—she's pretty cool. A little freaky. Laughing a lot in odd moments. Really loudly. Really crazy laugh. Tall! Like a model. Dyed-blond hair—dyed-blond-as-hell–platinum hell. Keeps looking over her shoulder like some kinda druggie. But turns out to be kinda fun. Ironic, like. She gets jokes. I buy her a drink and I'm like, "What about you, you from Ukraine too?" "No," she says, doing the other girl's accent. "I from Massachusetts. Republic New England." "Ooh, the Bay State," I say. "Didn't know they had hookers there." I get really embarrassed—really red in the face. Oh my God, I wanted to die. Obviously, you don't say it, right? You don't refer to the fact. That must be, like, Hiring a High-End Hooker 101. Solicitation for Dummies. I am so over my head here. It made *dating* look good. But she gives me this deadpan look and finally—finally—she laughs. Finds it funny. That freaky laugh. So I buy her another drink—a cosmo. Cosmos were in then—had just gotten in. She could put it away. Drained the second one before I finished paying. I get her another, tell her to slow down, I can't afford drinks at these prices. Again—what a thing to say. How was I gonna afford her, right? We went back to Chris and his chick but it wasn't that fun—Chris has to, like, be the star of it all, you know? And he starts eyeing my girl and I'm like, fuck this, and I think she was too. Yes, like a mega-dork, I thought she liked me. Liked *me*. We kinda go off by ourselves and I lose track of Chris. (Chris, by the way, just to let you know how that worked out, passed out on the subway, woke up at the end of the R line with no cash in his wallet, and, get this, his *Blockbuster video card* gone. Five hundred bucks and free rentals, I guess. No idea how he got there. Sun's rising. Stamp on his hand from a Chelsea nightclub. Said the last thing he remembered was getting in a black car with Lisa, the hairy guy, and the sycophantic girl. That was my buddy Chris's night.)

So I go off with this girl and I'm starting to relax but that wasn't good enough for me, apparently, 'cause this wave of determination comes on, as it sometimes does, and I'm like, fuck it, I'm gonna get seriously, seriously hammered. I was so stressed. So stressed. We're working these crazy hours, you know. We were second-year analysts—working eighty- or hundred-hour weeks...I had a share in a house in Hampton Bays, seventy-five hundred bucks, I went out for one night all summer—that's how that amortized. I was supposed to be dating this Greenwich girl—Vivi, who I met through Angie Frye who was on the desk with us—and it was just so…beat. "If you don't want to be in a relationship, Guy, just tell me!" "Well, I guess I am sort of—" "What? What, you think something's wrong with me? You don't know how lucky you are!" Whereas this hooker's the coolest thing ever. A revelation. She didn't talk too much but she wasn't, like, the silent/judgmental type either. I mean, obviously, I guess. Not much in it for her if she was judgmental…but you felt like she actually thought everyone was a fucking compromised asshole—except for me. I felt like I was really entertaining. Like she really, really liked *me*. We had a bunch of gin and tonics and we tried to go out dancing down in the West Twenties but we got dissed by some shithead bouncer said I was too corporate. I started screaming my head off at him. "Prone to overreaction"—that's what my year-end evaluation said that year. I said, "Fuck it, let's go back to my place." She's all, "Yup." I was too wasted to start stressing but I wasn't totally sure she was a prostitute. I.e., I wasn't totally sure she was going to put out for money. It was confusing. I kinda felt like I wanted to date her…but at the same time I was worried—I'll admit it—I was worried about the actual transaction. She smoothed that over, though. We go back to my place—honestly, I was embarrassed to be taking her there, call girl or no. Place was suuuuuch a fucking sty. I had blown off my roommate a few months before and moved into a studio on West Eighty-Seventh 'cause I patronized a bar near there. I had a cleaning service come once a week and dig me out but I think they hadn't shown up or something 'cause there were pizza boxes everywhere and Chinese food open—in the bed! It was seriously gross. I started cleaning up, throwing shit into the trash, I was trying to explain that while I was gross,

I wasn't *that* gross, and she's like, "Don't worry about it, *Guy*." "Take it easy, *Guy*"—she'd been kinda riffing on my name all night. I felt like an idiot having given her my real name. "Hi! I'm Guy DeGroat and I'll be your client for the evening!" My name's pretty uncommon and I knew she'd remember it. But for some reason—for some reason, I don't know...God, I don't know what's wrong with me—bluhhh! I wanted her to know my name. I wanted to make a connection with her. I wanted—I *wanted* her to remember me. I was still thinking I'd, like, pull a Richard Gere, ha, and save her from all that—still thinking I'd be dating her...except I knew somehow she wouldn't date me. I knew I wasn't good enough for her.

I had a cane from when I hurt my foot playing squash at the River Club. She found it lying around somewhere. I put on a Velvet Underground CD and she was dancing around to it. She was dancing around using the cane, kinda vaudeville, modeling it...then she turned it upside down and she sang "Sweet Jane" and then she sang "Oh, Sweet Nuthin'," just totally deadpan, staring at me...it kinda freaked me out. It was turning into kind of a downer vibe so I changed it up, put on some hit music station, and she sang that Ace of Base song that was so big. God, it takes me back, that shitty music—that radio station, when I got to the city..."Everybody hurts!" And then we did a duet too...we're both leaning into the cane/microphone. She was really good. Not a great singer, her voice was kind of low and breathy, but a fucking amazing presence. Then she made me do something. "Come on, *Guy*, what are you—scared?" So I did "Over the Hills and Far Away" really loud—mega–air guitar—oh my *God*, kill me now! Look at me—I'm turning red just remembering it! We polished off the Famous Grouse and then we did it on my futon. But before we did it, she's like, "You're gonna have to pay me, you know." "Oh, shit—right." She told me it was five hundred dollars. "No shit." "Well, what'd you think?" "No, no—it's cool." I had eighty bucks in my wallet and I had left a hundred in the drawer for the cleaning people who hadn't come. I talked her into letting me give her a deposit. By then, of course, I didn't want to have sex with her so I just sat down on the futon, turned on the TV, started flipping channels. But as I am watching TV she's, like, unbuckling my belt. She starts giving me a blow job. Holy shit, she's an actual prostitute. She's a prostitute! And right then I realize she's beautiful. I'd been talking to her all night and thinking she was fun and kinda cool and then suddenly I saw she had this perfect face, perfect features under all the makeup, and just—well, to see her degrading herself... She got me turned on, though, so I hauled her up and had sex with her. Kinda glad to get it over with, to tell the truth! She was pretty quiet, didn't say much during it, looked kinda blank. She was on top...she was *reeeealllly* quiet afterward—I mean, dead silent, staring, her arms around her knees, and I thought, *Oh no, this is gonna be like the other week when I cheated on Vivi,* and it was fun to a point but then after I fucked her, this girl starts crying and telling me she wants to transition laterally from the account side to creative and she doesn't believe in Santa Claus. Those were the days, man... Then I fucking remembered I had the Series 7 exam in the morning and I dragged out the binder to study. Big surprise, I couldn't concentrate. I got the brilliant idea to take some speed—not real speed. I'd ended up with my roommate's bottle of ADD drugs and I took a couple here and there so I could cope. I offered her some and she looked kinda mad and said, "I don't do drugs." I sat there trying to study with my eyes glazing over, and I did that for maybe five minutes while she wandered around looking through my stuff. Finally she starts flipping channels and there's this movie on, you know, one of those flicks chronicling someone's "descent into alcoholism." *Days of Wine and Roses,* I think it was Jack Lemmon—I know it was. Great flick! Great flick... 'Course I started watching it with her. She was way into it—she'd shush me if I tried to talk. We sit there drinking Ricard with water—that's all I had left in the cupboard—and watching this movie. God, what a crazy night! What a fucking crazy night! Sometimes I'm sitting on the couch with Ann staring at *Seinfeld* and my mind flicks back to some incident from my twenties and I just can't believe that what I remember happening happened. We actually sat there and watched this Jack Lemmon film for, like, two hours. Then she found this backgammon set I had stowed away somewhere—monogrammed leather backgammon set; Vivi had way level-jumped on the relationship and given it to me for my birthday like two weeks into dating. "You wanna play?" I asked her. We sat there and played backgammon till three in the morning. She wasn't bad but I still crushed her—ha. I ordered my usual hangover cure from the deli—got one for her too—two bacon-egg-and-cheeses on a hard roll. We decided to eat at my kitchen table. That and my futon—first furniture I ever bought. We ate there, all civilized. She put on my Dartmouth Squash T-shirt. She's like, "Oh, were you friends with George Voorhees?" I'm like, "What the hell? How the hell do you know him?" Turns out she went to Dunning. *Dunning!* The hooker I hired was a day student at Dunning. I don't even know what day it is anymore. How the hell did you get into *this?* I ask. So she told me.

When she was little she wanted to be a model and her mom wanted her to be a model. She didn't remember whose idea it was originally. Point was, it's not like her mom made her do it. They both thought she should do it. Although she did say she was doing it before she could remember. Her dad was an older guy—really old—and he died, and the mom, who sounds like a real piece of work, raised her and her sister. Before long she's getting into all this weird shit with me—Guy DeGroat! I must've had some nice-guy aura. Like, it wasn't her real father, her real father was some hookup in a roadside bar who she never met…and I'm telling her about my evil stepmother, how my parents had to give me growth hormones so I wouldn't be five two…she tells me the photographer in her town who her mom took her to at ten was always all over her and, like, devirginized her at thirteen, but she got really pissed when I asked if it had scarred her for life. "Would I be talking about it if it had scarred me for life?" Though she did say that when she told her mom she wanted to quit, her mom shut her right the fuck down. They needed the money, maybe? Big, rambly, falling-apart house…She was doing print ads for local stuff—car washes, pizza places. I don't know. One day she went to New York on a bus. I still remember weird facts about that night…When Ann and I were living in Tokyo years later, it all came back to me, her spiel about the modeling over there. That's where she ended up; she lived in Paris for a year but she got big in Japan. "We'd get there and we'd just work…it was brutal. They'd take you from the plane, put you in a van, and drive you right to a shoot. You'd work twelve- or fourteen-hour days." And I guess, unlike the other girls, she was drinking and going out to clubs and one day she was hungover and she lost her shit at some big-deal Japanese photographer and she started screaming at him, telling him he was trying to mind-fuck her, and that he was fucked and Japan was fucked and all the people were fucked and she started throwing shit and called the other girls cunts—whipped the *c* word right out—and she went so crazy, kicking people and scratching and knocking over camera equipment and ripping her clothes, they had to drag her away and sedate her. Not a hugely great move, career-wise. She was hospitalized for three days and her agent called her up in the hospital and dumped her. She called home and her mother chose that moment to tell her her father, who she'd loved, wasn't her real father. Like she'd been holding that little bomb in reserve in case she needed to drop it, ruin a life. She didn't know what to do and she was scared about money. When she got out of the hospital she called a girl she knew from New York, an Australian girl, not a model, just someone she knew from partying in New York. The girl was living in Tokyo, working as a hostess at one of the men's clubs. They wait on the men and flirt with them and the men say titillating things to them—it's a form of relaxation in an uptight society. The girl got her a job and to be more popular, she dyed her hair blond because they like blondes. She slept with a few of them. It just sort of segued into that. Sounds like she was kinda checked out. Kinda numb. When she got back to New York she thought that phase of her life was over. She'd gotten her BA somehow, doing it part-time wherever she was, correspondence, I don't know, and a friend was supposed to be helping to get her a paralegal job somewhere. She was lonely, lonely, lonely, though, and one night a man she knew from Japan—call him a client, I guess—came to town and called her and since she had nothing better to do, she got all dressed up in some high-fashion outfit and lots of makeup and went to meet him in some fancy midtown place...He stood her up, though. She was really, really miffed because she'd been getting attitude from the bartender, and her tab by the time she realized the guy wasn't going to show was large. Hell, one drink in one of those places is twenty bucks. I really don't understand what money she was living on at this point. She said she borrowed some from her sister but then her sister got pissed and cut her off and she didn't have any anyway. Another guy started chatting her up and from some odd comment he made it sank in, even though she was pretty wasted, that he thought she was a prostitute, so she went with it. Partly just as a joke to herself, partly to see how it would pan out—roll the dice, you know—she did nothing to correct the impression. They went back to his hotel room—some cheesy conference hotel like, you know, the Hyatt on Sixth Avenue—and in the morning when she woke up there was a thousand dollars on the bedside table. In hundreds, I remember she told me. It was in hundreds. She thought about returning the money or just leaving it there in the hotel room, but it didn't really resonate as some watershed moment for her so she kept it. That was maybe a year, year and a half before I met her. I didn't ask her how many times she'd been back to the place. She said she went there sometimes, and that she got hooked up with Petra Annikov—Google it if you don't know—but that this paralegal job was really supposed to materialize. I still remember what she said. She said: "I think I would enjoy working in a corporate atmosphere." Isn't that funny? Sweet, really...I just kept going back to the fact that she had gone to Dunning, even though she didn't graduate, and she got on that bus to New York. I was floored! I mean, we played them! "But you must meet people you know from there!" I said. She said no, the worlds were pretty different. That was back in the days of, you know, Eurotrash, and the city was different then. There was no e-mail, people could get lost, and they did get lost. She said knock wood, she'd never run into someone she knew. "This is a generation whose only reference is to college," she said—I got the feeling she was quoting someone, that someone had laid this line on her—"and I didn't go to college." I don't know what it was, but talking about Dunning and boarding school, she was asking me what sports I played—it was such a turn-on. The speed must've kicked in, I was wide, wide awake, so we did it again and it was—

It was so fucking late, maybe four in the morning., and fuck it if I didn't still have the goddamn Series 7 test in the morning. I started to sober up the minute the night faded. In a way—in a *way*—I felt a little cheated. You know, I wanted my "I hired a prostitute" story and instead I felt like I'd paid a friend of a friend to have sex with me. I—I got kind of dickish. I was like, So, what do you charge for this, what do you charge for that. I'm like, What would you do if someone wanted to have a threesome with you and another girl. What would you do if someone wanted to have anal sex with you. She gave me this blank look and said, "Charge more, *Guy*. Charge double."

At dawn I went out to get money from the ATM. I came back to the apartment and I paid her what I owed her but I only had twenties from the cash machine and I also owed her for the sandwiches 'cause she had paid and I couldn't come up with exact change. By this point I was trying to get her out of there, so I'm going, "Keep it, keep it, keep it." "Nope, I won't." "Well, then I'll keep it!" Back and forth like that. Finally she takes a twenty-dollar bill and rips it in half. Starts laughing this crazy laugh. I'm like, "What the fuck? That's American currency you're destroying! I could report you!" That was the last thing I said to her—what a weenie-ish thing to say, huh? I hated myself for it. Chris called then, from a pay phone in Sheepshead Bay. "Dude, you gotta send a car service out here to get me." And when I hung up, she was gone.

I sat there shaking, I felt so bad, and trying to study and I showered and shaved and went in and somehow, mercy of God, I passed.

Chris and I went out for drinks the next weekend and after a couple beers, I told him I slept with her. I wanted to correct the impression he had that I hadn't gotten laid. I shouldn't have. You couldn't trust Chris. I felt really bad. But what did *I* do? I was tired of his always having the upper hand, you know, ragging on me about Vivi. I was gonna leave the stuff out about Dunning, keep that to myself, but Chris is a fucking bloodhound—he could get anything out of me even if I knew he was gonna turn it against me. And Chris had a chip on his shoulder about boarding school, so I knew it would come back to bite me in the ass. He's like, "Man, oh man." The rumor got around the office. I was scared shitless. They'd fired a guy for going to a strip club, for God's sake. Okay, he'd tried to expense it—I wasn't that stupid. But I lived in utter fear for weeks on end. I felt nauseated all the time. I ended up with an ulcer! Twenty-three and I had an ulcer! When the gossip faded, Chris asked me about her and I said I hadn't seen her again and he said he'd dug her up and *he'd* seen her and he'd passed her on to this complete fucking shithead John Curtis. It was, like, the worst day of my life. Chris was annoying, but man, I hated John Curtis. A real vile, despicable person. He'd walk around with this expression on his face—smuggest motherfucker. I just wanted to kill him. I don't even know how we knew him. He wasn't in the training program with us. You know what I did? It was so pathetic. I *went* to 5757 to try to warn her about the guy. 'Course she was nowhere near there. No one was—no Russian girls, nothing. I got a twenty-dollar gin and tonic and didn't even drink it. I wasn't gonna ask Chris if Curtis ever called her, so, I mean, I never found out what happened to her.

Except then I did.

Eighteen months ago she showed up at the new-parents night at school. She wasn't new—she already had one through. But her second kid was starting. I was new, though. Ann and I were new, so excited to be there among the chosen...It took a minute—a few minutes—because of course she's actually a brunette. Mrs. Davidson was talking and I was staring across the room at her—and when I got it, when I figured out how I knew her, I almost shat myself.

I acted like a total dick, I'm sorry to say. I didn't say hi to her—well, I pretended not to know who she was. I cut her. I was so jittery I couldn't talk to anyone, couldn't concentrate on anything. I kept refilling my wine, couldn't talk to Ann at all, was kind of a jerk to her too—we had it out in the cab going home. Not that I mentioned *her*. I was just wigging out, to be honest, totally wigging out. I'd wondered what had happened to her once or twice—okay, a thousand times—but I mean, it never occurred to me that she would go mainstream. If you'd asked me, I'd have said she'd leave New York and live in some second-tier suburb—you know, condo near the train kind of thing—piece something together. Get old quick. Or some alterna-life in Europe. Married to somebody who couldn't see past the American. I would have figured that that'd be all she could have gotten. Shows you how shallow I am. After I'd brushed by her a couple of times and pretended not to see her looking at me, I noticed Jed Skinker—he'd come in late. Think I overheard somebody say, "The Skinkers," and I still didn't get that they were a couple. Not till the end of the night when they took us on a tour through the halls to see the kids' artwork did I grasp it. I mean, not merely mainstream but *Skinker*. Jedediah Hussey Skinker. I *interviewed* with them. It was new-parents night, I guess I said that...Anyway, at some point I'm alone, just kind of staring into space—supposed to be looking at collages on the walls—and she comes over and just says, "Hi, Guy." She looks—I don't know—so beautiful…Like an utter tool, I go, really loudly: "It's very nice to see you again," like all formal, all stiff, like I don't know her. I'm all, "Please take your seats; the concert is about to begin," you know? God, how lame. How frigging lame. "Hi—hi! It's nice to see you again." She says quietly, "It's nice to see you too." I got up in the middle of the night that night and snuck into the bathroom. I've got gold taps and leaping-zebra wallpaper in there and framed photos of Ann's coming-out ball in Newport, and I—I cried like a motherfucker. I just *bawled*. I think in some way I always thought she was holding out for me.

I'm still in investment banking. I've been a managing director for two years. I cover the oil and gas industry. I have three kids, ages four, two, and six months. Ann and I have been married eight years, and we live on Park and Seventy-Eighth, though we're looking for a bigger place because with the baby, it would be nice to have live-in help.

Chapter Fifteen

T he playground's empty," Mary observed, hesitating at the gate. Gwen glanced at the swings and slides, the jungle gym beyond where a toddler entertained himself by climbing rapidly away from a lackadaisical weekend nanny.

"Can't get me! Can't get me!"

"Well, good. You can swing as much as you want."

However neutrally Mary might have intended it, Gwen felt the need to counter her daughter's statement. She pressed through into the playground. "Come, Mary!"

Manhattan at nine a.m. on a chilly April Sunday. Heading for her usual bench, Gwen felt it too, the disenfranchisement of a day and time that in other towns meant church or the running club or a bake sale, whereas the city seemed freakishly deserted, a post-storm wreck of a place, trash on the streets, overflowing the cans; hardened mounds of snow so old and dirty they were unrecognizable as nature. She stood in front of the bench and beckoned to Mary. "Come, honey!" Gwen had spent the two weeks of spring break up in Massachusetts, returning with Mary a week ago; Easter, coming late this year, was still a week away. After any hiatus from it, the city was capable of asserting its peculiarity in her thoughts again. *How odd,* she'd thought, taking the elevator up with their suitcases, *to live in little boxes stacked above the ground, this is not how I pictured myself at all.*

Mary was considering her mother as if a strange woman had addressed her in a language she didn't speak. With a "Whoosh," now she flapped her arms and flew through the playground gate and off to the bigger kids' jungle gym. Taking a seat, Gwen watched her daughter with only a hint of the anxiety that sometimes beset her, that Mary's tractability meant something dire— that she would be forever overlooked, that she would always dwell, polite and not requiring all that much attention, on the sidelines of this city, which ran on vocal selfishness and greed.

"Can't catch me!" cried the toddler. "Can't catch me!"

"I coming to get you!" the Latina nanny called perfunctorily, not stirring from her bench or looking up from her phone. She was young and pretty, in jeans and boots and a sheepskin-trimmed leather jacket, her hair pulled back in a sleek ponytail. "Coming to get you, Miles!" When she did look up, she and Gwen briefly acknowledging each other, she had the expression of mild disbelief in her eyes that some of the more put-together caregivers got, which seemed to reflect the preposterousness of the job. No doubt the woman who employed her had some big career, resulting in a need for "couple's time," as people called it, on the weekends. Gwen looked at the young woman until she risked being rude.

Another lifetime ago, she herself had interviewed nannies—half a dozen of them, from an agency a colleague of Dan's had recommended. It had never been one of Gwen's expectations, to have a nanny. The term embarrassed her with its false, aspirational connotations of uniformed Irishwomen and FDR's childhood. But she'd come to understand that that's what young mothers with her educational background and professional status did in this city in this economy in this decade. She never had gone for the PhD, but she'd been promoted up and out of the lab at Taurus into project management. The media flak about the conflicts of working moms failed to rile Gwen. When she got pregnant, she felt detached; later, she wondered if the medicalized birth had augmented her sense of being at arm's length from motherhood. There'd been a relief in breastfeeding not having worked out. When Yengsum, from Tibet, started, Gwen felt awkward and stagy taking the baby from her when she returned from killing time on some invented errand (as recommended by the agency, the nanny was doing a two-week trial period before Gwen went back to work), as if the facade of some primal connection might crack before the caregiver's enlightened gaze.

The two weeks had been endless. Gwen counted the hours till she would be released from pretending to have somewhere to go, to have demands on her time. She was much too organized to appreciate having help when she wasn't actually at work. When she read some platitude along the lines of "Nobody ever dies wishing they'd spent more time in the office," Gwen had let out a bark of laughter, thinking she'd be the first. She remembered it vividly: She was standing in the old Lexington Avenue Barnes and Noble. She'd wandered into the store to get out of a persistent rain and was turning over the self-help books stacked on the tables in the front of the store, checking her watch too frequently. With an hour to go, and surprised to find herself missing the baby, Gwen headed, on an inspiration, back toward the children's section to buy *The Velveteen Rabbit* for Mary.

There she saw a sight that unnerved her.

Sitting on the spongy-alphabet floor, sitting in the aisles with their backs up against bookshelves, sitting on the two steps of a makeshift stage propped up in the corner of the room in varying attitudes of boredom, relaxation, enthusiasm, and irritation were a crowd of mostly Caribbean nannies. Playing beside them, climbing onto their laps, crawling over their extended legs, sleeping in newborn prams, were the small white babies and toddlers. A few were laughing; a few were whining; one—somewhere—was crying outright, the sort of desolate childish wail that makes one look twice, just to be sure.

Gwen paused uncertainly. A little girl close by began to whine. She was protesting being strapped into her stroller, back-diving and crying, "No! No, no, no, no!" as a heavy, beleaguered-looking nanny pushed her chest down and struggled with the straps. "We got to go! We got to go, Eleanor!" The woman straightened up and took a breath. "Eleanor, I said we got to go! Mommy's waiting for us!" Gwen wanted to offer to help but knew she must not. She stepped awkwardly around another nanny who was down on the floor on her hands and knees chatting with a friend as, on a mat laid on the floor between two bookcases, the former changed a diaper, pulling a little girl's legs up and out of the way and clapping on a Pampers with such a matter-of-fact motion that Gwen winced. She winced, and as she tried to push on toward *The Velveteen Rabbit*, she found she could not move. She stood there, squinting and listening to the crying, the wailing, the whoops of laughter, the chatter. A fetid smell of diapers and milk and wet cloth permeated the muggy room.

"No-wa, no-wa, no-wa, no!"

"We got to go, Eleanor! We got to go!"

"Sorry," Gwen said, flushing, to no one in particular. And she forgot all about *The Velveteen Rabbit*, turned, and fled the store.

It wasn't till weeks afterward—after she had told Yengsum apologetically that it wasn't going to work out, after she had given notice to her boss at Taurus ("I find I want to stay home with my child"), after she herself had headed to Barnes and Noble with Mary on a rainy Wednesday afternoon—that Gwen was able to ask herself what on earth had derailed her.

The children weren't suffering, after all. Some of them had better nannies, some of them had worse. Gwen Hogan dealt in constants and variables, in empirical evidence collected over time; the chances were slim that this discrepancy would affect them unduly in their later years. Nor was Gwen such a bleeding-heart liberal that she couldn't view a group of young- to late-middle-aged women making between $350 and $750 a week without wanting to start a picket line. (In fact, she was the inverse: a cold disparaging liberal, voting the straight Democratic ticket year after year out of a clannish loyalty that felt more and more like a vise.) Growing up, Gwen had never had anything material to be ashamed about—Camilla had made sure of that. But it was as if, in the moment that she paused in the bookstore, Camilla became obsolete. Gwen realized, quelling a convulsive sob, that her mother was no use to her now. Work hard. Do well. Gwen had done both—she had always done both. But shame had arrived in her life anyway, like some unwanted freebie that came in a package with her education, her career, her quick surprised slide into an urban life, when she saw a group of mostly black women working on their hands and knees as domestic servants, hired by people like herself.

Not that Camilla had destroyed her entirely. "Too lazy to take care of her own kid," she could hear her mother saying.

In no way did that fit into Camilla Babineau's moral diorama. It's not that Camilla would have found the hiring of immigrant help unconscionable. It was simply nothing she would ever have had anything to do with.

That night, Gwen told Dan that she thought she'd better stay home until Mary was in school. She called up and, trembling, quit the job she had trained years to do. She went on, protesting to her boss, "Maybe if it wasn't for the commute..." until she realized he hadn't argued. The conclusion was as predictable to him as it was cataclysmic to her. She felt mad, as if she were experiencing a lapse in the continuity of who she was. She kept waiting for someone to stop her—if not her boss, then—oddly enough—her mother, so proud, underneath the no-more-than-I-expected front, of the Ivy League degree and the master's! Or Dan. She realized, sitting in the playground with the baby a few weeks later—the surprisingly delightful baby, Mary, her consolation in all of this and, soon, her friend—in the very same park where she was sitting this morning—after having embarked on her new life as a stay-at-home mother that if she hadn't necessarily believed he'd argue with her (Dan's mother, Connie, had stayed home and raised five boys, after all), she had assumed he would at least be surprised, even shocked by the suggestion. "Are you serious?" she had expected him to ask, floored by the news. "You mean, just give it up? Quit? After all these years?"

In fact, Dan had absorbed the sea change instantaneously, as if he, too, had predicted it, his eyes sliding away from her as she prepared to defend the decision she thought he would want to grill her about. Instead, he began to talk quickly, and vaguely, about modern mores and the importance of making sure one made the right decision for one's own family and didn't simply get swept up in what everyone else was doing. She was about to thank him for that when he pressed on. "Just because some women are totally career-obsessed...After all, we want a big family, right?"

When, as a child, Gwen came home teary from some injustice another child had visited on her, Camilla had never failed to point out Gwen's probable role in the incident. And, to be fair, because she had anticipated Dan's objections, Gwen had made her voice very sure when she told him. She wanted it to be clear that she had already made up her mind.

There was a freestanding building on the south side of the park that housed the public bathrooms. When a door banged, both Gwen and the Latina nanny started. Someone was emerging from the women's side. Gwen put up the front page of the *Times* she'd brought so as not to stare at the resident homeless woman who, she assumed, would emerge, pushing a shopping cart.

On the jungle gym, Mary got halfway across the monkey bars, hung there for a minute with a philosophical look, then dropped to the ground.

But it wasn't the homeless woman. It wasn't the shopping cart after all. An incredible sense of luck stole over Gwen. She stared at the paper's headlines for a minute, as if the luck might evaporate were she to try to pin it down. At last, she—who never won so much as a prize at a raffle—had been singled out for favor. Tentatively, she closed the newspaper, leaving her thumb in her page. It was Philippa Lye. Philippa Lye in her fur hat and that amazing coat with all three children in tow. The boy was complaining that he wanted a snack, and Philippa had the oddest reaction. Normally when Gwen saw her with her children, she was short with them, peevish and even a little mean. But today she gave the boy a pat on the shoulder and said, in an ethereally calm voice, "I'm sorry. I wish I had something, darling."

Displeased, the boy began to cry.

Gwen stood and gave an ineffectual little wave. "I have snacks!"

Philippa froze, like a deer on the lawn of a house—and just as lanky—but when she saw Gwen, she closed her eyes briefly, as if in relief, as if some specific dread had been in her mind, not simply a reluctance to socialize in the park.

"Hello, Gwen." She made her way over. Again the voice was strangely calm—like the voice of a refugee, Gwen thought, who could not be shocked by any postwar trifle.

"Hi, Phil." To Gwen's surprise, Philippa kissed both of her cheeks. Not expecting the second one, Gwen drew back, and Philippa's lips caught her forehead.

"Oops!" said Philippa. "*Deux bisous.* I never got rid of the habit. So affected, I know."

"No, I'm just—does he want something?" Gwen said impatiently, as if she were annoyed. "Is he hungry—Sebastian?"

The four children, Mary and Philippa's three, had watched this adult encounter as if held in abeyance. Referred to now, they sprang again to life.

"I'm hungry, Mummy!" Sebastian took the cue.

"Don't complain, Sebastian," the older girl instructed promptly, shooting Gwen the quick apologetic look of a child used to making up for parental lacunae.

"Mo-om!" yelled Mary from the jungle gym, but when Gwen called, "Yes? What is it?" she didn't respond, as if she had merely been staking a claim.

The little blond one, silent in a misbuttoned toggle coat and rubber boots, edged closer, her eyes on the snacks.

"I've got edamame, pretzel sticks…oatmeal cookies!" Gwen flushed. She sounded like a barker at a carnival. She burrowed in her reusable Whole Foods grocery bag, suddenly aware of how unattractive it was, and drew out translucent snack cups with slow, stiff fingers.

"She won't mind?" Philippa said, nodding her head toward Mary.

"Huh?"

"She won't mind sharing her snacks?"

"Oh! No." Gwen understood belatedly. "She's not like that." Sebastian took handfuls of everything offered and shoved them in his mouth indiscriminately. "Do *you* want something?" Gwen asked the little girl, Ruth, and was appalled at how curt she sounded. "What would you like?" she tried more gently, but found her voice still came out sharply.

Ruth said nothing, blinking her large eyes at the food.

"Mummy?" The older girl's face was all twisted up. "Can we?"

"Go on, Laura!"

It was the older one who got her mother's grief, Gwen saw, who, perhaps too often, made up for her failures. "Go on, Ruth," Philippa said, "take a cookie."

"Take two!" Gwen insisted, in her barker persona, pressing them on the older girl, who said in an overmature voice, "Thank you very much." She turned to her younger sister. "Here, Ruth. Say 'Thank you' to Mrs.—"

"Hogan!" Gwen filled in. "Mrs. Hogan. But you can call me Gwen."

"Thank you, Mrs. Hogan."

Mary had started going manically back and forth on the monkey bars—hoping it would make them notice her, no doubt. "She's got so much energy," Philippa said, sitting down heavily on the bench and watching Gwen's daughter as her little girl and boy stood finishing their cookies, also watching Mary. The older girl lingered at the end of the adjacent bench, twisting herself uncertainly over the back. "Yeah, that's Mary for you," Gwen said, rather proudly, still holding the bag of snacks in case she should have to provide second helpings.

"Laura, come on." Philippa craned her neck around. "Go take them to play. If you stay with us, they'll never go play."

"And how old are you?" Gwen asked—she who never drew out a strange child.

"Seven," the girl said promptly but without the performative instinct that animated most children's answer to the question; it seemed to embarrass her to draw attention to the fact. She looked away. A moment later her eyes returned to assessing her mother.

"Mummy—"

"Laura, please!" Philippa cried, with enough volume so that the nanny looked up from her phone and over at them. She went on, aggrieved, at the girl, who seemed to shrink in her shoes. "Stop asking questions! Go and push Ruth on the swings, as I said! Stop loitering over here, for God's sake!"

With no visible reaction, the girl did as she was told. She trotted to her sister and attempted to pick her up, then half lugged, half dragged the now-giggling little girl toward the swings. "Come on, Ruthie! Come on, Ruthie! Let's go swing!" When Laura began to push her younger sister, Mary ran over and took the swing next to Ruth. "I'll swing! I'll swing too!" The boy Sebastian noted the girls but made no move to join them, eventually heading to the jungle gym, the ladder of which he began to beat with a stick he picked up, ignoring the toddler boy who, puppy-like, tried to engage him, calling from above, "Can't catch me! Can't catch me!"

Philippa eyed Gwen's bag. "Could I have one?"

"Oh, of course! I'm sorry."

Philippa took a cookie and ate it slowly. Gwen had never seen someone less interested in her children's play; most mothers furtively watched theirs all the time, pleased by their activity. Philippa might have been alone in the park for all the attention she paid them.

"Do you come here most weekends?"

"Oh, well—I mean, we live near here," Gwen said.

"Do you ever run into anyone from school?"

"Oh, no." Gwen laughed. "It's too far east."

Absently, Philippa reached into Gwen's bag and took another cookie. "I like it over here, though. I like Yorkville. I started out here."

"After college?" Gwen ventured.

"Oh, I didn't go to college. I didn't even finish high school. I took a Peter Pan bus to New York City—I wanted to be a model." She gave a little laugh. "It's funny that it all worked out. I mean, that was my idea—my ambition. And I just—did it."

Not thinking, Gwen managed to be wry. "I heard you were big in Japan."

But Philippa didn't seem to hear. She stared past the playground toward the river, though you couldn't see the river; it was hidden by the trees.

She broke the silence with a non sequitur. "Do you get lots of useless presents at Christmastime, Gwen?"

Gwen thought the question strange. "Not really, no."

"Don't you?" She looked at Gwen. "We do. Well, I mean, I don't—my husband does. People—they want to curry favor with him. They put him on their lists."

"I'll bet," Gwen said. "Big banker and all."

"We get these awful fruit baskets and totally inedible chocolates. The back office, the middle office, clients...we get terrible wine. Bottles of obscure liqueurs. Gift certificates to useless stores. He used to leave everything at work—give it to the staff or, I don't know, throw it out, I guess."

"Sure." Gwen nodded. "You don't want to have too much stuff."

Philippa frowned; apparently this wasn't the point at all. "One time I went into his office near Christmas and I saw it all sitting there, and I said, God, here you're getting all this stuff and I don't get a single thing. I mean, no one, but no one, feels he has to curry favor with me. Ever. Or ever has."

"Hmm."

"So I got him to promise to bring it home from then on."

Gwen made a broad gesture as if to say, *Why not?*

"I like it," Philippa said seriously. "I can't explain it; I enjoy having fruit baskets and wine baskets and all those presents around. It makes me feel Christmassy, you know? Cup runneth over!"

"I could see that," Gwen said, though in truth she was suspicious of any gifts not exchanged among family.

"Chocolate-covered cherries. I like knowing they're in the cupboard."

"Yeah."

"Peppermint hot-chocolate mix."

"Right."

"California wine, cheese, crackers, and grapes gift basket."

"Okay."

"What is it, April now?"

"April fifth," Gwen said primly. *Depend on me to supply the obvious.*

"Well, a few days ago, I climbed up onto a stool—I mean, I had to climb up on a stool because they were put away in a high cupboard—and I got down that box of chocolate-covered cherries. Here we are in April, right? And these were from Christmas. Can you imagine anything more disgusting?"

"They don't sound that bad," Gwen said diplomatically.

"I tore the package open intending to eat one or two, and I ate double that, even though they were just horrible. They were worse than I'd imagined. I must've been craving sweets. I don't know what got into me."

"Well, sometimes—"

"Anyway, I'm lying."

"Oh. You are?" Gwen shifted her position slightly, glanced out at the swing set.

"I didn't eat a few—I ate the whole box. I kept eating them and eating them... It was just bizarre, because if I had never kept them in the first place, I mean, they wouldn't have been *available* to me to gobble up. It never would have happened. It was so... odd... so pointless... to keep something like that in a high cupboard for three months and then gobble them all up on some random Thursday..."

Gwen felt warm in her fleece and down vest. "Well," she said, "no harm done, I guess."

They watched the children. Mary was swinging higher and higher, pumping herself to great heights, showing off. She looked wildly happy. Embarrassed by the rush of love she felt for the child, Gwen picked up the section of newspaper she had been reading and refolded it.

"It's how I feel about suicide," Philippa said.

"What?"

"It's how. I feel. About suicide."

"Suicide?" Gwen said hollowly. She was lost. She'd thought the story was the weight obsession of an ex-model surfacing.

"You see what I'm saying, don't you?" Philippa seemed to be

prompting her for an even greater degree of attention. The newspaper crumpled in her lap, Gwen made sure not to let her gaze drop to it. "I mean—it's not something I'm about to go and do!"

Gwen nodded uncertainly. "Okay."

"I just like knowing it's there." As Philippa warmed to her point, her voice took on a coquettish, self-congratulatory tone. The story became more of an act. "I like having it in the cupboard—just in case. Do you know what I mean, Gwen?"

"I don't know."

"Like an obscure liqueur. Or…or a gift certificate to a useless store. It gives me…yes! That same feeling of plenty."

Gwen said stiffly, "But you have three children."

"Right." Philippa sat back noisily on the bench. "That's the problem."

"The problem?"

"It's nature's way of calling you out."

Gwen shook her head to show she wasn't getting it. "I'm sorry, Philippa. This is beyond me." She felt even warmer now, as if she were being held too close to a fire. She was beginning to regret the encounter. She had an urge to collect Mary and go home as soon as possible, get on with her day.

Philippa went on imperturbably, "If you're childless and you kill yourself, people judge you as they judge anyone who gives up the fight, but they pity you too—they talk about the 'demons'…'the demons she must have lived with.' But if you're a *mother* and you kill yourself"—she paused; a rhetorical flourish, Gwen could see—"you're just a selfish shithead, aren't you?"

"More or less!" Instead of summoning her empathy, the performance was irritating Gwen. She forced herself to say, "I'm sorry, Phil. I'm sorry it's so difficult."

"Oh, don't be!" Philippa said in a rush. "Don't be! It's probably better. I don't really want to be dead. I don't *want* my eighty million-billion years of nonbeing to commence...It's only the gesture that's alluring. It *is* attractive, isn't it? You can't deny that. Not even you, Gwen."

"I can't?"

"It's damn attractive. It's so...definitive. The way that you can't argue with it. I love that about it. It's such a fuck-you. And they'll know—the people whose fault it is, they'll know it's their fault. They'll make all sorts of rationalizations—'She was always unhappy'—but they'll know."

"But don't you have a nice life?" Gwen said in a small voice. The bench was growing more uncomfortable by the minute, the slats digging into her thighs, her lumbar spine starting to protest.

"Oh, yes. Very nice. But, really, is living better than getting back at someone?"

"Huh."

"Some days it's a toss-up."

The conversation felt like a long setup for a zero-sum game Philippa was running in which Gwen would be inculpated no matter what she said.

"It's about the party, isn't it?" she said dully.

Philippa looked thrown by the specificity of the question, as if it hadn't occurred to her that someone might drill down on the grand statements. "The party?"

"At the Steins'. He—" Gwen swallowed. "John Curtis." She reddened as, with a sickening feeling, she recalled the moment she had attempted to introduce the two of them. But she said the name anyway, wearying of the melodrama and the vagueness. "Minnie's husband. John Curtis."

Watching her, Philippa said, "Of course. You were there. You saw me...see him."

Gwen nodded. "He's an asshole!" she sputtered suddenly. "He's the biggest asshole! I knew him in college." Philippa looked puzzled, but Gwen ran with it. "Confront him, scream your head off! Go to the police, but don't do it. Don't eat the fucking cherries, Phil." She added grimly, "Don't let him get away with it. Don't give him the satisfaction."

"I don't—"

"People like that—he'll never feel remorse. I don't care if you kill yourself ten times over." Gwen stopped. "I'm sorry. God."

Philippa hadn't moved.

"You don't have to talk about it. I'm really sorry."

After a moment, Philippa said quietly, "You know, I could have stayed home like Rose! I could be living in a condo where our old house stood, making ends meet, buying day-old bread and rotting fruit at the grocery store."

"Not you."

"No, but you see, Gwen, my point is, I fucked myself. I completely fucked *myself*. It was vanity that made me think I'd get away, do something..." She intoned without obvious emotion, "Everything that happened to me was my fault."

"But that's not true!"

Phil was shaking her head. "You don't understand."

"I do I'm telling you, I knew the guy! Do you hear me? Curtis. He's beyond...he's a—"

Philippa laid a gloveless hand on Gwen's arm. "You really don't know, do you?" she said incredulously.

"What."

"Are you always the last to know, Gwen?"

"What the hell?" Gwen said rudely, fed up with games.

"Oh, Gwen." Strangely, Philippa began to plead with her, giving her arm a little shake here and there for emphasis. "It wasn't that bad! You have to understand that! I promise you. It really wasn't that bad."

Philippa's trying to persuade her made Gwen afraid. Her eyes sought the children; she counted them to see that they were all there. One, two, three, four.

"I mean, sometimes I'd get this sort of...poverty of thought. It was as if I had nothing in my head. No thoughts. Just a blankness. I couldn't read. I stopped being able to read. Or else I'd become hyperaware of everything—you know, my brain would describe things nonstop: *You are rising from your bed, you are walking across the floor*...I couldn't go to the grocery store. I couldn't go out and buy the paper or a magazine. I became a shut-in. I didn't go outside for a few weeks one time. I know that sounds bad. But it wasn't—it wasn't all that bad. I don't know. I could have gotten over it. People have gotten over worse! But then I had the bad encounter..." She tilted her head back and her eyes searched the gray sky. "And it kills me," she said to the sky, "because I can't say anything. I can't complain." She turned back to Gwen—met her eyes. "Because it was my fault."

The girls had deserted the swings. They ran now, as a pack, to the jungle gym. Sebastian and the toddler boy stood and watched them as they darted up it, off it, circled the swings—some serendipitous game of tag without any rules.

"I mean, he did rape me. It was my fault, but—"

"It wasn't! Stop saying that!"

"No, you stop it, Gwen!" Philippa said viciously, seizing Gwen's arm. "He was *paying* me for it, Gwen. He was paying me for sex. He had hired me for the night! All right? Can't you get that through your naive little head?"

Across the way, the Latina nanny was watching the two of them eagerly, as if her day had brightened beyond all expectations.

Gwen knew she had to get the words out, she must get the words out, but they stuck in her mouth. In frustration, she shook off Philippa's hand. She heard herself pushing the sentence out—making the words audible one by one. "I'm telling you, I knew him in college. He raped a girl in my dorm."

A few girls—if you believe the rumors.

"He's a rapist—that's what I'm saying. I'm telling you, he's a known rapist!" Gwen half threw up her hands, as if the very act of trying to convince Philippa disgusted her. She sat back as if to give up, folding her arms across her chest, but a minute later, she was right back in it. "Did you hear me? This girl in my dorm—there were others. Everyone knew about it. But it was college. It was college," she repeated helplessly. Philippa had no discernible expression on her face. With a final, exhausted effort, Gwen said, "Listen to me, Phil. You've got to listen to me." She enunciated very clearly. "Just because he paid you—"

But at this Philippa sprang to life. "Oh, he didn't pay me!" she said hotly. "That's the thing! He *didn't* pay me, Gwen!" She made fists of her hands and pounded her thighs with them. "Fucking hell!"

In another minute, the children would notice and Gwen would have to go head them off—make up some story to satisfy them.

"He never paid me! Never fucking paid me."

"You mean..." Gwen shied away from formulating a specific question.

"He walked out without paying me! That's what I mean. He got it for free. Not only that, he—he passed me on to his roommates..."

"He never paid you," Gwen repeated slowly, focusing on the one fact.

"No." Philippa shook her head emphatically, like a child. "He left the apartment—he left me there. I thought he was coming back. But I didn't get paid up-front. It was—I don't know—an off night. One of those nights." She seemed to be talking to herself now, sorting her memories into logical order. "At the beginning, he was trying to impress me. He kept talking about his job. Bonds. He was talking about bonds. I just sat there tuning out. Then his two roommates came home—drunk. Real dickhead, one of them, and then a sort of follower-on. Well, the dickhead recognized me. And I knew him. Adam Durban. He'd been kicked out of my class at Dunning for drugs. He knew me and you could see that made—" Philippa hesitated. "It made *him* mad. It was like we were ganging up on him. Durban kept talking about school landmarks, people—you know, trying to piss Curtis off that he had a connection with me. Durban didn't know that we weren't—well, that I was working. The four of us, we all partied together. They had coke...the follower-on made drinks."

Her heart beating furiously, Gwen nodded, aware of the children, shrieking, running, shrieking. *I was just lying there and he was—he was fucking me...*

"He took me into the bedroom and he said, 'I'm going to date you. I'm going to make you my girlfriend. Should I marry you? Oh my God. Maybe I'll fucking marry you. I can see the headline now: "Yale Bond Salesman Marries Hooker." ' Well, I got sick of it. I wanted to get out of there. So I said, 'Please—I wouldn't date you in a thousand years.' Some guys—they like that. You know, you dismiss them and it becomes a game."

"Oh no." If only she had known, Gwen thought, about the polo shirts and the madras shorts, the seriousness with which he had pursued his new look.

The toddler ran toward a pair of pigeons that were pecking

at bits of trash near the park fence. At the last minute, they took off into the air, and the little boy squealed and clapped his hands.

"You see, Gwen, I had to allow him to do it, or he would have really brutalized me. He was yelling at me—'Private-school bitch! Model bitch!' And I had to sort of"—Philippa's voice broke—"pretend I was into it." She broke down and sobbed. "Hell, I don't know! Maybe I was into it!"

"Mom?" That was Mary, jumping from a low platform of the gym down to the asphalt—the first to notice, unused to emotional vicissitudes from a mother.

"Now's not the time, honey. I need to talk to my friend." When Mary hesitated, Gwen raised her eyebrows and repeated firmly, "Now's *not* the time." She found a packet of Kleenex in her bag and handed it to Philippa, whose face was a mess of tears and mascara. Looking directly at Gwen, she said, "I just tried not to complain or anything till it was over."

It was as if the gravitational pull on the bench had increased. Gwen felt so heavy on it that lifting her arm to pass over the tissues seemed almost more than she could do.

Philippa dabbed at her eyes, first one, then the other. Gwen made to say something, but Philippa cut her off, clearing her throat with a loud dismissive sound. "Everyone takes it up the ass at some time or another, right?" she said brightly. "I just happened to be one of the people who was destined to have it be *literal!*" She dragged a sleeve across her nose. Before Gwen could think of what to say, she asked, "Was that the case with the other girls? Do you happen to know, Gwen? Was"—she pressed her lips together before she could go on—"anal rape his signature move, or was that just for me? I always wondered."

At her show of bravado, Gwen put a hand to her mouth. *Don't cry. Now's not the time. Now's* not *the time.* She bit down on the inside of her lower lip. "I don't know."

"Well," Philippa said after a long minute, as if pointing out the silver lining, "with the other two—they just had sex with me. Durban couldn't even do it, he was too fucked up."

"Mom?" It was Mary again, with Laura now beside her, the two girls scrutinizing them from the jungle gym.

Gwen called to them, "Better enjoy yourselves, honey! We don't have too much time left!" The two girls sank to seated positions on the jungle gym platform, as if they'd agreed that the time for running was over.

"Can't catch me! Can't catch me!"

"Maybe I don't want to catch you!" shouted Philippa's boy.

"So, anyway...I never got the money." She attempted a matter-of-fact tone but her face contorted. "I didn't get the money, Gwen. I never got the money. If only I'd gotten the money—I was so poor in those days!" Philippa said. "You have no idea!"

Gwen didn't contradict this. She sensed that this, oddly, was the thing that got to her, that she couldn't stop from getting to her each time she thought about it. It always got to her, and it drove her to the contemplation of the chocolate-covered cherries.

"I was so poor, and he—he did that to me—and he never paid me!"

It was her opportunity, Gwen realized later, to be the voice of consolation and of reason. To tell Philippa that it wasn't, of course, about the money—*I can see what you mean, but...*—that what she needed was long-term psychological help to understand the *real* terrible wrong that had been done her for which not getting the money was only the substitute grievance. Or perhaps, more practically, it was the moment for Gwen to suggest prosecution. She was certain, looking back, that anyone else in her position would have handled the situation much more competently than she. None of those responses came into Gwen's head just then, however.

But the girl who remembered a dollar an older girl had promised her in fifth grade if she switched seats on the bus so the older girl could sit next to her friend; the babysitting family who gypped her because Mrs. Franklin didn't have change for a twenty; the cab she'd taken back to the city from New Jersey on the evening of a blizzard in the mid-'90s with three other Taurus employees but whose entire bill she'd gotten stuck with...

That girl sat stiffly on the park bench. "Well, that's not fair," she said.

"No," Philippa said, wiping under her eyes with her knuckles. The two women eyed each other. "It's not, is it?"

Chapter Sixteen

Their neighborhood Italian was one of those family-owned places that still appealed to a certain type of Carnegie Hill customer—checkered tablecloths, signed photos on the wall. Other patrons, Gwen thought, must have returned with expectations of warmth and recognition, the rosy red-wine glow you could never quite achieve at one of the trendier places. The Hogans dined there a couple of times a month. (Date night, the St. Tim's mothers called it—but the phrase encapsulated everything Gwen had hoped to avoid in marriage.) Tonight Gwen arrived first. The pouty, silver-haired maître d' welcomed her with false enthusiasm— *"Signora, buonasera!"*—and, with a pained flourish, showed her to a table. Dan, he preferred. Dan ran up the bar tab; Dan had a quick, contemptuous authority that people like Silvio recognized. *"Buon appetito!"* Silvio gushed when he seated Dan a quarter of an hour later, turning a kinder eye on Gwen now that he could pair her with Husband Dan. She smiled up at him; something touching and ridiculous about the man's prejudices.

Dan whipped his coat off and hung it on the back of his chair. "Sorry I'm late." Mary had gotten her Easter basket last Sunday;

Dan's Lenten regimen had ended. He had his hand up for a drink before he had fully taken a seat.

"It's okay." It really didn't bother her. She liked sitting in the restaurant, soaking up the setting with no demands on her time. And she still felt, fifteen years in, a sense of anticipation waiting for Dan Hogan—a pride of ownership that the years hadn't taken away.

"Silvio's funny," she said. "I'm pretty sure he recognizes me, but he pretends to be only pretending to recognize me."

"Ha!" Despite the laugh, Dan looked as if he wasn't concentrating on her.

She'd wait till he had his drink to ask him her question.

The place wasn't crowded yet, and their waiter appeared promptly. Dan ordered a vodka martini. "Let's get the wine now too—let it breathe." This was a joke, though one that only Gwen recognized. With an obsequious "But of course—as you wish, sir," the man went off to fetch their thirty-two-dollar bottle of Calabrian red.

Waiting for the drink, Dan drummed his fingers on the table, craning his neck around to the bar every couple minutes to gauge its progress. At last it arrived and he took a long sip from the glass, looked happier at once. Another big gulp and he actually seemed to relax. "We should come here every week. It's good to get out."

"Yeah..." She swallowed. "Dan?" She knew he wanted only to escape tonight and she felt a little ill going ahead with it. But she never got a chance to talk with him. He'd been working late, she went to bed early...

"What's up?"

"I've got to ask you something." It made her self-conscious to ask him for a favor. It wasn't part of their lingo. "It's about Philippa."

"Yeah?" Dan looked wary. "Okay."

Gwen pursed her lips. "God, I hate to bring this up, but—"

"You're doing an intervention? Ha-ha—just kidding. She could use one, though, boy."

Childish antics failed to rile Gwen. She went on, "You know, after the Steins', when we were talking, and we were assuming— well, it turns out it's all true." She glanced at him. "About Curtis, I mean."

"What's true?"

"He did rape her—"

"Wow," Dan said, and she knew at once that it was not a reac- tion to the fact but to her having brought it up.

"—just as we thought."

"O*kay!* Glad we're finally getting a chance to have a nice dinner out together!"

"And I was thinking," she persisted, "well, I was thinking—" Her sheepishness increased as she ventured into his world. "I was thinking she could prosecute him." She felt silly using legalese. "I was thinking maybe there's a chance it's not too late. Is it too late?" she asked softly.

Dan looked flabbergasted. "*She* could?" he said, sounding in- credulous. "*She* could, huh? *I* already am, Gwen! You realize that?"

"No, no, I know—I figured you were," Gwen admitted, "when you said...But I just thought—if *she* were to pursue a conviction of her own, it might help her to...move on. Not that, I'm sure, you ever *really* move on, but—"

"Oh my God!" He ran his hands through his hair. "You know I went after him before, right? I mean, what about me? *I* haven't moved on, for God's sake!"

"What's the statute of limitations on a—a rape? Is there one?"

"Oh! Huh. Jeez. I don't remember."

"No?"

"I mean, yes, of course there's a statute. I could look it up, okay?"

"Could you find out? 'Cause what I'm thinking is that even if it went nowhere, even if she didn't *win*, it would still..."

Ignoring her, Dan put his elbows on the table, his forehead to his palms. When she finished, he raised his head. "You mean for later, Gwen? You're talking about all this for later on, right?" He glanced toward the door in a supreme effort to control himself. " 'Cause, I mean, I've got to focus on the case at hand right now, in terms of John Curtis." Dan paused, thinking how he should phrase it. "You realize I've spent *months* putting this case together. You know that, right?" He saw Gwen opening her mouth to say something but he pressed on over her: "Listen to me, Gwen—I went after him before. Four years ago. When he was at his old firm. I never even told you 'cause we got *nowhere*."

Gwen had stopped talking, was watching him impassively.

"We got down the line, he was totally fucking guilty, and I couldn't do a thing about it!" When Gwen said nothing, Dan practically pleaded: "These guys—they're all so protected. Kerr's probably never done an honest day's work in his life! And what does he have? Billions. If I don't get Curtis this time around, I might as well stop going into work in the morning. I might as well—what'd you say?"

"I said okay."

"Oh! Oh, okay." Dan sat back in the chair, holding his drink. Beside them a young couple on a date were not getting any help with the wine list from the waiter. "Whatever you prefer, sir." "I could not say, sir." "That would be up to you, sir." Dan smiled to himself, remembering those days of youth and cluelessness, glad to be on the other side. Fuck fine wines.

"How is she, by the way?" he asked after a minute. "You seen her much?" He put down the now-empty glass and shook out his napkin. "How is Philippa?"

After a pause, Gwen said, "I've seen her here and there."

"How's she doing?" With studied offhandedness, not looking at Gwen but surveying the crowd that was slowly filling up the restaurant, Dan said, "She was pretty shaken up, right? Running into a guy who—you know." He winced. "That must've sucked, huh?" As if Gwen had responded, Dan said, "Cool, cool."

He was all a-twitch and a-quiver, Gwen noticed. He half rose and moved his chair a few inches; he carefully realigned the salt-and pepper shakers, squinting at them. "She never said anything about him? About seeing him that night, did she?" To the waiter he mouthed, *Another*, pointing at his glass, and to her he said, "I don't want wine yet, do you?"

Gwen's tone was fastidiously neutral. "What are you after, Dan?"

He made a comic grimace. "Sorry! Sorry. It's just—this case is beating me up. The evidence is all there," he said more seriously, "but there's something...weird about it." He rotated his plate a quarter turn, studied it, then looked up at her as if to make an appeal. "The guy *rapes* her and then he—" He stopped abruptly. "You know what? Never mind. Never mind—it's fine. I shouldn't be talking about it."

"But—" Gwen cocked her head to the side. "The Steins? *That* has nothing to do with your case, does it? *She* has nothing to do with your case." When Dan didn't reply at once, just looked highly uncomfortable, Gwen gave a short laugh and said, "I hardly think she's insider trading!"

*　　*　　*

They always got the same things, the chicken Marsala for Dan, the branzino for Gwen. Gwen would eye the ragù, but it was silly to order something like pasta that she could so easily make herself.

"Dan?" she persisted when the waiter had brought Dan's second vodka tonic and left them alone again. "There's absolutely no way, right? I mean, just to be clear?"

"What?" he said, distracted—or pretending distraction.

"I don't think she knows what the stock market is!"

That look from him—that silent sizing-up he was giving her! He fingered the glass but didn't drink. "Not her."

For a second Gwen misunderstood him. "Phew, because you were freaking me out there—" But her husband was watching her unhappily. His face—why, it had pity in it! "Dan?" All at once his meaning dawned on her. She heard the emphasis in those two little words. "No!" She gasped. "Not *him!* I don't believe it!"

But Dan was nodding, inexorably nodding. "'Fraid so."

"Him and Curtis?" Gwen was aghast. "How can that be?"

"Right?" Dan leaned across the table toward her. "It was killing me—killing me! I couldn't get my head around it. Skinker tipping *him* off? That scum of the earth? It was all backward. Then it hit me, Gwen: Oh my God! Curtis and the wife! The compromised wife! It's not your typical insider-trading case at all! You scratch my back, I'll scratch yours...It's blackmail! Curtis is blackmailing him!" He couldn't help but crow now: "We've known for a while."

Gwen looked stupefied. "Oh my God." She shook her head minutely back and forth. "Oh my God. Of course he is!" The young man diagonally across from her shot a look of consternation in her direction, but Gwen couldn't seem to care about whether she was ruining his date. Her voice dropped to a whisper. "Of course he is!"

"Yup. Yeah." Dan tried to catch her eye—he wanted to commiserate. He didn't care about Philippa, but he hated to see Gwen so shaken. "Nice, huh? Real lovely guy, Curtis, isn't he?"

"Does she *know?*"

Dan let out a breath. "I don't think so. I'm guessing no. Skinker's the kind of guy—he's probably kept the whole thing to himself, right? Trying to protect her. How would it benefit anyone for him to tell his wife? Why would he put that on her? She's already kinda fragile, right?" Or was it all an act? Dan wondered. Even without the enabling Skinker wealth, he theorized, Mrs. Skinker would do just fine.

"Right. Right..." Gwen said vaguely.

He drank his vodka tonic and watched Gwen's face, watched her go through a sped-up version of what he had gone through when he realized the Skinkers were involved. She gave a nod as if to herself. "Of course he is," she murmured sadly.

Waiting for their entrées, they talked of Mary. The results of the test she'd taken for a Gifted and Talented spot in public kindergarten would arrive any day now. "She'll ace it!" Dan predicted, glad that Gwen seemed amenable to moving on to other topics.

But when their food arrived, as he was hungrily eating, Gwen suddenly let her fork drop to her plate. "So, is there a way to shield her?" she burst out. "Does she have to take the stand against him? It seems so unfair! She's the victim in all of this."

"Well, I don't know if I'd call her a total *victim*..."

"What? You're kidding me! Why? Because of the prostitution? But she must have been desperate, Dan! Can you imagine how desperate? I don't think that's fair!"

Dan switched his fork over to his right hand and speared a bite of chicken. "The what?" he said so quietly he might have been talking to himself.

Gwen went on hotly, "It's unbelievable, this guy's luck. He hires a prostitute for the night who conveniently becomes Mrs. Jedediah Skinker. He could not have planned it better if he'd tried!" She added vehemently, "God, I hope you get him! I hope you kill him in court!"

Dan laid down his fork and knife. "The prostitution?"

"Well, yes, right? I mean, that's the blackmail—that's what Curtis has got on Jed Skinker, isn't it? On her, I mean." Gwen made a convulsive gesture. "Oh, and don't tell me, on top of all that, he gilds the fucking lily with nursery school, is that right? Did the Skinkers get them in?"

"Oh my God." The expression drained from Dan's face. "Oh my God."

"Excuse my French," said Gwen, who hardly ever swore. "But—"

"The *modeling!*" he intoned. "The *hostessing!*" His disgust with himself was total. His eyes looked as pained as when he had a terrible hangover. "She was a hooker!" he cried under his breath. "She was a fucking hooker!" He gripped his glass. He could have thrown it across the room. "I've got DiNapoli *telling* me those hostess girls sleep with their clients and I'm saying, 'Not her. It's not like that, Frank!'" He couldn't believe it. He had fallen for it. The Skinker mystique! He'd been had again! He could have cried at his sad, benighted state. He was so outraged and dismayed at his own idiocy that he barely noticed that across from him, Gwen had gone white. She was looking at him with horror.

"Some kind of Mayflower Madam situation, was it?" And though Gwen didn't confirm this, he swore again and said, "Jesus

Christ, I knew it! I *knew* it!" After a moment, he amended that to, "God*damn it!* I should have known it."

Her eyes were enormous. "You didn't know."

"What?"

She repeated dully, "You didn't know."

He looked at her—"Oh Jesus, Gwen!" He rushed to reassure her. "No—no! I would have found out!" His wife was going to cry; her face was crumpling. "This has nothing to do with you. I would have found out today or tomorrow! I swear to God, I would have found out! It's amazing I got this far—"

"But..." She faltered. "What did you think had happened?"

"Oh," said Dan, waving a hand expansively, "I figured he did something awful to her but on some—I don't know—one-night stand. Thought she was cheating on her husband...and Skinker was trying to protect her even though he was the cuckold. Didn't want it to come out. Who would, right?" He put his hands to his temples. "*How* could I *be* so fucking idiotic? How?"

At the funny strangled noise that came from his wife, Dan looked startled.

"I have ruined her life."

"*Ruined her life?*" Dan spat out the words. "Are you kidding? This is the best thing that could have happened! This is huge! Curtis is going to jail! He's toast!" He tried to make her see the logic. "Doesn't she want him in jail? For what he did to her?" He wondered aloud, "What did he do to her? I mean, how do you rape a *prostitute?* Never mind!" An accusing edge to his voice, he said, "Jesus, Gwen, *you* were talking prosecution a minute ago!"

Gwen said hollowly, "That was my idea."

"But doesn't she want—"

"I have no idea what she wants." *Well, now, that's not true,* Gwen thought bitterly. *I know she wants the money.* "Does it have to come out, Dan?" Half crazed, she seized on an unlikely salvation: "Can you forget I said anything? Just prosecute the case like you were going to before? Rewind the conversation—make it as if I never said anything?"

Later, in a reckoning she felt compelled to make, Gwen was grateful that at least he hadn't lied to her. At least he hadn't told her he would forget all about it.

"I can't." Dan drank his cocktail unhappily. He looked out at the restaurant, surveying the crowd. "I can't say the guy was blackmailing Jed Skinker for inside information and not say why. It's totally relevant. It's been the missing piece all along. It's of utmost relevance to the case." *And it's gonna be all over the* Post, he thought remorselessly, *the minute we go to trial.* Curtis would never let himself go down alone.

"People like that," he went on, "you'd be surprised. Sometimes they feel better having it out in the open—like a kind of confession, you know? This may be freeing for her. You'll be surprised, I swear. She'll enter a new chapter of her life when it blows over."

Gwen looked at him out of her pale blue eyes. "Really."

He tried with more facts: "Skinker'll talk, now that we've got this. He's got nothing to hide. He'll talk and he'll implicate Curtis. He'll get off with very little. Probably won't even do time. But John Curtis—*that* fucker's gonna go to jail!"

"Jed Skinker?" Gwen repeated. She looked as if she didn't recognize the man Silvio had seated opposite her. "That man will never 'talk.'"

"Yeah," Dan conceded, chasing some sauce around on his plate. "Maybe not. It almost doesn't matter at this point! Skinker is being blackmailed by this slimeball while trying to protect his damaged wife. He'll come off looking like a hero!"

Gwen's silence would have panicked him if he hadn't been so

271

elated by the news, now that his gross disappointment in himself was subsiding. He started shoveling in the remaining food, desperate for the meal to be over. He was itching for his Black-Berry and only by concentrating fully on cutting and chewing the chicken could he manage not to grab it and start e-mailing colleagues. "Jesus H. Christ," he said to himself as the fact presented itself again with all of its shocking ramifications. "Skinker's wife! A drunk and a whore! Who woulda thunk it?" He went on eating and drinking—what else could he do if she wouldn't talk to him?—splashing wine diffidently into his glass and gulping it down. But that look in Gwen's eyes! The alcohol was hitting and he feared...he feared for his soul! *But I didn't do anything wrong!* he wanted to plead. *It's my job! I have to prosecute Curtis to the extent of my ability.* So then why the hell did he feel so guilty? It was like that Saturday night last fall when he'd been passed out on the couch and Mary—Mary had come out of her room. "Daddy? I had a nightmare." He could barely bestir himself to sit up. Shit-faced, and his kid needed him. "Ish fine, lesh getoo badabed. Ish fine. Ish fine." "Daddy? Are you okay?" "I'm gray, honey. I'm gray. I'm gray."

"I've got to tell her!" Gwen half rose from her chair. "I've at least got to warn her!"

"Sit down! Gwen, sit down!" Dan gave a self-conscious glance around. "Please! Please, Gwen? Can you please sit down?" She did so—wordlessly—not so much obeying, he knew, as paralyzed, no longer trusting herself to act.

He reached across the table and seized one of her hands. "Gwen? Honey, you've got to promise me—you can't say anything to her or to anyone. Do you understand?" He pressed her hand tightly between his two. "Look, I never should've told you anything. It's my fault, okay? But I'm gonna convict this fuckhead. And it'll be way, way better for her, too, if Curtis goes to jail, right?" He scanned her expression to see how this was going down. "You don't want him to get off, do you?"

"No," she said tonelessly.

"Okay, well, I don't need to tell you it would look really, really bad for me if my wife—if you were talking to Philippa about this. You'd make me look really bad." He hurried on. "If she said something to you, and you became a witness—I'd have to recuse myself from the case!" Gwen didn't seem to find the possibility as much of a calamity as he did. Her gaze shifted minutely so that she was focusing on him instead of looking numbly ahead, but she said nothing. "You understand? You'd be compromising my investigation, Gwen."

In another minute he would excuse himself and go make a call to Frank DiNapoli. He felt giddy with his newfound knowledge. At last he could see it all. Prostitution, blackmail; at last it made perfect sense, the seemingly inexplicable elements of the case fitting neatly into place as they should have long ago. The possibility of the promotion to deputy chief of the unit asserted itself in his head again, coming back from where he had banished it a few months ago. He'd best Diane Costa after all. He glanced at Gwen. He'd get the promotion and he'd make it up to her. He'd make it *all* up to her. There she sat—stricken—a few feet from him. He hated PDA but he wanted to take her into his arms...It was touching, in a way, that she had kept this childhood loyalty to Philippa, nice when anyone had a childhood loyalty to anything these days. But Dan doubted Gwen's assessment of the relationship was all that astute. Women like Philippa Lye—they didn't do friendship.

Wrapping up his argument, he spoke in the low, gentle voice he used in court when his case was so strong it was almost embarrassing, knowing that no point of hers could trump his. "You have to promise me not to say anything and not to do anything that will interfere with the investigation. Your loyalty has to be to me, Gwen. It's our livelihood, remember," he added, in case she hadn't gotten the point. "Yours and mine—and Mary's." For something to do with his hands, he poured her a glass of wine. "Have a drink—you'll feel better. I'm gonna make one quick call and then we can look at the dessert menu, 'kay?"

The maître d', Silvio, looked over at table eighteen with surprise. The busboy was retreating quickly after having poured more water. The man, the big drinker, had excused himself, was stepping outside to make a call, the BlackBerry already pressed to his ear. Silvio looked harder, his surprise melting into an approving curiosity. The girl had put her head in her hands and was weeping openly. At last, from that lusterless tomboy—that "Gwen," who always made the reservation with her first name only; inelegant habit—a sign that she was a woman after all.

Chapter Seventeen

They were waiting for him. He was leaving the building, and as soon as Ray held open the door for him—"Good morning, Mr. Skinker"—he saw them standing in neutral loitering positions a little ways down the block. The thing was, in New York no one loitered.

"Morning, Ray."

They had been watching him all week and they knew what time he left the apartment. Today was Friday. They wouldn't wait till Monday—he very much doubted they would wait till Monday. They had not been there when he took Lolo to the school bus. They knew his schedule and he knew that they knew. He would have to pretend to be surprised when they approached him—goggle his eyes or give a start. It wouldn't do to seem as if one had expected them. They wouldn't, Jed felt instinctively, like that.

It was by chance he had noticed the Ford hatchback parked at the hydrant midweek. He'd been thinking about his old dog who used to make right for that hydrant the minute she was out of the building. He had thought of that little black dog in the context of Roxie's puppies, six of whom had turned out pure black. The litter was living over at Billy Flood's cottage; it was May now, Ruth's birthday less than a month away. Squirmers. Only two of them looked German shepherd at all. And then, from trying to guess what the father looked like, Jed had remembered his old, old dog, poor thing, ignominiously named Barkie by himself and Sallie, a funny-looking little black dog with a big head and a jaunty splash of white on his chest. They'd found him starving, collarless, in the woods some Danforth weekend, hidden him away in their bedroom for half a day, smuggled him into the car under blankets from which he promptly emerged, been told in outraged voices from the front seat that they couldn't keep him—"Your father will take it to the pound the moment we get home!"—and then woken to the surprise of their lives—their mother had relented: Barkie was theirs to keep. He'd always made right for that hydrant. Jed saw the silver hatchback again now and realized he'd noticed it the night before as well. He knew at once they'd come for him. The emotion he felt was mild alarm at his dull-wittedness—that he'd had to sleep on the observation to understand it.

He'd had a dinner that had gone late and had come ducking home through a warm spring rain, twenty blocks, to find Mrs. Sampson sitting up. "She told me to leave when she went to bed, but I thought I'd stay." She shook her head at Jed for not carrying an umbrella. "Look at you. You're soaked, Mr. Skinker."

"*You've* got an umbrella, haven't you, Mrs. Sampson?"

"I certainly do!" Mrs. Sampson looked scandalized. "I leave my house prepared!" As the graying older woman gathered up her needlepoint and her purse, his eyes fell on a stack of yellow envelopes on the coffee table.

"She stayed up late working on these. Wants to get them out

early this year." When Jed failed to understand, Mrs. Sampson said, "The invitations!" And when he still looked dim, she said, "For Ruth's birthday!"

"Already?"

"People need time to put it in their books!"

"Of course."

"If men had to take care of the details, I don't know where we'd be, Mr. Skinker."

"Nor do I, Mrs. Sampson. Nor do I." Jed accompanied her to the door. She had been their housekeeper when he was a boy, taken care of the three children as babies, and now babysat some nights or helped Philippa out.

"You've got your bank to run, I know, but it's the details we ladies have got to think about."

"So, did she finish them?" he inquired. "The invitations?"

"Oh, she finished them." Mrs. Sampson sounded gratified. "She's handing them out tomorrow at school. People have plenty of time to put it in their books."

Jed watched the woman wait for the elevator, unsnapping her long navy-blue umbrella and shaking it out with deft movements, and he thought of the latest board "initiative" at Skinker, whereby they were supposed to be focusing on management EQ—no longer would mere IQ do, it seemed. His head of HR was wont to ship everyone off willy-nilly to leadership seminars, but it occurred to Jed that she ought to have simply booked his staff a day under the tutelage of Beatrice Sampson, with whom Jed performed a nightly bit whose theme, doggedly upheld by Mrs. Sampson and himself both, was his long-suffering, irreproachable wife's having to put up with and somehow overcome his own wild ineptitude, his bumbling, his destruction of everything in his path.

That was EQ.

And the fact was, he was a bumbler. The two men had come in their silver Ford hatchback, parked in front of the hydrant, to explain how.

People presumed—sometimes to his face—something altruistic on his part in the union. (Not Mrs. Sampson; she had a much too subtle view of human relationships for an assumption like that.) The condescension didn't rile him. He knew why he'd married Philippa, after all. But it was tedious. (He'd married her for the same two reasons anyone, he assumed, married anyone else: because he wanted to spend a lot of time with her, and because she would leave him alone.) Perhaps he ought to have gone for one of those women who wore their children's names around their necks like dog tags. Then he could have been like the client's strategy man in a meeting a while back who, learning that Philippa was pregnant (failing to realize it was with their third), had leaned in and told him in beatific tones, "Jed, fatherhood will change your life."

He, for instance, presumed altruism.

Curtis did.

No; he presumed idiocy on Jed's part. He thought perhaps Jed had been duped. That Jed had not known about her past, the way his wife had once earned her money. Curtis was the kind of man who bristled with excitement over the chance to cast himself as Iago—to *tell*. Jed had clearly put him in irons with his swift response to the initial call: "Please tell me what you want."

The air gone out of his sails.

"I don't know if you know this, Mr. Skinker...it's rather delicate, you see. And I hate to be the bearer of bad news, but your wife—"

278

Men who thought to uphold some standard of "purity" were ashamed of themselves, Jed felt. He interrupted: "I have no interest in hearing anything from you about my wife." He was annoyed that his response sounded defensive when he wasn't. He was stating a fact, merely. Nor was he trying to protect Philippa with that phrase "I have no interest" when he really meant something else. It truly was a *lack of interest*. He knew, after all. Knew it had lasted about six months, poor thing. After a few years he had stopped trying to rearrange time and events in his head so that he got there sooner, got her out of it before it even started. Instead, the law firm had come as her salvation. Twenty-five thousand a year net, plus overtime. Enough to survive.

What sort of person would want more details?

People were certainly turned on by funny things. Why was knowing everything about everyone else such a stimulus nowadays? Perhaps it was all some people had. All these obsessives who apparently were constantly Googling themselves. In a confused period of his life, when he had left Harvard but not Boston, he had lived with a girl in a Somerville walk-up. It was a point in his life when he was lost. He was resisting Hugh's pressure to come back to the city and take a job at the bank but hadn't admitted to Hugh—or to himself, for that matter—that what he wanted was to be in Danforth. That same year, Sallie was hospitalized for depression—more incontrovertible evidence that the things that had made the Skinkers who they were, as the girlfriend relentlessly pointed out, were all wrong. When he woke up in the morning, his head ached with the knowledge. He consciously tried to be all of the things that people, peers—this girl—seemed to want him to be. He tried to be more "open," to talk about the ways in which his childhood—meaning his mother—had scarred him; also, to start sentences with "I feel..." rather than "The fact is, you've got to..." Years later he ran into the girl crossing Grand Central, shortly after he'd married Phil. She knew all about it—had Googled him, apparently. "Your wedding was in the paper, Jed—it's right there. Didn't you know? Don't you Google yourself?" He must have looked at her blankly, for he recalled the girl thought it crazy—suspicious, even—that he had never Googled himself. "Don't you want to know what you'll find?" No. He had no interest in what he would find. "My God," she'd cried, "I Google myself every day!"

Interest. The ultimate driver. The things that interested you, you pursued. Dogs. Drainage. The things that didn't you let go...

Curtis said, "Oh, you'll be interested in *this*, I think, Jed." The predictable smarmy leap to his first name.

And he, already weary of the game: "Please just tell me what you want from me." A mistake on his part. (You see, Mrs. Sampson, you have a point: no umbrella; no EQ.) He should have realized that he took the fun out of it for Curtis at his own peril. A simple transaction wouldn't do. Curtis had anticipated something more nuanced.

"Calm down for a second, Jed. I'll *get* to that. You don't have to get all up in arms. I'm just reaching out here. That's all I'm trying to do. This is actually a favor to you."

Reaching out.

And later, Jed predicted, glad his sense of humor wasn't abandoning him, Curtis would want to "touch base." No doubt when it was over, and Jed was ruined, he'd want to "circle back." In a reverent tone, he produced that most specious of corporate formulas: "For the safety of you and your family."

"Please tell me what you want from me."

"Jesus, dude. LDL!" Weenie's code for "Let's discuss this live." With distaste, Jed agreed.

But when they did meet in person, on a rainy night at a midtown steak house Curtis chose—he'd been working half in New York, half in London for a year while doing over an apartment, apparently—the man seemed to dither. He didn't seem to have followed the advice of the getting-ahead-in-business tomes to nail down one's objective *before* the meeting; was he there to blackmail Jed? Or did he in fact want to make a social overture?

Curtis seemed torn.

"So, my wife knows your wife." From the fellow's quick reveal, Jed guessed it was the truth, wondered briefly at the context. "From back in the day, I mean."

He was larger than Jed would have expected and fleshy with the slack, defeated gestures of a much less wealthy man, and his hair was too good. The heavy-lidded ennui he talked in lifted occasionally in the course of the conversation, revealing laser-focused rage.

"Hasn't seen her in years but turns out they worked together." An insinuating grin, which Jed stonewalled. "At the law firm, I'm talking, not, um, before."

Jed's expression didn't alter. "Please tell me what you want from me."

Curtis slapped his hand down on the table, making the flatware and glasses rattle. "Can't we just talk here? Can't we just have a conversation? Relax, Jed! Jesus Christ. Have a glass of wine. You gotta enjoy life, you know?" Curtis gestured to the bottle he had ordered. "This is good stuff." He picked up his glass and held it up to his nose in one of those rituals people were going in for now. "Really good stuff. One fifty a bottle *pre-markup*. You can imagine what I'm shelling out for it here!"

Aha, Jed thought, with a modicum of relief, *a man who goes through his days pricing things.* He knew the type. It was the same type of person who liked to take you on a tour of his house when he had you over, opening bathroom doors so you could admire his toilets. Surely Curtis would get around to the price Jed had to pay before long. Surely they wouldn't have to belabor this. *Just name a number, for God's sake.*

Yet a diffident, meandering spiel followed, during which Curtis did not once meet Jed's eyes, about how Curtis's wife had been lonely in London and how in New York she hoped to be more "socially active."

Jed—the bumbler—still not getting what the man was after. It was only later that the idea dawned on him, so absurd he would have dismissed it—he suspected vanity on his own part—that Curtis had wanted to establish a kind of friendship with him. From some comments he'd made, Jed gathered belatedly that he had envisioned a future in which the Curtises and the Skinkers might socialize together—dining out here and there, the wives chatting about nursery school, perhaps, while Jed tipped Curtis on the deals Skinker was underwriting, not blackmailee to black-mailer but chum to chum.

In the moment, though, he had sat perplexed and alarmed by the long digression. Curtis went on expansively about the square footage of the house they were buying in the Hamptons (Jed's mother snobbishly didn't recognize that entity, as if she were some grammar UN, referring instead to Southampton and East Hampton, where, growing up, she'd spent summers) and donations he had made unbidden to various schools ("including St. Timothy's, I might add"). He talked in a laid-back manner that in truth was supercilious and had a threat behind it, as if he still couldn't decide which tack to take—sycophancy or violence.

Eventually he popped the locks on an impressive-looking leather briefcase and withdrew a *Times* clipping that he pushed over the table toward Jed. When Jed did not reach for it, he pushed it closer—"Come on, man! Have a look!" The picture was of Philippa and himself. A benefit his mother had made them go to in her stead. Landmarks a pet charity of his father's, who was a good deal more troubled (tellingly, in Jed's opinion) by the decay of old buildings than by that of humanity.

"We saw this in London—my wife saw it." A grin at Jed, which Jed couldn't return, not understanding it. "She recognized your wife. She was so excited to see it."

The food arrived, and, contemplating the slab of tenderloin, Jed felt an oppressive, almost suffocating boredom set in. Dread enveloped him as they ate; the man's refusal to get to the point made Jed think he might never get home this evening. His idea of torture. Then panic seized him; he mustn't let Curtis know about the farm if he didn't already. He mustn't slip up and mention it. He and his family could leave New York—he had to get her out, he had known he had to get her out for years, because the time with her had never started in New York and it never would. All the time he was to have, to spend with her. But if he could get her out to the country, the time would begin. He was sure of it. He'd long been planning an escape, grooming Chip Noyes, who'd been a protégé of his father and who deserved to be CEO. He would do a much better job than Jed helming Skinker, Farr into the new millennium . . . he'd gone so far as to draft a press release one night. Chip was for selling the building, had scouted office space elsewhere. Then last year—2008—had happened. Worst luck. He'd had to put it off.

Curtis mentioned nursery school again—grade school.

"You'd like a spot at St. Timothy's," Jed guessed, failing to keep the impatience out of his voice. He was hoping to bring the man around to the point, help him get there so they could both call it a night.

Jed, the bumbler.

The man lost it. He had, as Sallie, who was fond of the '80s slang of their adolescence, would have put it, a conniption fit. Palms smacked on the table; he rose and loomed over Jed. Gripping his cutlery, Jed managed not to recoil physically.

"Oh, that's *among* the *things, plural,* I would *like*—yes!" Abruptly John Curtis sat back down and glanced out at the restaurant. He smoothed his luxuriant hair. After a minute, he picked up his fork and began eating, still half facing out from the booth. Now Jed bored himself—he couldn't not notice that Curtis didn't hold his fork right. It dangled lazily from his hand as, like a spoiled child, he picked at his plate.

"Your mother, Jed—your mother is such a well-respected member of the community," Curtis told the room.

Soberly Jed chewed a bite of steak. "Do you have something on my mother as well?"

Curtis laughed at this absurdity. "On Winifred Skinker? Beloved board member of Cleary Girls' School?" Tiresomely, he got the name wrong. There was no *Girls'* in it. "Jed—don't be ridiculous!"

The insinuation that followed was not new to Jed's ears either. Curtis, in his defense, if not to his credit, was hardly the first to suggest to him that Jed's mother must have hated his marriage. Must have tried to argue him out of it. He'd never heard the insinuation from a man, though; it was more a woman's tack, an ex-girlfriend here and there. The women thought they were paying tribute to Winnie with the notion, but in fact, they were underestimating his mother. No one would have gotten her approval. She had known the night she met Philippa that her son would marry her. He'd taken the two women out to supper, at the Madison Avenue Italian preferred by Winnie because they still used tablecloths and the wineglasses had stems.

Philippa, tactfully, went to the bathroom between courses to give them a minute.

His mother was trembling, blinking, as she looked at him. He reached out and patted her blue-veined hand.

"Must you?"

A rhetorical question, so he didn't answer.

"If you'd wanted—a different sort of life, Jeddie..." Her way of saying that he didn't have to keep the bank going—not anymore. It had been nearly five years since Hugh died. They were over the hump. She'd let him off the hook now. He had sensed of late that she was over it. "In the eighties, and then when Dad died—oh, I don't know, Jeddie—I didn't want it sold. They were all getting eaten up. Alex Brown, and Morgan, Grenfell...we were different. Skinker was different." This was a tenet in the family doctrine, one he'd been raised on but one that had proved inconvenient to uphold when he'd actually had to run the place. When, in order to retain Chip Noyes and two others of his ilk, he'd had to resort to a crude eat-what-you-kill arrangement, no subtlety in the compensation whatsoever—how different did Skinker, Farr seem then? From time to time he'd envied the unborn heirs of W. Burgess Farr, who'd been saved the headaches.

"It was important to me then, of course. But now, I'd be—"

"Too late for that." With his free hand, he speared a fried artichoke. "You'll get to like her, Ma," he predicted, "the longer you know her."

But he had underestimated Winifred too. She snatched her hand back. "*Get* to like her, my boy? Will I?"

If she wrung her hands after that, she wrung them privately, too proud to comment. No doubt she herself had faced down insinuations, probably many more than he, given how strongly people must have wanted to give her an opening —old friends, colleagues on the Cleary board. "New daughter-in-law treating you right, Win?"

As far as he knew, she'd never said a word against Philippa.

As for Curtis, the things, plural, he demanded up front were collateral obligations he had to keep to satisfy his wife before he got down to the money itself—or so Jed assumed. St. Tim's for her daughter, followed by admission to Cleary, and while we're at it, another social nicety: a board membership for Minnie, as she was apparently called, on the Landmarks Protection Society. But as the dinner wore on, Jed began to see it wasn't that at all. Curtis, he saw, had a vision of how his life in New York should evolve. It was he who wanted to place his wife and stepdaughter into various roles in order to round out that picture—not the other way around. This Minnie, Jed perceived, might not care a whit about schools or boards. The insight came when he happened to make a comment that Curtis took up unexpectedly. Jed mentioned Curtis's boss. Coffee came, and with a sense of despair that Curtis still hadn't gotten to the point, still hadn't demanded the last and biggest of the things, plural, which Jed was sure would come, Jed observed, maybe digging a little bit himself, "Your boss is on the Landmarks board too, you know. Marty's been involved for a while."

What was it he caught in Curtis's voice in that next moment? Pride? A sibling's rivalrous hate to discover that Jed had access to Martin Kerr? "I found that out!"—his nostrils quivering. "I found that out when we looked into it for Minnie."

Jed waited for him to explain why he hadn't simply gone to

Kerr for the favor. It certainly would have been simpler. But what Curtis said was "It'll be nice when my wife just turns up at a board meeting, won't it? Just turns up!" and Jed grasped the man's true desire. He didn't want to use Kerr to get the board membership; he wanted to use the board to get to Kerr.

"Can you picture Marty's face when he realizes I never even asked him for an in. Not once?" Curtis said. Kerr's irritable unsavory mien—the permanent tan and capped white teeth—flashed into Jed's mind, but he said nothing. "So, have you met him?" Curtis asked defensively, as if prepared to be hurt by Jed's reply.

"Here and there." In Jed's opinion, Kerr was psychotic. Twenty billion in the bank and still going into work in the morning. A persistent rumor that he encouraged his traders to take hormones to make them trade more aggressively.

"People think his reputation is exaggerated but it's not," averred Curtis. "He's utterly fucking brilliant." He seemed to weigh revealing something. Jed kept his eyes down and went on eating the steak. "You know he flew my wife and me down to Jupiter for the long weekend. On the jet, I'm talking! Not commercial. On the *jet*." When Jed didn't say anything, Curtis went on angrily, as if he'd been contradicted, "He came up from *nothing*. Ten kids in the family. Buttfuck, northern Minnesota! Can you imagine? And now he's got this—this spread down there. Owns a fucking former plantation!" Jed stayed quiet. He must not let on that he had been to the place. He'd been down there checking up on his mother's cousins, a favor to Winnie, had run into Kerr in town and been obliged to go over with Philippa for a drink. Kerr had started to harass her two minutes after they walked in the door—flirting and putting his hands on her—and Jed had cut the evening short.

"He took me out golfing—martinis at noon. Cracked crab!

He never drinks any wine that's not a grand cru...and his wife? She couldn't be nicer. People say she's a snob? She couldn't be nicer! I fucking hate snobs. What's the fucking point? I'm as smart as you. I went to Yale. I graduated Phi Beta Kappa. Fuck you, you know what I'm saying? Joanie swears"—Curtis laughed fondly—"sounds like a truck driver. She cracks me up. She makes margaritas in the blender...they don't *need* to be snobs!"

Jed observed him. He'd watched Curtis be rude to the waiter—"Bring it now. Got it?"—the way Martin Kerr was always short with his underlings. Kiss up, kick down. Modeling himself on Kerr. Father figure he could appreciate, apparently.

After specifying the temperature of Kerr's pool for Jed and enumerating Kerr's staff, Curtis seemed to lose track of the narrative. He seemed at a loss. The man's hand trembled as he stirred sugar cubes into his cup, laid the spoon in the saucer. Looking nervous, he took several quick sips.

"You know," Jed said stolidly, "I could help you."

"Ha!" A painful grin as he set the cup down. "I hate to tell you, buddy, but that's why we're here."

"I mean—I could give you a job." It was what he had to offer, so he offered it.

"What?" He flushed with anger. "Why would I want to work for you? Jesus, don't flatter yourself, Jed!" The longer Jed's offer hung in the air, the more indignant it seemed to make Curtis. "You think I need your charity? Wow, that's *some* arrogance. I don't think you get it—I don't think you understand!"

So Jed, finishing his coffee, awaited a number. He couldn't predict how much Curtis would demand, but he had put some thought into how he could funnel the money to him.

Bumbler.

The junior guys who traded on inside information—they

thought they were smart, smarter, smartest. Smart enough to get away with it. Get a numbered account for your father-in-law, buy ten stocks, not just the one about to be acquired—the way they'd buy ice cream and chips with the condoms. But this guy—it dawned on Jed at last—had a motivation beyond arrogance, beyond greed. With a sinking feeling, Jed saw that it was no mere lump sum he was after.

He wanted to impress the boss.

To be given cracked crab at noon and not hit it out of the park...that was a shame John Curtis couldn't stomach.

Swiftly, then, Curtis brought the conversation around to ATG, the microchip company Skinker was advising on its upcoming acquisition.

"Good day, Mr. Skinker. Good day. It's a nice one," the doorman observed.

He had just a second after Ray's parting words to size them up. The man who stepped forward first had salt-and-pepper hair and gaunt cheeks pockmarked from adolescent acne. He looked tensed for action, as if he was ticking off the last fucking second he had to kill. Whereas the one who held back looked like a man you'd be glad to know. He was taller, with a hairline that was receding in no big hurry from his pudgy baby face. He looked affable—a guy to tell a joke; a family man. He played the sideman, though, in reality, Jed sensed at once, he was the closer.

Some nonthreatening words of introduction Jed missed and then, "Look, we know you've been in touch with John Curtis of the Invictus fund."

Odd that when he was confronted with the fact, it lacked

drama. He had always known what he was doing, after all; there was no "reveal." Still, it behooved him to listen politely. Offering any excuse was risible. Better just to listen, hear them out, be on his way. Ray was watching them intently from the door of the apartment building—he didn't like it. To reassure him, Jed put a hand up: *It's all right.* The men followed his gaze, Salt-and-Pepper looking as if he wanted to punch someone. "We've got phone calls," he jumped in, "subpoenaed records, a pattern of trades."

"We just want to talk to you."

Salt-and-Pepper testily stated a few more facts. Baby Face punctuated these with a summary—Jed's takeaway, as it were. "Look, Mr. Skinker, it's not you we want."

"That's right. You, we just want to talk to."

The curious Latinate phrasing struck Jed's ear. *You, we just want to talk to. John Curtis and Martin Kerr, we'd like to lock up.* When Jed said nothing, having nothing to say, Salt-and-Pepper went on. "We know you guys met up at the Weisshaus and talked about the Nanotech acquisition, which Curtis later followed up about by phone. We got all that, Mr. Skinker."

At this moment Philippa was inside the apartment getting dressed to take Ruth and Sebastian to school. Jed acutely hoped that he would not still be here talking with these men when his family came out.

Baby Face again inserted the takeaway—a mild suggestion, as if it had just occurred to him. "This may be your only chance to cooperate, Mr. Skinker."

"We talked to Carol Ann Ritchek; we know she was putting through calls to you from Curtis."

Jed started. Baby Face, reassuring: "She was very upset, Mr. Skinker. She was in tears. She said you'd never get involved in something below board."

Jed found his voice. "I'm glad to hear it was that that upset her."

"That's good?" said Salt-and-Pepper, his sense of decency clearly offended by Jed's expressing relief.

"I was worried Ms. Ritchek had gotten some bad news about her health." The day, two months ago in March, when Carol Ann had requested a morning off, citing, when she never had before, a doctor's appointment. He'd worried it was the cancer that had claimed her baby sister—there was something brittle in the way she stuck to her story. She'd be the type to hide an illness from him, knowing he'd involve himself—would want to pay.

"A lovely woman—clearly loves her boss. Very loyal. Same as your doorman Ray, here—you got loyalty up and down the line. You wanna come in and explain how you got involved in all this?"

Baby Face said, again in that neutral tone, the tone Ray himself used when observing the day's weather, "No honor among thieves, Mr. Skinker. You owe him *nothing*. You know that, right? Nothing."

Well, but: that wasn't it. That wasn't it, though it was a pretty good guess. (Without thinking, he glanced up to the row of windows on the eighth floor of the prewar building: their apartment—his apartment his whole life—where Philippa was now getting the little ones ready for school.) The man, in profiling him, had successfully plumbed his psyche, for it was *part* of it. To go tattling off to the Feds: "Curtis made me!" It was true he couldn't picture it. In all of this, he'd never thought he'd be the tattler.

Meeting the man's eyes, he said evenly, "I won't be coming in." He gave what he felt was a pause of acceptable length before stepping carefully around them and continuing up the block.

"We know about your wife."

Jed took a funny step, his shoe striking the sidewalk strangely. The two men caught up smoothly. "We know you're protecting her. Shit's all gonna come out. Nothing you can do now to keep a lid on that."

The bumbler. He had betrayed her. Betrayed her with that glance up to the eighth floor. "You know?" he said, skeptically, suggesting, *What do you know?* Perhaps it was all a bluff. A rumor they'd seized upon. Fishing, to see if he would bite.

"We know about her former—" said the affable-looking man and then he stopped, pressed his lips together, and looked courteously away. "We know, Mr. Skinker." Jed appreciated the circumspection even if it was only a technique to get him to cooperate.

"How about you just tell us what you and John Curtis talked about for ten minutes on that first phone call," the agent suggested, pleading a little. He looked baffled. "What the hell did he say to get you to meet him in the first place? What exactly did he threaten you and your wife with?"

Salt-and-Pepper, grimly: "You're being blackmailed, Mr. Skinker—that's a crime on top of all the other crimes Curtis has committed and for which he's gonna go to jail."

Baby Face, more conversational: "It'll stay quieter if you come in now and shine the spotlight on Curtis. Focus everybody on John D. Curtis. Not Jed Skinker. You don't want to be in the spotlight. You don't want your family—your wife and your kids—in the spotlight, do you? That'd be exactly what you don't want, I would think, Mr. Skinker. A man like you." He made a gesture encompassing the apartment building—the block. "Private man. Family man."

They had found their way halfway through his psyche: He would never cooperate to save himself. He would cooperate to save her. Yet—and this was a subtlety he wouldn't have risked on Salt-and-Pepper alone . . .

"Even though you know—" Jed paused. He didn't want to sound glib or ungrateful for the offer to come in and talk. "You see, even though you know," he repeated slowly, willing them to understand, "*I* can't be the one to come in and tell you."

He could imagine the interview. "So, when your wife was earning money as—" "What sort of clientele—" "What acts were—"

No.

I never Google myself.

No.

Something puzzled Jed. There was no reason not to ask. "John *D.* Curtis?" he said. "I wasn't aware there was a *D.*"

"He added it," Baby Face said, not missing a beat. "Wanted to give himself more of a Rockefeller ring." In the moment of relative levity, he reached into his coat pocket. Jed flinched, expecting a subpoena, but the man held out a business card. "When you decide it's in your interest to talk, Mr. Skinker, you'll be able to reach us here."

Jed took the card. He had been expecting to be served from the minute he noticed the two of them waiting on his block. Who, he wondered briefly, was letting him off the hook?

"We just want to hear your side of the story," Salt-and-Pepper threw out as Jed hesitated at the curb.

"You're not a bad guy. I can see that with my own eyes," Baby Face said. "We just want the truth."

Strange, that that obvious play for his cooperation should itself have the ring of truth.

With a glance back at his building, Jed went into the street and hailed a taxi. He always got one right away at this hour.

We hardly ever had real news—a real story to tell. Who does? Everything is known. Each day is uneventful, unless it bears some minor disappointment, some minor joy. Even the little mishaps that once colored our hours—waiting for someone at the wrong bar, spending an extra hour at the gym after work because we had no plans, only to arrive home to a message blinking on the machine about a party. "Oh my gosh, I was in my sweats, microwaving dinner, when I played your message and I somehow managed to shower, put an outfit together, and make it down to the East Village in thirty-five minutes!" Even those funny little ripples in our days as single girls had been flattened by our phones. Probably the most exciting moment in the past few years had been meeting, well, one another, as preschool parents. Now, though, our world had yielded an actual story that bore repeating—if only we could have gotten a word in.

It was frustrating to us afterward that people who hadn't actually been there—and very few of us had actually been there—did not defer to us but rather usurped control of the narrative. For months they went on with their factual errors and embellishments, both of which merely reflected their own biases and had little to do with the Skinkers. When the story told became so far removed from what had happened that day (and even began to be conflated with

294

another story, about a school admissions scandal), we ceased talking about it. We felt as if we had undergone behavior modification. We, who liked nothing better than a good gossip, a coffee-hour rehash of the latest embezzlement or divorce, had absolutely nothing left to say.

For starters, the word sodomy *was not used that morning. The conjecture, never confirmed, arose later. She, as she kept stating, simply wanted him to give Philippa the money.*

Skinker was not present, it's true, but he was not off "being arrested," as some people claimed. In an unlucky coincidence, he had been approached that same morning by the FBI and had declined to reveal the very information that an hour later was broadcast so loudly on Sixty-Third Street. But as Emily Lewin, JD, grew tired of explaining, an approach is not the same thing as an arrest.

Nor were we impressed by the commentary we heard many times in the aftermath of the event—commentary that frequently ended "And in front of her children!" We *are the only ones entitled to shake our heads and mutter reprovingly about the fact that the whole thing happened in front of her children—her younger children—because we saw that they didn't understand what was going on. How could they have? They were small children. The boy four, the girl turning three in a couple of weeks. Children pick up on themes—love, anger; more basically, warmth, cold. Tell yourself it's the details that scar children for life and you avoid the inconvenient truth that it is in fact the ongoing themes. Control. Disappointment. Entitlement. Narcissism. Deprivation. Frustration. Sorrow. Or, as our children used to call out from the M5 as it passed the lions who guard the main branch of the New York Public Library: "Patience and Fortitude! Patience and Fortitude!"*

That morning, her mother was handing out the invitations to the little girl's birthday party, not throwing the party that afternoon. The party occurred later on. Despite everything, she was determined to throw the little one's party. She was determined in the wake of the scene that took place outside St. Timothy's the Preschool (not St. Timothy's the Church; please don't try to inflate the symbolism) that late May (not June) morning, when the lovely weather had put us all in a good mood.

The scene did not include the word sodomy *or* prostitute — *all right, there might have been a* fuck *or two, but as an active verb not as a swear none of us who were there could be sure. It all happened so fast, in the ten minutes before Mrs. Davidson called security.*

His wife did not get into a catfight with her. There was no hair-pulling. There was no shin-kicking or, as Betsy Fleming started to say — when the recounting of the recounting of the recounting got so far removed from the truth that we began meeting solely in order to refute the latest outrageous embellishments — there was no female mud-wrestling on Sixty-Third Street that morning. It is true that when he failed to produce the money, she yanked Minnie's Chanel bag from her arm and started to go through it, apparently looking for the wallet. It is true that it was Mrs. *Curtis who paid her eventually — Minnie, as you may remember, liked to carry a lot of large-denomination bills for the same reason most people who carry a lot of cash do: it gave her a feeling of plenty.*

It was not the last day of school. It was the last chapel, a day when parents were invited to attend along with their children. I'm mentioning this because if you think that school ended and the parties involved never saw one another again, you are wrong. It was the Upper East Side. We continued to see them; they continued to see one another — for a time, any-way. Philippa. John Curtis. Minnie. Gwen what's-her-name. The children. As for us — some people, irritatingly, assumed that we shunned Philippa after this. We didn't shun her. Why would we shun her? We had noth-ing against her. We liked her. Please — we would but ask, stop casting us as some reality-television version of ourselves. We weren't the neuroti-cally jealous type of Manhattan woman who signs up for every new diet to come down the pike. When we got ice cream for our kids, we often got cones for ourselves — with sprinkles. We participated in book groups that chose higher-brow novels than you might have thought. Yes, we read The Kite Runner *but we also read Rushdie, we read Murakami, we read Ian McEwan. The reason we didn't send our children to the little girl's birthday party that occurred a few weeks later was not that* we *didn't want to associate with the Skinkers. It was for the sake of our* children *that we reluctantly declined the invitation. Our children . . . our children . . . the meaning of our lives and all that we had left! Was it fair to them to force them to be friends with the child of the most scandal-ridden family in New York after the Madoffs? Was it fair to them to blithely drop them off at an apartment now associated with insider trading and prostitution? Fair to our innocent children? To paraphrase Dr. Seuss, would you have dropped off yours?*

Despite all of this, when the day arrived and we did not go to the party, we were overtaken by unease. It was the day a mild paranoia started that we could never afterward wholly shake. We relaxed over the summer, maybe, but the feeling returned, worse, in the fall when we came back to the city and school started up again, the cycle of drop-offs and pickups and schlepping to extracurricular activities. It had never occurred to us that they would leave. *But leave they did—he one way, she another. And we were left behind. We were bereft. Without the Skinkers, our lives seemed like fading copies—Xeroxes of Xeroxes—the outlines growing fainter all the time. That fall after Jed Skinker died and Philippa left town with the children, we understood that what we were doing here in Manhattan a decade into the new millennium was going through the motions. Though our lives had many joys and small satisfactions, we could never fully believe, once the Skinkers were gone, that they* were *our lives. Surely, there must be something more! Something to show us that we were not merely parasites. Not merely good mimics. And although at first we scorned the Polo store that opened in the former Skinker, Farr building on Fifty-Fourth just west of Fifth, pushing by with a scoff and a remark out the sides of our mouths (unless, of course, Emily Lewin was there, since her husband's family, the Simons, had added the building to their vast real estate portfolio), ultimately it was too conveniently located for us not to buy the occa-*

sional shirt or bathrobe or tie there, especially for those of us whose husbands worked nearby.

They had the place all decked out with old pictures and Princeton oars and varsity pennants and sidesaddles, as they have at all of the Polo stores, so that it exuded old money. Well, Ann DeGroat went in one day to pick up some khakis for Guy, and hanging on the wall at the back of the men's section—what do you think she saw? A black-and-white photograph of Mrs. Hugh Skinker standing on the beach in East Hampton holding the hand of her little son, Jed.

Chapter Eighteen

Toward the end of May, St. Timothy's School held a last chapel, which parents were invited to attend. Fathers came. The block saw more men on that morning than it saw all year. Loving their children, for this generation, wasn't enough; financial security that in some cases would last generations wasn't enough. These men had to be hands-on fathers as well. Yet in the way they stood beside their wives, half facing, half ignoring one another, Black-Berrys clutched in hands should conversation falter, eyes darting up, darting down to their devices—all of them urgently in de-mand at their places of work, apparently—the men seemed like unwieldy accoutrements, the wrong choice in handbags some of the women had made and would now have to tote around all day.

Philippa Lye for once had arrived early, so early that no one had actually seen her come. She was wearing a short-sleeved denim dress grommeted all the way down the front. Her hair was tied back in a ponytail secured with an ancient-looking Her-mès scarf. Perhaps the men's discomfiture (they checked their devices even more frequently when she began to drift among them) arose from the fact that though she was strikingly beautiful, she did not seem to have dressed with them in mind, as most women would have, but rather at the whim of some eccentric muse. They testily said to themselves that if they ever did stray, it would be with fun, busty Betsy Fleming or angular, bitchy Heather Baird, certainly not with *her*. In fact, Philippa had worn the dress because her daughter Ruth had asked her to, had stood in front of her mother's closet and said, "My favorite—please?" but only Philippa and her children would have known that. Her little boy and little girl clutched at her legs as she walked from couple to couple handing out invitations—against explicit school policy—to the little girl's birthday party. She looked quite proud of herself, had quite the spring in her step as she shuffled through the bright yellow cards. "Now, let's see. Ann, where did we put yours?" Mortification at Philippa's apparent ignorance of the rule made the women redden. Quickly, they stuffed the yellow envelopes into their bags, mumbling their thanks and inventing reasons for turning back at once to their husbands. "Oh, Tommy, I forgot to tell you—" But Philippa said distinctly to each one of them, "Ruth and I *really* hope you'll come!" But while the mothers were embarrassed and tried to downplay the invitation-giving for the sake of those who had not been asked, they stopped short of actually refusing the invitations. That never would have occurred to them; it would only have attracted more attention; they could always say no later on . . . though the truth was, it was gratifying that the Skinkers were throwing a party at last. Philippa had always been the kind of mother whose children came to one's parties—indeed, were the very last kids picked up from one's parties—but who never reciprocated with so much as a playdate. Suddenly, on a May Friday, there she was, handing out envelopes. It caused a very minor stir when Philippa stopped in front of Gwen Hogan and her daughter, and Mrs. Hogan refused to accept the invitation. Pretending to keep up conversations with their spouses, the mothers watched this intently, wondering whether Gwen Hogan was actually that much of a brownnoser that she wouldn't bend a school rule to accept an invitation for that sweet goofy daughter of hers.

"I can't, Phil. I can't accept it." She spoke with a gravity that one might have been forgiven for finding, in this setting, comic.

"What? Don't be silly!"

"I can't, Phil." Gwen Hogan put her hands by her sides, curled them into fists, and refused to take the envelope in hand, as if she were being served a subpoena. "If you knew," she said grimly, "you wouldn't want me there."

Philippa looked hard at her. "I can't imagine!" She scrutinized Mrs. Hogan, who just stared shamefacedly at the sidewalk, so that eventually Philippa knelt and handed the envelope to Gwen's daughter herself. "You'll take it, won't you, Mary?"

"Mom, an invitation!" exclaimed the girl, and Gwen Hogan said dully, "Thank you."

It was time for Mrs. Davidson and Ms. Babcock to come to the door to invite everyone in. The conversation among parents had happily crescendoed, spurred on by the expectation of another hour to come in which the choices they had made in their lives would be validated again, in ways large and small.

The Curtises were among the last to arrive, walking up the block from their idling car, Arabella between them with that sharp-eyed weasely expression on her face. The Curtises had sat waiting in their car rather than joining the expectant throng. It wasn't that they were above the self-congratulation that came with belonging to a little Upper East Side nursery school that was ferociously hard to get into, but they maintained a distance from it. They didn't *love* their school the way the rest of the parents did. Minnie gave the mothers the nervous-making sense that she was in this to win, not to have the opportunity to prove herself worthy of the honor; that St. Tim's was there to serve her purposes and not the other way around. (Was it true that, through connections, John Curtis had virtually forced Mrs. Davidson to take his stepdaughter, even though she had passed her fifth, if not her sixth, birthday? It couldn't be . . . yet the girl had *told* everyone she was six.) And now here Arabella was, off to kindergarten at Cleary, and Minnie herself apparently halfway to a board position at the Landmarks Protection Society. All this registered with the parents, though not on the polite, welcoming faces they turned to John and Minnie. It was the first time most of the parents had seen the couple together. Curtis had made a late appearance at the Steins' party, of course, but they had turned out to be the type of couple that socializes independently, priding themselves on never giving each other so much as a nod, she courting Lally and her group, he deigning to speak with one or two of the bigger-deal dads, including their host, Ron Stein, who, today, noticing Curtis emerging from his car, had started up the block in the other direction and made a spurious work call, holding up an index finger when Lally hissed, "You promised, Ron!" The man frankly gave Ron the creeps.

With uncharacteristic determination Philippa pushed through to Minnie with a yellow envelope in hand—her last one. "Excuse me! Excuse me! Ex*cuse* me." A strange, punctuated exchange followed—muted, because at that moment the door did open and Mrs. Davidson cried, "Welcome to you all!"

Philippa had handed the invitation to Minnie and was now addressing Minnie's husband directly, as if she had independent business with him—a sufficient-enough oddity to attract glances. "Please come in!" Mrs. Davidson exhorted them. In the pause before the parents started in, not a single one of them failed to hear the remark Philippa made:

"I said, you owe me the money."

One or two of the parents rubbernecked; most of them pretended not to have heard. But as the argument escalated, the procession toward the building was forced to halt. The Curtises had walked right into the front of the crowd when they arrived, so now the three adults and the three children had taken center stage, as it were, Arabella clinging tightly to her mother's hand, Ruth and Sebastian, ignored as usual, sitting themselves down on the lowest step of the school.

"Look—I only want my money. You owe me the money. You at least owe me that."

A collective shiver went down the parents' spines. This was no bake-sale or raffle-ticket discrepancy; it was still Curtis and only Curtis she was addressing with barely a tremble in her voice. An affair gone bust; the assumption was transmitted through the crowd on some telepathic frequency. Minnie said sharply, "What are you talking about, Phil?"

"I just want my money," repeated Philippa, but she seemed to falter, as if the surreal-ness of the request had hit her.

Things began to happen so rapidly then that no one afterward could be completely sure about the order.

"Please come in!" Mrs. Davidson cried again. This time she gave a little peremptory clap of her hands. "Our program is about to start!"

"Phil, what the hell are you talking about?" Unhampered by doubt, Minnie simply tried to get to the bottom of it.

"I want to get my money, that's all!"

"What money? What are you talking about?"

Curtis seemed to think that if he didn't acknowledge her, it would all go away. A look of disgust on his face, as if a crazy person had assaulted him on the subway, he tried to push by, but Mary Hogan's mother, who had appeared from nowhere, stepped into his path. She put a hand out to stop him, said coldly, "Give her the money."

"Gwen! Gwen, what's going on?" Minnie said plaintively. She was so demure that day, dressed up in a pastel wool suit and yellow spiked pumps with flowers on the toe, the black handbag dangling incongruously from her shoulder. Curtis kept her in clothes, all right. Tightfisted, the man was not—but for the one, fatal exception.

"Give her the money, John," Gwen Hogan repeated.

"The fuck?" His expression seeking to make a joke of it, Curtis cast an eye toward Mrs. Davidson, as if his record of donations to the annual fund—short but robust—ought to perhaps have spared him being publicly impugned in front of the school. Mrs. Davidson gaped at him.

"You *owe* her the money. It's that simple."

"That's right!" said Philippa. "It's simple."

"Get out of my way! What the hell? Ex*cuse* me!"

"You owe her the money!"

"Yes, you do! You do!"

"Gwen?" Now Gwen Hogan's husband came hurrying up the block, probably hoping to sneak in, stand at the back, and leave before the end of chapel but still get some kind of marital credit for making an appearance. He scooped up his child, who was standing watching, and cried "Gwen!" when he saw whom his wife was addressing. "Get over here, Gwen! What are you doing? Get over here!" *Gwen* might have been a dog that had taken off after a squirrel. *"Gwen!"*

Gwen Hogan had no reaction at all to hearing her name called.

She didn't so much turn, though Mary Hogan said sternly, "Don't yell at Mommy."

Perhaps because of the tension in the air, Philippa's boy had started to whine and wail. Ann DeGroat knelt and tried to comfort him but he actually whacked at her when she came close. "I want Mummy!"

"You want a good smack," Betsy Fleming muttered. Unfortunately the remark rather hung in the air because by that point, everyone had gone still, even the children. As with any public scene, the crowd's first emotion had been surprise, yielding to a spark of glee that others were going down today and not oneself, then a moment of fear that one would somehow still be implicated in the offense, and, finally, irritation and boredom with the kind of people who made public scenes.

"What the hell? Can someone—" John Curtis looked around for sympathy, the two crazy women so close he was hemmed in and unable to move. But Gwen Hogan had the calm, unbudgeable presence of the good parent. Insistent, firm, unembarrassed by repetition—"You owe her the money." Shaking her head no at him. "She's not leaving till she gets the money, *John*." Now Gwen had her hand on Philippa's arm as if she weren't *letting* Philippa leave.

The first look of doubt crossed Minnie's face. "Oh my God," she spat at her husband. "Are you having an affair? Are you having an affair with her?"

"Me? What the hell?" Like any guilty man accused of the wrong thing, Curtis was incensed. "No, I'm not fucking having an affair! Please! Give me some credit!"

Minnie looked at Gwen. "Gwen?" she said tentatively.

"He owes her money, Minnie."

Minnie's dark eyes flashed her uncertainty. "You know what?

You can all leave us alone!" she announced, trying to block for her husband as they pressed forward. "We're going in!"

"Please do come in!" Mrs. Davidson said valiantly. (She had never looked so old or so frail, though the next fall, she secured a seven-million-dollar gift for St. Tim's—an unprecedented number in preschool donations in Manhattan—and decided to delay retirement.)

"Oh no, you don't!" Gwen said simply. "Not till he pays her."

"We don't owe you anything!" Minnie cried but the waver in her voice suggested that she would, if proven wrong, be prepared to negotiate.

"Not *me*," said Gwen.

"Get the fuck away from me, you freak," Curtis said to her.

"Gwen, come on!" urged Dan Hogan, who had managed to muscle through the crowd, child and all. He set Mary down and lunged for his wife's elbow. "Let's go home, Gwen! Let's go right now!"

That's when Gwen Hogan went into a frenzy. She threw off her husband and attacked Curtis, flailed at him with her fists, shrieking, "Give her the money! Give her the fucking money!"

Curtis's hand flew up to defend himself. It connected with Gwen Hogan's jaw, and she fell to the curb so precipitously it was as if he had flicked a speck off his bespoke suit. Dan Hogan went so red with fury he had to be held back by the Flemings and Ron Stein, who locked him in a wrestling hold. "Easy, man! Easy!" Mary Hogan started silently to cry. But before Mrs. Davidson could dispatch Ms. Babcock to break up the fight, Gwen had clawed her way to her feet. She yanked Minnie's purse from her arm—broke the chain strap right in two. "Where's your wallet? You pay her, Minnie, if he won't. You pay her." She started rifling through the bag but Minnie snatched it hysterically back.

"What's this about, John? What the hell is this about?"

"I'll tell you what it's about." Gwen jerked her head toward Philippa, who was standing watching with pursed lips. "He *hired* her, and he never paid her. He never fucking paid! And now he's going to pay. Today, right now, he's going to pay her what he owes her. Or you're going to pay for him, Minnie." She wasn't a pretty sight, Gwen Hogan—red-faced; her hair, slipped from its holder, falling all over her face and shoulders, and just the way anger didn't suit a tranquil demeanor like hers.

"This is extortion!" Curtis yelled. "I'm going to have you fucking people arrested!"

Minnie's eyes swept over them—Philippa, Gwen, Dan, her husband. Survival is often equated with stamina but has more to do with speed. In the seconds that followed Gwen Hogan's declaration, Minnie's face was like a time-lapse video of the skies when the different weather systems rush through. She faltered; she blinked; she weighed the odds; she came to some internal conclusion. "Pay her, John," she said evenly. "Pay her the money."

"I'm not paying that fucking whore!" Curtis exclaimed petulantly, perhaps not realizing that with the insult he'd hurled, he'd confirmed the debt he owed. "Fuck that!"

Minnie felt for her bag. Breathing quickly, she removed her wallet from the ruined purse. Of course she had no idea how much Philippa was owed. She and all of the parents seemed to freeze as her hand hesitated with a neat, new-looking stack of hundreds in it. Even Gwen Hogan didn't seem to know where to take it from there. Her face froze. She hadn't thought that far ahead, apparently. But then Philippa plucked the entire stack from Minnie's hand.

"This'll do."

Minnie didn't say a word as Philippa divided the pile of bills and stuffed half into one coat pocket and half into the other.

Mrs. Davidson had recovered from her initial, enervating shock. She was exclaiming, was still trying to get everyone inside, was calling security, yelling for security, though it was unclear whom she was planning to have escorted off school property.

Dan Hogan was overheard to say flatly, "Security's not gonna help."

Philippa had gone to gather up her children. "We're not going to go to chapel, darlings—not today." Her voice trembled. "We are done with school for today!" She walked up the block toward Park, a small querulous child's hand in each of her hands. "But why, Mummy? Why?" People said afterward that she held her head high—but then, she always held her head high. She had a long, ground-covering stride, and as she walked away, one or two of the hundreds escaped her pockets and floated down, then several at once, and when she didn't stop to stuff them back in, they trailed behind her like the magic dust that follows the Disney princesses. In this society where capitalism was seen as a straight-forward good, forty parents watched the bills flutter through the air and start to skitter away and didn't move. Only Curtis moved, saying pridefully, "Well, I'm going to the car!" Minnie didn't even look at him. A hand to her head, she sat down on the lower step of the school entrance, recently deserted by the Skinker children. Her feet must have hurt because she removed her pumps and held them in her lap, her stockinged feet flat on the curb. Curtis's door slammed, the car moved off, and no one seemed to know what to do till Tommy Fleming burst out, "God, shouldn't we at least pick them up?" Then the St. Tim's parents chased the money down like crazed kids when a piñata breaks, and there were a couple of awkward moments when two parents from different families stopped the same escaping bill, one with a stomp of the foot, the other on his knees, shooting out a hand.

* * *

Dan got home late that night, long after Mary was asleep. Gwen didn't see him when he came in because he went straight to the bathroom. She could hear him washing up, splashing, the tap running. She got off the sofa, where she'd been reading, and called to him, "You want me to heat up some lasagna?"

"Nah. We got takeout."

When he emerged, he drifted awkwardly around the living room, picking up a magazine and laying it down, straightening a picture book on the round table, and finally sitting noncommittally on the edge of one of the hard chairs, as if he were only stopping in for a minute. Gwen came and sat across from him as she always did. She couldn't bear to broach the subject. It was so painful to her—to think that she had hurt that part of him that had never been hurt: his career. To think that she had set him back, gotten in his way, brought him down. She had never wanted that. She never bothered him at work, and she hadn't called him today either, fearing the worst. Better to apologize in person. Odd how uneventful her day had been, after the morning. Except for one impromptu stop she'd made on the way home from school, she had spent it the way she always spent it—tidying; a load of laundry in the building's basement coin machines; a call home to Camilla, who was disgruntled about a neighbor's habit of mowing his lawn early on Sundays. Then pickup at St. Tim's, at which she was the sole mother.

Today, it seemed, everyone had sent the nanny.

Dan was clasping his hands, opening them, then reclasping them. He took off his glasses and placed them on the table.

Her stomach churning, she waited for him to take her to task—

explain in no uncertain terms what her behavior had cost him professionally.

"Looks like I'm gonna get the promotion—deputy chief."

She was so astonished, she couldn't absorb it. "What?"

He gave a funny non-grin, with his lips only. "Yeah. I got back to the office, and Mira had put in a call to see me. Went right in and gave her the play-by-play—what else could I do? I told her exactly what had gone down. She calls Matt in and the three of us sit there working it all out, and Nast points out that, I mean, it's not the worst thing to have my main suspect accused of something else and tried in the court of public opinion. How's that for jury appeal, right? 'The insider trader who also rapes prostitutes!' Awesome." Incredulous, Gwen watched his little performance—his set piece. "Even those annoying juries— you know, Mr. Upper-Middle-Class Fuckwit who's all 'Even though the defendant is a reprehensible human being, *I'm* going to consider only the evidence'—even that guy'll take note of a *rapist*. And, hey, if you—you do become a witness for some reason, and I have to recuse myself—"

"Dan, I'm so sorry."

"Nast'll take over for me and—" As if his forgiveness made him ashamed, Dan said, realigning the napkin holder in front of him, "You always did stand up for the girlfriends. In college. 'Member? You'd be all—what's the girl equivalent of 'Pals before gals,' huh?" He rushed on. "Anyway, it turns out Mira hadn't called me in about the, um, event this morning—that hadn't gotten downtown quite that fast! She called me in to tell me I got the promotion."

"Oh, Dan..."

"Yeah, I beat out Diane Costa." He screwed up his face. "She doesn't have the trial experience I do.

"I was thinking..." He pressed an index finger and a thumb

to his eyes. Then he lowered his hand and, with a brusque movement, rose and went over to the window, clearing his throat. He spoke to the window, to York Avenue, not looking at her. "I was thinking—even though it's off-season, it might be fun, when school's over...we could take Mary to Disney World." He turned around and tried on an optimistic little grin. "You know, before she gets too old." His voice broke on *old*. His shoulders slumped.

"Dan, you know I—"

He sank down to the floor, drew up his knees. "I'm sorry, Gwen." Choking out the words, he said, "Fuck! I'm sorry." He put a hand up to shield his eyes as he cried.

Gwen sat at the table, knowing that in this situation a normal person would reach out to him physically. Such a gesture struck her as false, though, so she sat at the table waiting, averting her eyes so as not to put him on the spot. When he was able to take a breath, she said, "I think I saw something online the other day for a package deal. Some kind of discount. Hotel and air together."

He raised his face. "Yeah?"

She nodded. "Seemed pretty good."

"Yeah," he said, wiping his nose with his wrist. "Screw paying through the nose for the resort. We'll find a bargain place—Mary won't care." He blinked at her. His mouth opened. He said, "You cut your hair."

Embarrassed, Gwen looked away, but she couldn't help it—she broke into a grin. "Yeah. You like it? On the way home from school today. Just walked right in, said, 'Cut it off.'" She mumbled, "I figured it'd be easier for running. Dry quicker—you know." And though she blushed, he wouldn't stop looking at her, just looking at her, marveling, until finally she protested, "Dan!"

Chapter Nineteen

It was June 10. Laura had the realization as she was sitting on the toilet staring at the interlocking tile pattern of the bathroom floor, the hexagons upon hexagons upon hexagons. She had to get Mummy up and get her making the cake. Ruthie's friends would be coming at lunchtime and they had quite a lot to do. They had to do the streamers and the place cards and they had to put the things they had bought at the art store into the goodie bags and write the classmates' names on the bags.

She flushed and skipped washing her hands; it was so tedious and time-consuming, she could never make herself do it unless someone was watching. How dirty did your hands really get if you carefully wiped yourself after number one?

She walked quickly down the hall in her nightgown and peered into the kitchen, expecting it to be empty, but Mummy was already up.

"You're awake."

"Morning, Lo." Mummy was distracted but not because she had a headache. She was not sitting at the kitchen table in her bathrobe squinting and sipping coffee. She was dressed; she had an apron on over her shirt and pants. The kitchen was a royal mess. Open bags of flour and sugar were spilling out on the counter. A stick of butter had melted and was pooling on the table. Laura had to resist an urge to run and clean it up, since she knew Mummy would snap at her if she did. Gammy's ancient electric eggbeater was plugged into the corner outlet and resting on its side. Mummy herself had flour all over her apron and on her hands and a large speck of something on her cheek, which she wiped at with the back of her wrist. She was concentrating on a recipe in the cookbook splayed open on the counter and held there with a saucepan. "'Pour batter into prepared pan,'" she read aloud. "Christ—the pan."

"Are you making Ruthie's cake?" Laura didn't want to push her luck but she couldn't resist asking the question. She could *tell* Mummy was making the cake but she wanted to hear her say it anyway: "You're already making the cake?"

"Well, I thought I'd better. The kids are coming at noon."

"What kind is it?"

"Angel food. I thought we'd dye the icing pink."

"Ooh—she'll like that."

"Can you grease the pan for me, Laura? The butter's over there. Oops—you'd better get a new stick out of the fridge. No, wait—here's one."

Laura had a moment's conscience-wrestling and then she submitted and said, "I have to wash my hands first." She washed them carefully with soap at the kitchen sink. It was funny that when you did wash your hands, it felt pleasant and you were glad you had.

"I hope Sebastian doesn't wreck everything," she said conversationally as she peeled back the paper wrapping from the stick of butter.

313

"He won't," Mummy said with a vehemence that Laura found encouraging. "I won't let him."

"But what if he has a temper tantrum?"

"Then he'll go to his room and stay there."

"Who's coming?" Laura said, starting to grease the pan.

Mummy didn't answer—she went on reading bits of the recipe aloud, talking to herself. "Middle rack? One, two—there is no middle of two. I wonder if I ought to go with the top or the bottom."

"Is Willie Haskell coming?" Laura asked. He was a boy in Ruth's class whom Ruth mentioned frequently. "Willie won't eat the cake," Ruth had predicted. "Willie doesn't like cake."

"He's not—no. He can't make it," Mummy said. There was a tightness in her voice when she answered. Laura glanced at her.

"Are Lila and Dickson coming?" The twins, with the strawberry-blond hair. Funny to have a hair color named after a fruit. It was such a specific color—everyone knew what color hair you meant when you said it.

"They *just* called to say they can't make it." Mummy coughed and looked away. "They had another party, apparently, and their mother got the dates mixed up."

The angel-food pan was complicated to grease—it was high, or deep, depending on how you wanted to put it, and it was hard to get to every spot of the tall, sloping central tube. Laura checked carefully for empty spots in the butter coating, mushing on more where she found one. "Is Peter F. coming?"

Mummy took a sip from her coffee mug before answering. "I hadn't realized, but Peter's family goes to the country every weekend. Which of course I understand! If Daddy weren't so busy right now, we'd be in the country, right? And if somebody else had a party, *we* wouldn't be able to go to it."

314

Laura turned the pan carefully around, checking it a final time. While she was inspecting it, tears started to fall on the buttered surfaces.

"Laura."

"No one's coming, are they?"

Mummy hesitated. "Some people can't make it." She went on, with too much gusto, "But that's always the way it is! It's to be expected, Lolo! No one can ever come... all the time."

Laura nodded. She knew it. It was because of something her family had done. There was something about the Skinkers that had made them like Millie Cromer, the fourth-grader at school whom no one liked, whom people said was going to leave the school. "People don't like us anymore, do they?"

Mummy didn't deny it. She wiped her hands on her apron and came over and put them on Laura's shoulders. Laura's throat ached but she stopped crying at once. Mummy's sympathy made her not want to cry. Mummy said some things about the people not being their friends anyway, things Laura already knew, and already knew Mummy would say to her, as she knew most things adults would say to her, with the exception of Daddy. Daddy could still surprise her. She would have liked to ask him because she knew she would have gotten a straight answer but he was too busy right now and he was mostly gone. He and Mummy sat up at night at the kitchen table talking. Sometimes they mentioned the farm. Her aunt Sallie had been down to stay with them for a few days (arriving right from Mass upstate in the black shirt with the white collar that meant you were a priest) to help Mummy because Daddy was so preoccupied with whatever was going on at work—and something very big was going on, Laura knew—that some nights he couldn't come home at all. First they talked of *lawyers, his lawyer, the lawyer.* Then *he, Hogan*—"He says..." "He thinks..." Catching her listening one night, Mummy smiled and said, "Do you know that we are talking about the father of a girl at St. Tim's? Mr. Hogan? Mary Hogan's dad?" And they looked pleased about including her in this and Laura smiled wanly, though of course it wasn't interesting. Laura didn't care who anyone's father was—only parents cared about other parents. It was the adult world and so it was boring.

Then one night at supper she asked Aunt Sallie if Daddy was with the lawyers, and she said no, he was with the "bidders," or maybe the "buyers." Laura didn't know what Daddy was selling so she didn't pursue it. That night he slept at the office and then he went to his club, which was right next to the office, and he had been sleeping there ever since, if he was sleeping at all. Sallie had to leave to go home for some emergency "with one of my girls" upstate; Mrs. Sampson came in to help Mummy, and Laura didn't like to ask Mummy questions because Mummy was so distracted with coping. That night Mrs. Sampson told her, "Now, don't you pay any attention to anything anyone says because it's not true. People make stuff up, you know?" Laura would have liked to ask which specific accusations were not true but she knew it would be wrong to take the remark like that, for Mrs. Sampson had meant it to cheer her up, so she smiled and said, "Oh, I know!" Laura recalled her conversation with Daddy when they had been making pancakes that morning at the start of March break. Perhaps it was now—the moment when he had to choose between the bank and the family. Perhaps he was choosing this very day. He'd already told her when they spoke on the phone that he couldn't be home for Ruthie's party. "But the big surprise is, Laura—now, don't tell her—I'm driving up *tonight* to get the puppy. I'm driving up and getting him and I'll be back before Ruthie wakes up tomorrow, which is her actual birthday, after all."

316

Laura still felt tickled to be trusted with such a giant secret especially since *she* had been the one to choose the puppy from Roxie's litter of seven; he was all black with a white spot on the edge of one of his front paws, as if he had dipped it into white paint. She was a little anxious that Ruth wouldn't be all that great at raising the puppy, that she would spoil him and not understand the importance of discipline. People overindulged their puppies and then they were surprised when their puppies turned into huge, unmanageable adult dogs that jumped all over their owners. (She got that from a school library book called *How to Raise a Puppy.*) She was also worried that Ruth would give the puppy a dumb name, the way her nursery-school class had named its tadpole American Idol. Daddy assured them that the puppy was for all three of them but that it was exciting for him to come on Ruth's birthday.

She withdrew from Mummy's embrace and went back to checking the pan. "Do we have to flour it too?"

"We'll be fine, Laura."

Laura nodded briefly. "So, we do have to flour it?"

At school Veronica L. had said to her when they were taking their jumpers off before gym, "We all feel so sorry for you, Laura, and for your grandmother. It's not her fault that Cleary is being tarnished." It was the first Laura heard of it.

Dismayed, she managed to get out, "I've always felt sorry for you, Veronica, and that tacky little woman you have to live with"—a comment of Mummy's she happened to recall, though it was not actually about Veronica's mother but about someone else.

Yet she knew she hadn't really won, she knew Veronica was still one up on her, because she sensed that their situation was bad. She suspected Mummy had done something—given her opinion too loudly, perhaps, at a time when you weren't supposed to give your opinion at all. Yelled at someone in public. Worse. She felt ashamed, knowing it was true. All week she felt the mothers looking at her at pickup. They were looking at her and because they were looking at her, there was nowhere she could look. If she looked over or up or around or just tried to look straight ahead of herself, she would meet the eyes of some mother whose gaze would flit away and who would then smile patronizingly at Laura. With a sinking feeling, she understood that Veronica L. was right: people felt sorry for her. Some of the nicer mothers said "Hi, Laura!" too heartily, as if she needed cheering up. She said "Hi" quietly back. Deirdre's mother walked right up to her and squeezed her hand, which embarrassed Laura, and she said, "Deirdre tells me what a nice singing voice you have, Laura. She said she really likes standing next to you in chorus." "Thank you," Laura said weakly, understanding that this was code for some-thing but not knowing what, given that it was Deirdre herself who had the pretty voice—indeed, was known in the class for it.

Now Mummy inspected her pan. "This looks good, Lolo."

Laura watched her mother pour the nearly white batter into the pan, then tip the bowl up and scrape determinedly with the spatula to get all of it. There was a forcefulness about Mummy today, and these last few days, that Laura hadn't seen in a while. It both relieved and alarmed Laura, though she didn't like to ad-mit to either. Mummy got that way sometimes when she cooked. She got a look in her eye and you knew she would get it done. The cake would come out. It was as if someone had told Mummy she couldn't do it and she was going to prove the person wrong. At the same time, it was alarming. It took too much out of her. She might not notice you getting done whatever it was she had to get done. You had better steer clear...it was nothing like when

318

Gammy cooked. When Gammy cooked, she was the one telling the recipe what to do, not the other way around. "Star anise? Oh, please. I don't think we'll bother with that, Laura, will we?" She kept up a conversation with Laura while she moved around her tidy kitchen and she never panicked the way Mummy did—"Oh God, is it done or not? How am I supposed to tell? Why don't they explain it better? They assume you know all these things!" Gammy was no-nonsense and confident. She was tough. Once when Laura was over visiting, she got sick to her stomach and told Gammy she might have to throw up. Right at that moment, she felt her stomach heave. Gammy snatched her arm and dragged her to the bathroom, crying, "Not on the Oriental, you don't!" Perhaps that was what the Cleary parent meant when she said, of Winnie Skinker, the oldest member of the board, "They don't make 'em like that anymore." The only time Laura had ever seen Gammy look old and defeated was the Christmas when Mummy knocked her glass over at the dining-room table and broke it and spilled red wine all over the tablecloth and she and Daddy argued and Mummy had to go lie down in Gammy's bedroom despite the fact that she kept saying, "I don't want to fucking lie down! For Christ's sake, stop treating me like an invalid!"—resisting the way Sebastian would have. But that was only because Gammy thought she was alone in the kitchen and she didn't know Laura was looking at her and when she realized it, her expression changed right away; she smiled, showing her crazy old-person teeth with the greenish hue and the gold fillings, and said, "Now, weren't you going to help me whip the cream, Laura? Come on, let's be quick about it. We don't want the pie to get cold, now, do we?"

*   *   *

By noon, the cake was done and frosted, after only one mishap with the first batch of icing, and the streamers were up in the dining room. Standing on a chair, Ruth had helped twist the two colors, pink and white, together while Mummy held the end and Laura, on another chair, taped it up with duct tape. Now Sebastian was playing with his plastic barnyard, and Ruthie, in her ballet leotard and tutu, was plunking out jangle sounds on the piano. Laura went into the kitchen to tell Mummy that it was noon and the party should be starting and she found Mummy crying.

"I'm sorry, darling," Mummy said, which made Laura afraid. Some parents apologized all the time to their children, but Mummy never apologized. "It's possible no one's going to come." She blew her nose into a Kleenex. "Now, I'm going to smile and be really happy for Ruth but just for a moment, I felt bad, as it's not poor Ruthie's fault."

Laura didn't know what to say so she repeated something Mummy had said earlier: "We'll have fun anyway. There's cake and everything." Oh, but she wanted to die.

"That's right. The cake came out perfectly, didn't it?"

She felt it, worse than ever—the thumb pressing on her—and she knew that it was bad, whatever Mummy had said or done. She felt herself drawn into it; she knew she was to blame too—all the times she had been mean to Ruth and fought with Sebastian and said she hated him. "I wish Daddy were here," she said, even though she knew it would make Mummy mad.

But Mummy only squeezed her hand and said, "Me too."

Then the phone rang. Mummy said nervously, "You pick it up, Laura."

Laura heard Ray the doorman saying, "A Mrs. Hogan?"

"Send her up, please!" Laura said smartly. She didn't even tell Mummy who it was. She knew exactly who the Hogans were from the park. She ran into the living room and told Ruth: "Ruthie, your friend's coming! Your big friend who's five! *Mary's* coming! Remember Mary?"

"Oh, it's the Hogans?" Mummy called. "They came?"

Ruth immediately deserted the piano and ran to the door. "Mary's coming!" Ruth told Mummy, who'd come out of the kitchen.

"Isn't that nice?" Mummy looked nervous and happy.

"Mary's coming!" Ruth repeated.

Even Sebastian left his barnyard and joined them, looking expectant and pleased.

As they waited Laura looked at her mother, who raised her eyebrows conspiratorially, and she wondered if Mummy knew that an older friend, a five-year-old friend, was worth two or three younger friends.

Mrs. Hogan came with Mary. Mrs. Hogan was one of those moms who looked so young and who wore no makeup and whose clothes were so plain you thought she was one of the babysitters. She looked even younger today and Laura was so surprised, she said directly to her, without thinking, "You cut your hair!"

Mary said, "You're right!" and Mrs. Hogan said, "I did! I cut it all off, Laura. Time for something new, I guess."

Mary, Laura could see, was a nice child who wouldn't be mean about playing with a three-year-old. "We can show you our room," Laura decided, and Mary Hogan said, "Okay," happily enough.

"It's my birthday!" Ruth announced.

Embarrassed, Laura cried, "She knows that, Ruth!"

But they all giggled, even Sebastian, as the mothers greeted each other.

"We're getting bunk beds," Laura announced, allowing herself the one small brag. "Now that Ruth's old enough." She wanted to tell Mary about the puppy but she couldn't because it was a secret.

Mrs. Hogan had hesitated just inside the door, and instead of a cheek kiss followed by a lot of rapid chatter, Mummy had given her a hug such as she would give Laura and then kissed her cheek. "You're staying, aren't you, Gwen? Of course you are. You'll have cake with us." Vaguely, Laura felt Mrs. Hogan must have something to do with the bad things that had befallen them, for she looked at Mummy meaningfully before she said quietly, "Yes, I'll stay." When Laura went back into the kitchen a while later, to get teacups for the stuffed animals, she heard Mrs. Hogan saying, "Oh, thanks, but Mary's going to public school," and Laura wondered if it was true what Veronica L. had said, that Cleary was tarnished and no one would want to go there now. But she never found out because then they started talking about the cake. Mrs. Hogan said admiringly, "Oh, you do that complicated icing," and Mummy replied, "It's easy!" as the mothers always said, though Mummy had thrown out an entire bowl of frosting—her first try—and had said something like, "Fuck! Fuck! Fuck this fucking fuck!" when she realized it was past saving.

When they were about to have lunch, another girl arrived. She brought a huge present for Ruth, so a big man—her driver—had to carry it in for her. He made a joke about its being very heavy as he set it down in the entryway. "Good thing my back's not bothering me!" Laura felt jealous and hoped that when Ruth opened it, it wouldn't be all that great, the way some big presents were not all that great. The girl's name was Arabella, and Laura took one look at her and didn't like her but she kept that to herself, and she was glad she was able to be mature because Ruth was very excited that there was not one but were two older girls at her party. Laura was embarrassed that Ruthie hugged Arabella because she thought Arabella would say something mean but instead the hug made the girl speechless and embarrassed, a little bit the way a dog looked if you watched it going to the bathroom. "Happy birthday, Ruth," she said stiffly.

Mrs. Hogan and Mummy came out of the kitchen and they both stared at Arabella's mother, who had finally come in after talking angrily on her cell phone in the hall for several minutes. She came in and said softly, "I don't know if I'm welcome here." Laura knew why they stared at her: it was her outfit. "I don't know if I'm welcome but I got dressed and put on my makeup for the first time in ten days, and, well—I decided to come." Mrs.—well, Laura didn't know what to call her because when Mummy introduced Laura to her, after assuring the woman that she was very welcome, Mummy said, "Mrs. Curtis," but Arabella's mother jumped in: "Not anymore. I'll be going by Colón now. For the time being, anyway. That's my maiden name. John's—John's going to jail." Her lip trembled, and she said, "I thought all that was behind me. I've got a brother who's in jail. I thought when I came to Manhattan..." She took a moment and then she went on in that voice mothers used to convince you everything would be fine, only she was convincing herself. "Colón will be really easy, you see, because I can keep the initials—I don't have to re-monogram anything." She did sound cheerier now. "The towels, I mean, and Arabella's backpack and all that." She was a funny one, Laura decided. She looked as if she had tried to dress casually but her casual was a movie version of casual. She wore matching ruby-colored velvety sweatpants and sweatshirt and her hair was perfectly combed and she had fine manicured hands painted satiny orangey pink that Laura wished longingly Mummy would have but Mummy never painted her nails because it reminded her of when she had to wear nail polish for a living. Despite the disguise of the casual outfit, Laura could tell that she was much too fancy for the party—for the apartment—for them. But despite the bad thing Mummy had done, she had come to the party and she sat at the end of the sofa with her ankles crossed and very good posture and she seemed to be trying to make polite conversation with Mummy and Mrs. Hogan. When Mummy asked her if she wanted water, if she wanted champagne, if she wanted anything at all, she hesitated before saying yes, and when she did say yes, she said, "Yes. Thank you. Champagne would be nice," in such a quiet polite voice that it made the back of Laura's neck tingle, and Laura started making up excuses for why she had to linger in the living room because she longed to hear Mrs. Curtis Colón answer again. Mummy handed her the bottle of champagne and said, "Could you?" and at this, Mrs. C.C. perked up a little more and she said, "I used to waitress!" and she popped the cork almost professionally good and said, "Who wants some?" And then it was funny because Mummy, who always said yes to champagne, who said she would bathe in champagne every day of her life if she could, looked anxiously at the bottle and said maybe she'd have a little but then withdrew her glass and said no, on second thought, she would have lemonade for now, but Mrs. C.C. made Mrs. Hogan have a glass with her—practically forced her to take one—saying, "I need a drink and I refuse to drink alone, Gwen!" The glasses poured, Mrs. Hogan looked like Laura felt when she went on a playdate and the mom gave her junk food—sort of embarrassed but excited at the same time. Then Mrs. C.C. asked, "Is it just us three? Where is everyone else?" and Laura froze, but Mummy just said, "Not coming." And Mrs. C.C. said a bad word—no, not *Fuck*, she said, "Bitches," and they all laughed, but Mrs. Hogan the loudest. Mrs. Hogan laughed the way Marguerite Chang in Laura's class laughed—as if she had never laughed before. She went from dead serious to uproarious uncontrollable laughter. Laura loved to make Marguerite laugh for just this reason.

When the adult conversation got boring, Laura said, "Can we have lunch now?" and the three women fell to helping the children, though Mrs. C.C. didn't really do anything—she dithered inconsequentially and then retook her seat on the sofa next to the bottle of champagne and poured herself another glass and checked her phone. Mummy didn't believe in having the token bowl of raw carrots at a birthday party so they had hot dogs in buns with bright yellow mustard, peas, which were only a pseudo-vegetable and provided not for their nutritional value but because Ruth loved them, bowls of cheese popcorn, and chocolate milk in the pink-tinted holiday glasses. Then they had the beautiful pink cake, which everyone exclaimed over, with mint chocolate chip ice cream, which made a nice color contrast, Laura thought, and they had bowls of M&M's and of Hershey's Kisses. Laura ate so much that she felt sick and had to lie down on the sofa with her knees pulled up to her chest. Mummy forced them to play just one game, pin-the-tail-on-the-zebra; the zebra had been Ruth's request. She liked striped things generally. When it was Arabella's turn, Sebastian went red in the face and yelled, "You're looking! I see you looking!" Laura had also noticed Arabella cheating, and in the most obvious way—by pretending to adjust her blindfold—but had been too embarrassed to say anything. Her brother, she perceived, would go through life irately pointing out its unfairnesses.

Chapter Twenty

Of her brother, Sallie Skinker would never have expected suicide.

Yet a conversation they'd had in their twenties came back to her as she lay in bed of a summer dawn. The day before, she had gotten the news from her mother that Skinker, Farr had been sold—sold one enervatingly humid June afternoon to one of the midsize American retail banks.

It was when she had been hospitalized for depression. Jed had come to visit her and had admitted to having endured his own dark night of the soul. "Funny, though," he'd said cheerfully at some point during that long-ago visit, forcing her outside into the hospital garden for that family panacea, fresh air, "you're not the type to kill yourself, sis." The kind of thing a sibling knew intuitively. "Nope," she'd agreed, glad to have it clarified nonetheless. "I don't have that bone..." She realized, though, looking up at the water-stained ceiling of her bedroom, following its cracks with her eyes, that she ought to have asked herself at the time what her brother's remark implied about himself. She could guess that Jed might have had a soft spot for self-sacrifice if it would cancel shame.

She pushed herself to sitting in the iron bedstead, the springs creaking beneath her weight.

Of course, there was suicide, and there was *suicide*.

Uncle Reg's spoiled fit wasn't something anyone, least of all Jed, would have wanted to imitate.

She'd been so tempted to wait up for him last night; she knew he was driving up late. "The morning, it'll actually be," he'd predicted, meaning after the closing with the buyers. "I won't leave the city till after midnight. One—two. I can't predict it." He was coming for the puppy. His plan was to get the puppy, turn around, and drive straight back so Ruthie would wake up to it on her birthday. The way they had woken up as children to find Barkie given a reprieve from the pound—theirs to keep.

When you were having what would become your happiest memories, you didn't know you were having them. Only later could you look back and add the surprise of that black head appearing around your bedroom door to a top-ten list—realize it had rarely been better than that. "Barkie's still here?" Sternly, grudgingly, as in *Don't take this as precedent:* "Your father and I decided you could keep him after all. *As long as…*" An exacting list of provisions had followed. Just as well: this morning Sallie couldn't seem to dwell on the happy memory. It fled from her. Then for some reason it made her afraid. She glanced toward the window—she never bothered to pull down the shade, as she was a morning person, someone who reliably woke up optimistic; if her spirits flagged, they flagged after dark—but the dawn light for the first time in her life since that week in the hospital so long ago gave her a sense of misgiving.

She turned back the sheet and quilt and rose—no use trying to go back to sleep. Infernal irritation with the sort of people who told her she should take a nap. Wrapping her terry robe around her, she listened for sounds—from outside, from Billy Flood's—as if Jed would still be there. She walked downstairs to the kitchen, where she put the stovetop espresso pot she favored onto a burner of the stove, sat down at the Formica table, and waited for it to boil.

The phone call she'd had with Winifred yesterday came back to her, her mother trying to control the shaking in her voice. "Sold! After ninety years! Sold in one day. Not even to a New York bank! First National Bank of Texas! What the hell is that?"

"All right," Sallie had said. "So he sells it to a Texas bank. He found a buyer! Good for him. That sounds like the right thing to do, doesn't it, Mother?"

There was a worrisome silence as her mother tried to take a breath. Winifred might have been fighting down hysteria. "But the name, Sallie! The name! Think of your father, Sallie—think of his seeing Skinker on a bank that's got nothing to do with us! I can't get my head around it. It never occurred to me they'd keep the name. Can that be legal?"

"I suppose..." Sallie spoke carefully, considering how to phrase it. "I suppose it's flattering in a way. A testament to Jed's good work." He had kept Skinker together—hadn't let the bank atomize. He'd taken himself out at once, before they could lose confidence in his ability to lead. Chip Noyes was to run the place; the partners were mostly staying. This didn't seem to register with her mother. "But it won't be owned by us anymore! We *are* Skinker! Without us, there is no Skinker! It doesn't mean any-thing!"

"An empty signifier. Yes."

"Well—yes! They want to keep the brand! But we're the brand, for God's sake! Your father—your father—" She grasped at a conclusion.

"Dad—yes," Sallie acknowledged. "But Dad's died." She purposely used the gentler present-perfect tense. "And he said *we* ought to be Husseys more than Skinkers, remember? Jed and I? We were always more farm than bank. Jed just got the Skinker thrust upon him."

With a prideful clearing of her throat, her mother changed the subject, as if she didn't want to admit to being remotely cheered up—or perhaps the woman was not ready to consider her role in the trajectory of her son's life. "Your brother's driving up tonight, Philippa told me. Honestly!" She clicked her tongue but Sallie could tell she approved. That gung-ho, stop-at-nothing mentality was part of the family's self-defining image. Sallie was guilty of it too. *Of course I'll sleep at the center tonight after Midnight Mass Christmas Eve and do three services tomorrow . . .* "I *told* him to wait," Winifred said, as if she'd been accused of something, "but he said he had to get up and back before any of the lawyers noticed he was gone."

Sallie smiled to herself when her mother couldn't resist asking, referring to the puppies, "So, what are they?"

"Farm mutts—shepherd, from Roxie, and some little black dog, judging by the color. Seven of them. Laura picked it out. Exact choice I would have made. Real animal kid," Sallie said fondly.

"Sallie," Winnie said, plaintive again, "you should be more involved in their lives! You should take them under your wing in this time of trouble."

Sallie took a breath. "In the first place, I'm not their mother. They have one, remember?" She fought off an interruption. "In the second, I don't have a lot to say to a two-year-old."

Winifred said hastily, "It's not too late for you, you know, Sallie. Even after forty, a lot of women are—"

"*Mother.*"

Soon they would all be together. Philippa would bring the children up for the summer. And Jed? Sallie didn't know what he meant to do when this trial ended.

In the still dawn of a summer morning, though, "before any of the lawyers noticed he was gone" seemed to take on a nefarious meaning. She had to force herself to wait for the coffee to boil, to microwave the milk, pour the two together, sit down with the mug. She was being ridiculous. Succumbing to the panic that had seemed to grip Winnie and that had made Sallie wonder if, after the blow of the past month, her mother's days of 100 percent sanity might be nearly over. Surely Jed had already come and gone, just as planned. It wouldn't do to call his cell phone shouting, "Jed, are you all right?" Not after what he'd gone through this week. In another half hour she could run over to Billy Flood's on some pretext, find out what time Jed had made it to the farm, when he had slipped away again. She sipped the coffee quickly, scalding her tongue. She'd felt this whole week as if she were watching her family's denouement on television—she had that sense of remove that one got from the small screen. She did watch some of it on television; it was all over the news. But she simply couldn't feel bad for her family for having to give up the store. For generations now, the Skinkers had had far more than their share.

As for the name—she believed descent ought to be matrilineal. She'd known enough women with three children, each with his or her own surname, those names themselves long gone.

THE SOCIALITE WAS A CALL GIRL. SCANDAL SCUTTLES SKINKER, FARR.

Sallie thanked God every day that the little ones were too young to understand. She worried about Laura, knowing the seven-year-old would be getting bits and pieces of it, bearing the brunt at school. She suspected it was for her as much as Ruth that Jed was doing this crazy round-trip.

Since the story had broken, Winifred had called her daily to dump the latest painful press on her, gnash her teeth, then click off before Sallie could form a response. Sallie, meanwhile, had been calling Philippa at home in the evenings after the children were in bed. In a funny way, her brother's wife seemed able to withstand the onslaught better than anyone Sallie knew would have—much better than she herself would have taken it. Philippa didn't, actually, care what people thought.

As the sound reached her, Sallie started, splashing coffee onto the Formica. She realized she had been hearing the sound for a few moments now but not making sense of what it was. She wiped at the spill with the sleeve of her robe, telling herself it was nothing—for it never was anything. Someone was calling the main house—that was all. It was a sound she normally wouldn't have been able to hear sitting here in the kitchen of the little house and that's why it had taken her a minute to identify it. But it was the stillest of summer mornings, and with the good weather predicted, the housekeeper had thrown open the windows of the main house a couple of days ago to air it out. It was getting stale inside, with Jed and his family not having made it up in a while.

Someone was persistently ringing the Skinkers at the listed number. Looking for Jed, no doubt, wanting a comment. Given the storm of press, she was surprised the media hadn't found the farm before now. She'd give them a comment, all right—to call this early in the morning! The ringing stopped and then it started again. Whoever it was had called back: *Make no mistake, I am trying to reach you!* The last time someone had called the house, it had been the police. The herd had gotten out when a rail broke after a storm and a dozen cows were strolling down Route 20. The sergeant had called her and they'd had a good laugh about it. The police couldn't call the little house because Sallie had gone cell phone only, cut the landline off completely there. So they had called the main house to reach her about the cows.

That fact comforted her, for a moment, that it was the town police who had this number. Then her mug dropped clear to the floor, as if someone else had been holding it. She rose, trembling... her limbs didn't seem to be working, but somehow her body and her mind on top of it were exiting through the screen door of her kitchen. She was trying to run, trundling awkwardly and slowly, wincing barefoot along the ridges of dried mud to the main house, her lungs burning, her face afire.

Now she did yell her brother's name. "Jed! Jed!"

She banged down the front hall and through the kitchen and into their father's study, making every promise to God there was... her life... her soul...

Forty years old, and her brother was still the most precious thing on earth to her.

Just before she picked up the phone she sensed God in the dark, dusty room. She checked herself—let the ringing continue. She closed her eyes and breathed one word: "Yes." Then she opened them and grasped the receiver. "Sallie Skinker here."

Chapter Twenty-One

Y ou knew you were getting close when you turned onto Rural Route 20 and saw the lights from the gas pumps of Pete's. Pete was long gone, and his impatient, city-minded son had sold the garage to an Albanian immigrant whose wife ran an upholstery business out of the back. But Pete's lived on through the painted script sign, the lights on the gas pumps like beacons at four thirty in the morning. Jed's mind never failed to clear when he got off the highway and the quiet, uncrowded road ran away before him. He checked the mileage on the old Volkswagen, a habit of his father's, who would announce, satisfied, when they pulled into the farm, "Two point nine," as if the distance from the highway might have changed in the interim since Hugh's last visit. The Volkswagen's odometer read 29,000, but it had already turned over once. Jed had gone out and bought a new car a few years ago, as you did when your old car was falling apart and could no longer fit your family comfortably. But the built-in navigation system had driven him crazy. "And the beeping when I parallel park! It's as if all the skills one's acquired are being taken away...planned idiocy," he grumbled to Sallie. "You can turn all that off!" she said, unsympathetic. A technological whiz, Sallie told him something he already knew—"You'll go obsolete yourself if you don't watch out. You'll start collecting typewriters and rotary phones." With the greatest dignity he told her, "Phones? I prefer the telegraph, my dear."

But—dawn at the turnoff onto Route 20.

He had seen more dawns in the past month than he had seen since college, but a country dawn in June was its own particular marvel. The stillness and the emptiness of the road, the dark farmhouses with one light on against burglars, the lumpy fields stretching away from him on either side...He liked this part of Danforth, closest to the highway—a bit of barbed wire, a new-built house here and there on an acre the farmers had sold off—better than the pristine rolling acres of horse farms with the five-bar fences farther north. Something southern about the latter; they belonged in Virginia hunt-country, he felt. He didn't have much tolerance for shining up a place...The blue, hopeful light of dawn; he'd never become jaundiced to it. He got that from Hugh. Hugh, with all of his limitations, his idiosyncrasies (the amateur's interest in architecture that had become an obsession), had had a knack for the basics—and his mother had too—of instilling those values, perhaps superficial, but something a boy could grab onto and not have to think about: One said please and one said thank you. One ate the food on one's plate. One got up early. Maps were cool. So was swimming in cold water. Dawn was good, but you had to catch it. And if you did catch it—"Keep it a secret," Hugh told him. "Don't brag."

Superficial.

That was the word she had used. *That was all superficial.* How he had stirred when she said that. How he longed for it all to be over so they could start. But he couldn't think of her—couldn't allow himself to think of her. Wouldn't think of her. Not yet. The time with her was about to start but he had to get the puppy for Ruth, get back, go to work, close the whole thing down. And then the unfolding of the time would start. Consciously, he drove a little faster along the curving road. Like anyone who speeds, he was aware of it yet didn't think of it. Tiresome, to talk about the near misses. "I almost..." But you didn't. He was very, very short of sleep but his reflexes were sound. The truth was, he had to hurry. He was pushing it. Ruth wouldn't sleep past seven thirty. He wanted to be there when she opened her eyes. Sallie had volunteered. "*I'll* drive it down." He refused her offer; didn't tell her that the only thing that had gotten him through the last seventy-two hours was thinking of alighting at the farm, taking a few breaths of the farm air, resting his eyes on the barn and the house—with any luck getting a glimpse of the herd. Needed his fix. Soon—soon they could all come up together.

No doubt it was the sleep deprivation, the days running into nights running into days, but his thoughts had become a Joycean monologue...the time and the time and the time and the time. That's how he thought about it, was thinking about it now. He had never seemed to have time with her, this past decade. The children, with all their joy and chaos; his work, which one couldn't neglect; managing his mother...Odd, that that odious man should be the catalyst for the rest of their lives together. He'd tried to speak the truth to her on the phone when he called to see how Ruthie's party had gone. But even though he'd tried very carefully, somehow he lied—there was falsehood in his statement. "These past few weeks, we've been apart a lot," he said, when he meant "These past ten years." He wanted to correct himself but they got on to other topics, as one did with one's wife. The time and the time and the time; the cake and the minutiae—Lolo, she said, had been a sport. Sebastian was coming down with something maybe. The boy had lain down on his bed and fallen fast asleep at six p.m. No fever but he seemed exhausted. There was something going around...she talked a little too much, gave too many rapid-fire details. He suspected she was made shy by her own performance—embarrassed by the fact that she had come through. All through the crisis, she had been up early, focused. Containing the drinking. Almost as if she'd only been waiting for an opportunity to come through. Idleness didn't suit her. Made her feel useless, nervous. Brought out the worst.

Marriage to him. Had it brought out the worst?

No. Banish the thought. Don't go melodramatic. Hurry. Hurry. Soon—

Would she be better off without him?

So much to prove and no way to do it in the context of the Skinker family. Didn't want to be told she was a lily of the field. Too much emphasis on looks, which had been her cross to bear. What would her life have been like if she hadn't looked the way she did? Happier, probably. Although...he was glad Sebastian had gotten her looks, not the girls. God, but Lolo was a firecracker. She could be anything, do anything. She was Grandfather Reg...buying the building for a hundred grand in 1973. He hadn't told Winnie that part. The Simon brothers had called. Skinker, Farr—or the entity that would be known as Skinker, Farr—would shortly be moving to four floors in a midtown office tower. Meanwhile, Herb and Stephen Simon were prepared to offer a hundred million for the building—wanted to raze it. He'd been obliged to remind them of its landmarked status. Hugh had seen to that. If it hadn't been landmarked, they could have torn it down and built. Instead the Simons would buy it for twenty million and rent it. Jed hoped for a family foundation, something that wouldn't piss him off when he walked by. All you could hope for with your second half century: that things wouldn't piss you off. You rarely got that.

He sped along the road...2.0 on the trip meter. Less than a mile to go. He decided that when he arrived at the farm he would say aloud, "Two point nine," in tribute to Hugh. Nearly there. He pressed the pedal. He had wasted time. A sickening amount. He knew that now. He wished he had taken them with him when he left the bank a few hours ago—the bank he no longer owned, the building he would sell within a week—woken his family up, the hell with the time, and put all four of them into the car with him so he didn't have to go back to the city at all. He wished it so badly he felt an agony in his side. It was illogical. Today and tomorrow he had meetings noon to dusk, then dawn to dusk. More unwinding. Another six weeks to do it properly—he hoped not six months. Then he had to testify. That he wasn't going to jail himself a stroke of luck his own lawyer could hardly believe. Hogan in the U.S. Attorney's Office, indignant on his behalf. "You were blackmailed!" He liked the guy. He still cared. About the score, the refs, the playing field...it was narrow, Hogan's focus, but there was a dignity to it. It wouldn't take a year, would it? He despaired briefly. He kept his eyes focused on the road...He saw himself as a massive tank rolling through a siege, buffeted by bullets, fire, whatever they could throw at him. He had to keep on rolling, rolling, rolling, no matter how they strafed him. And it really would start then. The time together would start. It was like when you wait so long for something—half a lifetime—but the last five minutes are unendurable. He had to hurry.

He took the turn as fast as he dared—put a little flair in it—show they hadn't gotten him, not yet. He glanced at the speedometer. "Ha!" That'd be one to keep from Sallie—his record was forty-seven. This would be over fifty, for sure. He felt that jolt one always felt around this particular turn, that, just when you thought you'd be coming out of it, the road seemed to commit more deeply to the curve, to curve more sharply when it couldn't possibly have any curve left. Serve him right—with his lofty thoughts. *Drive, man!* He recalled what Philippa had said on the phone last night. Last night or maybe this morning. He could no longer remember time. At the end of the call, he had managed to come back around to the point he was making. "We've been apart," he'd repeated, only this time he said firmly, truthtelling, "these past ten years." He wrenched the wheel as hard as he could as the farmer's stone wall rose up before him. "Oh," he heard her saying, her voice puzzled, "but that was only superficial. Underneath it all, darling, we've always—"

Epilogue

She looked, Ann DeGroat remarked, as if she *knew*.

"Knew what?" Ann's husband, Guy, asked irritably. They were sharing a cab whose air-conditioning didn't work down Fifth Avenue to the Seventies, where he would drop her on their block and continue alone to his office in midtown. But Ann only shook her head. "Just knew, you know? Like Eve or something...It's like, she has the knowledge now—Philippa does—and the rest of us are just...clueless." She turned to Guy. "Didn't you notice?"

The long, vaulted nave of Heavenly Rest had been packed, the side pews bulging, throngs of latecomers standing in the back, every printed program taken, forcing people to share. "Hell of a memorial service," Guy heard someone mutter. At the long, rather upbeat reception in the parish hall afterward, Skinker's secretary, Carol Ann Ritchek, had been mobbed by the financial services crowd in front of the coffee urn so you could hardly move. But always he had been aware of *her*, of the long, slim, motionless back way up in the front pew; of the willowy woman in black they all went to pay homage to, as if, suddenly, they all needed her blessing, her composure, her quietude, her kindness—her beauty, which seemed a blessing in itself—as she shook hand after hand after hand, accepting the tributes. But not his, not Guy's. He never went over to say hello, couldn't bring himself to, snatched glances at her from across the room like the dope he was, hoping she would bestow a little of her strength on him, with a look, an acknowledgment...

Rather than take up Ann's point, Guy swore at the heat, cranked his window down, and went into a pedantic explanation that people were always misquoting that passage, that Eve had eaten from the tree of *knowledge of good and evil,* not the tree of *knowledge, full stop,* to which Ann replied, in that same calmly speculative tone, "That's exactly what I'm talking about."

Her intensity dissipated as the traffic increased, and she went on idly, "She's moving upstate—taking the children and moving up to Danforth. I was surprised to hear that. Were you? The Skinkers seem so New York, don't they? So New York. The apartment's already on the market. Betsy told me. Halstead has the listing—'estate condition.' You better believe it! Oh my gosh, wasn't Sallie Skinker wonderful?" Ann gushed, enjoying herself—a chat with her husband in the middle of the day. "At first I was confused, because I hadn't realized she was a priest. And I thought, *Who is that talking up there all presumptuously, as if she knows the Skinkers?* Ha! Joke was on me. But wasn't she great? What was it she told them, the three kids? 'So much to look forward to...dogs and—' Dogs and—something. I can't remember, but it was good, wasn't it? She was really good. She—"

"Dogs and dentists and daffodils," Guy said curtly, fearful that Ann would ruin the line. He looked out the window as the light turned green, at the lush green park. "That's what she said."

"I suppose they'll live together up there and sort of jointly..." She became distracted, looking at her phone.

The paper program lay crushed on the seat between them where Ann had relinquished it. *A Celebration of His Life,* it said.

"Here it is! Wow, it's a real rambler." She had managed to find the listing for the Skinker apartment and was swiping through the interior photos. She held up her phone so they were visible to Guy as well, who reluctantly tallied up the costs of a total gut.

Acknowledgments

My greatest thanks to Lee Boudreaux and to Brettne Bloom for getting me to Lee.

For help in research I would like to thank Florence Wu, Gus Christensen, Lisa Korologos, Jessica Illuzzi, Ursula Wallis, Rern Lau, and, most particularly, Lisa Baroni, formerly of the U.S. Attorney's Office, Southern District of New York.

About the Author

Caitlin Macy is the author of *The Fundamentals of Play* and *Spoiled*. Her work has appeared in *The New Yorker*, the *New York Times Magazine*, and *Slate*, among other publications. The recipient of an O. Henry Award, she lives in New York City with her husband and two children.